I0637898

Heavy is the Crown

JAMES E. LORRAINE

Publisher: Crown Cipher Publishing

www.crowncipherpublishing.com

Printed in the United States of America

This is a work of fiction. Names, characters, places, and incidents are the product of the author's imagination or are used fictitiously. Any resemblance to actual persons, living or dead, events, or locales is entirely coincidental.

☐ Dedication

For the ones who bled in plain sight
and were called strong instead of saved.

For the ones who smiled through the wreckage
because rage wasn't allowed, and grief had nowhere to go.

For the souls who laid in the dark
not to rest, but to disappear
because disappearing was easier than explaining the ache.

For those who ran to the needle of the tattoo machine,
not for ink—but for proof they could still feel something
when everything else had gone numb.

For the women who stayed too long.
For the men who never got chosen.

For the hearts that were cracked open
and handed back as if they were just glassware.

This book is for the ones who learned how to suffer
beautifully, quietly, violently.
And still showed up.

You're not alone.
You were never alone.

Welcome to the Kingdom.

Table of Contents

Prologue: The Kingdom Was Always Burning

There was no crown. No coronation. No scroll declaring them rulers. Only a city that bowed when they walked in, a silence that broke when they touched, and a legacy that started not with a kiss, but with fire.

Los Angeles wasn't kind to lovers. It was a stage lit in neon, drowning in liquor, dripping in secrets. Club Noir was just the beginning. A basement bar posing as royalty that pulsed just off La Brea. Low ceilings, red light, leather, sweat. A sound system that turns whispers into confessions. No windows, just darkness, mirrors, and a thousand whispered reputations.

They weren't royalty. But they owned every inch of silence the city gave them.

James King. A name that echoed across boardrooms and darker rooms. Muscles that looked like they were carved from regret. A mind sharp enough to encrypt your soul and still leave you wanting more. A man who moved like he already knew the outcome, and took what he wanted like it was owed.

Ellie Sinclair. Therapist and empire-builder. Mouth like honey laced with arsenic. This was before she disappeared, before the silence she left behind started sounding like scripture. She didn't fall in love. She dismantled it, piece by piece, to see what survived. And when she chose you? You didn't feel chosen. You felt seen.

Together, they didn't just bend a room. They set the temperature, and everyone else adapted. James King and Ellie Sinclair are brilliant, ruthless, and already broken in the ways that matter.

This isn't safe romance. It's power, obsession, and the price of letting someone close enough to hurt you. If you want soft edges, close the book.

If you came for war dressed in lace and sin, welcome. The kingdom was always burning. And some thrones are earned, only in blood.

https://open.spotify.com/playlist/583LHhF5JblEI82CRfbPdj

Chapter 1: The Throne of Smoke and Silk

Tucked beneath a liquor store off La Brea, Club Noir's entrance was discreet: a single black door behind a heavy curtain, unmarked and uninviting. If you didn't already belong, you walked past it without ever knowing.

Dim red and violet light carved long shadows across leather booths and half-empty drinks. Bodies moved without shame. Pleasure here was public, expected, and worshipped. But the rules were simple: you paid, you obeyed, you didn't pretend it meant nothing.

In the center of this pulsing chaos, the room bowed visibly and spiritually to one pair. The King sat, a predator disguised as royalty. His frame overflowed the throne-like couch, arms stretched along the backrest, chest rigid beneath a fitted black shirt that hugged his powerful build. Inked skin peeked just beneath the sleeve, black waves and ciphered patterns. Never above the neck or below the wrists.

His boundaries were marked in muscle and silence. Thick fingers curled casually around a crystal glass of bourbon, the liquid untouched. His caramel skin gleamed beneath dim lights as if brushed by oil and shadow, his sharp beard enhancing his commanding presence.
But it wasn't his formidable stature that silenced the room, it was how he held his Queen. She sat sideways across his lap, pale and luminous against his fire. One heel rested casually on the couch edge, the other dangled seductively from her toes. Her body was carved temptation. Her dark hair fell in sensual waves, teasing just above nipples pressing against sheer fabric. She sipped from his bourbon. Not because she wanted it, but because she could.

The music slowed, allowing moans to resurface more clearly. Around them, indulgences intensified, with women touching themselves openly, and lovers moving rhythmically against furniture. But eyes watched the King and his Queen.

She adjusted herself on his lap, pressing her thigh firmly against his hard length, clearly defined through tailored pants. Her hand traced along his chest, dragging nails slowly before brushing over his belt.

"You're tense," she murmured against his ear.

"I'm in control."

She laughed softly, dangerously. "Not the same thing."

His jaw tightened. "I don't need this place."

"Then why are you hard?"

His gaze burned into her, unflinching. "Because you're sitting on me like you want to be taken in front of them."

Her laugh was dark, indulgent, hips grinding subtly forward. His breath caught slightly.

"Let them watch," she said, defiant.

He looked away briefly, tension rippling through powerful shoulders. She reached up, caressing his beard.

"Give them what they want."

"I don't perform," he growled.

"No," she whispered, lips brushing his. "You rule. Tonight, let them see their King."

He downed the bourbon swiftly, set the glass aside, flexed his neck, and exhaled.

The Queen rose from his lap, standing directly before him. Every eye followed her, tension thickening through the club. She spoke softly, "Do you see anyone worth watching?"

He looked up at her, eyes dark. "No one touches me."

"That's not what I asked."

He shook his head.

"I do," she murmured, scanning the crowd.

Her eyes landed decisively on a caramel-skinned beauty, curves inviting sin beneath black lace, thighs strong, lips glossy and parted. The Queen raised a finger slightly, beckoning. The woman obeyed silently, kneeling before them both. The King's fists clenched tightly.

The Queen circled the new woman slowly, fingers tracing the curves of her shoulders, cupping her breasts possessively. The woman trembled, moaning softly as the Queen kissed her neck.

"You're here," the Queen whispered to the woman, loud enough for him to hear clearly, "to feed a god."

She glanced back to her King, smiling wickedly. "Do you trust me?" she asked.

"I always have." Her smile deepened. She kissed him fiercely, possessively, before returning to her chosen prey.

Kneeling behind her, the Queen slid her fingers between the woman's thighs beneath the black lace. The woman gasped, body arching, moans growing louder as practiced fingers found her rhythm.

The King remained still, watching intently, silent. But his grip tightened. Watching was power, but this was perilously close to worship. His discipline unshaken, his claim absolute without a single touch. His jaw tightened visibly, but he remained still, his eyes fiercely locked onto her.

She locked eyes with him, her voice thick with desire and power. "Now," she said clearly, letting her hand tease deeper, "let's make them beg to be us."

The club's breath stopped at her command. Her words were more than an invitation; they were law. The King sat immovable, tension coiled like a storm within him.

The Queen's fingers moved expertly beneath delicate lace, driving her muse toward an undeniable climax. Moans filled the space, urgent, uncontrolled, echoing openly. She leaned forward, whispering to the writhing woman beneath her, "He's listening. Don't disappoint him."

The muse's moans spiraled higher, louder, reaching a breathless climax that shook her visibly. She collapsed, shaking and spent.

The Queen stepped back slowly, licking glistening fingers as her gaze met his again, unwavering and hungry. The club erupted in applause, awe-driven and worshipful.

She approached her King deliberately, lips brushing his ear. "Your throne is waiting."

He rose, towering over everyone, stripping off his shirt in one motion, revealing muscle, ink, dominance. The Queen's eyes glowed, fingertips grazing his carved abs reverently.

"You were made to be worshipped," she whispered, awed.

"I was made to serve you," he replied, dropping purposefully to his knees before her. Gasps filled the club.

He pulled her closer roughly, burying his face between her thighs without hesitation. She cried out instantly, gripping his head as his tongue devoured her mercilessly, relentlessly, bringing her swiftly toward release.

Her climax shattered through the room, raw and unrestrained. And as the Queen trembled under his mouth, a single stranger watched quietly from the edge, eyes fixed intensely upon her: unafraid, uninvited, undeniably aware.

The King lifted his head slowly, lips glistening. Their eyes met across the room. The air shifted with dangerous possibility.

The Queen then guided her King effortlessly into the heart of Club Noir, threading through corridors that dripped with shadows, where bodies writhed slowly, whispers merging with moans into a sensual symphony. Her fingertips trailed lightly along his lower back, the subtle touch a silent assertion of claim. They moved as if they owned not only the place, but the air itself.

Their destination waited: a blonde temptress with honey-toned skin and curves that spoke softly of submission, but whose eyes glittered dangerously with forbidden curiosity. She leaned languidly against a pillar, a vision in sheer and lace that promised sin beneath innocence, her presence begging to be unraveled.

Without hesitation, the Queen approached, heels clicking like a heartbeat of anticipation. She leaned in close, her lips brushing the woman's ear, voice dripping like venom-laced honey. "Do you know what you're asking for?"

The woman's breath hitched visibly, pulse fluttering at her throat. She nodded eagerly, eyes wide and filled with promises she was too naïve to fully comprehend.

"That's it, beautiful," the Queen whispered, voice both comforting and cruel.

She turned slightly, glancing toward the King, her gaze sparking with silent challenge. He watched her with dark intensity, and restraint. The Queen smiled knowingly, reaching out one hand toward the King, a silent request, one he understood immediately.

He didn't hesitate, stepping closer, tension radiating from every inch of his massive frame. His chest strained against the thin barrier of his shirt, tattoos vivid beneath sweat-glistening skin, eyes alight with molten anticipation.

She pressed herself against him, her body molding into the hard lines of his frame, fingers tracing the sharp angles of his jaw. Her voice was silk, edged with venomous command. "She's waiting, my King. You could taste her…if I allowed it."

He reminded her, "You know the rules."

A smile ghosted her lips, wicked and knowing. "Yes. And I made them."

He didn't move, didn't flinch. But tension tightened, his eyes darkened, and storm clouds gathering in their depths. She stepped away slowly, savoring the battle that played behind his carefully composed expression.

She circled back to the temptress. Her fingers grazed down the woman's bare arm, eliciting a shiver, before leaning in and kissing her throat softly. The woman moaned quietly as the Queen's mouth explored upward, along her jawline, finally claiming her lips.

The kiss deepened, ruthless and demanding. The woman melted beneath the onslaught, legs trembling, knees weakening. She fell back onto the plush cushions and didn't fight for air. She surrendered it.

The Queen glanced at the King once more, eyes glinting with challenge. "You won't touch her?" she asked softly, taunting him gently, provocatively.

He gave a slow, deliberate shake of his head. "This is your game."

"Then watch me win," she purred.

She lowered herself gracefully, silk pooling around her knees, mouth finding warm skin, teeth biting softly, leaving red marks of ownership. Her hands explored gently at first, then harder, more insistent, leaving trails of red marks that spoke of promises the woman hadn't known she was asking to fulfill.

Her lips met the temptress's mouth, deliberately slow, ruthless in their dominance, a claiming kiss. Her tongue explored, tasting submission, drawing whimpers, fueling desire until the woman beneath her was breathless, dizzy, helplessly undone.

Still, the King didn't move. But his eyes never left her. A primal growl, nearly inaudible, vibrated deep within his chest.

The Queen withdrew, slowly licking the taste of conquest from her lips, before walking deliberately back to her King. He met her gaze, rigid but unwavering, disciplined restraint battling raw temptation beneath his dark eyes.

She straddled him without hesitation, claiming his lap as her throne.

"Now," she commanded softly, "fuck your Queen."

His control cracked, just slightly. He shifted beneath her, powerful thighs tensing. His cock, hard and impatient, pressed firmly between her parted thighs. His mouth found her neck, teeth grazing dangerously, hands gripping her hips with unyielding strength. His hips rocked up slowly at first, then harder and deeper, until pleasure spiraled through them both.

She rolled against him, rhythm building faster, matching the beat of the club around them. Their bodies collided again and again in primal rhythm, each thrust more possessive, more desperate than the last. She clutched his shoulders, her moans dissolving into cries of pleasure, nails digging into his skin as she rode him mercilessly.

Their climax shattered all pretense, a mutual surrender so intense it left them breathless, shaking, joined in sweat-soaked silence.

But afterward, as they caught their breaths and bodies cooled, something lingered beneath the surface: something sharper, colder.

His hands didn't hold her close. His breathing slowed, disciplined once more. A distance returned, more pronounced now than before, like a shadow slowly growing between them.

She rose silently, adjusting her dress. The King remained seated, eyes fixed forward, unreadable.

The room had gone quiet around them, the crowd sensing the fracture beneath the spectacle. She tilted her head slightly, watching the King carefully. "Are you satisfied?"

"Are you?" he replied, his voice deceptively calm.

She swallowed hard, seeing the barely hidden wound she had inflicted. Neither answered the other, not directly. And the club sensed it.

The Queen walked away, heels clicking against marble, leaving her King to the silence. Her pulse thudded heavily in her chest, pleasure replaced now by an emptiness she hadn't felt before. Something had changed between them. She just didn't know yet what had been lost.

The Queen's thighs trembled slightly as she rose from her throne, the King's lap, still damp with evidence of their climax. Her heart raced, her breathing shallow from lingering pleasure, yet beneath it coiled a tension she hadn't anticipated. A silence had fallen, heavier and colder than she'd ever felt between them.

"You didn't touch her," the Queen murmured softly, her voice laced with quiet accusation and subtle confusion, echoing intimately between them. "Not once."

The King's gaze, distant now, narrowed with a quiet intensity. "You didn't need me. You needed an audience."

His words sliced through her, sharp and precise, revealing a wound she hadn't intended to inflict. Before she could answer, the air around them shifted palpably, sensing vulnerability. From the shadows, bodies emerged slowly, emboldened by the fracture between them.

A group of men approached first: five powerful figures, boldly encircling her like predators drawn by the scent of vulnerability. Their eyes openly devoured the sight of her flushed skin, lingering over her breasts beneath the silk, the curve of her hips, the glistening moisture still visible on her thighs.

The King sat motionless, deliberately indifferent, a dangerous stillness radiating from him.

One man stepped closer, reaching boldly, fingers brushing gently along her bare arm, eliciting an involuntary shiver from her. The King's voice, deep and commanding, broke through the tension instantly.

"No one touches my Queen."

But even as he spoke, three women began to circle slowly toward him, their eyes heavy with desire and unmistakable intent. The King stiffened slightly, sensing their approach but refusing to break his focus on the Queen.

Jealousy surged fiercely inside her, hot and possessive. "No one touches my King," she echoed sharply, voice loud, commanding absolute authority.

She moved quickly, pushing past the circle of men, reclaiming her space. The three women paused in their approach, cautious but unyielding, their eyes challenging her silently even as they respected her command.

The Queen reached the King swiftly, reclaiming her position before him, facing him directly, her voice hard with command and possession.

"Strip," she demanded coldly, her gaze locked onto his, unwavering.

Without hesitation, he obeyed, removing every shred of clothing until he stood gloriously bare, his muscled, ink-covered body radiating strength and dominance that only she could command. She circled him slowly, deliberately, fingertips tracing along his powerful frame, reclaiming every inch as hers.

"You are mine," she whispered, voice lethal, possessive, daring him to challenge.

"Then prove it," he challenged quietly, voice edged with restrained anger and desire.

She sank to her knees before him—proud, dominant, and uncompromising. Her lips parted deliberately, tongue slowly tracing the hard length of him, savoring the taste of his arousal, reclaiming the territory she momentarily risked losing.

He groaned softly, fingers instinctively threading into her hair, guiding her mouth deeper along him. The room watched in rapt silence, the voyeuristic tension mounting.

Suddenly, he pulled her upward sharply, crushing her mouth with his. Then he turned her and bent her over the throne's padded edge, holding her there like a sentence.

"Tell them", he growled harshly against her ear, his cock pressing firmly against her slick entrance, teasing her cruelly. "Who fucks you? Who owns your pleasure?"

"You do," she gasped loudly, body trembling beneath his powerful grasp. "Only you, my King."

He thrust inside her mercilessly, deep, punishing, reclaiming her before the entire room. Her screams echoed through Club Noir, pleasure and dominance blending fiercely, unmistakably. Her hips bucked hard against his powerful thrusts, fingers gripping velvet desperately, losing herself completely in his ruthless possession.

Their shared climax ripped through them violently, voices mingling in raw, primal release, their bodies locked together fiercely in a public reaffirmation of their power. Yet afterward, breathing heavily, bodies still joined, he whispered darkly into her ear, "You tested the throne tonight. Next time, I may let you lose." Withdrawing from her abruptly, he left her shaken and exposed. He dressed quietly, refusing to look back, and left her standing alone: claimed yet abandoned, victorious yet defeated.

The room returned cautiously to life, whispers and speculative murmurs rising softly. The Queen adjusted her dress slowly, chin raised defiantly despite the vulnerability beneath. Her eyes briefly touched upon the five men still observing her hungrily from the shadows, and the three women lingering nearby—watching, waiting, sensing an opening.

She moved quietly toward her King, determined to repair the damage she'd inflicted, knowing their fracture might be deeper than she'd ever realized.

The King let a slow smirk tug at the corner of his lips, amusement gleaming in his dark eyes as he began to move. His powerful frame stalked in a slow, deliberate circle around the three kneeling women, his inked skin slick with the remnants of his queen. Each step was intentional, calculated, designed to feed the heat in his queen's belly: the fire of jealousy, of rage, of helplessness. And they knew it.

The three women had no intention of making this decision easy for him. They wanted to be chosen. Needed to be chosen. And they would make sure he knew exactly what he would be missing if he didn't.

The golden-skinned woman lifted her chin, her full lips curving into a knowing smile. Her red silk dress clung to her in ways that left nothing to the imagination, the curves of her breasts spilling out, nipples peeking through the sheer fabric.

"I will worship every inch of you, my King," she purred, voice dripping with seduction. "My mouth was made to serve you, to bring you to the edge again and again until you can take no more." She licked her lips slowly, deliberately. "I will take you so deep you'll forget anyone else exists."

The green-eyed woman was next, her soft, sculpted body wrapped in lace that barely held her. She tilted her head, her hands gliding down her own curves as if presenting herself.

"My King," she whispered, her voice velvet, her fingers tracing the swell of her breasts. "You have never known true pleasure until you have felt my tongue and my hands work in perfect unison to please you." Her legs shifted, parting just enough to reveal the wet heat between them. "Let me show you what it means to be devoured."

The dark-skinned beauty was last, her eyes simmering with wicked delight. She was a vision of pure temptation, hips full, thighs pressing together, her body made for indulgence. Unlike the others, she turned her gaze to the queen first, smiling.

"But why choose just one, my King?" she mused, her voice a sultry melody. "Wouldn't it be a shame to deny yourself the pleasure of all three of us at once?" She leaned forward, her breasts heavy, her scent intoxicating. "And wouldn't it be even more divine…if your Queen joined us?"

The air grew thick, charged with the weight of it all. The Queen stood frozen, her jaw tight, her body trembling. She was suffocating.

Her stomach twisted violently as she watched them, their shameless offers laced with sin, their bodies poised to take what belonged to her. She fought to keep her composure, but inside, she was unraveling. If he took them…if he let them touch him, taste him, claim him, she would never forgive him.

Her hands clenched at her sides, nails biting into her palms as the worst thought plagued her, what if he enjoyed it? What if he found something in them that she could never give? What if he decided he wanted more?

She bit down on her lip hard enough to taste blood, her heart hammering as she forced herself to breathe. But then she saw it. The King's hand.

Slowly, he moved as if to grab his thick, perfectly-imperfectly curved manhood, still slick with her essence, his tatted thighs glistening with their shared sins. Her vision blurred for a split second, rage and despair warring inside her.

She turned, her eyes landing on the man who had knelt before her, the one who had licked their combined juices from the floor. He was staring at her now, hope flickering in his gaze, a silent plea.

She sucked in a sharp breath. No. No, she could not bear this.

And as if sensing the depths of her agony, the King spoke, "Choose."

The word was a dagger to her chest.

He turned to her fully now, his voice steady, unyielding. "Choose one…or all three," he commanded. "And exact their pleasure, or their punishment."

The room fell deathly silent. A single tear slipped from her eye. She stiffened her chin, refusing to let the rest follow. Her breath was shaky, her lips parting, but the words wouldn't come. Before she could force them out, the women spoke again, desperation clinging to their voices.

The golden-skinned one pressed her hands together, pleading. "Let me make you forget, my King. Let me take all of your pain and turn it into pleasure."

The green-eyed woman's fingers ghosted over her own throat, her breath hitching. "Command me. Use me. Take me any way you desire."

The dark-skinned beauty smirked. "Or let me bring your Queen to her knees beside you, my King…let us both worship at your feet."

The Queen's hands trembled. Her throat was thick, her voice barely above a whisper as she finally spoke.

"Please…" Her voice cracked, her dominance shattered. "Spare me the pain of watching you take them all. If you must…let only one serve you with her mouth."

The room exhaled as if they had been holding their breath. The King, however, remained silent. His heart clenched at the raw ache in her voice.

He had brought her to this breaking point. He had reduced his Queen to this fragile, desperate thing. And though he burned with the need to comfort her, he wasn't done yet.

His eyes darkened, and he turned, not to the women, but to the man. The one who had looked at his Queen earlier. "Come forward," the King commanded.

The man obeyed instantly, rising from his knees. And as he approached, the Queen couldn't help but notice: his manhood was impressive, thick, hard, twitching with need.

A ripple of anticipation went through the room. The women's faces flickered with disappointment, realizing he was not being called for them.

The Queen, still trembling, assumed her King would use him to service one, or all of the women instead. Relief flooded her.

Until the King turned to her once more. "Whisper your choice to me," he commanded.

Her breath hitched. She hesitated. Then, with reluctant steps, she moved closer, her lips barely brushing his ear as she gave him her answer.

His body tensed. His tattoos stretched as his muscles clenched, the lion on his chest flexing, the spartan warrior on his back seeming to come alive. He pulled back, his gaze burning into hers.

"So you have chosen who you would deem worthy of my life force?" His voice was low, filled with an unreadable emotion.

Her throat bobbed. Slowly, she nodded. His jaw tightened.

He turned to the man. "Has she chosen?" he asked, though his voice carried no expectation of an answer.

The room was suffocating with tension. And then, suddenly, he exhaled, his voice turning sharp, filled with bitter disappointment.

"Is there any one woman that can equal my fucking Queen?!" he bellowed.

The women gasped, kneeling deeper, salivating, desperate. The Queen's heart pounded, her panic taking over. "No," she gasped, a strangled sound, stepping forward. "Please—"

The King's gaze snapped to her. His voice was razor-sharp. "How many men, including your selection, can match the bedding pleasures your King gives you?"

The silence stretched. Her lips quivered, then her answer came as a whisper. "All the men in this room, and it still would not be enough."

The air was electric. And then, he moved. He carefully selected five of the most handsome, well-endowed men from the crowd.

"Stand before her," he commanded.

The men rushed forward, their bodies chiseled, their excitement evident. The room vibrated with energy. The King's voice dropped to ice. "Do not touch her unless I command it."

He turned back to his Queen, his eyes cold, his pain raw. "Say your selection."

She shook her head. He clenched his jaw. Then, as if testing her further, he called forth two more women. His voice cracked with heartbreak. "Choose who you will share the life force of your King with, my love."

Tears welled in his eyes. She would not say. He glanced down. All were ready.

And the room waited. The King's voice split the air like a lion's roar. "If you wish to worship your Queen, my Queen with your mouths, drop to your knees."

The command sent a violent pulse through the room. Bodies shuddered in anticipation. All around them, the electric scent of sex, sweat, and sin thickened as the tension snapped into something raw, something primal.

And then, they fell. Five men. Five sculpted, powerful, well-endowed men. Five wolves kneeling before a Queen stripped of her throne.

The first was a towering god of muscle and dark, polished skin, his sculpted abs flexing as his hands rested on his powerful thighs. His cock—long, thick, veined like a warrior's blade—pulsed with hunger.

The second was golden-brown, a chiseled Adonis with tribal ink licking up his forearms, his tongue slowly tracing his lips, his dark eyes locking onto her exposed thighs.

The third's chocolate skin glowed beneath the club's heat, his dreadlocks falling against his broad shoulders as he exhaled sharply, his heavy shaft twitching as if he could already taste her.

The fourth was lean but lethal, abs carved like a Grecian god, his long fingers twitching in anticipation as he stared at the place between her legs that still dripped with the ruin of her King.

The fifth and others looking on were a perfect mix of strength and stamina, of wicked grins and hung cocks. They were already fisting themselves, as the sight of the Queen standing before them with her thighs quivering too much to bear.

Their Queen. They wanted to feast, and she wanted to be devoured. But not like this.

At first, her lips parted in pleasure at the sight of them kneeling, offering themselves to her in submission. Her body still hummed, her muscles weak from her King's brutal, unrelenting claiming of her. She should be reveling in this, in the hunger in their eyes, in the throbbing ache between their legs meant only for her.

But then she felt it. The disconnection. The chasm between her and her King. It was a subtle shift at first—an ache in her chest, a weight pressing against her ribs.

And then, as if the weight grew claws, it dragged her down.

She wobbled, her dominance flickering, her balance shifting dangerously. And he saw it.

The King stiffened from where he stood, his jaw locking, his muscles tightening. His heart screamed for him to yell, to stop this before it was too late. But he didn't move.

He was paralyzed, watching in slow, agonizing motion as his queen swayed slightly, as her legs shifted, as her thighs, his thighs, prepared to part.

And then, his mind betrayed him. The image hit him like a war hammer to the ribs. He saw it all: his Queen, pinned beneath their mouths, her head thrown back, her body offered to them. He saw them licking into her, fingers spreading her open, tongues diving deep, drinking every drop of her.

He saw her whimpering. Shaking. Taken. And then, the skulls on his chest ached. Another five. Another five deaths in his collection if she let them touch her.

The Queen's cold stare flickered. Then, it softened. And he knew that she saw his pain.

The club around them was a fever dream of sex and chaos: women moaning, bodies writhing, men groaning as they spilled onto waiting tongues. And yet, the stares of the onlookers were on them.

"Goddamn, she's gorgeous."

"I'd kill to be in their place."

"That's a fucking Queen right there."

But none of them mattered. Because her King was breaking.

The seconds stretched into minutes, and the entire world balanced on a single, fragile moment.

The Queen's mind flickered back to her king beneath the mouths of other women, their lips wrapping around the thick weight of him, their tongues exploring what belonged to her.

She saw them suck him. Worship him. She saw them stroke the pulsing length of him, their hands gripping his thighs, their mouths eager to claim his pleasure.

And then, she came back to herself. The King did, too. Their eyes finally locked, and their hearts ached to embrace.

She moved, stepping toward him. Toward her King, toward home. But she never reached him. Because in an instant, two of the men at her feet grabbed her thighs, their tongues darting out, tasting the sweat-slicked skin that led to her most intimate place.

A third moved in, mouth parting, breath hot against her swollen clit. At the same time, a man behind her groaned at the sight of her pink, gaping pussy, fully exposed, glistening, her full, untouched bush adorning the base of her pleasure.

The King saw red. He moved, with rage flooding his veins. But the three women stopped him. One gripped his thick, sensitive cock in her palm, wrapping her lips around the head, sucking him deep before he could push her away.

Another grabbed his massive arms, fingers running over the carved muscle as she tried to steal a taste of his lips.

His Queen screamed. Tears erupted down her cheeks. Her plea for reconciliation had become a battlefield of lust and betrayal, and it was too much.

They both ripped away. Clothes were snatched, bodies shoved aside. The King's voice was a death sentence. "Any man who touched her without my command, your punishment will be harsh. And unforgiving."

And they knew he meant it. The battle scars on his body were nothing compared to the war inside him.

As they dressed, the silence between them was so deafening it screamed. And then, she did something that shattered him. She reached for his hand.

And then he grabbed her like she was air in his lungs. He picked her up, his arms wrapping around her with a force so desperate it broke him.

And for the first time, the King wept. Not loudly, not violently. But silently. His tears slipped against her skin, his torment unspoken.

She kissed his lips, but he wasn't in the present. His mind was a battlefield. He saw her under them. She saw him under them.

It had only been moments. But it had felt like eternity.

"Are you okay?" he asked, his voice masking the storm inside him.

She swallowed her own despair and forced a small smile. "Yes."

But everything had changed. Her hand slid onto his thigh. His fingers curled against her skin. She kissed him again.

But neither could shake the truth. What had once been impenetrable now had a crack. And through it, something dark, something unspoken, something waiting to consume them both, was slipping in.

The Queen stood in silence, one heel still on the throne, her inner thighs glistening with the final traces of the King's worship. The heavy beat of Club Noir continued to pulse around them, but it felt distant now, like the sound of war drums echoing from beyond castle walls.

Her eyes remained fixed on the King, who had retreated several paces back, his breath still uneven, his broad chest rising and falling with the weight of what they had just done.

The crowd began to shift again. Lust hadn't faded, but reverence had been replaced by uncertainty. Something unseen had cracked beneath the spectacle. And the Queen felt it too. Felt it like the echo of a scream locked behind stained-glass eyes.

She stood tall, chin high, though a tremble teased her knees. Her body hummed with pleasure, but her heart felt like it had been scratched, just beneath the surface. It wasn't pain, not yet. But the knowing that pain was coming.

The King fastened his pants in silence, his hands slow and deliberate. The air clung to his sweat-damp skin, tracing the deep grooves of his inked muscles. His gaze remained low for a beat too long, as if something within him refused to meet hers just yet. And that alone chilled her more than a thousand jealous stares from the room.

She moved to him, slowly, the same way she had approached prey in the past, but this was no conquest. This was a plea.

"I meant what I said," she whispered, reaching to brush his jawline with the backs of her fingers. "They all want you. But only I own you."

He didn't flinch. But he didn't soften, either.

"You gave them a show," he said quietly. "One that might have cost us more than it earned."

Her hand dropped from his face. "Don't you dare put this on me. We were fire tonight. Untouchable. We made gods jealous."

His head finally lifted, and his eyes met hers: dark, worn, and glinting with something ancient. "Gods fall, too."

That struck her harder than it should have. For a moment, her breath stalled, her lip parting to offer a retort. But nothing came. The King turned from her again, retrieving his shirt from the back of the throne where it had been tossed. He didn't put it on.

She followed, bare beneath the lace that still clung to her curves like melted sin. "So that's it? You let me ride your face in front of a room full of sinners, and now you're too broken to look at me?"

His shoulders tensed. "I'm not broken."

"Then say something real."

He turned abruptly, the full weight of his body towering before her again. The intensity in his voice cut through her like a blade laced with history.

"You played the crowd like a violin. You invited a stranger into our space. You demanded I kneel like some conquered knight. And still, I gave you everything."

"I never took what wasn't mine," she snapped back.

He stepped closer, eyes narrowing. "And yet, you stood above me like a Queen proving to the world she could control her King."

The Queen's spine stiffened. "Isn't that what this was always about? Power. Pleasure. Spectacle."

"No," he said, voice now low, broken at the edges. "It was about us."

She faltered.

He pressed forward. "And tonight, it wasn't."

The space between them tightened. Not physically—they were still close enough to feel each other's heat—but emotionally, the chasm widened. And for the first time, she didn't know how to close it.

"You let that stranger stay on his knees longer than you kept me at your side," he said bitterly.

Her brows furrowed. "He was never a threat."

He didn't reply.

She whispered, "You're jealous."

"I'm betrayed," he corrected.

Her chest tightened. "No one touched me but you."

"And yet," he said, stepping back again, "it still feels like something was taken." His words hung in the air, heavy and raw.

She crossed her arms over her chest, suddenly aware of how exposed she was. "I can't undo it."

"I don't want you to," he said. Her eyes met his, confused.

He continued, "I just want to understand if tonight was about us...or just you."

She stepped forward again, brushing her lips near his ear. "I don't want anyone but you."

"Then stop testing me like you do."

That cracked something in her. She pulled back, blinking fast. "So what? You're saying I went too far?"

He nodded once. "I'm saying I don't know how far you plan to go."

That silence returned, the one that came not from peace, but from the threat of something sacred unraveling. She turned away first this time, adjusting her dress slightly, straightening her spine.

"You always said you loved how dangerous I was," she said softly.

"I did," he replied.

She paused, almost afraid to ask. "And now?"

"I'm wondering if I should've been more dangerous too."

That stung more than anything else he'd ever said.

She turned to him, tears fighting for purchase in the corners of her eyes, but she would not let them fall. Not here, not now. Not in the kingdom they'd built on dominance and desire.

The Queen stood still, arms wrapped across her body as if she could hold in the ache swelling beneath her ribs. The weight of his words echoed in her skull: 'I'm wondering if I should've been more dangerous too.'

She turned her head slowly, as if afraid that any sudden movement might shatter what remained between them. But he was already walking away. No fire. No farewell. Just silence.

She wanted to call after him. To grab his hand. To demand he not leave her alone in a room still reeking of lust and their unraveling. But the pride that had built her throne, that had made her Queen, kept her lips sealed.

He walked to the far side of the room, muscles taut, his skin glowing beneath the soft lighting. Women's eyes followed him, still dripping with desire, but now tempered by fear. Because they knew what had just passed between their King and Queen was not a performance. It was prophecy. Something sacred had broken. Something they'd all believed was unshakable.

The Queen turned back toward the throne, her heels clicking with finality on the marble floor. She sank onto the plush seat, not to rule nor command, but to feel something beneath her again that didn't shift. That didn't tremble beneath the weight of uncertainty.

Her fingers traced the edge of the seat, the same one where she'd knelt earlier, where she'd begged his mouth to remember every inch of her. The memory made her clench involuntarily, but the heat turned to ash.

She looked down at herself. Her thighs were still sticky with the remnants of his devotion, but instead of pride, she felt hollow. She had everything. And now, she wasn't sure she had him.

Her fingers trembled as she reached for her heels, slipping them off slowly, letting them fall to the floor with two dull thuds that seemed louder than the club's pulsing music.

Chapter 2: Kings and Queens and Quiet War

The drive home was usually filled with laughter, teasing, and stolen touches that promised the night had only just begun. After nights like those, their bodies burned for each other before the front door had even closed. Pinned against hallway walls, gasping between bites of lips and the frantic tearing of clothing. The world outside vanished in a haze of lust and love.

But tonight was different. The hum of the engine was louder than their words. Silence bled through the space between them like fog, wrapping itself around every thought they were too afraid to speak aloud. The drive resumed, but something heavier hung between them now. Not silence, something older. Something sharp.

Streetlights flickered past in rhythmic flashes, casting long shadows over their faces, both beautiful and unreadable.

The King drove, both hands on the wheel, posture upright, muscles stiff. A practiced calm radiated from him, but it was deceptive. Inside, he was on fire. Thoughts stormed through him, visions of the night they just left behind playing in relentless loops. One image, more than any, haunted him: The fourth man.

A sculpted warrior of masculine perfection. Broad-shouldered, thighs thick with power. His body inked with black fire, and his eyes locked onto the Queen like she was prey. He had watched her with open hunger, his cock twitching against his thigh, waiting. Waiting to taste her. To drag his tongue through the slick mess that still belonged to her King.

The King's jaw flexed again. He tightened his grip on the steering wheel, the leather creaking under his fingers. The taste of bile rose in his throat as his imagination refused to release him. He saw it all: the stranger parting her legs, dragging his mouth across her folds, sucking the remnants of the King's claim from her body.

Beside him, the Queen shifted, "Will you stop and get me something sweet to drink?" she asked, her voice light. Too light.

It caught him off guard. The mundane request felt almost jarring, like a needle dropped into the middle of a battlefield. For a moment, it cooled the fire inside him. He gave a brief nod and turned into the nearest gas station.

But as she looked out the window, her own mind drifted elsewhere: far from syrupy drinks and quiet car rides. She saw him, her King.

His hands tangled in the hair of the women from the club, his cock buried deep in the mouth of one, while the other stroked his chest, licking along his collarbone.

She saw him stretch them out like offerings, his teeth in their throats, his voice a guttural snarl as he spilled himself inside them. Her stomach flipped.

The car slowed, the tires crunching over loose gravel. The King stepped out, his frame towering in the gas station's flickering light. As he moved through the store, the Queen's eyes lingered on him: broad back, black shirt clinging to his damp skin, hands flexing unconsciously at his sides.

He had always bought her drink after a night like this. It was their ritual. He knew she needed the sugar, the rush, the normalcy. But tonight, the act felt hollow. Like muscle memory. Like a performance.

She watched through the windshield, eyes catching the way his lips thinned as he reached into the cooler. But what she didn't see, was the way his eyes flicked to the shelf of cookies…and skipped right past the oatmeal raisin, their favorite. The one he always bought for himself, even though she stole the first bite.

He came back to the car without it. She noticed. She also noticed the silence as he handed her the drink. She twisted the cap and drank half of it in one gulp before the car even left the lot. He noticed that, too.

The drive resumed in silence, but now there was something deeper behind it. A revelation, the kind you don't say aloud.

The King glanced over. She looked perfect: hair tousled, makeup smudged in the sexiest way, her thighs still glistening beneath her skirt. She was his. But tonight, she hadn't felt like it.

When they arrived at the house, she got out first, heels clicking against the driveway stone. The sound used to turn him on. Tonight, it echoed.

The Queen opened the front door. "I'll start the shower," she said over her shoulder, casual and unshaken. Until she saw it when he removed his pants: Lipstick, on his cock. Not her shade.

Her world tilted. She didn't scream. didn't crumble. She simply pointed. "Get that off you," she said, voice like broken glass. Then she turned away.

The King stood frozen for a beat. Then he saw it. Bruises, fingerprints on her hips. Deep, wide, male hands that weren't his, and his blood ran ice-cold.

He didn't follow her to the shower. Instead, he stood in the middle of the living room, staring at nothing, chest rising and falling with a slow, dangerous rhythm.

She showered alone. He cleaned himself in silence. When they crossed paths again, she tried to joke. "I guess you got everything you wanted tonight. No cookie. No pussy needed."

His voice was ice. "Mine washed off," he said, pausing just long enough to pierce her heart. "But your bruises, my love, will be there tomorrow."

And then, he walked away. No kiss. No reclaiming. No redemption.

She crawled into bed alone, curling around the pillow that smelled like him, aching in places she didn't have words for. He didn't come.

And when the morning came, it was polite. Hollow. No worship. No morning destruction. Just a peck.

And as he left, he muttered, "I'm late."

He drove straight to the gym, tension crackling beneath his skin. Not for pleasure, but for battle against the iron. A promise to himself if he could inflict such pleasurable pain, he can reward himself with a black coffee and a blueberry scone.

Ellie got herself together, and as she had always done since she discovered this gem of a café years ago, she stopped for coffee. Iced, sweet, and just the right kind of comfort.

"Hey there."

She turned. Man Number Four. His suit looked painted on. Shoes sharp enough to wound. That devastating smirk again. He looked like he had walked out of GQ and straight into her morning.

And for a moment, she saw him nude again. His cock standing thick and proud, his abs glistening, his lips parting as he groaned. She flushed.

"Oh, forgot me already?" he teased, his smirk devastating.

She stumbled over her words, shaking her head. "You must be mistaken." And then, she left. But the thoughts followed her. She condemned herself, forcing her King into her mind, into her body.

And then, a tap at her window. She startled. Man Number Four handed her the coffee she'd forgotten. A brief laugh. A small thank you. Then she didn't just feel it, but she saw it.

Her King, walked up and saw them. He kept his head cool despite the fire within. His fists clenched as he turned and walked away, but his expression remained unreadable. Calm. Controlled. Deadly.

She quickly got out the car and had grabbed his arm, his Queen, trying to explain something with her eyes, but he hadn't stopped, hadn't flinched.

He simply stared at her with a single tear dropping from his eye. He bowed slightly and simply said, "My Lady." Inside him, however, the battlefield raged.

The smug look on the stranger's face replayed over and over. That man, her admirer, had smiled like a man who didn't know he was already dead as he causally walked away.

And in the King's mind, he had already killed him. The vision struck hard and fast: He saw himself closing the distance between them. Slow, silent, and final. He saw the man's confidence falter, the smile fade, then crack.

One punch. The man's lip split, his head snapping back from the force of it. Blood spattered against the concrete. The suit, once pristine, darkened where it soaked in his humiliation. But the King didn't stop. The next strike shattered cartilage. His knuckles cracked. Bone met bone with the sound of drums.

By the time the fantasy ended, the man was unrecognizable. A bloodied ruin at the King's feet. And he whispered down at him, cold and calm, "Now you know."

Then, reality returned with a slow blink. The rage remained.

The King walked forward, jaw tight. His gaze swept over the man's tailored arrogance, the perfect shoes, the confidence of a man who had never faced a real god.

He didn't strike. Not yet. Instead, he "accidentally with purpose" knocked the coffee from his hand with a flick of his wrist. The cup spun midair. Splash. Lukewarm liquid sprayed across man number four's expensive suit. The man froze, shocked. Speechless.

The King stepped into his space, voice low, controlled, and dangerous. He said it calm, too calm, hoping for a reaction that would awaken the mighty warrior that told him to destroy him ten times over, "I think you may have spilled your coffee."

She stood next to him, waiting for a reaction that would not come. And then, he was gone.

He drove in silence. Classic Nas," Street Dreams" played low, a mockery of restraint. His jaw ached from grinding. His hands tightened on the wheel. Every breath was a countdown to the explosion he kept just beneath the surface.

The voices in his head screamed at each other: "She wanted it. She let him stand there, talk to her, look at her. She didn't stop it."

But another voice pushed through, "And you let them touch you. You let three women worship what belonged only to her. She stayed. Even then." His chest clenched. His temple throbbed. But he had made his decision.

The King shook the thoughts away as he arrived at work, slipping the mask of professionalism over his face like a shield. He smiled, but his eyes were hollow.

His admin Jean popped into his office, scantily dressed, leaning against the doorframe. Her perfume arrived before her voice, sweet and too eager.

"Everything okay?" she asked, voice laced with curiosity and something more.

A flash: His Queen, laughing across the dinner table, eyes alight with joy, stealing his fries, her warm giggles shaking the walls of his chest. That smile, his favorite thing in the world, his real world. The one he had cracked with his own hands.

"Sir?" the assistant called him back.

He cleared his throat, adjusted his suit, and gave a small, polite nod. "Apologies. A bit distracted." But there was no apology in the world for what he had done.

"Today is decision day for The Gemini Cyber project," Jean added. "You have been blowing this off, might I add, and not in the fun way. Today you are going to have to give it some of that good stuff too" The boardroom. A space of power. Of plans. Of masks.

He took his seat at the head of the table, surrounded by blank faces, power players and hungry executives. But only one pair of eyes held his attention: Green Eyes, the woman from the club. The one whose tongue had nearly touched sacred territory.

For a split second, a flash of her lips inches from his, whispering the filth she wanted to perform. How she had begged to worship him. How she had looked up at him like he was already hers.

He blinked, then refocused. His voice cut through the tension like a knife. "I have a hard stop at eleven. Let's get started."

But she knew he saw her. She knew because she had seen him, too. As the meeting blurred on, her mind was not on the spreadsheets or projections. She was back in the private room at the club. Watching him ruin his Queen, watching his body glisten with sweat, muscles tensed, veins pulsing.

She remembered how his fingers dug into his Queen's thighs, stretching her wide, breaking her in front of a worshiping crowd.

She had watched, aching to be in her place. And now, as she stood in front of him in her tight-fitting dress, her curves perfectly outlined, lips painted the same shade as sin. And she wondered, "what if?" What if he let her? What if his Queen slipped up again? Would he finally break? Would he finally take?

The clock struck 11:11 (Lucky Love). Her moment evaporated. His admin swept in like a storm, briefing him on his next obligation, her voice a blur in his ears.

No words for Green Eyes. No acknowledgement. But the electricity still danced between them like heat lightning, visible only to those who'd already been scorched.

After a day packed with meetings, the King loosened his tie as he neared the exit. He was ready to shed the suit. Ready to return to something real. Off came the jacket. His chest still looked lethal beneath the fitted dress shirt, shoulders broad, body crafted in sin and sacrifice.

His crown felt heavier than usual. His confidence? Not broken, but bent. Warped.

"Excuse me…excuse me!"

He ignored it at first. The voice was familiar. Soft. Sultry, persistent.

He turned. Green Eyes jogged toward him in heels, breathless. Slightly flushed. Perfectly disheveled. She smiled, calculated but radiant. "You move fast."

"I'm late for plans with my Queen." His voice was even, rehearsed.

She laughed lightly, tilting her head. "Lucky woman."

He smirked. But it didn't reach his eyes.

She leaned in just enough, her perfume catching him like a whip of memory. And then she mumbled under her breath, just loud enough: "Wish I was so lucky."

He heard her but pretended he didn't. She reached into her clutch, then handed him a card. No flourish, just an offering. He held his hand out instinctively. He glanced at it, then at her. "So your name isn't Green Eyes after all."

She smiled. "Guess not." He tucked the card away, uninterested. At least, that's what he told himself.

He turned to leave, and saw his phone had missed calls, messages. Then his phone rang. He answered.

Her voice was frantic. Shaky. Desperate. "My love?" she whispered. He barely listened. He heard everything, but it all sounded far away, like waves crashing beyond a closed window.

He simply said, "I understand, my lady." And it sounded softer than he meant. So much softer than she deserved after the sins they had both committed.

The silence between them was deafening. She whispered, "Am I your Queen, James?" He did not respond, not because he did not want to, but he did not hear her clearly.

Then, "AM I YOUR FUCKING QUEEN, BABE!?" she screamed.

It rattled his spine. His throat tightened. His voice cracked. "Yes, my lady. But your King…"

He paused and turned his back from Green Eyes. He stopped. Sighed. The silence swallowed them both whole.

She sat on the edge of their bed, gripping the phone like it was her last lifeline. Her heart was beating wildly. Her chest hurt. Her fingers trembled.

Then his voice returned, gentle and broken, "My Queen."

Her breath caught. "Yes."

"Indulge your wounded and humble King for a moment."

Her tears came faster. "Anything." She scrambled, fixing her hair, reaching for something sexy, some form of hope.

"Read Proverbs 6: 34-35." His voice was sharp now, carrying an ancient kind of ache.

And then, "My Queen." Click.

One final look at Green Eyes before saying, "It's been somewhat of a pleasure," and before she could speak, he was already walking off with his back turned The Queen stumbled to the nightstand and found the Bible. Her fingers shook as she turned the pages, whispering the verse aloud: *For jealousy is the rage of a man: therefore, he will not spare in the day of vengeance.*

Tears blurred her vision. She continued: *He will not regard any ransom; neither will he rest content, though thou givest many gifts.*

She sobbed, deep, gut-wrenching sobs. Because she knew what came next. And he was already halfway home.

In his Bentley, playing softly Nina Simone's "Don't Let Me Be Misunderstood" blared from the speakers.

He gripped the card in his hand, his chest rising like a battlefield drum, and without a second thought he put it in his inside pocket.

The King had fallen, and only war remained. At home, the door clicked shut behind him. James didn't speak. The faintest trace of lavender oil, cocoa butter, and sweat. The kind that lingers on skin after a fight. The kind that could make a man drop to his knees if he wasn't careful.

He moved through the hall like a soldier returning from war, unsure if the kingdom he'd fought for still stood, or if it had turned to ash in his absence. Then he saw her.

She stood barefoot in the kitchen, his shirt clinging to her frame like it had been designed to be ruined. It barely contained her curves: those full, aching breasts pressing against the cotton, hips draped in a sin that only he was ever supposed to taste.

She didn't turn around and didn't have to. She felt him watching and felt the thunder of his regret in every footstep.

Her hands shook as she stirred the sauce on the stove, and that alone made him ache. Her hands didn't shake. Not even when she was angry. But now? Now they trembled like they'd been touched by ghosts.

He cleared his throat. She didn't flinch. "I'm late," he said. His voice was sandpaper: gritty, dry, worn.

"You didn't text," she replied, barely above a whisper.

"I didn't think I needed to." Silence. And then she turned, slowly.

Her eyes were red. Her lips slightly swollen. But it wasn't mascara or leftover heat from a fight. It was from crying. The kind that doesn't just leak down your face, it pours from your soul. "I waited," she said simply.

And that broke him. He stepped forward, slowly, as if any sudden movement would cause her to disappear. "Ellie…" Her name felt like a prayer in his mouth. Like a sin wrapped in salvation.

She didn't move. Just stared at him. And then she whispered, "I didn't touch him."

He struggled within, but finally he said with his hands slightly trembling. "I know."

"You didn't even ask."

"I didn't have to."

Her throat bobbed. "Then why did you act like you hated me?"

His voice cracked. "Because I hated myself." The words dropped between them like a guillotine.

She exhaled, and her hands dropped to her sides. "Say it again."

"I hated myself," he repeated, eyes never leaving hers. "For letting them touch me. For thinking, even for a second, that anyone else could ever take your place. I hated myself for what I made you feel because of my moment of jealousy I agreed to."

Her breath caught, and for the first time since he walked in, she took a step toward him.

"I made dinner," she said softly.

"I'm not hungry." He paused "For food."

She lifted her chin. "Then what are you hungry for?"

His eyes darkened. She saw it. Felt it. That shift. That coil tightening between them. "Say it," she whispered, voice shaking now. "Tell me."

"I'm starving," he breathed. "Starving for you."

She stepped into him, placed her hand on his chest, fingers splaying over the lion tattoo that had once meant fury, but now only held her name. "Then take what you need," she said. "Because I need to give it."

He grabbed her. Not rough or tender. Desperate. Their mouths collided with a fury that had been building since the moment they walked out of Club Noir. Since the moment they let others into the spaces only they had ever filled.

She gasped into him, her hands diving into his curls, gripping tight as his tongue parted her lips and stole every ounce of air from her lungs.

He walked her backward, gripping her thighs as he lifted her effortlessly onto the counter, the pots still simmering behind them, forgotten.

"You still taste like mine," he growled into her mouth.

"I never stopped being yours."

His shirt, her shirt, was yanked up and over her head, exposing her breasts, nipples already hard, skin flushed with heat.

"Goddamn," he whispered, falling to his knees, his hands spreading her legs.

"James—" she gasped, but he didn't give her the chance to finish. His mouth was on her. Tongue thick and ravenous, dragging through her folds like he was reclaiming territory that had never truly been lost.

She cried out, her thighs trembling as he moaned against her, the vibrations nearly making her collapse. "I'm gonna cum—"

"Do it." And she did. Right into his mouth. Right onto his tongue.

He stood in one motion, undoing his pants with a speed that bordered on savage, freeing his cock and slamming into her in one long, brutal thrust.

She screamed. Not from pain. From worship. From being found again. His hips moved like war drums, his cock spearing into her with punishing precision, her body jerking with every impact.

He grabbed a handful of her hair, pulled her mouth to his, and kissed her like he'd never kiss another woman again. And he wouldn't. Because she was home. She was always home.

And as he spilled inside her, pulsing deep, grunting into her throat, he knew that no matter what came next, this moment was holy. They collapsed against each other, breathless. Silent. Not from distance, but from something sacred.

He kissed her temple. "We're not fixed."

"No."

"But we're not broken yet."

She nodded. And then, as the sauce on the stove began to burn behind them, she smiled.

Because even in the ash, there was still fire. Awake. Distant. Together, but frayed.

The Queen stared at the ceiling, one hand resting against his chest. The King watched the door, as if expecting ghosts to enter.

Neither of them noticed the clock. They had all night to feel everything they didn't know how to say.

Chapter 3: Whispers in the Club

The Queen sat on the edge of the bed, sunlight streaming across her skin like molten gold. It should have felt warm, holy even, this afterglow. The scent of their night still lingered in the air: sweat, sex, surrender. Her thighs ached in the most delicious way. Her lips still tingled from the weight of his kiss. And her heart…for a moment, it had felt steady again.

He'd kissed her goodbye just hours ago, voice laced with something between teasing and truth. "Make your fucking coffee at home today." It was meant to sting and soothe all at once, a whip cracked over silk.

She had smiled as he said it. Smiled when he turned back and kissed her one last time, deep and slow like a warning. Smiled when she pressed her face into the pillow that still smelled like him, still smelled like them. Her King, her storm.

She moved like she always did after a night like that: deliberate, elegant, humming under her breath as she gathered his things. It was ritual, really. A kind of intimate routine that made her feel grounded, cared for, in control.

She picked up his suit jacket, still draped across the barstool from where he'd dropped it mid-kiss. The memory made her smile again. She could still hear the hunger in his voice, feel his hands on her waist, remember how fast he'd lost control the moment she started undoing his buttons.

Her hands moved automatically, folding the blazer neatly, fingers brushing down the lapels. Then, habit took over. She reached into the inner pocket, fingertips sweeping for receipts, loose change, the usual clutter of a man who never fully unpacked.

The sheets still held his scent. Her body still bore the bruises of his grip. And her mind was a battlefield, but it hadn't gone to war yet. Not until that moment when her fingers, reaching for his suit jacket to send it to the cleaner, found something foreign in the inner pocket: A card. Sleek, clean, corporate. *Gemini Technologies*.

She frowned. Not uncommon. He met people everywhere. Deals happened in clubs, in lounges, even on rooftops if the skyline was right. She barely glanced at it at first, flipping it onto the counter with little thought. She had never been one to question the things he brought home from work.

But then, it flipped over. And on the back, handwritten, a personal number. A cold thread coiled around her spine. She picked it back up, inspecting the name printed neatly on the front. It wasn't familiar. But the personal number? The ink? The way it sat alone, untouched, as if it was something meant to be hidden?

Her lips pressed into a thin line. Her rational mind told her this was nothing. A professional contact. Someone from a meeting. But her instincts told her otherwise.

The nagging feeling wouldn't let go. And before she could talk herself out of it, she dialed. It rang once. Twice. Then a voice: soft, sultry, laced with something too knowing. "Hello?"

Her stomach tightened. She steadied herself. "Who is this?"

A slight pause. Then a quiet chuckle, smooth as silk. "Oh, you must be the Queen."

Her blood ran ice cold. She gripped the phone tighter, voice razor-sharp. "Who the fuck is this?"

Another laugh, low, entertained. "How lucky you are."

The Queen's breath stilled. The woman continued, her voice dripping with amusement. "We, met again yesterday. A coincidence, really. Business, but familiar." A slight hum. "Your King is quite the presence. He certainly left an impression."

Her heart pounded. She could hear the smirk in the woman's voice. The unspoken implications. And then, the final dagger: "I do hope to see you both at the club again soon."

The line went dead. She stood there, the silence pressing against her chest, the phone still in her hand. Her fingers tremble as her sorrow turned to anger.

She refused to let this feeling consume her. She glanced at the time. Barely an hour had passed since he left for the gym.

Her body moved on instinct. She tore the card apart, shredding it into pieces, then placed the remains exactly where he would see them when he returned.

That word: "Lucky." As though he'd been some prize handed to her by fate. As if she hadn't built the man. As if she hadn't poured her soul into shaping him from the wreckage he once was into the god he had become. As if she hadn't stood beside him when he was only a storm of ambition and rage and made herself lightning to match it.

Lucky? She was there the night he bled through his button-up after fighting three men who tried to shove her outside a bar. She had kissed the bruises, massaged his swollen fists, whispered his name like it was holy.

She had protected his reputation when he couldn't control his temper, and he had silenced every demon inside her with a single word.

"Mine."

She wasn't lucky. She was chosen. And more than that, she was the reason. And now some background player in their kingdom, wanted to reframe her legacy like it was chance? Her jaw clenched so hard her teeth ached.

She hadn't planned to go out that morning. She was going to clean up, maybe light a candle, replay last night in her head a few more times. But now? Now, she wanted coffee. And maybe war.

She moved through the bedroom like a weapon preparing for unsanctioned battle. Silk robe off. Dress on. Not too short, but enough to make them stare. Heels with a purpose. Red lips. Straight spine.

She didn't need to look in the mirror to confirm what she was. She was fire, forged in betrayal and sharpened by pride. And someone was going to feel her burn.

As she grabbed her keys from the entryway table, her eyes flicked once more to the trash bin. The card was in there now, ripped to confetti. But the rage wasn't.

It still throbbed under her skin like a second pulse. She opened the front door to full sunlight and stepped out without hesitation.

'Lucky' was the word the woman had used. The word that refused to stop echoing inside her skull. Not loved. Not worshipped. Not chosen. The word simmered, spreading through her bloodstream like poison. Her jaw clenched so hard her teeth ached. She laughed out loud.

Was she lucky when she poured everything into a man just to be questioned? Was she lucky when she kept her body loyal, her mind sharper, her kingdom intact while he waded through temptation and trials? Was she lucky when she gave up sleep, sanity, and her soul just to keep the fire burning?

No. She wasn't fucking lucky. She was forged. She had earned that man with blood and brilliance, with submission and steel. Her mouth was dry, but her voice inside was screaming. Who the fuck does she think she is?

Her eyes flicked to the iced coffee she'd made for herself that morning: hazelnut oat, his favorite scent on her breath when she kissed him goodbye. She lifted it without hesitation, peeled the lid off with a grace that bordered on violence, and poured the contents directly over his suit.

The jacket soaked, staining instantly, dark liquid cascading down the rich wool in jagged streaks. It wasn't just about the card. It was the principle.

The woman's smug tone. The way she had said his name. The way she had said "we met again." Again? Again?!

The cup clattered to the floor as the last of the coffee slipped from her fingers. The Queen stood there, chest heaving, anger humming beneath her skin like a second heartbeat.

And then…stillness. A single breath. Her reflection was calm and radiant. Dangerous. Today, she wasn't going to cry. She wasn't even going to scream. She was going to remind the world who the fuck she was. And she was going to start with coffee. The same kind she was told to make at home. Not today. Today, she would take it outside. She was coming for answers, or war. And whichever came first? So be it.

The Queen didn't strut. She stalked. The heels clicking beneath her were a declaration: measured, deliberate, and without apology. Her dress clung like wet sin to every curve, and her hair, pinned just loose enough to hint at recklessness, framed her face like a storm cloud promising devastation.

She'd worn it on purpose. The same look she'd once used to silence an entire room. The same look her King had once said made him forget his own name.

But today, she didn't wear it for him. Today, she wore it for war.

The coffee shop came into view like a stage waiting for its drama. Clean, curated, glass windows gleaming in the morning sun, the scent of espresso and cardamom thick in the air.

The place was nestled between a boutique fitness club and a bank. Modern, neutral, and just pretentious enough to have customers who thought they understood power because they wore tailored joggers and carried MacBooks.

She pushed the door open and was instantly met with the warm clatter of conversation, the low hiss of steamed milk, and that all-too-familiar gaze from the barista behind the counter. It flickered from her face to her legs, then to her mouth, like he was scanning for the part that might hurt him most. Good. She let him look.

She didn't say a word at first, only stepped up to the counter, eyes scanning the menu like she hadn't already memorized it. The barista snapped to attention, fumbling slightly with the tablet. "Welcome back. What can I get you?"

Her lips parted, slow. Controlled. "Cold brew. Extra ice. Light cream."

He blinked. "Same as—" He caught himself. "Coming right up."

She offered no thanks. Just swiped her card and turned to survey the room. She didn't see him at first, not the man from the club. Not Man Number Four. But she did feel it.

That tight, slippery sensation in her gut. The one that said she shouldn't be here. That she was already playing with fire. That she was about to touch something her King would never forgive her for even thinking about.

And still, she stayed. Her hand tightened around her phone as she waited, her fingers drumming silently against the screen. That woman had said, "Lucky."

The barista called her name. She didn't even look at him as she took the drink, her gaze still cutting through the room like a blade. She took a seat near the window, strategic. The light hit her just right, glowing on her skin, catching the gold in her eyeshadow. She crossed one leg over the other, her dress sliding just enough to stir a response from a man two tables over. She didn't look at him.

She was watching the door. Waiting. Her fingers wrapped around the chilled plastic cup. She sipped slowly, ignoring the sting of betrayal still lodged like glass in her throat.

He hadn't betrayed her. Not really. He hadn't fucked that woman. Hadn't kissed her. Probably hadn't even looked at her twice. But he had left that card in his pocket. Had brought it home.

Had let that woman's voice, her smug fucking voice, reach her ears. And now, no matter how she tried to spin it, no matter how tightly she wrapped her pride around her shoulders, the wound was bleeding.

He had said: "Make your fucking coffee at home." And she had tried. God, she had tried. But rage tastes better with ice and caffeine.

The bell above the door jingled. She didn't move at first. Just lifted her eyes through her lashes. And there he was: Man Number Four.

Same smirk. Same posture. Crisp white shirt rolled at the sleeves, revealing forearms that tried too hard. No tie today. Just casual arrogance.

He saw her. And that grin returned like it never had a reason to leave. "Well, well…" he said smoothly, standing. "didn't think I'd get this lucky two days in a row."

There it was again. *Lucky.* Her spine stiffened, but her face didn't change. "Is that so?"

He stepped closer. Too close. "Back for more coffee," he teased, "or did you actually miss me?"

Her blood went cold. The words were wrong. The voice, too familiar. She turned slowly, spine straightening, expression unreadable. She didn't blink. "Do you always mistake silence for permission?"

He chuckled, not phased. "Only when the silence comes with heels that loud and a dress that tight."

Then she leaned in, her mouth inches from his ear. "Didn't you get enough coffee yesterday?" she whispered. He had no idea who he was talking to.

But, before the next words could leave her mouth, before the chill in her stare could be unleashed, a memory overtook her. It crashed through her like a tidal wave. Sudden and violent. A different man, a different night.

The King and Queen had been walking from a bar, his hand warm in hers. Laughter from strangers filled the air, the city buzzing around them. Then the voices started. "Hey, pretty thing. Drop the old man, come ride with a real one." The King ignored them.

She squeezed his hand, urging him forward. Then, the mistake. A hand reached out. Fingers touched her hair, and he offered her his cock. The silence before the storm was terrifying. She had seen many sides of him. The ruler, the lover, the warrior. But that night? She saw the executioner.

The air shifted, thick and suffocating, and before she could speak, before she could stop him. It was destruction. A man reduced to nothing in a matter of seconds. Blood. Silence. The King's breathing, slow and even, as if he hadn't just ended something.

She had begged him to stop. But he hadn't heard her, and would only stop when there was nothing left to destroy. And her King: calm, controlled, and efficient. A surgeon with violence.

He stopped only when she grabbed him from behind, whispering that she was okay, that he could stop, that she was safe. He turned to her then, eyes wild and glassy with fury. And when he saw her trembling, he had gone still. He had looked at her like she was the only anchor in the world that could hold him in place.

She blinked, snapped back into the café, the aftershock of the memory still pulsing in her chest. And suddenly, she saw Man Number Four with different eyes. He wasn't dangerous. He was clownish. A child trying to play chess on a battlefield he didn't understand.

Her smile turned sharp. He walked toward her like he knew her body already. Like the exchange in the club had earned him the right to tease her. Like he didn't know that she wasn't a woman, but a Queen, and that he was treading in holy, dangerous territory.

"You looked like you enjoyed the show," he said, inching closer. "Just thought I'd offer you the solo version."

She stared. There was no shame in his gaze. No fear. But she wasn't unclaimed. She had never been unclaimed. Even when her King wasn't in the room, he was still everywhere.

"I see you're still confusing attention for affection." Her voice turned icy. The man blinked, clearly thrown.

She took a step closer, heels clicking like punctuation. "You think a smile makes you memorable? You think a compliment makes you dangerous?" Her voice dripped with condescension. "You're not a wolf. You're a dog barking at a Queen's chariot."

His smirk faltered. She stepped back, her gaze ice. "Don't flatter yourself," she said. "You are definitely no King."

"You done?" he asked. Trying to recover his edge.

She tilted her head again. "Actually, yes." And with that, she turned and walked away, every eye following her. None of them were him.

And that, more than anything, was the ache behind her calm. She didn't care what expression he wore, didn't care if his ego bled all over the floor behind her. She was already gone.

Outside, the sun had brightened. But it didn't touch her. Not this Queen. She walked back to the car like she was made of flame and fury, her nails biting into the leather strap of her purse. She didn't regret going. She regretted needing to go.

Because now she didn't just feel betrayed, she felt dirty. And it had nothing to do with him. The man from the club had nothing on her King. But that woman, and that voice, had managed to get under her skin in a way that few ever had. The word would echo for days. But not forever.

Now she knew exactly what she was fighting for. That was not war though. Not even close. But when it came? She'd be ready. Crown or no crown.

Meanwhile, the King stood in his office, adjusting the cuffs of his suit. The fabric stretched slightly over his broad shoulders, the muscles beneath flexing as he moved.

He felt good. His Queen had been warm this morning. The weight that had been on his chest felt lighter.

"You're glowing today," his admin Jean teased.

He smirked. "Am I?"

"Suit's fitting you extra nice. That a new workout routine?"

"Something like that."

She chuckled. "Whatever it is, keep doing it."

As she turned to leave, she paused. "Oh, before I forget. The CEO selected Gemini Technologies for your project."

His body froze. His mind snapped back to the card. Panic surged through him. Without a word, he bolted from his chair, rushing to his car. He had to get rid of it. But as he tore through the vehicle, flinging open compartments, and checking everywhere. He realized it was gone.

Back at the Estate, the Queen sat on the couch, laughing at the television. The King walked in, kissing her head. "I'm gonna shower. You joining me?"

"Of course," she said, barely looking at him. He smirked, pulling out his hardened length.

"Hurry up."

She hummed in response.

He entered their sanctuary, then stopped. His suit: coffee poured over it, and the business card shredded. Before he could react: A fist connected with his jaw. Then another. Slaps, violent, furious. "GET THE FUCK OUT!" she screamed.

He tried to explain. She wouldn't let him. Her voice rose, shaking the walls, her fury unchecked. And finally, broken, he left. Her sobs followed him.

The sound of the door slamming echoed in his mind long after he drove away. The weight of her sobs had settled into his bones, a cold ache that no amount of distance could shake.

He should have turned back. Should have pulled her into his arms and made her listen. Should have told her that he would never betray her, not in the ways that mattered, not in any way at all. But he hadn't.

Instead, he let the war inside him rage as he gripped the wheel, the city lights reflecting in his tired, hollow eyes. The night was clear, cruelly beautiful, as if the world had the audacity to carry on while his own had just collapsed. His mind spun, voices arguing, warring for dominance.

"You did nothing wrong."

"Then why does it feel like I have?"

"Because you let another woman put doubt in her mind. Because you let that card exist between you, let it poison what was sacred."

"She was the one in that coffee shop. She was the one with another man's eyes on her."

"She never once wavered. Never once let her heart stray. She stood before you in that kitchen, shaking, eyes pleading, asking if she was still your queen. And you—"

His hands tightened on the wheel until his knuckles turned white. His mind flashed back to that night. Her voice, cracking, desperate.

"Am I still your Queen?" He had seen the fear in her, the devastation at the mere thought of losing her place at his side. He had given her his everything: his loyalty and devotion, his body and his soul. And yet, here they were. Again.

A bitter laugh escaped him. "And you still had to prove yourself to her. And she didn't even listen to you tonight."

The battle in his mind was endless, but the outcome had already been decided. He had nothing left to say. Nothing left to fight for. He drove on.

Meanwhile, the Queen stood at the window, arms wrapped tightly around herself, waiting, hoping. Her fingers trembled as she clutched the fabric of her robe, her bare feet cold against the floor. The night stretched on in an agonizing silence, and she felt the weight of her own actions crushing her.

Had she gone too far? Had she let her anger rule her instead of reason? Then her eyes fell to the bed. The shredded card. The very paper that bitch had touched. A sickness rose in her throat. The very thought of another woman's presence infiltrating their home, their bed, made her stomach churn.

She stormed toward it, snatching up every trace of the night's devastation: the suit, the torn pieces of the card, the sheets that had been tainted by doubt. It all had to go. Her breath came in sharp, shallow bursts as she carried it outside, barely feeling the cold as she threw it into the trash bin with shaking hands.

He had brought it home. Brought her into their sanctuary. And suddenly, the regret, the sorrow that had begun to seep in, was washed away by another wave of fury. How could he? How dare he?

Across town, the soft chime above the door barely registered as he stepped inside McClendon Studios and Ink, the scent of antiseptic and ink thick in the air. Jazz played in the background, low and smooth, but it did nothing to calm him.

Kevin looked up from the counter, his smirk already forming, until he saw the king's face. The smirk vanished. "Damn, man," Kevin muttered, stepping forward. "What happened?"

The King exhaled, rubbing his hand down his face. His throat was tight, his chest even tighter. "Kev…" His voice was rough, raw. "You got time to inflict some much-needed pain on an old friend?"

Kevin studied him for a long moment before nodding. "I got you." The station was prepped in silence, the hum of the tattoo machine filling the space as Kevin worked.

"So what are we doing tonight?"

The King leaned back, staring at the ceiling. "Something that speaks of heartache," he said. "The fall of a mad king."

Kevin let out a long sigh. "You ever gonna get something happy? A damn butterfly, maybe?"

The king let out a humorless chuckle. "Not tonight."

They settled on the design: a heart wrapped in thorns, a dagger driven through it, bleeding. The shading deep red, except for a small part left untouched: a sliver of hope before the heart bled black and cold.

The pain was a relief. He welcomed it.

In the morning, the sky outside softened. Gold, blush, lavender: the cruel beauty of dawn. A new day rising over the ruins of a kingdom. The Queen curled into herself, silent sobs wracking her body as the first light of dawn crept through the windows.

The roar of his car's engine pulled into the driveway just as the world shifted from night to morning. She bolted upright. Her heart raced. Adrenaline replaced oxygen. She didn't have time to compose herself, didn't have the courage to meet him head-on. Not yet. Not like this.

She sprinted to the couch and collapsed against it, pulling the blanket back around her, angling her body to mimic sleep. Shallow breaths. Stillness. Pretending.

She heard the door open, heard the slow, uneven steps of a man who had been drinking, a man who had spent the night exorcising his demons. His footsteps were uneven. Slow. Heavy.

She smelled him before she saw him: Angel's Envy whiskey clinging to his skin, sharp and sweet and dark. Beneath it, something else. A different kind of scent. Metallic. Clean. Fresh. Ink.

Her lashes fluttered open just enough to catch a glimpse of him as he passed. He was shirtless, pants hung low on his hips, belt undone, muscles taut and rippling under the hallway light. His eyes were red-rimmed. His beard unkempt. There was something wild in his stride, something that had once been tempered by her touch, but not anymore.

And then she saw it: The tattoo. Her breath seized in her chest. A heart, wrapped in thorns. Pierced by a dagger. Bleeding. The edges were still raw. Angry, freshly inked. She couldn't breathe.

"Hi," she whispered hoarsely, before she could stop herself.

He didn't respond. Just grunted something low, unreadable, and disappeared into the bathroom. She hesitated only a second before rising. Her body moved before her pride could catch up.

The bathroom door creaked open. She stepped inside as the steam billowed past her, cloaking everything in a warm, wet haze. He stood beneath the spray, facing away from her, the water cascading down his broad back, over his inked spine, across the muscles that still bore her bite marks from the night before.

He hadn't bandaged the tattoo. "Let it bleed", she remembered him once saying. "Pain tells the truth others won't."

Even now, bruised, broken and wrecked, he was breathtaking.

She swallowed hard, taking in the lines of his frame, the cut of his waist, the way his thighs flexed with every slight movement. Heat bloomed between her legs without permission, desire entwined with heartbreak in a vicious knot. Her body remembered him even if her heart was in pieces.

But then her gaze found his forearm. The dagger. The blood. The thorns. Her arousal vanished. Her chest caved in.

She stepped into the shower, still in the black silk nightgown she'd worn while curled on the couch: thin straps, fabric soaked and clinging like memory. Her bare feet slipped slightly on the wet tile, but she didn't care.

Her hand gripped his arm, fingers wrapping around the tattoo. His head turned slightly. Eyes met hers. Wrecked. Tired. Gone. "What have you done?" she whispered, barely audible above the water.

He didn't answer.

Her fingers traced the ink, shaking as they passed over the blade. "Does this mean your heart is guarded now?"

His voice came low. Hollow. "You wouldn't even let me explain."

Her throat clenched. "I was hurt."

"And I wasn't?" His tone was sharper now. Not angry, but lethal. "You think you're the only one who bleeds when we go to war?"

She stepped closer. The rain shower soaked them both. "I built you," she whispered. "I made you a King."

He laughed. Bitter. Shattered. "And then a god."

Her breath caught.

"I bled for you," he said. "I worshipped at your feet. I carved out pieces of myself to keep you warm."

Her hands trembled. "Then talk to me. Don't walk away."

But he was already moving. He stepped out of the shower without another word. Water streamed down his body as he toweled off with slow, deliberate motions, as if her presence no longer mattered.

He pulled on dark jeans, slid his arms through a crisp black shirt, one she had gifted him after their first international deal closed. The collar still carried her scent.

She clung to the doorframe, soaked and shaking. "Where are you going?"

He paused in front of the mirror. Then, without looking at her, he pressed his right fist to his chest, over the bleeding heart, and bowed. "To the battlefield, where this mere mortal belongs."

Tears spilled down her cheeks. He turned to her one last time. His voice was soft. Final. "The King is dead, my lady. The warrior has returned." He paused. "All from your doing"

She tried to move. Tried to speak. But the door opened and then closed. His footsteps faded. The car's engine growled. And then, just silence.

She collapsed onto the wet tile floor, her back against the wall, her crown slipping from her soul. He was gone. Not to punishment. Not to revenge. But to survive. And she was alone. Not as a Queen, but as a woman who had loved a god, and lost him to the war she created.

She sat in the middle of the bedroom floor, her nightgown now soaked through, heavy with water and even heavier with sorrow. The straps clung to her shoulders like accusations. The fabric clung to her skin like consequence. The cold had seeped into her bones, but it was nothing compared to the raw, echoing ache that pulsed through her chest like a second heartbeat: sharp, punishing, inescapable.

Her arms wrapped tightly around her legs, forehead resting against her knees, but no posture could contain the tremble in her limbs or the storm in her spirit.

Her mind wouldn't stop. It had become her tormentor. Her jailor.

"The King is dead, my lady. The warrior has returned."

Again. "The King is dead..."

Each repetition, each ghostly echo carved another wound into her.

And then came the image. That vicious, beautiful agony inked into his flesh. Her breath caught, her stomach twisting with such violence she nearly retched right there on the floor.

She had once adored every tattoo on his skin. She'd traced each one like scripture, whispered prayers into the dark as her fingers glided over the symbols of his past. Each line had been earned. Each shadow told a story. But until now, none of them had been because of her.

This one was. A heart, once open, now strangled by thorns. A dagger, not just piercing, but buried. Deep and unforgiving. Blood pouring from it: Not red, not a metaphor. But black, a void. He had left a piece of it uncolored. Not out of hope. Out of finality. As if to say: 'There is nothing left here to fill'.

She had spent years building him up: gathering the broken pieces of a warrior's soul and shaping them into something noble. Something majestic. She made him a King.

And now? She had cast him down. She had become the very thing she swore she would protect him from. She was his war now. His battlefield. The sanctuary he once found between her thighs, between her words, between her very breath, it had turned into a minefield.

She had not just wounded him. She had driven him back into the wilderness. Her fingernails dug into the soft flesh of her arms, the sting a distant thing, drowned out by the chaos in her head. Her breathing came in ragged pulls. Her mouth opened, but no sobs came anymore. They had already wrung her dry.

And then her mind dragged her back again. To the coffee shop. The way she had walked in that day like a goddess. Untouchable, alluring, worshipped. Men's eyes followed her like disciples. She had bathed in it. Power, vanity, and the thrill of control.

Now it felt pitiful, childish, cheap. How dare she? A man who had never strayed. Never wavered. Never hesitated.

And she…She had wavered. Her pride, so carefully sharpened over years of survival, had become the knife she turned against him. All because of a whisper, a card, and a woman who didn't even matter.

Because deep down she had wondered, "Am I still enough?" But he had never stopped choosing her. But she had made him bleed.

Chapter 4: The Edge of Devotion

The Queen applied her makeup methodically: concealer under her eyes to mask the faint bruises left behind by tears, blush to mimic the glow of vitality she no longer felt, mascara to lift lashes that still trembled from weeping. Lipstick last—ruby, deep and defiant. The kind he once said made her look like royalty and sin rolled into one.

As the final coat went on, her hand shook. She gripped the sink. Her breath caught in her throat. "Get it together," she whispered.

But the house had other plans. The silence was heavy again. Not peaceful. It screamed at her. Every polished surface in the estate seemed to reflect a life that was no longer hers. The marble countertops still bore the imprint of where his hands had once gripped during stolen kisses. The couch where he had sprawled, larger than life, seemed to mock her now with its perfect cushions and untouched throws.

She dressed slowly, selecting a fitted navy dress that clung to her frame with a kind of quiet desperation. It said, "I'm fine." It said, "professional." It said, "unbothered." And it was lying. She was dressed in grief and longing, with buttons.

By the time her assistant Danielle arrived, the Queen sat in the kitchen, sipping water with the poise of a poised executioner. The calm before collapse.

Danielle stepped inside without knocking, as she always did. Pumps soft against the hardwood, braids twisted into a tight bun, glasses low on her nose. She studied the Queen with the wariness of someone approaching a wounded goddess. "Morning," she said gently.

"Hey."

Danielle paused. The air between them had shifted. She could feel it. "You okay?"

"I'm fine."

"You're not."

"I'm functioning."

Danielle set her folio down on the counter. "Lying doesn't suit you. Never has."

The Queen looked down into her glass like it might drown her. "He left."

Danielle didn't flinch. "Was it the card?"

The Queen's lips twitched. "It was everything. And nothing. And me."

Danielle moved around the island and placed a hand over her arm. "Did he cheat? Then he's a fool."

"No," the Queen said softly. "He's not."

Danielle leaned against the counter beside her. "So what happened?"

"I broke him."

The silence was thick with understanding. Danielle didn't try to fix it. She just stayed.

"I said things," the Queen continued. "I did things. And he left with that…that tattoo. Like he needed pain to purge me."

Danielle's face fell. "Have you heard from him?" Danielle opened her folio and began listing the day's agenda, but the Queen was far away.

"Three sessions before lunch. Couples counseling at one, media consultation at three, solo grief support at five." The Queen nodded.

"If James calls—" Danielle began.

The Queen's head snapped up. "Come get me. No matter what I'm doing."

Danielle blinked. "Even if you're mid-session?"

There was a pause.

"You called him by name," Danielle said quietly.

The Queen frowned. "I didn't—"

"You did."

Danielle's face softened with a kind of sorrow that was too knowing.

"I haven't heard you say that name in years. Not even in private."

The Queen folded, breath catching in her throat. Danielle was there before the collapse fully came, catching her on the stool like a mother catching a child mid-fall.

Tears spilled freely now, staining her dress. "I pushed him away."

Danielle wrapped her arms around her. "You're still a Queen. Don't forget that."

"I don't want a kingdom without him." Danielle didn't answer. There were no words for that kind of ache.

By the time they arrived at the office building, the Queen had sculpted herself back into marble. Her heels echoed like war drums through the glass atrium. The silver lettering above the entrance: *On Second Thought*, gleamed cold in the morning light. The name felt cruel today.

She moved like she hadn't spent the morning whispering the name she'd sworn not to. Danielle walked beside her, tablet in hand. She glanced sideways. "You okay? Because that lipstick? That's a statement. Last time you wore that shade before noon, you were trying to win him back after that blow-up in Miami."

The Queen kept walking, but Danielle stopped her at the elevator.

"I'm fine," the Queen answered.

Danielle held up her hands. "Copy that."

The Queen's chin lifted, and she said again, "So, if James calls…I need to know. Even if I'm in a session."

Danielle nodded. "Okay." They rode the elevator in silence.

By the time the doors opened, the Queen was back in her armor. But Danielle looked down at the tablet, whispering under her breath, just loud enough to hear. "He still loves you."

The Queen didn't answer. But she clutched her bag tighter. Because she still loved him. Too much.

Across the city, the King was a machine. At the gym just after dawn. No playlist. No partners. No mercy. His beard two days thicker. His jaw sharp. His eyes dark as obsidian and just as cold.

The polished, suit-and-tie version of himself, the Vice President, the strategist, the empire-builder, had vanished. What remained was muscle and rage, forged in silence, coated in sweat.

His arms bulged, veins prominent as he threw the weights like they owed him something. His chest swelled. His back curved and tensed with each rep, each pull, each brutal drop. It wasn't exercise. It was repentance with weight. It was war.

By the time he stepped under the punishing spray of the gym shower, his body was quaking with exhaustion, red-hot from overuse, his breath ragged and uneven. Then he saw it: the ink. Still raw, still perfect. Still bleeding.

His breath caught. His hand lifted slowly, fingers hovering above it, not to touch, but to acknowledge. The dagger, the heart, the thorns, the gap. Her.

He braced himself against the tile, water cascading over his head, his shoulders, down the thick ridges of muscle that had been carved by time, by pain, by her. His mind betrayed him. She appeared behind his eyes. Drenched in the shower. Clothes clinging to her skin. Hands on his arm. Voice trembling. "What have you done?"

The way she looked at the tattoo like it had shattered her more than the fight itself. "Does this mean your heart is guarded now? Am I still your Queen?"

His eyes snapped open. He wanted to scream. He wanted to shatter something. But instead, he smiled. A slow, cruel smile that belonged to the man she had awakened, the one who didn't beg.

"I think…" he whispered to himself as he shut the water off, dragging a towel across his skin, "…I'm in the mood for some coffee."

At "On Second Thought," the Queen sat stiffly at her desk. Her posture screamed composure, but her fingers trembled beneath the wood. The office bustled around her, but it all felt distant.

She hadn't eaten. She hadn't slept. Her makeup was perfect. Her mask was flawless. But inside, the woman who had once ruled from the depths of her soul was crumbling.

Danielle peeked in, lips pursed. "Should I cancel your morning sessions?"

The Queen didn't look up. "No. Keep them."

"You look—" She paused. "You look tired."

Then, after a beat, "Did he cheat?"

A bitter scoff. "No."

"Then what…?"

The Queen closed her eyes. The silence that followed was unbearable.

And then, barely audible, she whispered, "James." The name. The man. No longer a King. Just a wound.

Danielle's face paled. "You two were—"

The Queen's fingers curled against the desk. "I don't know if he'll ever come back." The office air was thin.

James, now at the office, stood at the floor-to-ceiling window of Elliott Global Technologies, the morning skyline sprawling in sharp angles and cruel beauty. The city buzzed below, blissfully unaware that another kingdom was about to be reshaped.

His reflection in the glass was unreadable. Clean-shaven, crisp charcoal suit, gold cufflinks catching the light. Everything about him screamed control. Mastery. But under the surface? War.

Behind him, the door opened. Jean slipped inside with practiced ease, tablet in hand, her heels whispering over the hardwood. "Your 8:30 was rescheduled. They're pushing for after lunch."

He didn't turn. "Fine."

Jean paused, then tilted her head. "You okay, King?"

He hated how that title still lingered here. In this place, it didn't belong. Not anymore. "Just handle the meetings," he said, voice calm but cool.

She nodded. "Boss wants to see you. Now."

James inhaled deeply, but he didn't ask why. He already knew.

The CEO's office was nothing short of a modern fortress—brushed steel, imported stone, and enough surveillance to make the Pentagon nervous. James entered with shoulders squared and eyes steady.

The older man stood by the liquor cabinet, swirling a glass of something amber and unnecessary.

"Gemini Technologies," the CEO said without turning. "You haven't signed off."

"I'm aware."

"I need your signature today."

James's replied, "I'm not touching Gemini."

The man turned slowly, lifting the glass but not drinking. "Is this about the oversight committee again?"

"It's about boundaries. Ethics. Loyalty."

The CEO's brow lifted. "You're throwing away tens of millions over a personal slight?"

James stepped forward, slow, deliberate. "I built this strategy. Every win we've had over the last two years bears my signature."

"You're damn right it does," the CEO growled. "Which is why I can't afford for you to throw a tantrum over—"

"This isn't a tantrum." James opened his briefcase, pulled out a pristine sheet of company letterhead, and laid it flat on the desk.

Resignation: The word hit the room like a slap.

"You can't be serious."

"I'm done," James said, voice like a sealed tomb. "I won't be dragged through backdoor politics and forced to work with people who operate without honor."

"You walk away now, and everything you've built here? It burns."

James stepped back, buttoned his jacket. "Then let it burn."

The CEO stared at him, searching for weakness, but found only stone. Then, something shifted.

"Fine," the man said slowly. "What about this: It is still part of the Gemini project but there is a division that is in Southern California that could use you there. Two years. Quiet assignment. Full clearance. Team of your choice. You're still VP. Pay is untouched."

James didn't blink. "No Gemini. No Ava (Green Eyes). She works with this LA-based team and I will consider it, but I am not committing to either."

"Done." He turned to go.

"Your Queen will follow you," the CEO said, voice quieter. "If she still wants you."

James paused. "She won't even know where I went."

And then he was gone. Jean caught up with him outside the elevator. "You're leaving?"

"I may be temporarily relocating."

"Southern California?" Her eyes widened. "Oh my God, we're going to the beach?"

"You're going to the beach," he corrected. "I'm going to war."

Jean blinked, sensing the shift in him. "What about the Queen?"

James didn't answer.

"James—"

"Ellie will be fine."

Jean's voice lowered. "She doesn't even know you're leaving, does she?" His silence was the answer.

She reached for her tablet, trying to fill the void. "You want me to cancel the Cayman Islands trip?"

He turned, a shadow of something sadder flickering in his eyes. For a moment, he forgot they had a trip planned together before things fell apart.

He asked Jean, "You ever been?"

Jean quickly said "I will if you are sending my fine ass"

"Then it's yours."

Jean's jaw dropped. "Wait, seriously?"

"Take your man. Take ten days. Don't look back."

Jean grinned, surprised and touched. "Damn. You're really done."

James adjusted his cufflinks. "No." He looked out the window toward the sea of concrete and sky. "I'm just tired of bleeding for people who think I'm unshakable."

Across the city, Ellie stood in her office, hands clasped behind her back, her posture immaculate, her face unreadable as she stared out over the skyline.

She closed her eyes. She was ten again, in a chair too big for her, saying nothing while a therapist waited. Silence had always been her safest weapon.

In Ellie's office, Danielle entered quietly, placing a latte on the desk. "Anything from James?" she asked.

Danielle shook her head. "Not yet." The Queen's lips twitched, almost a smile. But inside? Something was unraveling. She didn't know he was already gone, didn't know that across the kingdom, her King had surrendered the throne. Not to weakness, but to silence. To freedom, and to war.

Ellie sat in her office, arms folded, staring at her phone. Still nothing. No call. No message. No apology. The ache that had taken root in her chest all morning had shifted. No longer just longing. Now, it was laced with something sharper, bitter. Something primal.

She hadn't cried since she walked through the doors of On Second Thought. Not once. Not in front of Danielle. Not in the elevator. Not in the silence that greeted her when she stepped into the sanctuary of her corner office.

But the waiting? The waiting had carved something out of her. Her phone screen remained black, taunting her with its silence. Where the hell was he?

Her arms unfolded slowly, fingers flexing with quiet restraint. She stood, heels clicking as she paced toward the floor-to-ceiling windows. The skyline stared back, indifferent. Glittering. She hated how beautiful everything looked. It felt cruel.

Her lips tightened. The last words he had said to her still lingered: "The King is dead, my lady. The warrior has returned."

But he hadn't left the battlefield. Not fully. Not yet. And that made the silence worse. If he was truly gone: if he had fled, or ghosted her, or cut ties clean, maybe it would have made sense. But this? This halfway haunting? It was unbearable.

She turned back to her desk. Snatched up her pen. Scribbled something across the top of a notepad, only to tear it off and toss it into the trash. Her mind wasn't in her work. It was still in the shower with him. Still replaying every drop of water as it slid over the black ink etched into his skin. His word, "You wouldn't even let me explain."

Her fingernails dug into her palm. "Why didn't I?" The thought struck her before she could cage it. "Why didn't I let him explain?"

The memory of the coffee poured over his suit, the way her fists had found his jaw before her words did, it all came rushing back in a single, searing wave. God. He hadn't even raised his voice. He had let her hit him. And then he bowed. She shook the thought away with a growl.

No, she wouldn't play the victim here. She wasn't the one who'd brought that woman's number into their home. She wasn't the one who let a stranger speak her name like it was a shared secret. She wasn't the one who needed to explain.

He should've fought harder. He should've called. And then came the pivot. Her heart stung. But her pride? It hissed like a wounded animal.

She walked toward the bookshelf, hands grazing the spines of titles until she reached the one she was looking for: *Emotional Strategy in Modern Courtship*. Her own writing. Her own words. Her own empire. She pulled it out, flipped open the inside cover, and wrote a note in flawless script.

Then she reached for the soft black leather box that had been sitting behind it. Inside: the Rolex she had gifted him after he closed his first million-dollar deal. Presidential Platinum. Custom engraving on the back.

It had taken her six months to design. He had worn it nearly every day since. Until this week.

She tucked the book and the Rolex into a gift bag, one of the white and silver branded ones from her signature client line and set it aside. Then she called for Danielle.

"Yes, my Queen?" Danielle's voice was quiet but sharp. Protective.

"Make sure this gets messengered to Elliott Global Technologies. Directly to James. No assistant interception. You understand?"

Danielle blinked. "Are you sure?"

Ellie nodded once. "Absolutely."

Danielle hesitated. "What message do you want me to include?"

"None," Ellie said coolly. "Let him interpret the silence however he wants."

Danielle gave her a long look. "Ellie…"

But there was no changing her mind.

When Danielle left to arrange the delivery, Ellie sat down, legs crossed, eyes dead calm. She didn't scream. She just waited, like a lioness sharpening her claws.

Let him feel it, she thought. Let him open that package and remember exactly who built his empire. Let him see the gift he never earned, given again like a farewell he didn't ask for. Let him taste regret the way she'd been tasting absence.

Across town, James sat in his office, one leg bouncing as he stared at the same damn file for the fifth time. He hadn't spoken to anyone since he walked in. Had barely looked up. His mind wasn't in mergers or expansion strategy, it was still in the steam-filled shower, in the way her voice had cracked when she touched the tattoo: "Does this mean your heart is guarded now?"

His jaw clenched. He hadn't told her everything. Not yet. Not about Southern California. Not about the doubts. Not about the fact that every inch of that new assignment made him feel sick.

Because none of it meant anything if she wasn't in it with him. And yet, he hadn't reached out. Because pride was a brutal beast. And love, when betrayed, wore teeth.

A knock interrupted his spiral. Jean entered, holding a white and silver bag with a branded logo that made his stomach twist.

"Delivery came for you," she said, setting it on his desk.

"From who?"

She shrugged. "Didn't say."

He didn't touch it right away.

Jean lingered. "It's from On Second Thought. You know. Her brand."

He already knew. His fingers moved slowly as he unwrapped the tissue paper. When he saw the box inside, his breath caught: The Rolex.

His eyes dropped to the book beneath it. His own inscription, penned by her hand: *To the only man who could ever wear this crown and still carry my heart.*

But nothing else. No note. No explanation. And the weight of everything he had already lost.

Jean spoke again. "You okay?"

James closed the box and set it aside. "Close the door behind you."

She hesitated, nodded, and left.

He sat there, hand over his face, unable to breathe. She had sent the watch back. And without saying a word, she had made her message loud and clear.

The Queen had stayed late in the office. Too late. Her session notes were stacked with obsessive order on her desk, and the lights had long since dimmed to their automatic nighttime settings. But she didn't move. She couldn't. She just sat there, one leg crossed over the other, staring at nothing while pretending it didn't hurt.

She delivered her petty act hours ago, and for a while, it gave her some sick satisfaction. A sting meant to bruise, not maim. A quick slap in the middle of their war to remind him that she could still draw blood. But, as the sun dipped behind the skyline and the last of her clients filtered out of the building, the venom turned on her.

Danielle appeared in the doorway, her expression unreadable.

"You have a delivery."

Ellie blinked. "A what?"

Danielle stepped inside, holding an envelope wrapped in cream linen and bound with a thin black cord. It looked regal. Funereal. Like something sent after death.

"There's no return address. Just your name."

Ellie reached for it with numb fingers.

"Who brought it?" she asked.

Danielle hesitated. "A courier. He said it was urgent."

She waited until the door clicked shut behind her assistant before breaking the seal. Inside, a single folded receipt.

The Queen unfolded it slowly, breath catching as she read the line item: *Donation: Presidential Platinum Rolex. Appraised value: $167, 000.* But it wasn't the amount that shook her. It was what was written at the bottom. Two words: *My Lady.*

Her entire body stilled. She had once watched him open it like a boy receiving his first crown. Now, it had been given away. Given back. Not to her, but to the universe. To charity. To strangers.

And he hadn't added a single insult. Not one curse. Not even a signature. Just a title. A vow, broken with grace. Her fingers trembled as she folded the receipt.

She stood, moving to the mirror, not to check her reflection, but to steady the Queen who had declared war against the one man who'd taught her how to wear a crown.

Her breath caught, and for the first time all day, her eyes stung.

What kind of warrior turns his sword on himself just to make a point? What kind of god allows himself to burn...just to light the battlefield? Her god of war.

She clutched the envelope to her chest, inhaling deeply. She had destroyed the only man who had ever been willing to die beautifully for her.

Across the city, James stepped into the lobby of a luxury hotel overlooking the skyline. He wore no tie, no armor. Just a black dress shirt with the top buttons undone and eyes that had stopped pretending to be indifferent.

"Reservation for King," he said smoothly.

The clerk blinked, then nodded. "Of course, sir."

When he entered the penthouse, he didn't bother unpacking. He moved to the window and stared out, the city glowing like the embers of a fire he had barely escaped.

Chapter 5: The Blood in the Bourbon

He hadn't returned the Rolex out of bitterness. No, this wasn't about revenge. It was strategy and precision. The most devastating kind of mercy. James hadn't just returned the memory of the gift, he had sanctified it. He transformed it into something charitable, noble, public. Irrevocable.

And in doing so, he had told her: I'm willing to destroy even the pieces of myself you once gave me, if that's what it takes to walk away clean. It wasn't an act of cruelty. It was an act of surrender. And it pierced her deeper than any blade.

Her tongue was dry. Her mouth tasted like regret. The war inside her, once so righteous and fiery, now felt suddenly grotesque and pitiful. Unworthy of the man she had nearly torn apart.

James had not sent a message of peace. He had sent the end of the war. And she, the great Queen, the empress of resolve and command, realized that her throne had never felt more hollow inside.

James stood at the penthouse window of The Langston, an ultra-modern glass-and-marble hotel perched above the city. His reflection stared back at him: dark-skinned, bearded, beautiful, and broken. The ink on his arm was still fresh. Still angry. He hadn't wrapped it and wouldn't. He let it breathe, let it bleed. He had nothing to hide now. The city lights blinked below like promises no one intended to keep.

Jean had booked the suite. She'd insisted, saying he needed to be above it all, to look down on the kingdom he once ruled and decide whether he still wanted the crown. She didn't say it with cruelty, but she said it more like a sister. Like the one person left who hadn't chosen a side.

But even now, with silence cocooning him and a bed big enough to swallow regret whole, James couldn't stop his mind from reaching for her: Ellie, his Queen.

The image of her mouth flooded his thoughts: moaning, commanding, pleading. That perfect lower lip that always curled just before she came undone. The weight of her thighs clenching around him, and her fingernails in his scalp. The way she'd whisper his name like it wasn't just a name, it was a prayer.

He unbuckled his pants slowly, breath heavy, desire and sorrow crashing like twin waves. His hand moved instinctively, rhythm matching memory, and soon he was trembling. Eyes closed, heart wide open, chasing a climax that felt more like punishment than pleasure.

He came with her name in his mouth. Not loud, just final. Then, silence again.

Across the city, Ellie lay sprawled across the bed they once shared. She'd changed into a fitted dress sometime after the shower, muscle memory, not intent. It clung to her now like consequence. She hadn't even unzipped it. She hadn't moved since collapsing hours ago, crushed beneath the weight of her own destruction.

But when her hand slipped between her thighs, it wasn't lust that guided her. It was mourning. Her fingers trembled as they moved, not out of desire, but devotion.

She imagined his mouth on her neck. His breath against her spine. The way he used to take his time, even when he was furious, especially when he was furious. Worship in every thrust. Ownership in every gasp.

She climaxed alone, his name falling from her lips in a whisper so cracked it could've been a sob. And when it was over, she didn't cry. She just lay there. Empty. Spent. And still completely, irrevocably his.

Neither of them reached out that night. But, as morning crept across the city in shades of lavender and steel, they both stirred within their separate silences: two halves of a war-torn crown, cracked down the middle by pride.

And somewhere inside the quiet, something began to shift. Not forgiveness. Not yet. But perhaps, readiness. To speak, to fight again, but not each other. To begin what neither of them knew how to finish.

The morning light slanted through her office window like judgment. It painted harsh angles across the floor, the same way truth now carved through her chest. Ellie sat still, unmoving, her hands wrapped tightly around a ceramic cup of tea she hadn't touched.

Danielle stood near the bookshelf, pretending to adjust the placement of a decorative vase, but her eyes kept flicking toward her Queen. "You didn't sleep again," she finally said. Ellie didn't respond.

Danielle sighed, stepping closer. "Would you like me to clear your day?"

Ellie blinked. Slowly. As if the question had taken a moment to register. "No."

"Ellie…" The use of her name was a gamble, but Danielle had always known how to walk that tightrope. "He's hurting too."

"Is he?" Her voice was quiet, flat. "He's the one in a luxury hotel, not me."

"You don't know that."

"I know what he sent me," Ellie whispered.

The receipt sat tucked inside her leather portfolio, folded with surgical precision. *Donation: Presidential Platinum Rolex. Assessed Value: $167,000.00.* At the bottom, two words handwritten in that unmistakable penmanship. She hadn't cried. Not this time. She hadn't screamed either. There was no rage left. Only devastation cloaked in grace.

She stood now, moving with that same eerie composure that had unsettled kings and broken boardrooms. "Where are the press kits for the grief symposium?"

"Waiting in Conference Room B."

"Have the team meet me in twenty minutes."

Danielle nodded but didn't move. "Ellie, it wasn't petty. What you did was emotional, yes. But this? What he sent?"

Ellie met her gaze. "It was war."

Danielle looked away, quietly retreating as the Queen turned her back and faced the skyline once more.

Across the city, James sat poolside at a luxury suite overlooking the hills. He hadn't touched the champagne they sent up. The bed was made, unused. His bags remained unpacked. Only the balcony showed any signs of life: a half-burnt joint still resting in the ashtray, and the scent of weed lacing the air like a whispered prayer.

He stared into nothing, shirtless, sweat from the gym still drying across his muscled chest. The city buzzed below, and yet it felt miles away.

Jean appeared at the patio door. "They're requesting confirmation of your final commitment to the SoCal transition. Want me to respond?"

He didn't turn. "Not yet."

Jean hesitated. "She hasn't called?"

James exhaled. "Wouldn't matter if she did."

Jean studied him for a moment. "You look like a man who's either about to fly across the world...or burn it to the ground."

James didn't move. "She taught me both."

"You know you love her?"

He finally turned, eyes dark, unreadable. "She's my beginning and my end."

Jean nodded. "Then stop standing in the middle." And she was gone.

——

Ellie walked the halls of her office like a shadow that demanded attention. She stopped only when her assistant handed her the updated Gemini Technologies proposal she worked on with James. He asked her to review it for errors before all this happened, and still it remained unsigned.

"Q1 was a fairytale," she muttered. "Now we're nearly in Q3 and the dragons are real." Still pending, still bearing his name. She flipped it open, scanning the details until she reached the list of project stakeholders. And there it was: *Ava Daniels.* Green Eyes: Her name sat on the draft, a dagger all its own.

Ellie's throat burned. She pulled out her phone and stared at his contact. No message. No call. Her finger hovered over the screen, but she didn't dial.

She closed the document, walked to her private office, and shut the door. Her heart didn't know whether to hope or to surrender. But her soul waited. Because love that deep never dies quietly. It goes to war. And neither of them had raised the white flag. Yet.

Ellie sat motionless in her office, long after her last meeting ended, staring out through the tinted glass as the skyline dimmed in shades of silver and blue. The city pulsed with life, but inside her chest was only the low, haunting throb of regret. She'd been so proud, so sure. So unwilling to bend. But now, her pride was a crown she could barely lift.

The receipt entered her mind. Because only he would know how to burn her with such tenderness. Only he could deliver a deathblow dressed as a farewell gift. Not with anger nor fury, but with restraint. Calculated. Controlled. Devastating.

It was the first time she questioned if she was truly prepared for war. Because when James fought, he didn't swing wildly. He dismantled kingdoms, even his own, just to prove a point.

And this time, she feared…the point was her. Her hands trembled. Her chest clenched. She remembered everything now.

All the ways she used to win small battles to hide the war within herself. The cold comments. The quiet punishments. The petty stings meant to remind him that even Kings must bleed. Her knees pulled in as she sat curled into her plush chair. And her mind opened the floodgates.

She had a flashback to months ago. They had disagreed, nothing serious. Something about scheduling, or maybe the way he prioritized her needs over his own. He had asked her to be patient, to trust him.

And she had scoffed and left the table early. She then posted a photo in a tight dress with the caption: Queens don't wait, we reign. She knew he'd see it. And he had.

But he said nothing. The next day, he still brought her coffee. Still kissed her forehead. Still told her he was proud of her.

And the guilt that gripped her then was back again now, sinking its talons into her ribcage. James had never retaliated. Never sought revenge. He didn't match her pettiness, he absorbed it, and met every jab with grace. Still loved her when she was acting unworthy of the throne he built for them.

And Ava? She was nothing. A set of pretty eyes and flirtation with no substance. A momentary ripple.

But Ellie had turned that ripple into a tidal wave. She had made it bigger than it was. She gave the woman weight that James never did. And in doing so, she cracked the foundation she swore was unbreakable.

"I should've believed you," she whispered. She blinked away the tears, only for another flash to crash against her. That realization burned so deeply she couldn't breathe. But then, her eyes widened. She scrambled for her phone and dialed his number.

Ringing. No answer. She redialed. Again. Five calls in five minutes. Still nothing. "James…" she whispered.

Her heart raced. She wasn't just worried, she was unraveling. He always answered. Always. By the sixth call, her pride cracked. Her voice rose, unsteady, desperate.

And then? It wasn't desperation anymore. It was rage. She hit record on the voicemail: "If you think this little game is going to scare me, you're wrong. You walk out, you disappear, and you think I'm supposed to chase you? You want to act like some tragic warrior with ink on your skin and silence in your mouth, fine. But don't pretend like I broke you when you walked away first. You said you were my King, then act like it, or stay gone. Just don't expect me to keep waiting for a man who can't even answer his damn phone!"

She hung up, chest heaving, the silence echoing louder than her voice ever could.

Across town, James stepped out of a sleek, high-rise boutique. He had the box in hand. Reacquired at nearly double the amount the charity had received. He hadn't cared. Money wasn't the point, redemption was. And now, as he looked down at it gleaming in the afternoon light, something unspoken swelled inside him.

He was ready. Not just to return, but to reclaim. He pulled out his phone, the Rolex still in hand: Six missed calls. His chest tightened. He played the voicemail.

And as the venomous tone spilled out of the speaker, Jean's eyes closed, her lips parting in a soft gasp of dread. She had frozen beside him, just outside the boutique, where she had been waiting quietly.

As the voicemail played, she winced. Then, after a heartbeat of silence, she did something she'd never done before: she reached forward and cut the message off with a gentle tap of the screen.

"I'm starting a support group," Jean said flatly. "It's called No, Not That Email. First meeting is now."

"I'm sorry," she said softly. "But you've never not called her back, James. And when you couldn't, I always did. I let her know you were tied up. You always made sure she knew."

Her voice trembled with that loyal, nervous grace of someone watching a divine force self-destruct. James didn't answer. His jaw was tight, eyes dark, unreadable. But not empty, just wounded.

Still, he slid the watch onto his wrist. Adjusted it. "My Lady," he murmured. And with that, he turned toward the car, his mind already deciding. He would not answer her voice with rage. He would not let the heat of her anger melt the steel of his love.

She had struck with venom, yes. But he would answer with fire. With grace. With a gesture that would rip through every wall she tried to build.

Across the city, Ellie still sat in her office, the voicemail message still echoing in her ears. Her phone screen mocked her: no missed calls. No returned messages. Just that same still silence, one she had filled with that voice. That tone. God, why did she say it that way?

She exhaled shakily, fingers trembling over her keyboard as she debated canceling the rest of her day. Something she never did. Her reputation was built on her composure, her ability to command even in collapse. But today, the weight of her crown felt heavier than her spine could hold.

Her mind whispered: "I messed this up. Again." She stood slowly, drifting to the window, arms crossed tightly over her chest, gaze distant.

And that's when Danielle entered, eyes wide. "My Queen," she said, out of breath. "You need to look out the east window. Now."

"What?" Ellie turned, confused.

"Just…trust me."

With reluctant steps, Ellie crossed the room and turned toward the east-facing glass. Her breath stopped.

Outside, lined across the street, the sidewalks, even the office parking loop were flower trucks. Dozens of them. Big white cargo vans, each overflowing with blooms. Roses in every shade and lilies with petals like silk. And sunflowers: her favorite. So many it looked like a field had exploded in the middle of downtown.

Gasps echoed in the offices below. Phones snapped photos. Onlookers paused mid-stride, tears in some of their eyes. And there, standing among it all, his hand resting on the hood of one of the trucks, was James.

The Rolex gleamed on his wrist. His smile? It cracked something open in her soul. Ellie staggered back from the window, trying to compose herself, but it was futile. Her hands shook, her knees wobbled, and tears stung at the corners of her eyes.

"I need to go down there," she whispered.

Danielle, who stood behind her, simply nodded, her own voice thick. "Go."

The elevator doors parted with a soft ding, and Ellie stepped into the lobby, heels clicking with precision and purpose. Heads turned. Some whispered. Others simply watched with wide, wet eyes.

James stood waiting. No words or grand speeches. Just a presence so undeniable it shook the walls of her restraint. She walked straight to him, slow and deliberate. Their eyes met, and everything else vanished. They headed to the building entrance. He held the door open, and she led him to the private elevator. Back up to her floor.

They entered her office. She closed the door and locked it. Then, moved to the windows. With one motion, the remote closed every blind, every sliver of sunlight shut out, until the room dimmed into intimacy.

She turned slowly, her back against the glass. He walked toward her, quiet, unhurried. The tension hung like a storm cloud between them: electric, thick, heavy.

He reached for her, and she let him. Hands met skin. Mouths met like fire on oil. Clothes peeled away in frenzied, reverent tugs.

But just as his hands began to slide up her skirt, her body tensing with the ache of need, she froze. A flash of memory stopped her. She saw herself in their bathroom mirror. Naked. Vulnerable.

The soft curls between her legs full, wild, unshaved, just the way he'd loved. Just as he'd once begged: "Grow it for me," he'd said, voice low in her ear. "Wear it like a crown. Your royal tapestries."

She had laughed at the time. Called him ridiculous. "What is this, the '70s?" But then she'd seen how serious he was. How reverent. And she had said yes and honored that vow like it was sacred. Never touching a razor again. Letting it grow thick and dark, a private symbol of her loyalty.

And now, as he reached for her, her hands caught his. She pulled back. "No," she whispered.

His brows furrowed. "No?"

She shook her head, breath ragged, tears pooling in her eyes. "I can't. Not yet."

His chest rose and fell, heavy with unsaid things. But he didn't push. He stepped back. Pain flickered through him. And then, understanding. But beneath it, fear.

She had never denied him. Not once. And now, she did. Setting the stage for the deepest betrayal yet to come.

James stood still, the city humming behind the tinted windows of her office, but all he could hear was the tremor in her voice as she whispered that single word. She had never denied him before.

Not in the kitchen, not in the car. Not on the balcony of that villa in the south of France. Not in the middle of a heated argument, when the tension between them cracked open like lightning across a battlefield. But now, she did.

He stepped back slowly, his breath heavy, lips parted as though he might say something. But nothing came out. His body was flushed with heat, arousal still visible against the fine fabric of his trousers, until it wasn't. Until the pulse of desire withered beneath the cold hand of confusion and dread.

He stared at her. Waiting. Hoping. "Ellie," he said, his voice low, unsteady. "Am I unforgiven?"

She opened her mouth, then closed it. Her eyes welled again, not from pride this time, but from something deeper. Something ancient and trembling beneath the surface of who she was before the war between them had begun.

But James didn't wait. He stepped closer and pressed his hand to her cheek. "I can't keep pretending I'm not starving for you. I want to drink you. I want to be inside you. I want to fill you, mark you, and remind you that no man could never, ever, take your crown."

She gasped, her fingers curling at her sides. And then, she flashed back to another memory: The mirror. The promise.

She remembered the day he'd stood behind her, brushing her hair aside as she admired herself in the mirror. She'd joked about her unruly bush, said it looked like a '70s porno. And he had stared into the reflection, his hand possessively resting at the base of her spine.

"I love it," he had said then. "It's for me, no one else. Grow it for me, and don't ever shave it. It's your crown. Your vow."

She had smirked. Teased him. But in the end, she agreed. And for years, she honored that promise. Until the razor met her skin.

She snapped out of it with a jolt of guilt and adrenaline. Her fingers trembled as she reached for the hem of her skirt. Slowly, deliberately, she peeled it up, then pulled down the lacy black panties that clung to her thighs, and then her skirt down to the floor. James's breath caught. His gaze dropped instinctively, the heat in his body surging in anticipation.

But then, everything stilled. The moment he saw it: smooth, bare, waxed clean, something inside him broke. Not a crack, but a shatter. As if burned. The erection that had been begging for her touch was gone in an instant, retreating like a soldier sensing ambush.

His lips parted in disbelief, not at her nudity, but at the absence of what had been sacred between them. That crown, that symbol. That quiet, intimate kingdom of devotion she'd once worn for him and only him.

"Why…" he choked. "Why would you do that?"

She swallowed hard, instinctively moving to cover herself, but it was too late. The damage was done. Her mouth opened, her voice trembling. "I just…I thought… maybe a clean slate, something new…"

But his eyes were distant now. Haunted. He didn't see her anymore, he saw him. Man Number Four bent over her. Tasting her, drinking the honey he once called his sacred nectar.

He blinked rapidly as if to purge the image from his mind, but it clung like a virus. His voice, when it came, was soft but razored.

"You threw it away." "You threw it away," he repeated. "What we had. What that meant."

She stepped forward, still half-naked. "It wasn't about anyone else."

"Don't lie to me." His voice dropped, guttural, broken. "Not about this."

"I wasn't thinking. I was hurt—"

He turned his back to her, pain folding through his body in waves. His tattoo, the heart wrapped in thorns, was still red and raw. He pointed at his forearm. "You see it?" he asked.

She nodded through her tears.

"You see the section I left unshaded?"

"Yes…"

"That was for hope. For light. For a way back to you."

Her knees buckled slightly as she sank into her chair, trembling.

But James turned, his chest rising and falling in waves of something far more violent than rage: betrayal.

"You remember what I said when we first talked about forgiveness?"

She looked up, tears clinging to her lashes. "You said you could always find a way back. Always."

"I did."

He stepped closer, crouched down, forcing her to meet his eyes. "But I told you one thing. One thing I couldn't forgive."

Her lips quivered. "James…"

"Deliberate cruelty."

The words were a whisper and a blade.

"That's what this was. You knew what it meant to me. You knew."

Her mouth opened. But she couldn't speak.

And then his voice dropped even lower, ragged and intimate in a way that tore at the soul. "Fuck you, Ellie."

She gasped, her entire body jerking with the words.

"You deserve the pain you so easily inflict. You don't deserve the kind of love that would bleed itself dry just to keep your crown polished. Fuck you."

She sobbed.

He stepped back, letting her dress, and when she finally stood, broken and disoriented, he crossed to the door.

With his hand on the knob, he turned and gave the most chilling performance of his life: "I'll see you at home, love," he said loudly, smiling like everything was fine. And he walked out.

In the hallway, Jean and Danielle were mid-conversation. Both turned at the sound of his voice.

But Jean's eyes locked onto his face. And she knew that something had happened. Something final.

Before she could speak, James turned to her, calm and steady as a blade. "SoCal back on the table but as definite."

Jean blinked. "You—what?"

He didn't repeat himself. He just walked away. The hallway behind him silent. The war was no longer coming, it had already begun.

Chapter 6: The Queen Who Walked

The silence had grown louder. Not the peaceful kind that follows closure, but the haunting quiet that slips in when words have turned to weapons, and neither party dares to reach for the blade again.

Ellie lay awake, sprawled across one half of the bed, the other untouched. His side still smelled of him: rich spice, warm musk, and power. It clung to the pillows like a ghost that refused to leave. She hated it. And she loved it.

The imprint of his body on the sheets mocked her, more than any voicemail, more than the echo of his voice as he slammed the door behind him with that faux-cheerful, "See you at home, love."

She hadn't cried after that. Not then. But now the tears came slowly. Silently. Not the sobs of a shattered woman, but the broken weep of a Queen who had discovered she was no longer a ruler, just a woman who had lost the one man who never needed her crown to love her.

Danielle had called twice. Ellie hadn't answered. There was nothing to say. No orders to give, no plan to craft. James hadn't called either. She could still feel the heat of his body when he walked into her office. The fire in his eyes that dulled the moment she stripped down and revealed the final, cruel truth.

She had done it. Cut away what she once called her crown. The sacred thing she had grown for him, for them. Shaved clean in a fit of anger and fear. She thought she was claiming herself, thought she was punishing him.

But the look on his face had told her the truth. She hadn't reclaimed her power, she'd thrown away her bond. She could still see the way he stepped back, and how his erection vanished in real time. That look in his eyes, that wasn't just disappointment.

That was death. The death of belief. Of faith. Of a man who had reshaped the entire world to orbit around a single woman, only to learn she had deliberately realigned the stars. And she'd done it with a razor.

Her breath shuddered as she remembered his final words: "Fuck you, Ellie." No one had ever spoken to her like that, not even her worst enemies. And yet, he didn't scream, didn't rage. He just shut down.

She could survive yelling. She could recover from a slammed door or even one of his brutal truths. But this icy, surgical rejection? It cut deeper than any outburst ever could.

Across the city, James stood in the steam of a rooftop sauna, hands braced on the cedar slats of the wall, head bowed, his breath slow and heavy. He hadn't touched his phone in hours. Jean had texted, Danielle had tried to check in, and he ignored it all.

The Rolex was still on his wrist. He hadn't taken it off. He couldn't. It wasn't just a timepiece anymore, it was now a reminder. Of beginnings, of loyalty, of all the things he once thought unbreakable. And of how easily Ellie had cut the final thread.

His muscles twitched as he shifted, the sting of his latest tattoo burning beneath the sweat: still fresh, still healing. The heart, wrapped in thorns. The dagger piercing it, just off-center. And the sliver of untouched flesh, left intentionally unshaded. Hope.

It had been for her. He had shown it to her, desperate to remind her there was still something left. But she'd shaken her head. Then disrobed like a woman offering a peace treaty, only to unveiled war instead. Her bare skin, the clean-shaven wound where his crown once lived.

She hadn't just changed her body, she had erased him from it. And still, he wasn't angry. Not in the way the world expected a man to be. He wasn't planning revenge, he was mourning. Because you don't burn down your own home unless it's already made you bleed.

And Ellie? She had left him bleeding on the marble floor of their kingdom. Now, there was only the silence. The terrible, hollow silence of two people too stubborn to reach, too wounded to rebuild, and too soul-bound to ever fully let go.

She stared at a drafted text she never sent: *I miss you, but I don't miss who I became with you.* Delete. Again.

Ellie didn't go into the office the next morning. Danielle called once, then twice, then finally sent a text: *You okay, my Queen? Want me to reschedule your morning?* Ellie never replied.

She lay curled on the living room couch instead, wrapped in one of James's hoodies, the one that still smelled like his skin and ambition. She hadn't eaten, hadn't even opened the curtains. Her palace, once a reflection of her dominance, was now just a dimly lit mausoleum of the man she couldn't forget. She hated that hoodie. And yet she clung to it like a lifeline.

Her eyes were swollen, her lips cracked, and her hands trembled when she tried to sip the water beside her. The Crown, once so heavy on her head, now just felt hollow. Like a decoration for a woman who'd forgotten how to rule.

She picked up her phone. The temptation to call him pulsed in her blood like a fever. But she didn't, because she knew he wouldn't answer. Because she didn't know what she would say, and she wasn't sure she deserved to say anything at all.

Instead, she opened her photo gallery: thousands of images of them. Intimate, wild, hilarious. Him shirtless in the kitchen, flipping pancakes in boxers and dog tags. Her bent over the balcony railing in Cabo, a sunset behind her and his hand on her ass. Their silhouettes in a mirror: sweat-slicked, grinning, entangled.

She paused on one. The night he gave her a crown of sunflowers and kissed her knees. She'd asked him why the knees. And he'd answered, "Because that's where you fall, and I want you to know I'll always honor you there."

The sob that burst from her chest was raw. She clutched the phone to her heart and screamed into the silence until her voice gave out.

James was dressed in all black when he returned to the office that morning, not a wrinkle in sight. Freshly shaved bald head, and tight beard without a hair out of place. But Jean could see it. Something had shifted. His movements were too sharp, too calculated. The silence between his steps had the weight of war.

"You good, King?" she asked softly. He nodded once, adjusting his cuffs.

Jean studied him a moment longer. She saw the Rolex back on his wrist. A flash of steel, a symbol of defiance.

"Got your schedule prepped. Gemini meeting is still locked in for Friday."

His jaw flexed. "I said no Ava on the core team."

"She's been reassigned," Jean said quickly.

He nodded. And then, he turned toward the floor-to-ceiling windows of his office, gaze lost on the horizon. His voice came low, almost unreadable. "I need that pain back."

Jean blinked. "Excuse me?"

"The hunger," he clarified. "I can't let it dull."

Jean exhaled slowly. "Are you sure that's what you want?"

"No," James said flatly. "But it's what's necessary."

Ava sat in her glass-walled corner suite two floors below, reviewing the upcoming presentations. She had plans. Big ones. Not just to seduce him, but to prove that whatever Ellie had squandered, she could savor.

And yet, beneath the predatory tilt of her smile, there was something else: curiosity, hunger, and the thrill of chasing a man the world said couldn't be caught. But Ava didn't believe in impossible. Especially not when it came to men with broken hearts. She was ready.

She waited near the central conference room, which was draped in silk the color of spilled wine. Her green eyes tracked his every step, her smile low and dangerous. She had tried subtle, she had tried professional. Now? She was trying one last thing: Seduction.

"I know you can go all night but you don't look like you have slept," she said smoothly as he approached.

James offered a single nod. "I don't sleep much."

"I could help with that," she replied, eyes glittering like jewels of sin.

He didn't take the bait. Just adjusted his cuffs and stepped past her, grabbing what he needed from the conference room. But Ava was quick. She followed.

"You know, I booked the top suite at the St. Valen tonight maybe you should pop by. You should see the tub: Marble, and big enough for two…three, if we're flexible."

James turned, slow and deliberate. "That supposed to impress me?"

Her smile deepened. "No. I think the part where I imagine you naked in it, that's what's supposed to do the trick." She stepped closer. Close enough to smell the spice of his cologne. Close enough to trail a finger along his lapel. He didn't flinch, but he didn't move either.

The office was quieter than usual. James hadn't noticed the time, as he made his way back to his office and left Ava right where she stood.

He sat behind his massive desk, documents spread out in perfect precision, a travel checklist glowing faintly on his screen. A bottle of his favorite bourbon rested nearby, untouched. Boxes were half-filled. Not just with things, but with decisions. Memories. Intentions he hadn't spoken aloud.

The move to Southern California was set in motion. Not finalized, but he'd drawn the line. His body might've still been here, but his heart? That piece had already started drifting toward the Coronado Bay, bleeding out one slow beat at a time.

He exhaled. His fingertips grazed the Rolex on his wrist, the weight of it both comfort and reminder. That's when the soft knock came. His door creaked open. Ava.

She stepped inside like she belonged there, hips swaying under the same emerald green dress she'd worn earlier. Only now, the neckline dipped lower, and the zipper had made progress. Her heels were too high for subtlety, her perfume too sweet for innocence.

She didn't speak. She didn't have to. The click of the door locking behind her was declaration enough. James didn't move. He simply watched as she crossed the room with a smile that dripped sin and desperation.

"You're really going," she said softly, perching herself on the edge of his desk. "You're packing up, and leaving all this behind?"

James didn't reply.

She tilted her head. "You don't have to."

So she leaned in, her voice barely a breath. "You deserve to be worshipped, you know. Not doubted. Not questioned. And I can worship you."

Her fingers reached for his tie. And that's when James's mind betrayed him. For a moment, one fractured and treacherous moment, he let it happen. He didn't stop her.

Her hands brushed down his chest, slow and reverent, lips parting just as she slid between his knees. Her breath was hot, panting. Her nails grazed the bulge in his tailored slacks.

The fantasy bled in: Not just Ava, but Ellie watching. Not angry, not horrified. Masturbating with her robe open. One hand between her thighs, eyes locked onto him as Ava began to unzip his pants. Her other hand pinching a nipple. Mouth parted in lust as she whispered, "Yes…show me how far you'll fall. Show me what I've broken."

The heat of that image scorched his blood. Ava's mouth moved toward him. James's fingers flexed as her hand slid up his thigh.

He snapped out of it. The spell shattered. "Ava, chill," he said.

Ava blinked, dazed by her own hunger. "What?"

James didn't move, but his voice dipped, quiet and lethal. "I would like to ask you a question."

She tilted her head. "Sure, ask your question?"

"Are you nice and tight?"

Her lips curved. "Oh, I am, very."

He stood. Full height. Full presence. Towering over her now. His next words were arctic. "Oh, well that's a shame, I don't seek to fuck tight pussy, that is a game for men with…. shall we say, size or ego issues." She stilled.

James took a step closer, adjusting his cufflinks as he spoke, his tone cold as polished steel. "I love my women grown. Open. Seasoned with the fullness that only comes from time, pain, experience...and thick cocks that are a bit above average." Ava's breath caught.

"See," he continued, his eyes unflinching, "any child can break delicate tiny tight things. But it takes a real man to dive deep into open waters and come up still breathing." She shrank.

"And by deep, I mean wide and deep," he said, eyes narrowing, "where kiddie conquerors drown, and big pussy energy is such a real thing for real men"

Only the hum of the AC and the sound of her pride disintegrating in the corner of the room could be heard. He reached for his blazer, slipping it on with slow, practiced ease. Adjusted his collar., smoothed his sleeves. Then one final strike.

"And neither of your lips..." he glanced at her mouth, then her core, "...are suited to my or my Queen's likings, but your tiny fist may prove delightful for my grown ass woman."

Ava opened her mouth to protest. But James was already walking past her. Before he reached the door, he turned his head just slightly over his shoulder: "Good evening." Then he was gone. Just like that.

And Green Eyes, the last temptress standing, was left sitting on the edge of a desk that didn't belong to her, legs pressed together, mouth trembling. Rejected. Dismissed. Unworthy. Because the King, even wounded, even betrayed, knew what real power tasted like. And hers couldn't hold a candle to the woman he still burned for.

He left to meet Ellie at one of their favorite rooftop dinner bars.

The elevator climbed slow and deliberate. Silent, except for the soft hum of its gears rising toward the top floor of the glass tower. James stood alone inside, a single bottle of top-shelf bourbon in one hand, the other tucked in his slacks. His muscles coiled beneath the smooth lines of his suit, tension laced in every breath.

He didn't know what would come of this meeting. Ellie had asked to talk, "like two adults," she said. "Like two people who had built a kingdom and knew how much had gone into the mortar."

And James, despite everything, said yes. But as the elevator continued its climb, his eyes drifted to the mirrored wall, and memory took him. She had been on her knees. Not because he asked. But because she wanted to be.

The elevator had just closed behind them, after a gala, maybe. She had looked at him with that gleam in her eyes, pressed the emergency stop, and then dropped to her knees like she was offering prayer to a god she made with her own hands.

Her lips wrapped around him slowly, reverently, taking her time, sucking him down inch by glorious inch until he could feel the heat behind his eyes. Her hand cupped his balls as her head bobbed, saliva dripping in strands as she worked him, messy, hungry, and in full command.

He had gripped the rail behind him, growling her name, before yanking her up, spinning her to face the wall of the elevator. Her gown flipped up. No panties. She had gasped as he bent her over and sank into her, her heels squeaking against the tile, her palms braced against the mirrored glass.

Alarms had gone off from the emergency brake. But neither of them gave a damn. He had taken her like the world was ending. Fucked her like she was the last woman on earth, and he was the last man worth praying to.

The way she moaned. The way her body bowed for him. And how afterward, she had collapsed against his chest, whispering, "This elevator will never be the same."

Ding. Snapping back into the present, the elevator opened at the rooftop. James blinked. The air was thick with memory and silence. A private table sat near the glass barrier, elegantly set for two. Crystal tumblers, a decanter of bourbon, and a single white rose.

She wasn't there yet. He walked to the edge, hand resting on the rail, looking out over the city. He ran his hand down his face and tried to breathe. Then, the door behind him opened. And he felt her before he saw her.

Hair swept back, face glowing with soft defiance, eyes that held storms and centuries behind them. She wore black, fitted, regal. Her cleavage teasing but not begging. Her stride was proud, heels clicking like a declaration. A Queen through and through.

She stepped inside the rooftop garden, saw him, and froze for a breath. Her gaze flicked down. His watch, her gift, still on his wrist. She swallowed hard. As she walked toward him, from the outside, it looked warm. Familiar. But to anyone who truly knew them? It was ice.

She sat first. He poured the bourbon. Neither spoke.

"I never touched anyone," she snapped. "You know that, right?"

He nodded. Quiet.

She continued, "And I know you're hurt. But enough of this. Come home."

He looked at her. The pain in his eyes wasn't sharp anymore. It was tired. "I miss you," he admitted. "All of it. The mornings, the wars. Even the damn coffee fights."

Her lip trembled. "Then come home."

He stared at his glass. Rolled it gently in his palm. "Maybe this break is what we need," he murmured. "Maybe we got too far from our core. Maybe it helps us get back there."

Her expression soured. "I don't need a break. I need you. And I haven't given myself to anyone. Not even a kiss."

He looked at her again. "I never asked for punishment," she continued, voice rising. "I don't deserve this. Not when I've been untouched."

His voice was low. Steady. "What do you think you deserve, Ellie?"

"I deserve a man who doesn't vanish every time it gets hard!"

"I deserve a woman who believes me," he snapped back. "Even when doubt whispers. Especially then."

She flinched. And then venom, born from pain. "If you starve a woman long enough of love, affection, and cock…don't be surprised if she's full and content when you return."

The words were poison. They sank into his bloodstream like acid. He set down his glass and stood. "You threaten the man who would've died for you?"

Her eyes were blazing.

"You threaten the King who found you when you were pieces and never once asked for the whole? You think content is something to boast about? I elevated you. You were my sky, my ground, my church."

She blinked. And he stepped closer.

"But maybe…" he whispered, "maybe I was too deep for you from day one."

He reached for the decanter. Poured the rest of his bourbon on the concrete. Then turned. "I'll see you when I get back." He took two steps, paused, and added, "Queen of mediocrity and contentment."

Ellie didn't move, didn't chase. She sat in silence, with her fingers curled around her tumbler. She drank. Alone.

And as she descended in the elevator, the same one that once echoed with their moans and pleas, the ding that signaled the lobby below sounded more like a funeral bell. The end of another round, and perhaps the final breath of a kingdom once made for gods.

The morning opened with quiet schemes whispered between two loyal women, Jean and Danielle, who, in another life might've ruled kingdoms of their own.

Jean leaned on the edge of Ellie's assistant's desk, her voice low but urgent. "If we get their meetings staggered just right, I can keep James in town for forty-eight more hours without breaking protocol."

Danielle blinked. "You're serious?"

Jean nodded. "He negotiated the right to return at any time. His same project. His same terms. It's still on the table. All of it. He made sure of that."

Hope bloomed behind Danielle's lashes. "So he's not gone forever?"

Jean sighed. "No. But he's leaving, for now. This time feels different, Dani. Ellie's pulled her stunts before. But he's never fought back."

She paused, looking down. "This feels like watching a dying soldier fight his final battle. Not to win, but to make peace with dying standing up."

Danielle swallowed hard and offered her an out. "You should come tonight," she said softly as Ellie wrapped up the last meeting of the day. "Some girlfriends, a little wine. Somewhere posh and grown, and full of beautiful women pretending their hearts don't ache." Surprisingly, Ellie said yes. Anything beat the silence at home.

James, meanwhile, went through his own rituals. An old playlist he hadn't touched in years poured through his luxury suite where after he left home this time would be home until SoCal. Wine, steak, a view of the skyline. And ghosts. So many ghosts.

He thought about the first time she ever challenged him in public. Thought about how she'd slammed the door of his Porsche and told him he didn't listen. But then how she came back ten minutes later, crawled into his lap and whispered, "I yell because I hate the idea of anyone else ever touching you."

He remembered their kitchen dance-offs and what they called "Kitchen talk", how she always cheated at cards, and how he always let her win anyway.

He remembered the quiet rules they built over time, the ones carved from mistakes and lessons, and the kind of pain that only comes from surviving things together. Rules that kept their kingdom whole. Rules that now lay broken, scattered like glass shards in a castle gone hollow.

He lay back on the bed, robe open, the city lights bathing his chest. The heart tattoo, still raw, throbbed under his skin. The unshaded piece in its center pulsed with quiet pain. He closed his eyes. He could still taste her.

Ellie arrived at the lounge in a sleek, backless dress that glittered like starlight. Her heels were sharp, and her walk was lethal. Heads turned. Whispers bloomed like perfume trails as she passed.

She sat with Danielle and the girls, sipped her drink slowly, and smiled on cue. But inside, she was ice.

Men approached: handsome, successful, charming. And none of them could see that everything she touched had already belonged to someone else.

She stayed for two hours. Smiled, nodded, laughed once. And then quietly excused herself. Danielle watched her go with a pang of grief. There was a woman pretending to hold a sword, while bleeding out underneath the armor.

Back at the suite, James stood on the balcony, staring out into the void. Tomorrow night, he'd be in Southern California, in a penthouse suite far away from this haunted city. And his Queen.

But for tonight, he was still here. Still tethered, still holding a sword, point-down in the dirt, wondering if any part of their love could survive the war they'd both waged. The next morning would bring movement. A relocation, a dividing line drawn in gold and grief.

But for now, they lay in separate beds, under the same moon, each drowning in memories. And neither one knew that what came next wouldn't just test their kingdom, it would threaten to reduce it to rubble.

Because distraction was coming, desire was waiting, and the cracks in the crown had only just begun to split wide open.

Chapter 7: Saints and Sinners

The first morning apart was the cruelest.

The Queen lay beneath her mountain of expensive sheets, the scent of him still clinging to the pillow beside her like a ghost refusing to leave. She turned her face into the fabric, desperate for warmth that would never come.

Her body ached, not from longing, not from absence, but from how intimately it still remembered him. The way he held her, the way he slept on his side, one hand always tangled in her hair like a claim.

She reached for her phone out of habit. Nothing: No call, no text, no whisper of a man who once couldn't go ten minutes without checking in on her, even in war.

Her fingers hovered. She could call. Just press the name. The contact was still pinned. Still royal. My King.

Instead, she rose. She moved like a ghost through the silent estate, her robe flowing around her like mist, her skin bare beneath it. Even in the silence, she refused to cry. Her kingdom would not see her collapse.

Three hours south and a world away, James stood barefoot on the balcony of his new penthouse suite, coffee in hand, ocean breeze tugging at his still-wet beard. The morning sun kissed his chest, the ink of his tattoos dark and alive under the golden light. His newest? Still sore, still healing. He didn't touch it.

His eyes were locked on the crashing waves below, but his mind was back home. In the house, in their bed, on her.

He hadn't slept, not really. His body had betrayed him in the middle of the night, twisting with need, every muscle remembering the sound of her voice, the rhythm of her thighs around his hips. The sacred heat of her body clenching around him like worship. He had tried to ignore it.

But the ache was too real. He had come here for peace, but what he found was purgatory.

Back home, Ellie dressed in silence, her hands shaking only once, when she clipped on her earrings. The final detail. The armor.

Danielle was already waiting for her downstairs, silent, holding a hot coffee and a file she didn't even glance at.

Ellie stepped into her heels. Paused. "Do I look like I'm dying?"

Danielle blinked. "No."

"Good." She grabbed the coffee, her expression tight. "Then let's go."

James arrived at the SoCal office early, earlier than anyone expected. He had skipped the usual parade of greetings, avoided the gawking young interns who whispered about his resume and his reputation.

Jean had flown down to prep the space, make sure everything was as he needed. She didn't speak at first, but she watched him. This wasn't the version of James she'd seen before.

This wasn't the polished, sharp-edged corporate god. This was a man in mourning. Quiet. Controlled. Dangerous. "Your Queen hasn't called?"

He didn't look up. "Not once."

Jean hesitated. "Maybe she's waiting for you."

His jaw ticked. "She'll be waiting a while."

That night, Ellie lay in the bath, her skin pink from heat. Her fingers trailed across her thighs, her thoughts drifting where they always did now: to his voice, to his mouth, to the way he used to pull her to the edge just to see her fall apart in his hands.

She touched herself. Slow, gentle, seeking. But when her climax came, it felt empty. Like laughing at a joke no one else heard. She whispered into the silence, "Come home."

Ellie stared at her phone for longer than she should have, thumb lingering over the screen, the message she'd written long deleted: *I miss you.* Too much. Too late.

The silence from James didn't just echo, it swallowed her whole. And when the ache in her chest became too much to bear, she wandered somewhere she hadn't gone in a long time. Her DMs.

One lustful message after another filled the space. Unread, ignored. Until she saw a name she hadn't seen in years. A slow smile curled across her lips, despite herself: Zion.

A built, Black man with golden-brown skin like toasted honey, high cheekbones and thick, artist's fingers that always seemed to speak more than his mouth did. He was eclectic. Artsy. A little dangerous, but not in a reckless way, more like the kind of darkness that made women curious enough to ruin their reputations.

He was in town. And it just so happened she was now free.

They had met years ago at a gallery opening. Innocent, but unforgettable. He always knew how to look at her in a way that said, "I see what you hide, and I want it all."

So, she responded, *Want to meet for a drink?*

He didn't wait long: *Midnight. The Winston.*

The Winston was dim, plush, quiet. The kind of lounge with expensive chairs and dark corners, perfect for sins whispered in silk.

Ellie struggled with the decision, but her mind was made up that anything would beat the silence and distance from James She arrived in a long black coat, heels clicking, lips red as fresh blood. She spotted him instantly. Zion perched like a panther, dreadlocks tied back, black turtleneck stretched across wide shoulders, the soft glow of a candle flickering against the silver ring on his finger.

"You still haunt my paintings," he said as she sat.

"I came for a drink."

He smiled slowly, his dark eyes dragging across her form like a paintbrush over canvas. "Then let's make it memorable."

Meanwhile, in Southern California, James lay back on his bed in the luxury hotel suite, his arm thrown over his head, towel across his waist. He hadn't answered Ellie's message: *I miss you and need you*, but he saw it. And it carved something open.

And then she appeared: Not Ellie, but the woman he had passed earlier that day: White and thick, with a golden-tan, and a body sculpted by desire and genetics. Her leggings had revealed the way her thighs hugged tight, but left that one space between her legs, just wide enough to make her pussy look wet before it even was.

He groaned softly and let his hand slide lower. But it wasn't just her. It was Ellie commanding the woman. His Queen had done it before, for him, and for her. He had watched her bend women to her will with only a look, had seen them melt under her mouth.

And now, in his fantasy, she was doing just that. The woman knelt between Ellie's thighs, lapping hungrily, while Ellie sat perched, back arched, hands in the woman's hair. James stood behind her, stroking himself, watching his Queen's fat ass rise and fall as she moaned through a climax.

"Would you like to taste your Queen off my lips?" the woman purred, her face drenched. James stepped forward and pressed his mouth to hers.

Ellie didn't miss a beat. She reached back and guided his cock into her dripping pussy, and the woman moaned watching him fill her.

The sound of skin meeting skin, of dripping heat and hungry mouths was perfect. James stroked harder. The fantasy woman reached between Ellie's thighs and rubbed her clit while James pounded from behind.

Ellie threw her head back, eyes rolling, coming around him hard. He grunted. His hand clenching around his thick shaft, until he finally exploded, cum spilling over his fist as he gasped her name.

And then: shame. Not for what he'd fantasized, but because it wasn't real. He didn't want fantasy, he wanted her. The real thing. The only thing.

Back in the hills, Ellie followed Zion to his private home: a sprawling space carved into the cliffside, moonlight cutting through wide glass panels.

Art was everywhere. She noticed cameras all over. He claimed the camera was just for reference, for the painting. She didn't argue, and she didn't ask where the lens was aimed.

Color. Chaos. Her. A portrait. Of her. Nearly finished, almost perfect: just like she used to be.

She moved closer, reached for the canvas, and touched it. And something inside her snapped. The coat dropped. Her dress followed. She turned to Zion, eyes burning. "Kiss me." He obeyed.

His lips weren't as full as James's, but they were warm, curious, eager. He kissed with exploration. James kissed with possession.

Still, she was soaked. She grabbed two handfuls of his dreads and guided his mouth between her thighs. He licked and he tasted. But not like he was starving, not like James. Not like the man who once whispered, "Let me drown in you."

She moaned, but it wasn't enough. She grabbed his wrist, dragging his fingers to her wet entrance. One slipped inside. It still wasn't enough. "More," she hissed.

Zion hesitated. "You want more?"

"All of them," she snapped. "Fill me. Stretch me."

James had mastered the art of worship through pressure. His thick fingers worked her open until she screamed, until her body surrendered fully. James never fucked her with his fingers, but instead he devoted himself to her.

Zion hesitated. She closed her eyes, frustrated. When it didn't come, she took control, and threw him onto his back, straddled his face, and rode it like a throne.

She came hard, but even that climax felt shallow. And when she looked down, she saw him spit her cum from his mouth. Not drink, not savor. She was a meal, and he acted like she was an inconvenience. And still, she let it continue.

Zion grabbed her, bent her over, and she heard the rustle of the condom. She waited, willing and eager. He slammed into her with the force of a beast. She gasped. He was big, yes, and aggressive.

But it was just fucking. No love. No reverence. No her.

James had fucked her, but he made her feel opened, known, holy. Zion slapped her ass. "Take this Black cock, you slut." She moaned, the degradation stirring something primal.

"I thought you had something for me," she growled, reaching back and spreading her cheeks. He slid into her ass. She screamed, coming hard around him. But again, it was empty.

She felt the condom swell with warmth as he groaned and collapsed against her. She reached for more. But he pulled out, removed the condom, and stood. "You wanna shower?"

She blinked, still catching her breath. "What?"

"I got an early day. You good?"

She found her clothes in silence and dressed. Then she left. No kiss, no tenderness, no closing gesture.

She rode home in silence, tears welling behind her mascara. She had been used, not chosen. The way James made her feel: like the dirtiest and most divine creature to ever walk, was gone.

She got home, showered, and collapsed in bed, Naked and still not satisfied. She typed out a message to James that she missed him and hit "send". Almost instantly, a reply. Not from him, just her phone: *Notifications silenced.*

On "Do Not Disturb." Her heart cracked. James had never blocked her, never silenced her, not until now.

Across state, he rolled over and read the message. Then he paused and placed the phone back on the table. No reply.

And for the first time, she realized he might not. The morning sun was ruthless in its honesty, streaming through the Queen's windows like a spotlight on the truth.

Ellie lay there. Her skin still tingled, her thighs still shaky. But instead of satisfaction, she felt only hunger. Not for touch or dominance. But for connection, for someone who could fuck her like a whore, and still hold her like a Queen afterward.

Someone who could whisper filth into her ear and still make her laugh like the world hadn't shattered. James had done that. James had been that.

Now, she was left craving something deeper than just being filled. She wanted to be seen while on her knees, held while bent over. Worshipped, even while being used. And the silence in her chest screamed louder than any moan she'd unleashed last night.

She showered and dressed for work, her makeup sharp, her heels sharper. But inside, her bones felt like wet paper. Still, she went. Because queens move, even when they're hollow.

Meanwhile, in Southern California, James moved through the gym like a storm in still waters. He was quiet, focused, layered in a sleeveless black hoodie and sweatpants, but his presence was impossible to ignore.

He had joined this gym to stay disciplined, to avoid chaos. But chaos had just walked through the door.

He saw her the moment she stepped inside: glowing, golden-tanned skin, a radiant contrast to her long black curls that hung just above a sculpted waist. Her tights were cream-colored, thin, and clung to her curves like desire itself.

No panties. And the outline of her lips: plump, juicy, unmistakably full, pressed against the fabric like they were begging to be freed. Even from across the room, James could see the hair. A full, natural bush. Black and thick beneath the thin tights, catching the sunlight like some kind of erotic halo.

His mouth went dry. His hand adjusted his hoodie, trying to hide the swelling beneath his sweatpants. But she saw it and smiled. She approached, confidently, a playful lilt in her step. She had eyes like storm light, and a rib tattoo that peeked out from beneath her sports bra as she leaned into the weight rack.

James glanced up. Her nipples were like bullets beneath the compression: hard, proud, unbothered by shame. Her hips? Wide, full. Built for grip.

She motioned for him to remove his headphones. He did.

"Morning," she said, voice like cool honey. "You don't remember me, do you?"

James smirked, wiping the sweat from his temple. "I try not to stare. It's a bad habit."

"Not that bad if it brings you back around." She extended a hand. "Thalia. Head of Global Accounts."

Greek name. Fit her. He shook her hand. "James."

She raised a brow. "Oh, I know who you are. Everyone here does."

He chuckled and touched his chest in mock humility. "Damn. No pressure, huh?"

She scanned him shamelessly, her eyes lingering at the impressive outline stretching his sweatpants. In her mind, she was already wrapping her lips around it, wondering if she could take every inch down her throat without gagging. Wondering how his fingers would feel buried in her curls while he fed her his legacy.

"You look like you're built to ruin a woman," she said, half under her breath.

He caught it but played coy. "You've done some work yourself. That ink…" His eyes traced the tattoo on her ribcage. "Beautiful."

She angled her chin. "So you have been staring." James grinned.

He was about to excuse himself. Too much temptation, too soon, when she stopped him. "Hey," she said. "I had a dream about you last night."

James raised a brow, caught off guard. Part of him wanted to share the fantasy he had of her. Of Ellie watching him take this woman and use her, while Ellie touched herself and came screaming from the sidelines.

But he didn't. Instead, he quipped, "In the dream, did you toss a few quarters in my cup, or chase me off the stoop before you called the cops?"

Thalia burst out laughing. The kind of laugh that echoed and pulled heads in the gym. James hadn't laughed like that in weeks. Maybe longer. "God, you're dangerous," she said, eyes bright.

"I should go," he said, collecting his towel. "Can't be late today."

She let him go. But not before her eyes followed the swing of his thick manhood beneath the cotton of his sweats. 'God help the woman who gets that,' she thought.

Later that day, Thalia knocked on his office door. He looked up.

She wore a blazer and high-waisted pants. But the confidence, the curve, the heat, was still there.

"There's a happy hour I love in the Gaslamp District," she said casually. "If you're not too busy tonight…"

James didn't hesitate. "I'll see you at six."

Ellie sat in her office, pretending to work, her inbox a blur. A knock on the door: Security. "Delivery for you, ma'am."

Danielle, wide-eyed, rushed over. "It's him. I know it's James."

But when they unwrapped the package from plain brown paper, with no bow or note, the smile slid off Ellie's face.

It wasn't flowers, it was a painting. Nearly life-sized, nearly naked, nearly divine. Danielle gasped. "Ellie, who the fuck did this?"

Ellie's face darkened. "Zion."

Danielle's jaw dropped. "From last night? He did this after one damn drink?"

A small, folded card was attached: *Everything I knew you would be.*

Danielle stepped back, arms crossed. "Ellie, that man is fine. But I can name five women in this city he's fucked just for sport. Don't fall for the tortured genius routine. You're better than that."

Ellie turned away, lips tight. "I needed something, Danielle. Something to remind me I'm still alive."

Danielle didn't reply. didn't need to. Because Ellie already knew. She walked to the security desk, voice flat. "Have the painting stored. One of the unused art rooms." And she left. Her heels echoed through the hall like gunfire.

Back in Southern California, James adjusted his cufflinks. His watch no longer gleamed with platinum arrogance. Tonight, it was the quiet confidence of a Patek Philippe. Timeless. Reserved for evenings that didn't scream but instead whispered power.

His shirt hugged his chest, his scent sharp and clean. He looked in the mirror. Not a broken man, but not yet whole either.

But maybe, just maybe, tonight was a step toward healing.

Thalia rested her hand under her chin, fingers curling slightly as she laughed at one of James's more clever responses. She had leaned forward over the high table of the intimate wine bar, her hips slightly twisted in her seat. Her long legs crossed, and her rib tattoo peeking from the hem of her silk top. Her breasts stretched the fabric, and her nipples now hardened from a combination of the wine and his voice.

And James? He was a storm contained in a man's frame: a black tee molded to his broad chest, arms relaxed but heavy with tension, like a panther just watching and waiting. His sweatpants, unfairly worn with effortless sensuality, did nothing to hide what she'd noticed back at the gym.

And now, under this table, her fingers had grazed his thigh accidentally-on-purpose. And then she'd felt it: thick, heavy, imposing. Not just big. Beautiful.

She shifted slightly in her seat, her voice low, eyes twinkling with intention. "I'm not gonna pretend I haven't been dying to know what that feels like," she said, gently pressing her palm against his thigh again, this time firmer.

"But not just because of what I see," she whispered, her voice softer now. "I want you, James. Because I've listened, because I see the mind behind the body. That calm, observant, stormy silence. The kind of quiet that only comes from someone who's battled himself and survived. I want that, the man beneath the ink. The man with the soft heart no one sees, unless they're lucky enough to hear you speak in the dark."

He didn't flinch, but he heard every word. It hit somewhere beneath his ribcage, a space Ellie used to occupy alone.

Thalia leaned in closer, lips just inches from his ear. "But I'll be honest," Her tone shifted to playfully apologetic. "I haven't shaved. I wasn't expecting this tonight. If I had, I'd take you home and show you how I'd worship a man like you."

James's lips curled into a smirk, his hand lifting his glass slowly. "I used to eat candy off the carpet as a kid," he said with a straight face. "Hair lint and all."

Thalia blinked. Then stared. Then burst out laughing. "Wait, what? You ate hairy candy? Why does that make me even hotter for you?" she gasped, covering her mouth, giggling into her wine.

"I'm just saying," James murmured, sipping his glass. "I've never been scared of a little flavor. Full and natural is a gift, with just enough grooming where I'd be eating."

She leaned back, visibly excited, almost blushing but too bold to show it. "That's a dangerous thing to admit, James. Because now I'm wondering how much flavor you can handle."

His eyes stayed locked on hers, the corner of his mouth twitching upward again. "Depends who's serving."

The sexual tension between them was electric: hot, charged, but somehow still tethered to something more intimate than just lust. James wasn't just looking for flesh, but he was trying to feel again. And Thalia was willing to offer herself for both, his fire and his heart. They clinked glasses, eyes never breaking.

And across town, the Queen curled into herself, alone in their massive bed, her body aching. Not from exertion, but from absence.

The man from last night had filled her, stretched her, fucked her. But the hunger remained. Worse now, because she remembered what it used to feel like to be taken. Devoured without being discarded after.

She stared down at what she was wearing: his shirt. Still. No lingerie beneath, just the shirt. Loose, oversized, swallowing her in scent and sorrow. It had dried now. Her body, her tears. But the silence screamed.

She grabbed her phone again. No messages. She closed her eyes and pressed it to her chest, heart pounding. She was spiraling. Trying to anchor herself to something. Someone. But the man she needed had always known how to drown her in love and lift her back up again. And she had let him go.

Her hand slipped between her thighs, the need returning, burning. But she couldn't. Not tonight, not with a stranger's taste still lingering in her memory. Not when her body had given permission, but her soul had begged for something else.

Her pleasure was now haunted, and her desire tinged with grief. The echoes of his mouth, his hands, his voice. None of it had been matched. Not even fucking close. She curled up tighter and wept softly into his shirt.

Meanwhile, James stood from the table with Thalia. Their laughter had faded to a slow hum, comfortable and relaxed. They walked out together, not touching, but the space between them electric: Two people working in the same world, orbiting the same building. But tonight, it had changed.

As he walked her to her car, she looked over her shoulder and said, "James," She bit her lip, then shrugged, her voice suddenly vulnerable. "Don't disappear."

He nodded once, slow and meaningful. "Neither should you."

She got into her car, as James stood there alone for a moment, heart suddenly unsteady. He pulled out his phone. Still no message, no missed calls. Just the cold, empty screen that used to light up with her name like the sunrise.

He slipped it back into his pocket. And walked toward his car. Not broken, not healed. But finally beginning to breathe again.

Back at the estate, the Queen walked to her closet, dragging James's shirt from her shoulders. She folded it with trembling fingers and placed it in the drawer where she kept her most sacred things. The shirt like a crown once worn proudly, now tucked away like a memory she wasn't ready to forget.

Ellie stood before the mirror. Unashamed, but alone. Still a Queen, but no longer certain if her King was ever coming home. She decided to give what she offered so many others a try, therapy.

The therapist's office was quiet, cloaked in warm neutrals and soft jazz. Nothing fancy, but rich with calm. Ellie sat across from him, her legs crossed tightly, skirt hugging her thighs, arms folded like she had something to defend. But it was her eyes that gave her away: Hollow, wary, hungry.

He listened with that kind of presence most men couldn't fake. Not just hearing but absorbing. She watched the way his brow furrowed when she mentioned regret. The subtle clench in his jaw when she confessed to sabotaging something beautiful.

It was the kind of attention she hadn't felt in weeks. Months, maybe.

She shifted slightly in her seat, thighs brushing. The movement drew her attention inward, her core already pulsing softly. Not just from lust, but from the vulnerability of being seen. Really seen.

Her mind drifted for a moment, just a flicker of a fantasy. His fingers around her wrist, guiding her onto the couch. His voice low, soothing but firm, asking her what she really wanted. Telling her to give in.

She blinked, snapped back. Her cheeks flushed.

And when she left the building, breath still shaky, her phone buzzed. James: *I miss you too. I miss everything we built and destroyed. You will forever be the forever.* A broken heart emoji.

Her chest tightened. She stared at it, thumb hovering. But she didn't reply. Instead, she slipped the phone into her bag. Her head high, lips tight, pretending the message hadn't splintered her insides.

James sat on the edge of the hotel bed, staring at the screen: *Read.* No response. The fire in his chest had dulled into something sharp and icy. Not rage but resolve. He dropped the phone on the mattress and grabbed his bag and headed to the gym.

Just as he predicted, Thalia found him there, smoldering in her tight black tights and sports bra, with her dark nipples pressing hard against the fabric. Her thick, natural bush visible through the light stretch of material as her hips swayed with purpose. No panties, no games.

He spotted her. She smirked. "I haven't shaved," she whispered, leaning in as he finished his final rep.

"And I still haven't forgotten that candy off the carpet," he replied with a crooked grin.

She laughed, pulling the waistband of her tights down just enough to let him see the deep, dark curls at the apex of her thighs. "Then come taste dessert."

A scrap of paper with her address appeared in his palm like an invitation to Eden. "Seven," she said. "Don't be late."

He wasn't. The lights were low in her penthouse apartment. Aromas of sandalwood and desire hung in the air. She wore nothing but a sheer robe. Her nipples poked through like pearls beneath silk. Her thighs glistened.

He stepped in, silent. He kissed her like he was reclaiming something stolen. Hands tore at fabric, lips collided. She pushed him onto the couch and straddled him, grinding slowly against the stiffness straining his sweatpants.

"I've dreamed of your mind," she whispered. "Your kindness. That quiet strength. I want your cock, but not just for how it fills me. I want it because it's yours."

James groaned. She slipped down, pulling his pants with her, and took him into her mouth. Wet. Skilled.

His eyes rolled back as she gagged and swallowed, spit coating his shaft. She looked up, eyes burning. "Does this taste better than that candy?" she asked, licking his tip with slow devotion.

He growled, grabbed her, and flipped her over. The robe was gone. That full, untrimmed bush was everything he'd imagined, thick and beautiful and hers.

He dove in, tongue tracing her folds like a man starved for sweetness. She exploded, shaking, and screaming. Her juices flooding his face. James pulled back only to gasp, licking every drop as if he'd just uncovered a sacred spring.

"I bet you can do more with those fingers," she panted. She convulsed again, squirting hard, eyes rolling back, mouth wide as she screamed into the sheets.

He reached for a condom, but she stopped him. "I need to feel you. All of you," she moaned. He hesitated, then slid inside raw. Her pussy swallowed him, walls gripping with intense pleasure. She was made to take it, all of it.

But she didn't want to be fucked. She wanted to be claimed. So, he flipped her again, missionary. He looked her in the eyes and gave her everything.

Thrust after thrust, sweat-slicked bodies colliding. Her fingers dug into his back. Her voice was a symphony of surrender. "I want to be your peace," she whispered through tears and moans. "Let me take your pain."

James came hard, deep, exploding inside her until she was overflowing. She smiled and curled her legs around him. He pulled out, cum dripping from her folds like warm honey.

But he wasn't done. He fed her his own release, pushing his soaked fingers between her lips. She sucked them clean, with soft, greedy moans. Then he bent her over. His cum still seeping from her. And fucked her doggy-style with a force that made the windows rattle.

He spit in his hand. Worked her tight asshole open with two fingers. And before he could put in another, she reached back and guided his cock up and replaced his fingers. Then slid him inside her ass, slow, deep, brutal.

She screamed as her next orgasm tore through her. Squirted again. Her body collapsed forward, ass gaping, holes leaking. James roared as his second climax surged through him, pumping her full, the primal fury of a broken king.

The phone buzzed. Thalia traced the tattoo on his chest with her nail. "She may be your Queen," she whispered, licking his neck. "But I plan to become your peace."

James didn't move, didn't reach for the phone. The screen lit up again. 4:02 a.m. Ellie was calling…again. He closed his eyes, sweat still dripping, lips still trembling. And let it ring.

The morning sun filtered through the gauzy curtains of Thalia's downtown apartment, casting a golden hue over the bed where they lay. James sat on the edge, one leg bent, his elbow resting on his knee, his eyes scanning the skyline.

Behind him, Thalia stirred. She stretched languidly, her bare skin a tapestry of bite marks, red trails from his grip still fresh on her hips and inner thighs. Her full bush glistened faintly from the aftermath of the night. She didn't try to cover up. She wasn't shy, she was proud, claimed.

"Hmm," she purred, running a single finger down the ridges of his back. "You don't strike me as the type to let anyone make you wait."

He looked over his shoulder, the corner of his lip twitching. "I'm not."

"But you waited for me," she whispered.

She sat up, kissed his shoulder softly. "You okay?"

James nodded, reaching for his slacks. "Better than I've been."

It wasn't a lie. But it wasn't quite the truth either.

The night had been a symphony: raw, aggressive, sensual. Thalia had taken everything he gave her. Demanded more. She didn't ask to be worshipped, she didn't ask for his love. She just wanted the storm.

And he gave it to her, twice. Once with his mouth, once from behind as she clawed at the sheets, moaning his name into her pillow while her legs shook from the power of his thrusts. She had begged for more, called herself his, told him she would be the woman who brought peace to his chaos.

And for the first time in days, maybe weeks, the silence inside James wasn't hollow. It was calm.

She kissed him again, lips brushing the ink on his shoulder. "You're not as hard as you want the world to believe."

James smiled faintly. "And you're not as patient as you pretend to be."

Thalia smirked, pulling the sheets around herself. "Touché."

He stood and buttoned his shirt, sliding the Phillipe Patek onto his wrist. Her eyes followed his every move, memorizing him.

"You free this weekend?" he asked suddenly, his voice lower, almost hesitant.

Thalia cocked her head to the side, her smile growing sly. "I am now."

He nodded once, firm, then leaned down and kissed her again. This one wasn't urgent or possessive. It was gentle, quiet. A whisper that said, "I see you."

As the door clicked shut, Thalia lay back on the pillows, satisfied and smiling. He wasn't hers yet, but she could feel the tide shifting. Slowly and strategically. She had time. She always played the long game.

James stepped into his private elevator, the morning hum of the city wrapping around him. He loosened his collar, letting out a breath.

It hadn't been love but it hadn't been empty either. Thalia wasn't Ellie. She didn't have her fire, her feral edge, her complete surrender.

But Thalia wasn't a disappointment. Not by a long shot. She could keep up. And maybe, just maybe, she could hold him for a while.

His phone buzzed as the elevator ascended. Five missed calls. All from Ellie. He hesitated, thumb hovering over the voicemail icon. He slipped the phone into his pocket and stared ahead at his reflection in the mirrored walls.

Back across the state, Ellie sat in her massive walk-in shower, the jets cascading over her like warm rain. Her back was against the wall, knees drawn in, arms wrapped around herself.

The silence after she repeatedly called him, was worse than any fight they'd ever had. And now, her voicemail wasn't even playing anymore. Just ringing, no answer, no reply. Just absence.

She had left him on read.

He'd answered with silence. They were both losing. But only one of them had tasted what it felt like to be discarded, ignored, unseen. Her fingers tightened around her knees.

She remembered Zion: the hands, the tongue, the roughness. She remembered how he let her moan and ache and cry in the dark, only to fall asleep without so much as

93

a kiss goodbye.

She remembered being filled but not claimed. Taken, but never wanted. She had tried to be strong and tried to move forward.

But James wasn't just a man. He was a god. And now, his goddess had fallen.

Ellie pulled herself to her feet, her muscles aching, her chest raw. She toweled off slowly, dressed in silence, and looked around her palace. It was pristine, and immaculate. It was empty.

Her hands trembled as she reached for her purse. She didn't need another meeting. She didn't need Danielle's wine nights. She didn't need Zion's paintings. She needed answers and healing. She needed help. And not the kind her current therapist could offer.

Because if she didn't find something soon, if she didn't break the pattern, the pain and war that lived inside her, she would destroy everything she ever touched. Her kingdom, her throne, and maybe even herself.

She didn't text him again. She didn't call. But for the first time since he left, she sought out therapy. Real therapy, not the kind that let her flirt and smile through the wounds. But the kind that would rip them open, piece by piece. Because now, the war was no longer between them. It was inside her. And she was ready to face it.

Chapter 8: The Ghosts Who Still Breathe

James didn't expect the morning to feel quiet. Not peaceful, not resolved. Just quiet. A kind of fragile hush in his chest, like a ceasefire he hadn't called for.

He allowed himself to recall the peace of earlier that morning, as he stood in the center of Thalia's condo. Shirtless, barefoot, coffee in hand, the scent of vanilla and roasted almond drifting in lazy swirls from the mug. The bed was still unmade, and her black silk robe lay draped over the arm of the couch, like it had decided on its own that it wouldn't chase him.

She was somewhere in the back, humming faintly, completely unbothered. Not pressed for declarations, not reaching for more than the night gave. And that surprised him.

Not because she hadn't earned more. Thalia was all grown-woman poise and intellectual sensuality. But because she was playing the long game, and she didn't hide it.

James watched the steam curl from the rim of the mug and allowed a rare thought to settle: She might be exactly what I need right now: Not a replacement, not a revenge body. Just a space to breathe, and to not be needed in the way Ellie had always needed him. Violently. Spiritually. Devastatingly.

Thalia reentered the room wrapped in nothing but her patience. A smile bloomed on her face. Not sly, not seductive, just warm. A woman who knew the rhythm of waiting. "You didn't sneak out," she noted, her voice low and smooth. "Pleasant surprise."

He smirked. "Didn't feel right."

"No," she agreed, walking past him, her shoulder grazing his bare chest. "You don't exit things that way. Even if they're temporary."

She took his mug, sipped from it without asking. Then looked at him over the rim. "You're still in love with her."

It wasn't a question. He didn't lie. "Yeah."

She nodded once. No drama. No performance. "I know."

He studied her. "Does that bother you?"

"I didn't ask you to come here to forget her," she said. "I asked you here because I want you to remember what it feels like to be wanted, without being weaponized."

His chest tightened. Damn. That line landed hard. He wasn't ready to admit how deep it hit.

Thalia stepped closer, fingertips brushing the tattoo just beneath his clavicle. "You carry her like scripture," she said softly. "That doesn't scare me. It just tells me where to kiss when you forget who you are."

James exhaled, sharp and low, slowly coming back into the present. She wasn't bluffing. She didn't just want him she wanted to understand him. And still, his soul whispered a name that wasn't hers.

Meanwhile, up the coast, Ellie sat on the edge of a beige leather couch in a cold, expensive office, legs crossed at the knee, ankle twitching. Her therapist, Dr. Lane, was too handsome for this setting. Clean cut, slightly younger than her usual type. Skin like coffee in a storm, and a voice that sounded like it had once led worship.

She'd chosen him impulsively, ignoring the gnawing feeling in her gut. He leaned forward now, eyes kind but firm. "You punish yourself because you think you deserve it." She flinched. He wasn't wrong.

"I don't need a sermon," she murmured.

"I'm not preaching," he said, softer. "I'm watching you drown in silence." Something cracked in her.

He moved too close, farther than the professional line allowed. She didn't move. His hand touched her knee. Warm, confident, present. "You don't have to suffer to prove you're still good."

Her breathing stilled. It was a moment pregnant with decision. She let the silence stretch. For a second, her body leaned in.

Then, she pulled away. Smooth, elegant, firm. "That's not yours to touch," she said, quiet but sharp. "And I'm not here for that kind of healing."

He nodded, stepping back, shame flickering across his expression. "I'm sorry."

"So am I," she whispered, grabbing her coat. She left without another word.

Back in the car, her hands trembled. But it wasn't Dr. Lane she was thinking about, it was Zion. The man she let inside during the storm. The one whose arms she used to erase the echo of James. It had started on her terms but ended on his.

Too rough, too fast, too much. She hadn't said no, but she hadn't said yes to that. And the shame lingered, curling in her belly like regret dipped in heat.

Her phone buzzed. Zion: *Thinking about you. Still.* She stared at the screen, with her breath held and then deleted it. But her hand stayed frozen over the screen.

Across the ocean of silence, James sat again in the gym locker room, phone in hand, thumb hovering over Ellie's last voicemail. He didn't play it. But he didn't delete it either. Some part of him believed that maybe, just maybe, the crown wasn't shattered beyond repair.

He still wore the watch. And sometimes, in the quiet, he swore he could feel her heart beating on the other end of the silence. It didn't happen all at once, no door slammed. No dramatic monologue, no final goodbye etched into a voicemail or text thread.

———

Weeks passed like soft avalanches: quiet, relentless, erasing the shape of what once stood tall. Ellie moved through the days like a shadow wearing a crown. Meetings, reports, phone calls, and project launches. Her calendar stayed full, but her eyes never did. The office buzzed as always, but her laugh no longer filled the hallway.

Danielle noticed first but didn't say anything. She didn't have to. She just stopped playing music in the mornings. Ellie had made a decision, silently and stubbornly. If the kingdom was crumbling, she'd hold the walls up herself. Even if they crushed her.

Her therapist, replaced now, was competent, professional, forgettable. The sessions turned clinical. Safe. She kept things surface level, never letting anyone reach the parts of her that bled. Especially not the places where James still lived like a ghost.

And still, every few nights, she reached for her phone. She never pressed "send." She couldn't. Because if she said it aloud, "I miss you. I need you. I was wrong too", that would mean it might be too late. And Ellie wasn't ready to mourn the end of something still breathing.

James buried himself in discipline. He'd been back at Gemini for over a quarter now. Same chaos, less clarity. Mornings began before the sun. Protein shakes, heavy lifts, conference calls, and daily briefs. The Gemini project was alive and moving fast, and he was driving it like a man with something to prove. To everyone, to her, to himself.

Jean hovered like an unspoken prayer, making sure nothing fell through the cracks. She didn't ask about Ellie anymore. She didn't have to. Sometimes, she caught James staring too long at the Rolex or thumbing the edge of a photo buried inside his briefcase.

He never mentioned her name. But it was in the way he trained too hard, slept too little, ignored his own body like it had betrayed him. It was in the way he refused to replace the key Ellie had once kept on her chain. It was still on the ring, still waiting, still home.

Thalia remained distant but present. She didn't press, didn't beg. She moved around him like smoke: touching, tempting, retreating. She knew she had made her mark, but she wasn't arrogant enough to believe she'd healed him. He smiled at her sometimes. And that was enough, for now.

Weeks later, James sat across from Thalia at a candlelit table tucked away in a quiet rooftop lounge. The view stretched behind her like a postcard: twinkling skyline, the hush of night, soft music drifting beneath the stars.

He was laughing at something she said. Not forced, not fake. Just light, easy. Thalia leaned in slightly, her hand resting on the stem of her wine glass. Her curls framed her face in soft waves, her skin catching the glow of the lantern between them. She looked breathtaking. A woman who could turn heads without even trying.

But as James leaned back and took a slow sip of bourbon, a flicker passed through his eyes. Not sadness, not guilt. Just distance. He wasn't here, not all the way. Thalia saw it. She always did.

She didn't get angry and didn't sigh. She simply reached across the table, curled her fingers around his wrist, and whispered, "Come back to me." Then she leaned in and kissed him. It wasn't desperate. It wasn't demanding and grounding. A kiss meant to remind him that she was here. Now. Present. Willing.

When she pulled back, her smile was gentle. "You don't have to be in love with me, James," she said softly. "Just don't ghost yourself."

He nodded, slowly. And for the rest of the evening, he stayed present.

But when he lay in bed alone later that night, it was Ellie's voice he heard in the quiet: "You'll always be my forever, even if we never speak again."

The days turned into a blur of polished smiles and avoided mirrors. Neither James nor Ellie said the words out loud: not to friends, not to assistants, not to themselves. But they both felt it. The space where the "we" used to be, was slowly filling with silence. The kind that didn't echo. The kind that stayed.

It was a Tuesday when the first crack appeared. Ellie was reviewing financials when her eyes lingered too long on a report James used to handle. His handwriting was still in the margins. Sharp, precise. She stared at it like it was scripture.

And suddenly, her body remembered the weight of his hand on her lower back. The whisper in her ear when she was about to panic over a presentation: "Breathe, baby. I'm right here." Her fingers curled into a fist. She pushed the folder aside.

The next morning, she sat in a different therapist's waiting room, this time with more care. The woman who emerged to greet her was not what Ellie expected.

She was tall, bronze-skinned, and impossibly elegant. Long, jet-black hair fell in gentle waves down the back of her tailored cream blouse. Her lips were full and matte, painted in a soft terracotta tone. Her eyes were almond-shaped, intelligent, and softly lined with kohl; dark pools that both welcomed and warned.

Her presence was arresting. Not sexual, but sensual. Like poetry wrapped in calm thunder. "Ellie?" she asked, her voice rich, low, and slow.

Ellie stood a little too quickly. "Yes."

"I'm Camila," she said, extending a hand. Her fingers were warm. Firm. Intentional. Ellie followed her into the softly lit office and sat down, trying not to fidget.

She could feel her pulse thudding just beneath her collarbone. A reaction she hadn't expected. Arousal? Curiosity? Intrigue? Maybe all three, and that annoyed her.

Keep it professional, Queen, she told herself. You're not here to chase distraction. You're here to heal.

Camila sat across from her, legs crossed, clipboard resting in her lap. "Where would you like to begin?" she asked.

Ellie kept it basic but honest and for the first time in weeks, she felt something stir beneath the numbness. A spark. Not for romance. But for reclamation.

James stood again in the gym locker room, phone in hand, thumb hovering over Ellie's last voicemail. And sometimes, in the quiet, he swore he could feel her heart beating on the other end of the silence His minded drifted to the day they met. It started with a handshake. Not the kind that changed the world, just a simple exchange between two strangers trying not to look too tired, too bruised, too uncertain.

Ellie was wearing her therapist badge: small font, understated title, nothing flashy. Just the way she liked it. She was a junior associate at a firm that barely knew her name, but her calendar stayed full because word of mouth spread quickly: She listens. She's kind. She doesn't make you feel broken.

But kindness, as she'd learned, came at a cost.

Her last relationship had left her hollow in ways she didn't know how to name. He'd wanted her body: paraded it in pictures, praised her curves, showed her off like a trophy. But he never asked about her mind, never stayed long enough to hear the tremble behind her silence. When she cried once in the dark, he'd said, "You're too pretty to be this complicated."

That was three months ago. Now she was at a conference, pretending to take notes, sitting in the back of a breakout session on emotional intelligence in cybersecurity. It was a packed room, but her mind was somewhere else entirely, until a voice beside her said: "This is either going to be brilliant, or a long hour of corporate buzzwords."

She turned. And there he was: Broad shoulders stuffed awkwardly into a too-tight button-down. Dark skin, bald head, tight beard. He smelled like something clean and simple, a cologne that didn't try too hard. There was a heaviness behind his eyes that she recognized. Worn and wounded, but still showing up.

She smiled politely. "Let's bet on buzzwords." He laughed. Not loud, but genuine.

"I'm James," he said, extending a hand. "DOJ. Cyber division."

"Ellie," she replied, shaking his hand. "Therapist. Mostly trauma and behavioral."

He looked surprised. "That's not what I expected."

"What were you expecting?"

"I don't know. More suits."

She chuckled, looking down at her jeans and blazer. "I like to keep it low-key."

"Well," he said, nodding thoughtfully. "Low-key works."

They didn't talk much during the presentation, but every now and then their shoulders brushed. Every now and then, their laughter overlapped. He never once mentioned her looks. And that was the first miracle.

After the session, Ellie packed up her notebook and tried to slip out. But then something stupid in her chest sparked and she turned. "Hey."

James stopped mid-step, blinking.

"You wanna keep talking?" she asked. "If you promise not to try anything."

He looked confused. "Try what?"

"Like, come on," she muttered, already regretting it. "You know what I mean."

James looked so genuinely lost, it stopped her. "I wasn't gonna ask for your number," he said, almost shyly. "I just liked talking to you."

And that was the second miracle. She softened.

He scratched the back of his neck. "I'm not really good at this part. I don't usually get approached. Not like that."

"You think I just approached you?" she teased gently.

"I mean, you stopped me."

"Because you were walking away," she said, rolling her eyes, cheeks pink now.

He laughed again, open, warm. "So…we keep talking?"

She nodded. "Yeah. But don't try anything."

He held up both hands, eyes wide with mock innocence. "Scout's honor."

And God help her, that dorky response made her stomach flip. They walked for hours. Past coffee carts, into quiet conference corners. Talking about music and movies and the strange way both of them always felt too much. James admitted he was just getting back into shape. That he used to hate mirrors, and that he had tattoos he never showed anyone.

"Why not?" she asked.

"Too dark," he said. "Too real."

She didn't press. She told him about her worst date: the one who asked her bra size before her last name. He winced in secondhand disgust.

"I'm sorry," he said.

"You didn't do it."

"No," he replied. "But I've probably been that guy. Before I learned how to shut up and listen."

She looked at him sideways. "You listen really well."

His voice dipped low. "You make it easy." She wanted to kiss him right there.

Their first touch. It was stupid, really. He handed her his hotel key card by accident instead of his business card, laughing at himself as he fumbled to swap them. She reached to hand it back, fingers grazing his palm.

And that was it. Not fireworks, not lust. Just warmth. But it stayed long after they stopped touching. He blinked. She held his gaze a moment too long. The air between them shifted. Their first goodbye.

They walked back toward their rooms together, after the conference was emptied out for the night. The hallway was dim and quiet, only the hum of soft lighting and tired laughter from behind distant doors.

James stopped at his door first. "Guess this is where the Scout says goodnight," he said, smiling gently.

She nodded. "Thanks for not trying anything."

He chuckled. "Thanks for not running when I said I work for the government."
They stood there. Awkward. Sweet.

"I hope I see you tomorrow," she said, almost a whisper.

"I hope so too."

And then, for one second, she leaned in. Her forehead touched his chest, barely.

His hand hovered near her waist, not quite touching. He didn't pull her in. She
didn't kiss him, but the pause held enough tension to rewrite gravity. And when
they stepped apart, something stayed behind in the air between them. Something
unnamed.

The next morning, Ellie woke early and spent extra time on her hair, though she
told herself she wasn't dressing for anyone. James hit the gym before dawn,
checking his watch repeatedly as if that would make her appear. They both walked
the lobby more than once that morning. Neither saw the other. But both looked.

Back in the present day, James sat alone in his hotel room, flipping through the
slides for tomorrow's Gemini presentation. But all he could think about was her
laugh that day, and the way it made the space between who they were and who they
could become feel possible. Ellie. Before the thrones, before the war, before the
armor. Just Ellie. And the man who hadn't yet learned to call himself a King.

——

The apartment was silent, save for the low hum of a ceiling fan, and the occasional
creak of old wood settling beneath time. Ellie sat curled on her couch in an
oversized hoodie, knees drawn to her chest.

The wine glass on the table beside her was still full. A soft flicker from the TV
played across her face, but she wasn't watching. She hadn't been for hours.

Her laptop sat open, some forgettable document half-finished. She was supposed to
be reviewing files. Client notes. Something clinical, something cold. But her mind
had gone warm. Gone soft. Gone back.

She hadn't meant to remember. But there it was, a flashback: She was shaking. Not
violently. Not visibly. But enough that James noticed. It was late. Maybe 2 or 3 in
the morning. Her breath had started coming fast, sharp. Her hands trembled just
beneath the blanket, as she'd tried to hide it.

He didn't ask what was wrong. He didn't ask anything at all. He just got up, went
to the kitchen, and started making breakfast food at 3 AM like it was the most
natural thing in the world.

Eggs, bacon, toast, black coffee. Soft jazz playing low from the Bluetooth speaker he always carried with him like a mood guardian.

When she finally stepped into the kitchen, drawn by the smell, and the sound, and the quiet devotion, she stopped. Because he wasn't wearing a shirt. And she had never seen his back before. Muscles roped down his spine like carved stone, thick and beautiful, flexing with each subtle movement. But what stopped her was the ink: his entire back was a mural of black-and-gray realism.

A Spartan warrior. Helmet down, sword at rest. Surrounded by ghosts. By fire. It was fierce, it was grief, it was beautiful. Her body responded before her brain could catch up. Arousal flooded her. But not just that. It was the way he was feeding her soul, not asking for anything back.

And suddenly she thought of the movie, "Baby Boy." That moment when Ving Rhames was cooking in the kitchen naked, muscles glistening, power in stillness. Except this wasn't fiction, this was her life, her kitchen. Her King.

He glanced back. "You good?"

She swallowed. "Yeah."

"You sure?"

She nodded, stepping closer. "You ever gonna tell me what it all means?"

He shook his head. "Not yet."

"You always cook when people spiral?"

"Only for the ones I plan to keep."

Back to the present day: The memory hit so hard she almost dropped the wine glass. Her breath caught, and the lump in her throat returned like an old enemy. She wiped her eyes. Once, twice. Then, closed the laptop and walked to her bedroom. She didn't sleep.

Elsewhere, James was alone in the hotel gym. It was late, nearly 1:00 a.m., and the place was empty. The kind of silence that invited ghosts. He moved through his circuit without music, without thought. Reps on autopilot, the pain in his muscles grounded him better than sleep.

Then, mid-set, his leg cramped. He dropped to the bench with a grunt, exhaling hard, face pinched in pain and frustration. And then it hit him. Her laugh. That laugh. That sharp, bubbling, head-thrown-back kind of joy that used to break into his day like sunrise.

It wasn't just a memory. It was grief. He sat there, bent over his knees, letting the sweat drip, letting the ache spread. He missed her in ways the body doesn't know how to forget.

More fragments of memory snuck in:

Ellie helping him with his blistered feet after he pushed too hard at the gym, her fingers rubbing ointment in slow, silent care.

James showing her a journal entry from his teens. The only thing he wrote that year: *I want someone to choose me without flinching.*

Ellie's first panic attack in his car, and how he simply pulled over, held her hand, and counted her breaths with her. The attacks had been so raw back then. The next morning, neither of them mentioned anything to anyone. James went back to meetings.

Later that night, Ellie sat in bed, with a blank journal on her lap. She hadn't touched it in months. She opened to the first page, stared at the empty space, and slowly wrote: "Ours." No explanation. No title. Just a word that still meant everything.

———

Ellie stared at her phone long before the sun rose. No coffee yet, no makeup. Just quiet and ache. She opened the text thread that hadn't been touched in weeks. The photo icon still showed his face, though it was buried now under silence.

Her thumb hovered. Then, without drama or ceremony, she typed: *I still see you. Even in the dark.*

She hit "send" before she could stop herself. No punctuation, no second sentence. Just that. She turned the phone facedown and whispered, "Don't make me wish I hadn't."

Across the state, James was locked in a Gemini planning meeting when the message arrived. He didn't notice at first. He was talking, focused, animated, until his phone buzzed twice in rapid succession. Jean moved to silence it, saw the name, and paused.

James glanced down, mid-sentence. First message, Ellie: *I still see you. Even in the dark.*

Second message, moments later, Thalia: *The most powerful kings are those that are strongest during their struggles with weakness. I love watching you war with passion and the grace that suits you.* He froze.

The table faded into silence. "James?" someone asked.

He blinked, cleared his throat. "I'll be back in five."

On the hotel balcony, the city stretched out below him, wide and golden in the morning haze. He opened Ellie's message first. Read it once. Then again, and a heat pressed into his chest. Not fire nor rage. Just that unbearable tightness that comes when someone sees your soul before you're ready to show it.

His fingers hovered, then he replied: *You are and will forever be my light, my love. But do not forget how I made friends with every monster I've met in the dark, and they have welcomed me back with the very open arms you so easily close on me.*

He hit "send," and closed his eyes. It was both a confession and a wound.

Then he opened Thalia's message and stared at it a long time. She didn't push, never had. But that message? It didn't feel like seduction. It felt like loyalty.

He typed: *Thank you. I'm looking forward to seeing you soon.* It wasn't a lie. But it wasn't the whole truth either.

———

Back north, Ellie's mind reminded her of their first fight. It had started over nothing: A missed call, a short text. James had gone silent for a weekend. Ellie had assumed it meant disinterest, that he'd changed his mind. And she didn't say anything.

She wanted to. She wrote long messages, then deleted them. She sat in the bath one night and almost called but couldn't bring herself to speak if he didn't want to hear her. She stayed silent.

And then the gift came. A small black box, wrapped in matte paper. A blood-red satin ribbon tied with care. Inside: a single CD. When she played it, the song began immediately. "Say something, I'm giving up on you…" By the second verse, she was crying. Hard.

Tears streamed down her cheeks like confessions she never spoke aloud. Because no one had ever fought to be missed by her. No one had ever said goodbye with grace and sorrow at the same time.

It was the first time she believed that maybe, just maybe, he was as afraid of losing her as she was of him. She called. And this time, she spoke. "I don't know how to be strong for you and myself at the same time," she said softly.

"I never needed you to be strong for me," James replied. "I just needed you to believe I was worth not walking away from."

He paused. Then added, "I've never had anyone care about losing me. So when you went quiet, I assumed it was my turn to disappear. But Ellie, if you want me, I'm already yours. My loyalty, my pleasure, my whole fucking heart. You can have it."

———

When Ellie brought her mind back to the present and re-read his message, the one about monsters and her closing her arms, it gutted her. Her hands trembled, but she didn't cry. She just sat there, blinking against the tears she refused to release, and let the silence sit between them like fog. She didn't respond, she just stared at the blinking cursor on a message that began: *You didn't deserve that.* But she never hit send.

Back at his hotel, James sat on the edge of his hotel bed, phone in hand. He had typed out a new message to her: *Do you still think of me when you can't sleep?* He stared at it. Waited. Then locked the phone, message unsent. They were both still reaching. Still aching. Still typing into silence. But neither one pressed "send.'

———

After a brief talk with Ellie, Danielle closed the door behind her with deliberate calm, smoothing her skirt before dialing Jean's number. "She's coming," she said without preamble.

Jean didn't ask who.

"She's landing Thursday," Danielle continued. "She'll be at The Pendry. Dinner is at Bice, 7:30."

There was a pause. Jean's eyes lifted from the screen in front of her. "She coming to talk? Or to start a war?"

Danielle exhaled. "That's between them. We just get them in the same room."

Jean nodded slowly. "And James?"

Danielle's voice was sharp and soft all at once. "You'll get him there. I trust you to know how." She hung up.

James was walking out of the gym, towel slung around his neck, sweat clinging to the back of his neck, when Jean fell into step beside him.

"Bice," she said like it was just another calendar item. "New sponsor dinner. Nothing major. Clean energy people. Light on speeches."

He raised an eyebrow. "It's not on the calendar."

"Last-minute. You know how these get. Show face, eat, smile. You're a professional, not a hostage."

James gave a short grunt. "Fine."

Jean hesitated. "Want me to call Thalia? See if she's free?"

He slowed to a stop in the hallway, towel in hand. She watched his mind churn. He hadn't seen Thalia in a few days. It hadn't been tense, just quiet. Comfortable. Too comfortable.

"Yeah," he said. "Let her know it's casual. Just dinner and conversation."

Jean nodded. "Got it."

Later that night, Jean lingered near the corner of the office floor, phone in one hand, mind in a tangle. Danielle's name lit her screen. She answered with a soft breath.

"I talked to him," Jean said.

"And?"

"He's coming."

Danielle hummed. "And the plus-one?"

Jean gave a tight laugh. "I talked him out of it. Said it'd be cramped. All work."

Danielle's voice dropped, amused. "You told Thalia?"

"Not yet."

Danielle laughed outright now. "Good. You'd be arranging a funeral."

Jean snorted. "You think I want to be anywhere near that crime scene?"

Danielle grew quiet for a beat. "You hear anything about Zion?"

Jean's face stiffened. "Hell no."

"Because that?" Danielle continued, "That would kill him for sure."

Jean didn't answer. She didn't need to.

James stood at the hotel sink, shirtless, steam curling around him from the post-shower haze. He wiped the mirror once and stared at his reflection.

His stomach was tight, his arms still humming from the gym. But the weight behind his collarbones, that wouldn't lift.

He hated the part of him that hoped Thalia would cancel. He hated that he looked for reasons not to go, even as he laced up the same dress shoes Ellie once teased him about, saying they made him look like a man who could ruin a room with a whisper.

He hated that he still wore the watch. And he hated most of all that he didn't know if he was walking into a trap. Not a betrayal. Just a memory. And some memories don't break you they pull you under.

James found himself thinking back to a simpler time: Him lying on the sand, sunglasses on, arms folded beneath his head, watching Ellie sunbathe facedown just a few feet away.

Her bikini bottoms were barely there. Just enough to meet legal requirements. Bronze skin shimmering in the sunlight, back arched slightly, her legs moving gently as if flirting with the tide itself.

He let his eyes wander. And then he saw it: A subtle patch of pigment, light brown, almost heart-shaped, on the lower curve of her ass. He leaned up on one elbow, smirking. "Babe."

"Mmm?"

"Is that…Texas?"

Ellie turned her head, squinting over her shoulder. "What?"

"Right here," he said, pointing lazily. "That's either Texas, or I've stared at too many maps."

She laughed, soft, honeyed, and belly deep. Then rolled onto her side and looked at it. "Oh my God, you're right!"

He grinned. "So, I guess every time I want a taste of that, what do I say? 'Let me visit Dallas'?"

She rolled her eyes. "No." Then leaned in, voice low and teasing: "You want what's back there, you ask for the Alamo."

They burst into laughter, and he kissed her neck. She pulled him down into the sand, and for that whole afternoon, the world didn't matter. Only the waves. And that damn Texas-shaped birthmark.

———

No arriving in L.A., Ellie stepped off the plane. Heels silent. Eyes forward. No hesitation. But as her foot touched the ground, the memory clung to her: James's voice whispering "Alamo" in her ear one night, his lips brushing the mark like it was sacred.

She swallowed. Pulled her sunglasses down and slid into the black town car waiting at the curb. In the backseat, her fingers tapped idly against the clutch in her lap, and her chest tightened with every turn the car made toward the hotel.

She inhaled. Then, softly, quietly, to herself: "If I see him, I'll say hello. Nothing big."

Another turn. "No, I'll say, 'It's been a while.' Something neutral."

A pause. Her hand trembled slightly as she reached for her lip balm. Then, quieter still: "Can I even be her again? That woman he met? The one he wanted without agenda?"

Her eyes welled, but she blinked the tears back hard. Because if this really was a reckoning, she had to show up as the one he fell for. Not the one who pushed him away.

Chapter 9: When Fire Walks Into the Room

James saw her before she saw him.

It was the kind of moment poets used to write about before language got lazy. The kind of moment that made time stop just long enough for the heart to stutter, for breath to lodge beneath the ribs, for memory and desire to crash into the now like it had never left.

She was at the bar, her back to him. She wore an elegant black dress that kissed every curve with the kind of familiarity only a lover should know. Her shoulders bare, skin aglow under the lounge's amber lights. Hair swept into a loose, regal updo, with soft tendrils framing the curve of her neck. The same neck he once bit softly while whispering, "mine" through clenched teeth in the backseat of a car they never told anyone about.

The bartender poured something dark into her glass, and James watched her fingers curl around the stem: slow, graceful, like she wasn't just claiming the drink, but the entire goddamn room.

He couldn't move. Not while the ache in his chest threatened to undo him. This "accidental" Ellie sighting was orchestrated. He pulled his phone from his pocket, screen glowing like it knew who he needed to speak to James: *I love you. But I'm going to kick your fucking ass.*

Three dots danced immediately.

Jean: *You're welcome. Do Not Disturb activated.*

At the bar, Ellie didn't notice him yet. Not fully, not with her eyes.

But something shifted inside her: an internal weather pattern that swirled the moment he walked in. It always happened when he was close. She used to joke that her soul wore a sensor calibrated to the weight of his presence. That sensor was going off now.

She reached for her drink, and for a moment, her thoughts wandered. Softly, and without permission. Suddenly, she was transported back. It was SoCal, this lounge, this bar, late summer. Jazz low, water just beyond the patio glass. They were laughing too loudly in a place too expensive to be that free.

James had just ordered oysters for the first time. They arrived with lemon, cocktail sauce, and way too much flair. Ellie watched him hesitate. "You sure about this, King?"

James held the shell like it was evidence in a trial. "It's a texture thing, right?"

She nodded. "I can't do it."

James raised an eyebrow. "The queen of 'fill my mouth' doesn't want to swallow?"

Ellie gasped, nearly choking on her wine. "James!"

He grinned. "I'm just saying. For someone with such…impressive oral confidence…"

She covered her face, laughing so hard her cheeks flushed. "I hate you."

"You love me."

"Shut up."

Still giggling, she picked up an oyster and, against her better judgment, slurped it down. Eyes wide. "…That's not bad."

"Told you."

He looked so smug, so proud. And the way he watched her, like she was magic and he'd known it all along, made her want to crawl across the table and climb into his lap. That night, they didn't make it to dessert.

Bringing herself back to the present, her fingers tightened around the glass, grounding her in the now. This bar, this nigh. The burn of the bourbon was smooth, sweet. She smiled faintly.

And then she saw him across the room: still and sharp. A king wrapped in tailored charcoal, no tie, collar open just enough to whisper danger. The Rolex still gleaming on his wrist, his eyes set on her like no time had passed.

Her body betrayed her first. A rush of warmth at her core. A tightening across her chest.

The air in the room thinned. People noticed. Not just them. The room noticed. Heads turned, conversations dipped into pauses. Even the bartender slowed, as if aware he was watching two solar bodies caught in orbit again.

James didn't smile. He didn't need to. He was already walking toward her, and every step he took felt like a vow.

Ellie rotated slowly on her stool, knees crossing just enough to hold herself together, lips parting like a woman caught between instinct and regret.

He stopped just close enough to scent her perfume: vanilla and soft smoke. The one she only wore for nights she wanted to be remembered.

His voice came low, teasing, laced with amusement he hadn't earned but would absolutely wield. "Fancy meeting you here. At this event, that isn't an event, but smells a lot like a setup."

Ellie's lips curved, slow and sharp. "Doesn't everything around us smell like strategy?"

Their first smile cracked at the same time. He nodded toward the seat beside her. "Would the lady prefer I join her here and we look like two old friends catching up?"

She arched an eyebrow. "Depends."

"On?"

He leaned in, just enough to make her pulse jump. "Or," he said, eyes locked on hers, "may I interest the Queen in dinner this evening?"

Then her voice, calm as ice melting against flame: "You may."

The table between them might as well have been a fuse. The wine glasses had been refilled, but the hunger in their eyes had nothing to do with food. Ellie sat like a woman who knew what power tasted like, and James watched her like a man remembering how it felt to be conquered and crave it.

"You're still wearing the watch," she murmured, running her fingertip along the rim of her glass.

James didn't blink. "It still fits."

She cocked her head slightly. "Does it?"

"It fits better than ever," he said. "But it never left, Ellie. You know that."

The silence between them wasn't awkward, it was loaded. Under the table, her heel grazed the inside of his calf. Not accidental.

He held her gaze. Said nothing. "You shaved," he said, voice low, reverent. A question, a memory, a dare.

Ellie's lips curled faintly. "You let it bleed."

———

As they sat, she remembered being pressed against the hotel window, the night sky at her back, with her legs around James's waist and dragging him in with a moan that shattered the quiet.

His suit pants were still halfway on, undone, the belt hanging open as she rolled her hips against him, bare, wet, hungry. Her hands on his head and rubbing the hair on his beard. His mouth moved along her throat like he was searching for a vein to drink from.

She ground down, slick and bold, whispering into his ear. "No one else gets this." His grip tightened. "Say it," she breathed.

"Yours," he groaned.

"Say it again."

"Yours." He tried to pull her higher. She held him there, pinned, pulsing, every motion precise.

"You'll never beg like this for anyone else." And he didn't. He broke for her. Right there against the glass, moaning her name into her shoulder while she came like a storm that refused to be tamed.

James thought back to another time: The bathtub overflowed, water spilled in waves over the edge, hitting the tile floor with a slap. He barely noticed. Ellie was on top of him, straddling him in the steaming bath, skin dewy and flushed. Her thighs clenched around him as she rolled her hips with a rhythm too sinful to be taught, only born. Her hands braced against his chest, her body glistening as she rode him with eyes locked on his.

He was groaning her name already. "Shh," she whispered, pressing a hand to his mouth. "Take it."

The water slapped with every motion. Her nipples brushed his lips as she leaned down, panting into his neck. "You don't need to breathe," she teased. "You just need to stay under me."

She bit his collarbone. He came undone, back arching, hands gripping her hips like lifelines, mind blank with pleasure. She smiled when he came. Like a goddess satisfied by her worshipper.

——

James exhaled, slow and hard. His eyes were glazed with memory.

Ellie shifted in her seat: subtle, but enough to let him know she felt the aftershock too.

"You keep looking at me like that," he said, voice low and dangerous, "and we're leaving early."

"You keep sitting like that," she fired back, "and the room's gonna figure out what I'm remembering." He smirked.

"I'm not the one shifting every time your leg brushes mine."

"I'm not the one licking his lips like he forgot how I taste."

He leaned in, his breath fanning across the linen. "You still taste like ownership."

Ellie's breath caught. Before she could respond, both of their phones lit up, simultaneous vibrations cutting through the tension.

Ellie glanced first. Text preview: *Just thinking about how wet you used to get…* She opened it. Full screen. A picture of his erect dick, hand wrapped around it, thick, dark, proud. Underneath: *Don't pretend I didn't ruin you a little. We both know you loved it.* Ellie's jaw tightened.

Her pulse didn't race it dropped. Just like that, the desire shriveled. The tone collapsed. She stared at the image. At the arrogance. The presumption. Her hand moved without hesitation. Blocked. Gone.

James checked his. Thalia sent three photos. The first: Her bent over a black marble vanity, bare back arched, thong tugged down around her thighs. Her skin glistened, body oiled and waiting.

The second: Her breasts cupped in her hands, tongue teasing her bottom lip, the words "Still wet for you" scrawled across her lower stomach in red lipstick.

The third: Thalia on her knees, mouth open, fingers between her legs, one name typed below: *King.*

Swiped through them once. And then again, slower. Not because he was tempted. But because he was measuring the distance between what looked good and what felt empty.

He put the phone down, didn't reply, didn't even sigh. He looked at Ellie instead. She met his gaze, her expression unreadable. Neither asked. Neither answered.

James stood slowly. Offered his hand. "You said I could have dinner," he said softly, watching her eyes. "I didn't say we had to finish it here."

Ellie didn't smile. She just placed her hand in his. The rest would burn.

Upstairs, the door clicked shut behind them with a finality neither of them questioned.

James tossed his blazer onto a nearby chair. Ellie slipped off her heels without looking at him, her bare feet silent against the hardwood as she walked toward the window. The city glowed below her: indifferent, golden, alive.

He watched her for a long moment. The line of her spine. The arch of her silhouette beneath black silk. She didn't glance back. Just stood there, letting the silence drip into the room like melted wax.

"You still look at me like you own me," she said, her voice calm, almost detached.

James moved behind her, close enough to feel her warmth but not touching.

"I never stopped," he murmured. She turned slowly. Their eyes met. The kiss wasn't gentle. It was claiming.

Teeth and heat. Her fingers clawed at his shirt. His hands gripped her waist, dragging her into him like she might vanish if he didn't hold her fast. He kissed her like it was the last oxygen on earth, and she let him because she needed to drown.

She bit his bottom lip. He groaned into her mouth. They broke apart, just for air. "Take it off," she said. He stared at her. "My dress," she clarified, voice dipped in hunger. "Take it off like you remember how."

With reverence, he slid the straps off her shoulders slowly, watching her eyes, fingers tracing every inch of exposed skin like an oath made flesh. The fabric pooled at her feet. No lingerie. Bare. Glowing. Waiting.

She reached for his buttons next, unfastening each one with deliberate care. Between each snap, she whispered: "I used to dream about this. You. Undone."

James's chest rose beneath her touch, his skin warm, dark, branded by memory and need. His pants followed: unzipped, unbuckled, until he stood before her only in briefs that did nothing to hide how hard he was for her.

Ellie dropped to her knees. She kissed the head of his cock through the fabric, lips lingering just long enough to make him hiss. "You missed this?" she asked, voice sultry.

He looked down at her, jaw tight. "You have no idea."

She tugged the briefs down with one hand, and when he sprang free, she licked her lips, then smiled.

They fell into the sheets like warriors returning from exile. Ellie on her back, legs spread, one arm above her head like a queen awaiting a crown. "Remind me," she whispered. "Remind me what I gave up."

James dropped between her legs, mouth hot, tongue merciless.

He licked her slow at first, teasing and tracing the lips he'd kissed before, but it didn't stay soft for long. He devoured her like scripture. Hands holding her hips steady, tongue circling her clit in tight, practiced rhythm. When her moans started to break, sharp and strangled, he slid two fingers inside and curled just right.

Ellie arched. Gasped. "Fuck, James." And when she finally released, body jerking with heat and relief, she opened her eyes and watched. Watched as he swallowed every drop of her, tongue working like a man dying of thirst. His mouth stayed open, chasing the last of her on his lips, his face glistening, sucking like a straw when there was nothing left but ice and noise.

And she pulled him up to taste it on his mouth. He kissed his way up her body: lips on her stomach, her ribs, her collarbone. She grabbed his cock and guided him in herself. Slow, deep. Until they both gasped in unison. "You still fit," she whispered, breath shaky. "Like I was made for you."

His head dropped to her shoulder. "I never fit anywhere else." They moved together like they were trying to rewrite history with sweat. Every thrust was a sentence. Every moan a chapter. And when James was close, he pulled back, slowed down.

"No," Ellie panted. "Don't stop. Don't you dare stop."

And when she came again, he followed, groaning into her neck as she clung to him like shelter.

They didn't speak at first, they just lay tangled. Bare and slick, breath catching against skin. James brushed the curls from her face. Pressed his lips to her temple. "If this was the end…" he began softly, "would you regret letting me back in?"

Ellie didn't answer. She turned onto her side, closer. Grabbed his hand. Placed it on her breast. Then whispered, like it was nothing and everything all at once: "Put your dick on my butt."

James let out a stunned chuckle: deep, full, half groan. He moved behind her and let his softened length rest where she wanted it.

They lay like that. Together. Breathing.

The room was still wrapped in the blue-gray hush of early morning. The city outside stretched quiet, golden, and half-forgotten. James stirred behind Ellie, the weight of his body soft against hers, his arm still draped lazily over her waist.

She was awake and smiling. Not because of anything said, but because of what had just been shared, again. James's length was still nestled right where she asked him to put it, warm and heavy against the curve of her ass, heartbeat syncing with hers.

She whispered to the ceiling, half-laughing. "That wasn't even the first time I said that."

James shifted behind her, voice rough with sleep. "You said it like it was normal."

Ellie grinned, eyes still closed. "It became normal. With you."

James thought back now, to the first time he heard her say that: A private rental, tucked just off the coast. The ocean air was warm and heavy with salt, the windows cracked open to let in the slow crash of waves.

They had made love hard that evening, twice. Ellie was already melting into the mattress, naked, sated, the sheets twisted beneath her like soft knots. James lay behind her, his chest rising against her back, hand on her waist.

She was half-asleep. Boneless. That sweet post-orgasm daze humming behind her ribs. And then, without thinking, she grabbed his hand, slid it over her breast, and whispered, "Put your dick on my butt"

Blinking. He said, "Wait…what?"

She giggled. "Just do it. I like the way it feels. You rock my world and I want to sleep, but I still need to feel kept. Wanted. That's my signal."

Still blinking, still dazed, James obeyed. He slid closer, let himself rest between her cheeks: soft, satisfied, completely bare.

And then, without meaning to, he started to gently grind against her. Slow, no urgency. Just the warm, pulsing rhythm of skin on skin. The weight of him along her ass. The quiet sound of breath and body. Not sex, not even teasing. Connection.

Ellie moaned softly. Her fingers curled into the sheets. And just like that, she came. No penetration, just the weight of him. The safety of it.

Later, lying in that sleepy afterglow, James had whispered: "That was the first time anyone ever wanted me to hold them."

Ellie turned in the sheets, eyes soft. "What do you mean?"

He hesitated. Then spoke carefully. "Most people I've been with, they wanted something: Sex, money, comfort, status, a warm place to escape. But once they got what they came for, they went cold, like I didn't matter."

She looked at him. Held his gaze. "You weren't a man to them. Just access."

James nodded. But then his voice shifted. Lower and more certain. "But you wanted me. Just me. No script, no transaction. You let me hold you because I made you feel safe."

After a brief pause, he continued, "I fell in love with you that night. Not just because of what you gave me, but because you didn't ask me for anything. You just wanted to be loved by me."

Ellie blinked hard. She couldn't speak. But in that moment, both of them got what they'd never had before. She made him feel like enough. And he made her feel like everything.

The memory faded like a sigh, and Ellie was still smiling, curled against his chest, their bodies tangled under the sheets. James's hand remained where she'd placed it, resting over her breast. They didn't speak. Then, his phone buzzed on the nightstand.

He glanced at the screen. A simple message: *Good morning, King.* With a soft-pink heart.

James let the phone buzz once more. Then he flipped it facedown. didn't sigh. He just tucked his chin into the crook of Ellie's neck, pulled her in tighter, and let the warmth of the only place he ever truly fit swallow the morning whole.

James watched Ellie sleep, soft against his chest, her breath warm on his skin. He could still smell her on his fingers, still feel her pulsing around him. The sun was barely rising, and yet his mind was already fighting with his heart over how easy it was to forget the world when she was beside him.

She stirred, blinking her eyes open with a playful, sleepy smirk. Her hand grazed down his stomach, but she didn't reach for more, just anchored herself to the skin she used to call home.

Then, with a voice straight out of a Saturday afternoon VHS classic, she asked: "Well, Daddy, where do we go from here?"

James laughed low, sliding into the Goldie impression like second skin: "To the top, if you not afraid, baby."

Their laughter folded into the covers. That line, their line, held more weight than it ever had. The moment softened, then stilled.

"I'm serious," Ellie said, quieter now.

"So am I," James replied.

She rolled away slightly, sitting up with the sheet against her chest. "I'm gonna go see how good the shopping is in this town, before I make any decisions."

A beat passed. Then she laughed, glancing back at him. "I just got here. You think I don't realize there's nothing easy about leaving you—even with you sending me on a shopping spree?"

James smirked, walked over to the desk, and dropped his black card down like a royal gauntlet. "Anything you like."

Steam fogged the bathroom mirror as James stood under the water, letting the night rinse off him, at least what Ellie hadn't decided to keep.

Her fingers trembled as she reached for the door. She remembered the last thing he said: "Your silence is louder than my rage." Months later, it still echoed.

Outside the door, Ellie stood in nothing but the oversized towel, thighs still sticky with his memory.

She picked up a delicate pair of panties and stared at them like they were holy. "I'm not washing you off," she whispered under her breath.

As she slid them up and crossed her legs, she held the heat inside like a secret. "I'm keeping you with me today."

James toweled off and dressed with focus, his mind drifting to Gemini, the venture that needed him sharp, fast, visible. His phone vibrated.

Jean: "You missed an important meeting this morning. I covered for you. I suggest you get in soon before someone else tries to."

He sighed, nodded to no one, and sat on the edge of the bed. He thought of Ava. Her attempt, her boldness, and the easy way he shut her down.

And then, Thalia. Still in the picture. Still patient and waiting. He unlocked his phone. Heart emojis.

James: *You're sexy. That for me?* Just before he could lock the screen again, dots appeared. Thalia was typing. Eager, immediate, there. James didn't wait to read the reply.

He opened a new text to Jean: *Still recovering from the Gemini dinner. I'll be in shortly. Don't let the place burn down without me.*

———

James then let his mind drift. He leaned back on the bed, still half-buttoned, and closed his eyes. Thalia. Ellie. Ava.

Ellie on her knees, hair wild, mouth open, eyes needy. Thalia stood behind her, toned and gleaming, her strap-on glistening as she pounded Ellie from behind with a snarl in her throat.

Ellie moaned, arms trembling. James sat in a leather chair, watching it unfold, cock heavy in his hand.

Thalia leaned forward, gripping Ellie's curls, angling her head toward James's lap. Ellie opened her mouth, licked the head of his cock with need.

From the corner, Ava sat on a soft chaise, legs spread, one hand between her smooth legs, breathless as she watched.

Then, Thalia leaned into James's ear, her voice low, primal: "You are a fucking King. This bitch is the submissive. She should be thankful you feed her this cock."

But just before his climax, as the image of Ellie's lips sliding lower, something in him cracked. Then he snapped out of the fantasy. His eyes shot open, and his breath caught. The whole thing vanished, and he was left with a pulse in his throat and a pit in his stomach.

———

Danielle's phone lit up. She didn't even glance. "Danielle," she answered flatly.

Zion's voice came in sharp, venomous. "Tell her to call me back. Or I'll tell her King exactly how I soaked his Queen. And you know it won't be pretty."

Danielle's mouth curled into a slow, deadly smirk. "You really think she hasn't told him about you?"

A pause. She kept going. "I heard you were…childish. Couldn't even handle the mess she made. Big boys drink their milk and grow up big and strong, Zion. You? You spit it out."

Zion barked something. Half insult, half panic.

"Maybe next time she should wait until she has to go to the bathroom and give you something more suitable to drink."

"Fuck you, Danielle—"

She ended the call and dialed without hesitation. Jean picked up on the first ring. Danielle's voice was tight. "He's coming, Jean. Zion just tried me."

Jean didn't waste time. She opened James's inbox. There it was. Subject: *Thanks for the loaner.*

She clicked. Screenshots: Ellie and Zion's flirty DMs. Enough to sting. Enough to twist.

Then came the images: Ellie, at Zion's place, gazing up at a portrait of herself, mouth slightly open in awe. Another: her dress half-off, back to the camera, clearly in the moment before being taken.

She didn't know he was recording. Jean didn't think, she deleted it instantly.

And just in time. The elevator dinged. James stepped out, buttoned, calm. He walked into his office, humming slightly. His mood was light, lifted. He opened his phone. He saw Thalia's reply. Quick, eager, soft. And typed: *You forgot to tell me what my next meal will be…*

Jean glanced over just as the screen lit up with the message. She caught the grin on his face. Then whispered under her breath: "I know this motherfucker just didn't…"

And with that, the story of their loyalty, and how far they're willing to go to protect what James and Ellie built, was no longer a subplot. It was a line in the sand.

Chapter 10: The Calm Between Explosions

The Teams call began with silence. No corporate greetings. No "can you hear me?" Just Jean, in her signature black-framed glasses, staring at Danielle through the screen like they were the last two soldiers left in a crumbling empire.

Danielle finally spoke. "He can't find out like this."

Jean didn't blink. "If he finds out from anyone but her, it's not just betrayal. It's humiliation."

They didn't have to say his name. They never did. "I'm worried about her," Danielle said quietly. "But I'm terrified for him."

Jean nodded once, her voice low. "We loved them before they knew how to love themselves."

They sat in that truth for a long beat. Then the flashback began to roll through Jean's mind like film through a projector.

She didn't belong in the building, let alone the room. Her resume was a Frankenstein of real experience, borrowed titles, and complete fiction. She had no idea what the hell "Skype for Business" even was when she said she'd used it for three years. And spreadsheets? Sure. If copy-pasting gossip into a group chat counted.

James sat across from her: young, sharp, and already magnetic. He listened politely as she rambled about collaboration systems and cross-functional alignment. But she could see it in his eyes. He'd made up his mind. Before he could cut her off, the door opened.

The CEO stuck his head in with no knock, mid-sentence, looking to interrupt. Without missing a beat, Jean spun in her chair and snapped, "Excuse you. I know you see we're in an important meeting. You can come back in fifteen minutes. And next time, try knocking. It's called manners."

James froze. A slow smile broke across his face. He stood and reached for her hand. "You're hired."

Jean blinked. "Wait...what?"

"You're hired," he repeated, nodding.

She lit up, practically bouncing in her seat. "I won't let you down, I promise!"

As she reached for the door, he stopped her. "One thing. Be honest with me from here on out. If you can do that, I'll pay you double what you're asking."

Jean grinned. "Deal."

She started to exit, then looked back, grinning wider. "Oh, and my resume? I lied about all that shit." She winked and then walked out.

Jean snapped back to the present just as James ended his current meeting. "I need you to get the action items out," he said without looking up. "And book me a lunch with Thalia. Somewhere I won't bump into Ellie." Jean nodded, hiding the churn in her chest.

As he walked away, she pulled out her phone and messaged Danielle: *We've had two fiscal reviews and a team bowling night since she left, and you still look like someone stole your bourbon. And not the cheap kind. Like, that D'USSÉ Beyoncé bottle-drop type of loss.*

Jean: *He's meeting Thalia for lunch. You got eyes on her?*

Danielle: *Of course. I'll keep the Queen in motion.*

Then, it was Danielle's turn to remember her earlier days, when Ellie was nothing like the woman the world now feared and adored. She was beautiful, yes, but hesitant. Fragile under her brilliance.

"I want to be honest with you," Ellie had said, eyes on the desk. "I'm new to this. Still learning. You'd be taking a chance working for me, and I can't promise it'll last."

Danielle didn't blink. "Well, it's almost certain I won't last," she said flatly, "and neither will you with that bullshit attitude."

Ellie looked up, stunned. Danielle stood. "Stand on your damn empire. You're the one building it. Give me a space to help you do it, and that's the last fucking time you mention failure. Not until or unless we fail." Ellie blinked, then smiled. She hired Danielle that second.

Back at his desk, James sat, frowning at his phone: *Unknown number.* He declined the call. It rang again. Still, something gnawed at him.

"Jean," he called out. "Some number keeps calling me. It's a nuisance. Probably spam."

"Let me see it," she said casually, walking in. She took one look. Her stomach dropped.

"Give me a second," she said, voice tight but steady. Jean stepped into the hallway, phone already dialing.

"Verizon? I need this number permanently blocked. Now."

Jean dialed again. This time, a cop back home. "I need someone to pay a visit. No violence, just...presence. Threat of a restraining order."

A pause. Then, "His name's Zion. You'll know when you see him."

———

Meanwhile, Danielle was frantically trying to reach Ellie: *Urgent. Call me now.*

Danielle: *Ellie, I'm not playing. CALL ME.*

Danielle: *He sent something. It's bad.*

Ellie froze in the middle of the boutique she was shopping in. Her fingers tightened around the dress hanger. She made the purchase in a fog and walked out onto the street, then hit "call."

Danielle's voice was shaking. "It's revenge porn, Ellie. That fucker sent images to a burner. We don't know how far it's gone."

Ellie stopped walking. Her heart dropped into her stomach. "I didn't even know he took anything," she whispered.

Tears filled her eyes. "He can't see that. James can't ever see that."

"I've already got the lawyers on it. Citing revenge porn. This is war now, El."

Over at Zion's apartment there was a loud banging. He yanked the door open, ready to yell. Two cops stood there. Not smiling. One shoved him into the doorframe with just enough force to knock the air out of him. They said nothing, then walked away. Zion stood there, heaving.

On the other side of town, Jean's phone buzzed. One word: *Handled.*

———

Danielle stood in her office, still shaking. The gallery alert had pinged her line. The painting had sold at $50,000. The portrait. That portrait.

She didn't waste time and made a call. "I need a jet." Her voice was steel to the assistant on the other end of the line. "Corporate resources, platinum access, no questions asked." Within fifteen minutes, she was on the way to the airport.

Inside the car, her hands trembled as she opened her messages and attached the image. She dialed Ellie. It rang once. "Danielle?" Ellie's voice was light, laced with confused warmth. She hadn't seen it yet.

Danielle's own voice cracked. "I'm so sorry. I'm on my fucking way."

Ellie laughed softly at first, like Danielle was exaggerating. "What? The painting? I already—" Then the second attachment loaded. The footage. Her voice disappeared. Her eyes stayed glued to the screen. The painting was stunning, breathtaking.

Ellie's bare back, honey-lit skin, hair falling like a storm down her shoulder. Her face wasn't visible, but it didn't need to be. It was her. Anyone who knew her, loved her, studied her, could tell in an instant. But it wasn't the painting that killed her breath.

It was the caption beneath it: *$50,000. Sold. For being deep in the heart…clap clap clap…of Texas.* And just above her curve: subtle, perfectly shaded into the soft tones of her hip, was the unmistakable shape of a small state: Texas.

The same one James had once kissed on a beach, years ago. The same mark she once said gave him access, if only he remembered the code. "Anytime you want it, just say 'I wanna go to the Alamo'." Her lips parted, but no sound came.

Her phone vibrated in her hand, calls and messages pouring in like rain. She said nothing. Just sat there, breath caught in her throat, shame flooding in faster than the tears.

The car ride back to James's suite was suffocating. But her body had gone completely still. Numb, except for the fire rising behind her ribs. Her phone vibrated again: Danielle. Jean. The lawyers. Even Thalia, maybe.

She didn't care. She let it buzz. She let it scream. Because the only thing louder than her phone was the silence James hadn't yet broken. And that silence was a fucking war drum.

The portrait had gone viral in the right circles. Art blogs. Investor threads. Black-label collectors whispering about Zion's "return."

CJ, James's childhood friend from back home, saw it in a thread before the gallery even announced it. He didn't know the full story, but he knew James. And he knew that body. He texted immediately: *I know she's your Queen, brother. But some other man just painted her like he owns her, and the world's clapping. You good?* Attached: the portrait.

James stared at it on his phone while seated across from Thalia at a rooftop lounge. At first, it looked like another tribute. Fans painted Ellie all the time. She was a muse to many. But this wasn't admiration. It was ownership.

His eyes froze on the birthmark. The exact one. That birthmark. He looked back at the image. And downed the rest of his drink.

"Everything okay?" Thalia asked, soft, sensing the shift.

James turned to her with a smile that didn't reach his eyes. "Yeah. Just remembered I've got something I need to handle."

He stood, leaned in, and kissed her cheek with practiced tenderness. "I'll reach out a bit later." Then he walked off. Thalia sat frozen, watching the back of a man walking away like gravity had changed.

Jean sat at her desk, rereading an email thread for the third time when her phone buzzed. A missed call from James. Then a voicemail. She tapped it open, but it was just static. He must've pocket-dialed. She called him back immediately. Voicemail. Called again.

She stood quickly, grabbing her tablet with shaking hands, scrolling for another angle, something she could do to undo what was done.

Then her phone rang again. She didn't even check. "Hello?" she answered, voice taut.

Danielle's voice exploded through the speaker: "This motherfucker has a—"

Jean cut her off, voice cracked, crumbling beneath the poise she wore like armor: "He knows, Danielle." Then softer. "He fucking knows."

Ellie sat in James's suite, curled on the edge of the couch. His bourbon sat on the bar untouched. She had ordered it like a peace offering, like prayer. But prayers don't land when you forget how to kneel.

She didn't cry anymore. She was past that. Now it was just the long, sharp ache of hope with nowhere to go.

Minutes passed. Then an hour. Then two. No knock. No key in the door. Just the kind of silence that grows teeth.

James was sitting in his own thoughts elsewhere. He didn't rage. didn't call, didn't plot. No destination. No music. Just city lights and his own thoughts chewing through him. Not about revenge. About reflection.

He told himself he wasn't angry. And maybe he wasn't. Maybe, like Ellie, he believed somewhere deep down that he deserved this pain just as much as she did. That somewhere along the way, they both broke something sacred. They were just waiting to see who would be brave enough to admit they still wanted to fix it.

The bourbon sat on the bar, untouched. The bed not slept in. The light in the hallway blinking like a metronome of disappointment.

He never came back. So Ellie went to him.

She didn't bother announcing herself. Danielle handled the logistics. Jean handled the clearance. And now, she sat in the quiet of his SoCal office, surrounded by the evidence that she still lived in this man's world, even when he didn't speak her name.

A pair of cufflinks she gave him for his first keynote. A framed, wrinkled napkin with a doodle she once drew when they first talked about buying land.

And then, on the bookshelf, a leather portfolio. Black. Subtle. Her company's logo etched in the corner in platinum foil. Then she opened it. Inside were pages. Poetry. Scribbled lines. Love letters never sent.

Her name appeared again and again like a prayer he didn't have the courage to say out loud anymore. Jean knocked once, opened the door slowly. "He's downstairs. Be up in less than a minute."

Ellie stood quickly, closing the portfolio and adjusting her blazer. She didn't want to look like she'd been reading old prayers. Not when she was the reason they were unsent.

James stepped in, fresh from morning meetings. Calm. Crisp. His eyes flicked to her and didn't linger. He walked to his desk, leaned on the edge, and spoke casually. "Would you like some coffee?"

Ellie blinked, unsure if she heard him right. "No…no thank you."

He nodded, poured himself a glass of water. She stepped closer, eyes pleading.

"James, I—"

He held up one hand, gentle but final. "I never expected you would let your bed get cold. That's not who you are."

She stopped breathing.

"But to be made a spectacle…that was a bit of a surprise."

She swallowed. "It wasn't like that. I—"

Jean's voice cut in from the doorway, neutral but undeniable. "It's not like your bed has been cold either, from what I understand."

Ellie looked down. James didn't deny it. He sighed. "Even now, even in sorrow and apology, you muddy it with justification."

His voice softened, almost mournful. "It's okay, love." He took a step toward her. "I once cried at the privilege to hold your sandaled feet in my hands. My beauty of all beauties."

Ellie's voice cracked. "And now?"

James smiled without joy. "Now? I stand in our royal court, no longer a King, but as a jester. And the laughter is louder than ever, love."

She clenched her fists. "So now we're not King and Queen anymore? Because your feelings are hurt by a nobody?"

He didn't raise his voice. He didn't flinch. "A nobody with access to a Queen makes it worse, love."

She couldn't stop the tears this time. They streamed before she could bite them back. James stepped closer, pulled a tissue from the box on his desk, and reached out. He wiped her tears softly.

Then tilted her chin up, he way she used to do for him when he felt small. "Head up and face forward, Queen."

His voice was warm, but distant. "I have no rage left in me. Not for you. Not for your artist."

"Helen of Troy was never taken, El. She acted on her own accord. And no one needed to war for her. The chaos came because they chose it." He let go of her chin and stepped back.

"I'm not guiltless in any of this," he said, straightening his jacket. "Don't think I've forgotten that."

He walked around the desk, gathering his laptop and phone. "You're everything you've ever wanted to be."

Ellie looked at him, her voice barely above a whisper. "So are you...King."

James gave a ghost of a smile. "Not yet, love."

He reached for his briefcase. "But I'll take my public humiliation. And I do it with pride."

He paused at the door. "But know this, an old friend has returned."

Ellie's spine straightened instantly. She knew: The dark passenger. The version of him that used to rule without warmth. The man who'd built his empire with scars and silence. Before her. Before love. Before softness.

James opened the door, stepped out, and looked over his shoulder once. "I have to get to work."

He didn't wait for a goodbye. He didn't need one. "Safe travels back home," he added as he turned the corner.

Ellie stood frozen. And just before the door shut completely, she heard his voice in the hallway. A whisper. A prophecy. A warning. "Something wicked this way comes."

———

The sun was starting to lean low across the sky, brushing gold across the glass exterior of James's Southern California office. Outside, Jean and Danielle stood just beyond the rotating doors, catching up. Shoulders eased a little, laughter still tucked in their throats.

It had been a long day. Danielle sipped her iced coffee and leaned against the sleek stone pillar beside Jean.

"You brooding in silence like you dropped a J. Cole album nobody asked for," Jean muttered.

"She doesn't say it, but El's breaking," she said, voice soft.

"She's not the only one," Jean replied, just as James pushed through the glass doors behind them. He looked fresh: tailored, crisp, skin kissed by sunset, but Jean caught it. The sharpness in his movements. The narrowed serenity in his gaze.

He was focused. Dangerously focused. "Danielle," James said, voice warm, smile genuine. "It's been too long."

Danielle blinked, then smiled wide. "Too long, indeed."

He gave her a soft hug, one hand to her back like an old friend he trusted once and maybe still did. She looked him over carefully, no rage. No regret. Just…steel.

"Jean," he turned. "Move the eleven-thirty to Friday. Reschedule Gemini's pitch for next week. I want to be on-site."

"You got it," Jean nodded. "And, uh…Thalia pinged a dinner invite. You want me to decline?"

James paused, adjusting his sleeve cuff. "No. Tell her I'll be there."

Jean didn't flinch. But Danielle gave her a look the second James turned. "I don't like how still he is," Danielle muttered.

Jean replied, nearly soundless. "Still waters don't drown you. They wait for you to walk in, then never let you back up."

———

Ellie sat on James's office couch, the leather still warm from his morning. She hadn't moved much: legs crossed, hands knotted together, trying not to replay their conversation from earlier.

When the door opened, it was Danielle who entered. She took one look at Ellie's expression and didn't speak. Just moved toward her with calm, precise steps.

"You ready to go?" Ellie nodded once. As they gathered her things, she looked around one last time: at the bourbon untouched on the shelf, the leather-bound portfolio still slightly ajar, the ghost of him in every polished surface.

They stepped out together, leaving the office cloaked in the kind of silence that feels final. The hallway was quiet, but not empty.

Thalia stood by the elevator in all black, elegance draped over her curves like a tailored vow. Hair pinned high. Confidence draped low. Her presence wasn't loud, it was composed, like someone who never needed to raise her voice to win a war.

She looked up as Ellie and Danielle approached. Their eyes locked. The air held its breath. Ellie's voice was even, quiet. But every syllable carried weight. "You'll never have my King. No matter what you may think."

Thalia didn't flinch. Her voice came like honey laced with quiet thunder. "No one will ever have your King. I've never met anyone more in love and loyal to someone in my life." Ellie blinked.

And then Thalia added, softly but without hesitation, "You're just as stunning in person as you are in your pictures…and your portrait." Then, she flipped her phone around for her to see the portrait Zion posted as the screen saver in her phone. She stepped into the elevator and didn't look back. The doors slid shut like a punctuation mark.

The private jet was quiet. Ellie and Danielle sat side by side, neither speaking. The hum of the engine was the only sound. Not even music. Just altitude, tension, and the thick silence between women who had just seen a shadow of what might come next.

Ellie didn't cry. Danielle didn't prod. But in the dark of that flight, it became clear: Thalia was no passing flirtation. She was playing the long game. And she had every intention of making James hers, without ever taking what wasn't willingly given.

——

That evening, James stood at Thalia's door with the war of the week still clinging to his skin. He hadn't expected comfort. Maybe relief. Maybe release. Probably sex. But when the door opened, everything in him paused.

Thalia stood barefoot, wearing nothing but an apron tied tight at the back and a pair of red-bottomed heels that looked both elegant and wicked. The scent of something simmering behind her was so warm, so rich, it softened the edges of everything he was carrying.

Her smile was soft, not seductive. Inviting. "Give me your jacket," she said simply, stretching her hand toward him. He shrugged it off, and she draped it over the hallway chair like it was made of silk.

Then she handed him a crystal tumbler with an amber pour already waiting. "Johnny Walker Green," she said. "Not your usual. But I think you'll like it tonight."

James took a sip. Smoothed his palm over his jaw. His eyes still held weight. She stepped close, not to kiss or question. Just to stand near him. "The shower's running," she added. "Robes are in there. Dinner's almost ready."

She turned on her heel and walked back into the kitchen, humming softly as she stirred something aromatic. She didn't ask about Ellie. didn't mention the portrait. She didn't ask what he needed. She just became peace, without ever announcing herself as the answer.

James's shoulders dropped just enough to register. His heart didn't lighten, but it slowed. He placed the drink down, gave her a soft kiss on the cheek, and moved toward the bathroom which felt like a retreat.

Steam clouded the air. On the counter sat a folded, thick robe, dark gray pajama bottoms, and a black tank top. The soap was a milky, high-end bar wrapped in silk paper. The lotion was sandalwood and citrus, already uncapped for him.

James stared for a moment. This wasn't just thoughtful. It was intentional. He let out a long breath and stepped into the shower, letting the water run over him until the ache behind his ribs began to loosen. He didn't think about war. He didn't think about Ellie. He just let himself be.

———

Ellie stepped off the private jet into the heavy quiet of the California night. The black SUV waited, engine humming beside the tarmac. Danielle walked a few feet behind her, giving space where words had failed.

As the car pulled up to the curb, Ellie reached for the handle, still silent. Danielle stopped her with a hand on her wrist. "Not my place," she said, voice calm but unshakable. "But y'all both been on that bullshit for no good reason."

Ellie looked at her, exhausted and unspeaking. But Danielle pressed on. "At least he acknowledged his fuckups too. So either be silent or not, but I think you know he's definitely worth fighting for. He's an impossible find these days. Nobody is even close."

She hugged her briefly, then stepped out and shut the door. The SUV pulled away from the plane. Ellie stared out the window, numb.

A flash struck her mind like lightning: Zion. Her bent forward, cheeks spread, asking for something, anything, more than the nothing she received. "I thought you had something for me." Her own voice echoed back in shame.

The car stopped. She blinked herself back to reality. Home.

———

Back at Thalia's, dinner was quiet. No small talk. No tension. Just warmth. James devoured the food on his plate, fork scraping ceramic in the most comforting way. He set the empty dish down, wiped his mouth, and leaned back.

"I really needed this," he said simply, his voice carrying more weight than gratitude alone. Thalia smiled but said nothing. She cleared the plate, disappeared into the kitchen, and returned with soft eyes. "If you don't mind," she said gently, "would you meet me in the bedroom while I clean up and shower?" No pretense.

He walked into the bedroom, candles already lit, the scent of fresh-cut flowers pulling him deeper into calm. He slipped off the pajama bottoms, stretched his limbs, and lay face down on the bed. He wasn't only preparing to take, he was also bracing to receive.

Thalia entered the room like a slow inhale. Now in a tank top with no bra and boy-cut shorts that revealed everything and more. Her thick, wild bush crowned beneath the waistband, unapologetically visible.

James turned his head to look at her, the corners of his mouth twitching toward something warm. He moved to sit up, to kiss her, to take. She kissed him back softly, then stopped him with two fingers against his lips.

"If you want to fuck me," she whispered, "you may have me any way you want right now."

"But if you indulge me just a bit, maybe I can give you something a little more filling first."

She pulled off her top and shorts slowly, revealing all of her, nothing theatrical. Nothing performative. She straddled his back naked and reached for the soy wax massage candles.

One by one, she tipped them over his skin: his shoulders, his back, his thighs, the base of his neck. The wax kissed him warm, then her body followed. And in the softest, most angelic voice, she began to sing: "This may come…this may come as some surprise…but I miss you." Sade. "Is It a Crime."

James melted. Not just his muscles, but is mind, his grief, his walls.

She glided over him like water: never hurrying, never distracting. Just touching, singing, becoming. When she whispered for him to turn over, he obeyed. She stretched his arms gently.

Her lips didn't touch his cock, but her movements made it stand in reverence. Still, she never climbed on. She moved like music itself, hips swaying, lips humming. She didn't need penetration to seduce. She only needed presence.

And as the third Sade track began, he finally closed his eyes and drifted. Not from exhaustion. But because he trusted her touch.

———

James woke to sunlight cutting through sheer curtains and the scent of coffee in the kitchen. He rose slowly, dressed, and made his way to Thalia, who was humming softly, barefoot again.

He kissed her goodbye, but this kiss was different. Not polite, but grateful. He whispered something into her ear that made her close her eyes. Then he left, without his armor, without his ache. But still with something burning quietly beneath the surface.

Chapter 11: The First Alamo

James walked through the Gemini headquarters like gravity obeyed him. Every step was exact. Every blink calculated. The suit on his back wore him, not the other way around.

He had already cleared four meetings and hadn't touched the coffee Jean brought him. Not because he didn't want it, but because he no longer needed fuel. He was running on silence now. And silence was more than enough.

When he reached his private floor, Jean was already waiting by his door, tablet in hand, her face unreadable. She said nothing as she followed him in. He sat, powered on his screen, and clicked the new flagged message from internal systems.

There were no words in the body of the email. Just three attachments:

The first was a screenshot of Ellie, mid-laugh, admiring the portrait on Zion's wall, the one that sold for $50,000.

The second was a still from Zion's security footage: Ellie stripping down in what she thought was privacy, her back turned, moments before Zion would take her, unaware he was taking more than her body.

The third was a DM log. Ellie and Zion. Friendly. Familiar. Too familiar.

Jean stepped forward slowly, reading over his shoulder. Her hand went to her chest, and her body froze. "Oh my God…"

Still, he didn't blink. "I can tell she didn't know," he said finally. His voice wasn't angry. It was something worse. "And what kind of coward does such things?"

Jean didn't speak. She knew better. James leaned back in the chair. Looked out the window at a city that had always taken more from him than it gave. "Nonetheless," he murmured, "what can I say that would matter, and what could I do that wouldn't result in his absolute destruction?"

He chuckled softly, without joy. "People have never treated me much like nothin' unless I had a bunch of somethin'."

Jean didn't dare interrupt. But her eyes were glassy now. This was a man unraveling while looking like he was sewing himself back together. "Give me a moment," he said quietly.

Jean nodded and left the office, closing the door behind her with the care of someone backing away from a ticking bomb.

James thought about a time when having someone seemed like it would be easy. His mind brought an image of a ten-year-old James, standing on the porch of their tiny duplex. The Bible his mother had just read from still lay on the table inside. His socks mismatched. Face unsure. Heart wide open.

"Mama," he said, arms folded. "I think I want a girlfriend." His mother didn't laugh. She didn't tease. She came outside, drying her hands on a towel, and sat next to him on the porch steps. She took her time, and let the silence settle between them like wisdom.

"That means you gotta like her like she likes you, Jay," she said gently. "Don't bother with no girl that don't like you back just the same or more." He nodded slowly.

She looked him over, gave him that look, the one that knew more than he ever said. "And if you get you a pretty one, you better be ready to fight for her. 'Cause everybody else gonna want her too."

She let that sit. Then, her smile curled like a warning dressed as love. "One more thing."

She leaned in, tapped his chest with her folded towel. "Don't never let your girlfriend see you get your ass beat. She'll never forget it."

James's eyebrows rose.

She stood, stretching. "So if you serious about this," she added, "you better get out here and be scrappy."

Her eyes met his again, firm and final. "Never fight to win, Jay. Fight willing to die for whatever you deem worth fighting for. You'll never lose."

James blinked, snapping out of the memory. He didn't flinch. didn't pace. Just hovered his mouse over the attachments and deleted them. Then emptied the trash and shut the laptop.

He stood slowly and buttoned his jacket. Jean stepped in just as he reached for his keys. "Give Kev a call," James said, voice calm. "Let him know I'm on my way."

Jean nodded. "Where are you headed?"

James gave her a half smile. "A nice drive up the coast sounds just like what the doctor ordered…"

He paused, then added: "…and some pain to dull this bee sting."

Jean's throat tightened. "You want me to reschedule—?"

"Everything."

She nodded again, and he walked out.

Jean didn't even blink before texting Danielle: *He's on the way to Kev's. Ink therapy. But he's too calm. Too quiet. Trying too hard to smile. He's a goddamn time bomb.*

———

Meanwhile, Ellie sat on her balcony in a white silk robe, legs tucked beneath her, phone in her lap, untouched coffee on the table beside her. She hadn't seen James since the office. And her guilt had twisted itself into something that looked a lot like grief.

A notification pinged. Dr. Lane: *You crossed my mind this morning. Hope you're doing okay.*

Ellie read it twice. Three times. Then tapped into his contact profile and paused. They were no longer bound by sessions. No rules or boundary violations. Just silence, and a small, open door. Maybe he's just what the doctor ordered.

———

At work, the glass in Danielle's office trembled as she slammed her phone onto the desk. She didn't scream, she didn't cry, she moved.

Legal counsel was already on standby, and Danielle didn't waste a breath. "I want every charge possible," she snapped into the receiver. "Revenge porn. Unauthorized commercial likeness. Emotional distress. Violation of trust. Defamation. I want his name shaking."

The attorney on the other end stammered, "We can build the case, but it might take time—"

"I don't have time," Danielle interrupted. "I want traction. I want headlines. I want every collector who bought his bullshit art wondering if they're next." She hung up, checked her email, and shot over photos. Attached NDAs.

———

Three hours away, Jean stepped out of a small corner store just outside downtown. She had already paid in cash, no paper trail. A prepaid burner phone in one hand, cold soda in the other.

She peeled open the package, powered on the phone, and dialed her first cousin in Compton. "Hey, Larry. I need a checkin on someone. Not hurt. Just watched."

Then a second call: Inglewood this time. Her voice dropped lower. "I need eyes, pressure, subtle intimidation. No arrests. No mistakes."

Both cousins knew the tone. They didn't ask questions.

Jean stepped to the side of the alley, pressed the power button long enough to shut off the phone, snapped it in half, and tossed it into the trash bin. War had begun. And Zion had no clue it was already at his front door.

Danielle called Jean, and their voices crackled like fire. "He's not just hurting her. He's waking up the part of James that doesn't know how to feel pain without making someone else bleed for it."

Jean said, "And if James spirals, he won't rage, he'll retreat. And this time? He might not come back."

They fell silent for a moment. Then Danielle added, "We're not just protecting them. We're saving what the fuck they built. That kingdom may be cracked, but it's still holy."

Jean nodded in quiet agreement, staring at her dark screen.

Up the coast, James drove fast. Music off, eyes locked on the horizon. The Pacific shimmered to his left. The wheel trembled under his grip. His phone buzzed. James answered on the third ring. "Yo."

"Man…" CJ started, his voice softer than usual, "That portrait. It's some bullshit, bro. You don't deserve that."

James said nothing, eyes fixed on the dotted line blurring beneath his tires.

CJ kept going, trying. "I mean, Ellie…that woman had your name in her breath. But now?" He sighed. "I don't know, man. Maybe it's time to stop bleeding for people who only cut you deeper."

Still no response.

"I'm not saying she's the worst. But you? You got people lined up that would worship the ground you walk on. You ever think maybe love ain't supposed to hurt this much?"

James finally exhaled, slow. Controlled. "I'm headed to Kev's."

"That's good. Get some ink. Let it out. Hell, get a whole sleeve about heartbreak."

James ended the call without a goodbye.

———

Ellie sat in her parked car outside a quiet café. Her hands trembled, not from fear, but from how long she had tried to hold it all in. A message draft sat on her phone: *I keep punishing myself like it'll buy me forgiveness.*

Delete.

Then: *Do you believe in redemption even if the person you love no longer sees you?*

Delete again.

Instead, she texted Danielle: *I'm scared I ruined him. And I don't know how to fix it.*

The message hung in digital silence.

——

James pulled into the alley behind the shop, the tires crunching over gravel.

Kev was already waiting out back, smoking a toothpick, not a cigarette. He knew the signs. James stepped out of the car, dark sunglasses on, jaw locked.

Kev nodded. "You ready?"

James didn't hesitate. "Yes. And plenty."

Kev tilted his head, reading the expression beneath the armor. James stepped closer, lowered his voice.

"Let's not only shade that light in the heart, let's remind me of this insanity, and the clown I've become once again. For love."

Kev just nodded and held the door open. Inside the shop, James stripped to the waist. Laid down on the table. Chest exposed. Shoulders broad, already marked with old battles and victories. But this time, he wasn't here for a masterpiece. He was here for the pain.

Kev dipped the needle. James didn't flinch. He carried a grief so heavy, so silent, it could have powered a city block.

His phone lit up on the counter beside the table.

Jean: *5 missed calls*

Danielle: *URGENT*

Thalia: *Just say the word and I'll come.*

He turned it face down. And the needle kept singing.

The sharp buzz of the tattoo machine filled the dimly lit studio, a rhythmic hum that resonated deep within James's bones. He sat motionless, his left arm extended as Kev meticulously brought the new designs to life.

Each puncture of the needle was a welcome distraction, a physical manifestation of the emotional turmoil churning inside him. On the opposite side of his forearm, a sad-faced clown began to emerge, a haunting reflection of James himself.

The clown's makeup was pristine, its smile wide but devoid of joy, with glistening trails of tears streaming down its cheeks. Above his wrist, directly beneath the heart tattoo that now received its final touches of crimson, another image took form: a series of open-mouthed faces, each one screaming into the void, cascading into an abyss of silent agony.

The thorn from his original heart tattoo now extended, intertwining with both new designs, binding all three together in a perpetual testament to his intertwined experiences of love, pain, and madness.

Kev paused, wiping away excess ink and blood, inspecting his work. He glanced up at James, his voice steady yet inquisitive. "You sure you want me to fill in all the heart? No more light?"

James, even in his most wounded state, felt a flicker of hope. He nodded, then hesitated. "Well…leave just a tiny bit of light, barely visible. There's still some love in this bleeding heart left."

Kev gave a slight nod, understanding the depth of the request, and resumed his work.

As the ink seeped into his skin, James's mind began to drift, the pain unlocking doors to memories long tucked away: The sun hung high in the sky, casting its golden glow over the neighborhood. James, around eleven years old, had just mastered the art of popping a wheelie on his weathered BMX. He was a solitary figure, often finding solace in books and solo rides, navigating the world on his own terms. Then there was CJ.

CJ possessed a quiet magnetism. He wasn't the loudest in the room, nor did he seek the spotlight, but there was an undeniable allure to his presence. Other kids gravitated toward him, sensing the depth beneath his calm exterior. Yet, CJ was selective, keeping most at arm's length.

One afternoon, as James pedaled past the chain-link fences of Country Circle, CJ appeared, effortlessly hopping over a fence to land beside him.

"Yo," CJ greeted, his voice smooth and measured. "You live around here?"

"Yeah," James replied, curiosity piqued.

"I'm just over there," CJ nodded toward a nearby house. "There's a trail by the swamp. Ever ridden it?"

"The swamp?" James echoed, a mix of intrigue and apprehension.

A subtle smirk played on CJ's lips. "What, you scared?"

James met his gaze, determination flaring. "Hell no."

From that moment, an unspoken bond formed. They became companions in adventure, riding through trails, sharing stories, and navigating the complexities of adolescence together. CJ's reserved nature balanced James's introspective tendencies, creating a friendship rooted in mutual respect and understanding.

One lazy afternoon, they lounged on CJ's front porch, the remnants of a snack between them. The conversation meandered, eventually landing on the topic of relationships: a subject neither truly understood but both were eager to explore.

CJ mentioned a girl he claimed to be seeing, his tone nonchalant. Not wanting to be left behind, James chimed in, "Yeah, I got a girlfriend too."

CJ's interest was piqued. "Oh yeah? You two...done it yet?"

James hesitated for a fraction before nodding. "Yeah. Just today, actually."

A pause settled between them. Then, with a raised eyebrow, CJ inquired, "Clothes on or off?"

James blinked, processing the question. Realization dawned, and with a mix of horror and humor, he exclaimed, "Clothes on! Do you want me to go to hell?"

For a heartbeat, silence. Then, laughter erupted, genuine and hearty, echoing through the neighborhood. They laughed until their sides ached, the innocence of their misconceptions binding them even closer.

In that shared moment of youthful naiveté, their friendship was solidified, a connection untainted by the world's complexities.

The hum of the tattoo machine drew James back into the present. Kev paused, wiping away excess ink and blood, inspecting his work.

"Something funny?" Kev asked, noticing the ghost of a smile on James's lips.

James shook his head slightly. "Just remembering old times."

Kev nodded, understanding that some memories were best left unexplored. "We're almost done here."

As Kev resumed his work, James felt the weight of the past and present intertwine. The ink etched into his skin was more than art, it was a testament to his journey, the pain endured, and the memories that shaped him.

James exited the tattoo parlor into the crisp night air, the fresh ink on his arm pulsating in rhythm with his heartbeat. Parked along the curb was CJ's Lexus truck, its sleek frame illuminated by the dim glow of the streetlights. CJ remained seated, understanding that the tattoo parlor was James's sacred space, a realm where he confronted his demons alone.

As James approached, his stoic facade crumbled. CJ stepped out, meeting him halfway. They clasped each other's forearms in a firm, brotherly grip, a silent testament to their unbreakable bond.

The weight of James's sorrow became unbearable, and he collapsed into CJ's embrace, his body shaking with silent sobs. No words were exchanged; none were needed. CJ understood the depth of his friend's pain.

The stillness was interrupted by the persistent buzzing of James's phone. He pulled it out to see Ellie's name flashing on the screen, accompanied by a series of desperate text messages pleading for him to answer. His thumb hovered over the screen, the internal battle evident. With a sharp exhale, he silenced the device and shoved it back into his pocket.

———

Jean sat cross-legged on her bed, the ambient glow of the city skyline casting elongated shadows across her room. Her fingers traced the edges of an old photograph: a candid shot of her and her ex-fiancé, Marcus, laughing amidst a backdrop of autumn leaves.

The memory was a double-edged sword, both cherished and painful: The aroma of vanilla candles filled the apartment as Jean returned home earlier than expected. Humming a familiar tune, she pushed open the bedroom door, only to be met with a sight that shattered her world. Marcus lay entangled with her best friend, their laughter dying the moment they noticed her presence.

"Jean…I can explain," Marcus stammered, scrambling for the sheets.

"Explain?" Jean's voice trembled, a mixture of rage and heartbreak evident. "My best friend, Marcus? In our bed?"

Her best friend avoided her gaze, hastily gathering her belongings. Tears blurred Jean's vision as she backed out of the room, the betrayal cutting deeper than she thought possible.

Snapping back to the present, Jean wiped away a stray tear. Her past pain fueled her determination to see love triumph for others. She reached for her phone and dialed Danielle.

Danielle reclined in her plush apartment, the remnants of a tense phone call with her lawyer echoing in her mind. She had just finalized the dissolution of a business partnership, a venture she had built with her ex-girlfriend, Naomi.

Days turned into weeks with no word from Naomi. Concern morphed into desperation as Danielle scoured social media, only to find a recent post: Naomi, arm-in-arm with another woman, captioned: *Out with the old, in with the new.*

The cold dismissal shattered Danielle, leaving her to pick up the pieces alone.

The shrill ring of her phone jolted Danielle from her reverie. Seeing Jean's name, she answered immediately.

"Jean, hey."

"Danielle, we need to talk. I'm worried about James. He's spiraling, and I'm afraid of where this might lead."

Danielle sighed, running a hand through her hair. "And Ellie isn't faring any better. She's been canceling appointments left and right. If this continues, she'll lose everything she's worked for."

"We can't let that happen," Jean asserted. "We know the depths of this kind of pain. We have to intervene."

Danielle nodded, determination hardening her features. "Agreed. Let's come up with a plan."

Meanwhile, Ellie sat curled up on her couch, clutching her phone as if it were a lifeline. Her text conversation with Dr. Lane had been unexpected.

Dr. Lane: *Ellie, I've been reflecting on our sessions and my approach. I realize I may have crossed professional boundaries, and for that, I apologize. Beyond that, I genuinely care about your well-being. Would you consider meeting,* not as doctor and patient, but as friends? Maybe dinner?

Ellie: *I appreciate your honesty. Dinner sounds nice.*

Dr. Lane: Great. *I'll make reservations for tomorrow evening.*

Ellie exhaled, a flicker of hope piercing through her gloom. Perhaps this was the distraction she needed.

———

Back outside the tattoo parlor, James's subdued cries escalated into guttural howls, a king brought to his knees by love's cruel jest. CJ held him firmly, absorbing the storm of emotions.

After moments that felt like eternity, CJ pulled back, gripping James's shoulders. "Get it out, then get it together, motherfucker. Let that pain out."

James's cries subsided into deep breaths. "You done, brother?" CJ's eyes searched his friend's face. "Are you fucking done?"

James wiped his face, a steely resolve replacing the anguish. His phone buzzed again, but this time, he didn't just silence it. He looked at CJ, his eyes burning with renewed determination.

"The mad king has returned," James declared, his voice firm. "There will be no mercy, only furious intent going forward."

CJ's lips curled into a smirk. "Welcome back, King

———

As the first light of dawn painted the sky in hues of amber and rose, James guided his car along the familiar highway back to Southern California. The rhythmic hum of the engine provided a soothing counterpoint to the tempest that had raged within him just hours earlier. With a renewed sense of purpose, he reached for his phone and dialed Jean.

"Good morning, James," Jean answered, a hint of surprise in her voice. "Everything alright?"

"Morning, Jean. I need you to adjust my schedule for today. Push things around to accommodate my arrival by 10 a.m.," he instructed, his tone calm and measured.

"Of course," she replied, concern evident. "Are you okay?"

James's gaze remained fixed on the road ahead. "Jean, it's not like my bed has been cold. What Ellie did wasn't betrayal, it was just her being herself." He paused, sensing her hesitation. "Before you say anything, please make a reservation at the finest Italian restaurant in San Diego for me and Thalia tonight."

Jean quickly searched her mental catalog of upscale establishments. "There's 'La Bella Vita', it's renowned for its ambiance and cuisine."

"Perfect," James affirmed before ending the call.

His next call was to Thalia. She answered on the first ring, her voice a blend of concern and relief. "James, it's good to hear from you. I've been worried."

"I appreciate that," he replied, his voice softening. "Would you join me for dinner tonight? Wear something that shows how much you've missed me."

A smile was evident in her response. "I'd love to. I'll see you tonight."

Accelerating down the highway, James felt a surge of determination. The past was behind him; the future awaited.

———

Meanwhile, Ellie sat curled up on her couch, her phone resting in her lap. Doubt gnawed at her. Agreeing to dinner with Dr. Lane, was it a mistake? She recalled his confident demeanor, the way his deep brown eyes seemed to see through her defenses. Perhaps a distraction was what she needed.

Her phone buzzed, breaking her reverie. A message from James. She opened it to find a link to a song: "Fuck It (I Don't Want You Back)" by Eamon.

As the chorus played: "Fuck what I said, it don't mean shit now; Fuck the presents, might as well throw 'em out; Fuck all those kisses, they didn't mean jack; Fuck you, you hoe, I don't want you back." Tears welled up in Ellie's eyes as the final words echoed through the room.

———

The morning sun cast a golden hue over the city as Jean settled into her office, the aroma of freshly brewed coffee filling the air. Her thoughts lingered on James and Ellie's abrupt decisions to move forward. The suddenness was unsettling. Danielle entered, her expression mirroring Jean's concern.

"Did you notice how quickly they've both decided to move on?" Jean asked, breaking the silence.

Danielle nodded, taking a seat opposite Jean. "It's almost overnight. Do you think something happened that we're unaware of?"

Jean sighed, swirling her coffee absentmindedly. "With those two, anything's possible. I just hope they're making choices for the right reasons."

At precisely 10 a.m., James strode into the office, exuding an air of renewed determination. His crisp white shirt clung slightly to his frame, a subtle hint of discomfort in his movements. Danielle approached him, concern flickering in her eyes.

"James, your shirt…there's blood seeping through," she pointed out gently.

James glanced down, noticing the faint crimson stain. Without hesitation, he rolled up his sleeves, revealing the fresh, intricate tattoo now adorning his arm. The design was striking: a thorn from his heart tattoo now intertwined with other elements, symbolizing an eternal bond.

Danielle's breath hitched at the sight, a mix of sadness and horror washing over her. She chose to remain silent instead, handing him his coffee.

"Your 10:30 meeting is in the conference room," she informed him.

James nodded appreciatively. "Let's get to it."

———

Ellie stepped into the office, her demeanor poised yet betraying an undercurrent of turmoil. Danielle greeted her, ready to discuss the day's agenda.

"Good morning, Ellie. Here's the rundown for today," Danielle began, handing over a neatly organized planner.

Before their conversation could progress, two uniformed police officers entered the office, their presence commanding immediate attention.

"Ms. Ellie?" one officer addressed, his tone formal.

Ellie exchanged a quick glance with Danielle before responding. "Yes, that's me. How can I help you?"

"We're here regarding an incident involving Zion. He was assaulted at a local bar last night and sustained significant injuries. We need to ask about your whereabouts during that time."

Ellie's eyes widened in shock. "I was at home all evening. Are you insinuating that I had something to do with this?"

The officer maintained his composed demeanor. "Not at all, ma'am. We're simply gathering information. Do you know anyone who might have had a motive to harm Mr. Zion?"

Ellie's mind raced, immediately thinking of James. "Was it James? Did he—"

The officer interrupted gently. "Mr. James was accounted for. He spent the evening at a tattoo parlor; his alibi checks out."

Danielle, who had been listening intently, interjected with a sharp edge to her voice. "Look, neither Ellie nor anyone here has any involvement with Zion. Frankly, we don't give a damn about him." She gestured toward the door. "Now, if there's nothing else, please see yourselves out."

The officers exchanged a glance before nodding. "Thank you for your time."

As they exited, Ellie turned to Danielle, a mix of confusion and relief evident. "Who could have done this to Zion?" Ellie mused aloud.

Danielle shrugged, a sly smile playing on her lips. "Karma has its ways."

———

Meanwhile, Jean's phone buzzed, breaking her concentration. She glanced at the caller ID: her cousin. Answering, she was met with a cryptic message. "Hey, heard homeboy got beat up pretty good last night. Some fingers broken. Guess he won't be painting anything anytime soon." The line went dead.

Jean gasped, a mixture of horror and regret washing over her. She quickly composed herself as James approached. "Everything okay?" James inquired, noting her pale complexion.

Jean forced a smile. "Yes, just some unexpected news. Nothing to concern yourself with."

James studied her for a moment before nodding. "Alright. Let's keep things moving."

As he walked away, Jean couldn't shake the uneasy feeling settling in her chest.

———

As the sun dipped below the horizon, casting a warm glow over the city, Ellie stood before her bedroom mirror. She adjusted the delicate silver necklace around her neck, its pendant resting just above the neckline of her elegant black dress. The anticipation of the evening ahead with Dr. Lane was a welcome distraction from the turmoil that had consumed her in recent days.

A sharp knock at the door signaled his arrival. Ellie took a deep breath, smoothing the fabric of her already perfect dress before opening the door "Good evening, Ellie," Dr. Lane greeted, his smile warm and genuine. "You look stunning."

She felt a blush creep up her cheeks. "Thank you. You clean up nicely yourself."

He offered his arm, which she accepted, and they made their way to the awaiting car.

———

Meanwhile, in San Diego, James adjusted the cuffs of his tailored suit as he approached La Bella Vita. The restaurant exuded sophistication, its ambiance a blend of classic Italian charm and modern elegance. Stepping inside, he scanned the room until his eyes settled on Thalia.

She stood near the entrance, a vision in a deep emerald gown that accentuated her figure. Her dark curls cascaded over her shoulders, and her eyes sparkled as they met his.

"James," she breathed, a smile gracing her lips.

He closed the distance between them, taking her hand and pressing a gentle kiss to her knuckles. "Thalia, you look exquisite."

She laughed softly. "Flattery will get you everywhere."

A waiter approached to guide them to their table. As they followed, James leaned in slightly and asked the waiter in fluent Italian if he could please ask the violinist to come to their table and start playing.

The waiter nodded with a knowing smile. "Certamente, signore." (Certainly, sir.)

Seated at their candlelit table, the soft glow highlighting Thalia's features, James reached across, his fingers lightly grazing hers.

Moments later, the gentle strains of Sade's "Is It a Crime" filled the air as the violinist approached their table, playing with heartfelt emotion.

Thalia's eyes glistened with unshed tears. James stood, extending his hand toward her. "May I have this dance?" She nodded, placing her hand in his.

There was no designated dance floor, but that didn't matter. Right beside their table, amidst the softly clinking glasses and murmured conversations, they began to sway together, lost in their own world.

As they moved in harmony, James leaned in, his lips close to her ear. "You deserve so much more than what I've given you," he murmured. "Thank you for your patience with me."

She rested her head against his chest, her voice a whisper. "I'm here because I want to be. Let's not dwell on the past tonight."

They continued to dance, the music weaving around them, binding them closer.

———

Ellie and Dr. Lane arrived at an upscale waterfront restaurant in Costa Mesa, the moon casting silvery reflections on the gentle waves. Their conversation flowed effortlessly, touching on topics ranging from art to travel.

As dessert was served, Dr. Lane reached across the table, his fingers lightly grazing Ellie's. "I'm glad you agreed to dinner tonight," he said, his voice sincere.

Ellie met his gaze, a mixture of emotions swirling within her. "Me too. It's been a while since I've felt this…at ease."

He smiled, his thumb tracing gentle circles on the back of her hand. "I'd like to see you again. Tomorrow, perhaps?"

She hesitated for a moment before nodding. "I'd like that."

As they exited the restaurant, Dr. Lane walked her to her car. Ellie turned to face him, her heart pounding. "Thank you for tonight," she whispered.

He leaned in, his lips brushing hers in a tender kiss. When they parted, she smiled. "I'm free tomorrow," she said softly before slipping into her car.

Dr. Lane watched as she drove away, anticipation building for what the future might hold.

———

In San Diego, James and Thalia remained close, their dance slowing to a gentle sway. The violinist concluded the song, offering a respectful nod before moving to serenade another table.

James looked into Thalia's eyes, a newfound determination evident. "Let's get out of here." She nodded, her eyes alight with desire.

Hand in hand, they left the restaurant, the night stretching out before them, full of promise and new beginnings.

The night had unfolded with moments that hinted at new beginnings. James found solace in Thalia's embrace during their intimate dinner in San Diego, while Ellie sought comfort in the company of Dr. Lane over a meal in Costa Mesa. These encounters offered brief respites from their recent tribulations, suggesting the possibility of moving forward.

However, beneath these glimpses of hope, unresolved tensions lingered. The assault on Zion cast a shadow over the evening, intertwining their lives in unforeseen ways. Jean's cryptic phone call hinted at deeper complications, and the fresh ink on James's arm served as a constant reminder of wounds not yet healed.

As the city settled into the quiet of the night, James and Ellie stood on the precipice of change. The paths they had chosen, while offering moments of joy, were also laden with the weight of their past decisions. The echoes of their actions reverberated, a constant reminder that while one could attempt to escape the past, it often had a way of catching up.

In the quiet moments before dawn, both found themselves reflecting on the night's events. The warmth of a new connection, the allure of a fresh start, and the promise of happiness were tantalizing.

Yet, the shadows of their past loomed large, whispering caution. The journey ahead was uncertain, and as they stood on the cusp of a new chapter, the only certainty was that the past was never truly behind them.

Chapter 12: Painted Betrayals

The next day, Ellie settled in at her therapist's office, and noticed there was something dangerously composed about her: intelligence cloaked in honeyed tones, skin like burnt caramel, lips painted with a shade that sat perfectly between scandal and restraint.

Camila crossed her legs, slow and effortless. Ellie followed the motion without meaning to, mirroring it, and instantly regretting it. The shift reminded her of the heat pulsing low in her stomach.

'Why am I wet every time she crosses her legs? ' It was involuntary now. A sensory betrayal. The scent of jasmine on Camila's blouse, the commanding energy that came without raising her voice.

In her mind, Camila was feeding her, sliced fruit on a silver fork, slow bites, guiding the food between her lips. She imagined her licking a drip of mango juice from Ellie's chin, then whispering: "Be still. Feel it."

She snapped out of it when Camila blinked: professional, unaware or simply choosing not to acknowledge the mental spiral.

"Progress isn't always linear," Camila said, tone silk over steel. "But honesty always moves the needle." Ellie nodded slowly.

That same afternoon, she messaged Dr. Lane and confirmed dinner. Lane was safe. Lane was kind. Lane made her feel…normal.

But Camila? Camila made her feel like prey, and she liked it.

Danielle picked her up not long after the appointment ended. Ellie got into the car with a distant smile, her legs still pressed tightly together.

"How'd it go?" Danielle asked, sunglasses covering a suspicious brow.

"Fine," Ellie replied quickly.

"Uh-huh." Danielle smirked but didn't push.

James adjusted the cuffs on his soft gray Henley, the sleeves pushed to his forearms, veins rising like river paths along sun-kissed skin. Charcoal joggers, jet-black sneakers, no watch, no jewelry. He looked like a man ready to train, but his mind was far from the gym.

The scent of rosemary and thyme coaxed him toward the kitchen. And there she was. Silk robe tied loose at the waist. Nothing beneath it but her, the kind of nothing that made silence heavy.

She stood in heels, slicing citrus with a blade that gleamed in the morning light. "Hungry?" she asked, with a glance over her shoulder that could turn faithful men atheist.

James leaned against the entryway. "Always," he said.

She smiled, walking toward him with purpose. "A king shouldn't serve. He should feast."

"And how," he murmured, voice lower now, "should I be served?"

She stopped in front of him, let her robe part just enough to reveal her full, untamed crown. Then slowly opened her mouth and said, "However you choose, my King."

James didn't move, didn't speak. His eyes trailed over her, the self-made sanctuary she offered, not as a distraction, but as a palace.

She continued, her voice honeyed but deliberate. "I'm not here to talk about anyone who's ever left you bleeding. I'm here to build, to war with you, and anyone who has betrayed you is an enemy of our court."

He stared at her for a long beat. She didn't flinch, didn't flutter. Just stood there, fireproof and patient. 'She's not a substitute,' James thought, 'she's an offering.'

As she turned back toward the kitchen, hips of sin, James followed her with his eyes.

And Thalia thought, 'Let the Queen mourn her crown. I'm polishing the throne.'

———

Ellie sat at her desk, screens glowing before her but unread. The email with the conference details was still open. She'd been selected as a featured panelist for the Cybercore Security & Wellness Summit, an elite gathering of thought leaders and tech giants.

The moment was supposed to feel like a crown returned. But her fingers hovered above the trackpad like the acceptance might burn her.

Danielle walked in, caramel curls pinned high and heels announcing every stride. She dropped into the chair across from Ellie and crossed her legs, tablet in hand.

"Looks like it's official," Danielle said. "You're on the wellness leadership panel. Morning slot. The PR team's already losing their minds."

Ellie nodded once, guarded.

"And before you ask: Jean said James hasn't accepted. So, you're clear to be brilliant," Danielle added, with a knowing smile.

Ellie breathed easier but didn't smile. "Good. I need this to be about the work."

Danielle raised a brow. "It should've always been about the work."

Ellie gave her a sharp look, one that softened just as quickly. Danielle knew how to throw the truth like a dagger but wrap it up softly, just in time.

———

James flipped through the digital invite on his tablet while Jean stood across from his desk, arms folded. His expression was unreadable: focused but detached.

"They want you for the keynote," Jean said. "Gemini. AI innovation. Cyber leadership. You'd be opening the entire summit."

"I already told you to decline," James replied, setting the tablet down.

Jean didn't budge. "And I didn't. I told them I'd confirm once I dragged your ego out of the corner and reminded it what ambition looks like." James gave a slight smirk but said nothing.

She stepped closer, her voice calm but fierce. "This isn't about her. This is about you finally doing what you've built for. You've waited too damn long to let someone else steal your fire. You don't need permission to shine, King." He leaned back in his chair, his jaw tight.

"She'll be there," Jean added, more softly. "But she's not the moment. You are."

James looked past her, toward the skyline, and let the silence stretch. Then finally he said, "Accept it."

Jean nodded. "Already did."

Later that night, James sat on the balcony, the ocean breeze cool on his skin. The city lights blinked beneath him like stars trying to compete. He wore a fitted black v-neck and soft charcoal trousers. Barefoot. Composed. Dangerous.

Thalia moved toward him with two glasses of deep red wine. Her robe slid against her skin like silk poured over fire. She handed him a glass, then sat close, her thigh touching his.

"You said yes," she said softly. "You're not going for her?"

"I'm going for me," he answered.

Thalia smiled, pleased. She turned her body slightly, pressing closer, "Then go and remind them who they should've never bet against. Go and build the kingdom that doesn't need saving."

She paused, her voice lowering, thick with promise. "With me at the gates, and our enemies outside them." James looked at her, and the war in his chest stilled. He lifted his glass to toast.

But before he could sip, Thalia leaned in and whispered, "No, my King." She set her glass down slowly, then dropped to her knees before him with the grace of royalty. "Tonight, I serve."

Her voice was reverent, her gaze unwavering. "And when the throne is rebuilt, I will rule beside you." James didn't speak. But the way he looked down at her, like a storm had just remembered its name, was louder than anything words could deliver. The city below blinked in a slow rhythm, like it too was waiting for something to erupt.

James stood barefoot, shirtless, still in the soft charcoal trousers that hung perfectly on his waist. The ocean breeze danced across his inked chest, the candlelight behind him catching the lines of pain and art that marked his body like scripture.

In his hand, the last of the deep red wine. He took a final sip, then leaned back into the plush chair, setting the glass down gently on the nearby table. Eyes closed. Breath held. And the fantasy began: The wine blurred the edges of the world, and the room, and his mind began its descent. The room was gone, replaced by a grand chamber of smoke and silk, drenched in gold and crimson.

Before him, both kneeling, Thalia and Ava. Dripping with oil and reverence. Nude, their skin shining with devotion. Eyes wide as they stared at him like he was a god, a judge, and an executioner in one.

Thalia stroked him from base to tip, her lips parting as she whispered, "Let us worship you…"

Ava, already on her knees, slid him into her mouth with a moan, the warm suck of her lips coaxing a growl from James's throat. He grabbed her hair in his fist, while Thalia pressed kisses to his chest, then his ribs, then his abs, kissing down toward Ava's chin until their tongues met around him.

The Mad King gripped them both, pulled Ava up, and bent Thalia over a chair. He took her hard, one hand on her neck, the other guiding himself inside. Deep. Unrelenting.

Ava moaned behind him, begging to taste again, begging to serve. James turned, pinned her down, and filled her mouth with himself. Over and over. Again and again.

Thalia's cries. Ava's choking. His hips, punishing. His voice, commanding. "You serve me now."

They nodded as he fucked them both. Two at once, rotating like chess pieces on fire. When he released, it was a flood. Across lips. Thighs. Tongues. He made them kneel again and opened himself once more, feeding them another stream, each swallowing drop after drop, whimpering in gratitude.

"You are a god," Ava whispered.

"No," James muttered. "I'm the end of gods." And the beginning of war.

Reality and the candlelight returned. The chair, the glass, now empty. He sat there stunned, for once, not by the intensity of his fantasy, but by the absence. Ellie wasn't in it. Not even a whisper of her name.

Just as he let that realization sink, steam curled into the bedroom as Thalia stepped out of the shower: damp, radiant, and deliberate. His robe hung loosely around her, one shoulder bare, the top of her breast teasing the edge of fabric, her toned legs shimmering beneath the hem.

She walked to the speaker first. Tapped. And then came the music: "All you gotta do is say yes…"

The voice of Floetry floated through the room, warm and rich like melted chocolate on silk. James looked up. Thalia untied the robe, letting it fall without flourish, because she didn't need theatrics. She was the show.

Full bush, dewy skin, nipples pointed like prayers, she moved toward him, barefoot, eyes burning. "However you choose, King," she said.

James opened his thighs, his hands resting on the arms of the chair. "I want it slow."

She obeyed. Climbing onto his lap, she hovered. Her soaked lips teased the tip of his cock, rubbing against him rhythmically. She rolled her hips, grinding until he was rock hard, twitching beneath her.

"I've been ready," she whispered. "All you had to do…was say yes."

She kissed him deep, mouth open, letting him taste the heat she'd been building for hours. Then finally, she lowered herself onto him. A moan. A gasp.

His eyes fluttered shut. "Don't deny what you feel. Let me undress you, baby"

Thalia rode him like scripture, like gospel. Long, fluid strokes at first. Then tighter, deeper. Her nails etched soft crescents into his chest as she leaned back, watching him come undone beneath her.

James gripped her hips, thrusting up as she moved down, their rhythm locked in carnal perfection.

"You feel that?" she moaned.

"I do."

"And it's all mine."

James didn't speak. He couldn't. He surrendered to her rhythm, her worship. To the fire.

And as she rode him to the brink and back again, her lips grazing his ear, she whispered: "This kingdom is yours now..."

And James believed it. Even if it was built on ash.

——

Ellie sat in the back of the black car, her legs crossed high, silk dress gathered just enough to showcase the curve of her thighs. The scent of jasmine still lingered from her bath, her curls pinned into a graceful sweep that bared the nape of her neck.

She wore no panties tonight. Not because she planned anything, but because she wanted to feel something.

Dr. Lane had been texting her throughout the day, soft, playful checkins like: *Tonight, I promise to only ask one question, and it won't be clinical.*

Ellie: *And what might that question be?*

Dr. Lane: *Do you want another glass of wine?*

She chuckled when she saw it. Her stomach flipped, not just from nerves, but a quiet kind of hunger. The kind she hadn't fed in far too long.

The rooftop restaurant glowed in amber light. They were seated at a corner table overlooking the coastline. Everything about it felt warm. Intimate. Undemanding.

Dr. Lane, wore a dark tailored suit, unbuttoned at the collar. No tie. Still polished, but relaxed. As he poured her wine, he offered her a softer version of the smile she was used to. "Call me Ken," he said.

Ellie arched an eyebrow. "Dropping the title already?"

"We're no longer doctor and patient," he said, tilting the bottle. "I'd like to get to know you now, not your trauma."

She sipped her wine slowly. "And what if I still like calling you Doctor?" she asked, the words layered with teasing edge.

He leaned closer. "Then I may start calling you 'Queen' just to stay even."

Her smile cracked wider than expected. She forgot how much she missed being flirted with by someone who didn't want to conquer her, but instead honor her.

After dessert, it began to rain lightly. The kind of drizzle that kissed skin instead of soaking it. They paused under the overhang near valet, the night stretching out around them.

"I'm not ready for the night to end," Ken said, brushing a damp curl from her cheek.

And then he kissed her. Not timid, not greedy. Just right. It lit her up in places that hadn't been touched in weeks. When he pulled back, she was breathless.

"Come with me," he whispered. They didn't speak as they entered his place: sleek, warm-toned, with books stacked against one wall and jazz humming low from built-in speakers. A glass of wine was poured, but neither touched it.

She kissed him this time. And when his hands lifted her dress, her body arched like it had been waiting for him specifically.

She tried to take control, and pushed him toward the bed, hands already sliding beneath his shirt. But he paused her with two fingers on her chin.

"You always lead," he said softly. "Just tonight, let yourself follow." She stared into him, resisting. Then nodding.

Ken laid her down like something sacred. He peeled her dress back slowly, inch by inch, until her breasts, her belly, and the soft mound of her pussy lay exposed under the ambient golden light.

He kissed the center of her chest and whispered, "You don't have to give me anything. Just take this." Then he trailed his tongue down her stomach.

Ellie reached for his head, tried to guide him harder, but he caught her wrist gently and pinned it above her head. "Let it happen," he said. "Don't grip it. Don't power through it. Feel it."

When his mouth covered her, she felt it. He didn't devour her, he savored her. His tongue was smooth, steady, knowing.

Ellie gasped, her legs involuntarily parting wider. Every time her hips rolled, he adjusted just enough to make her want more, but not enough to make her finish.

Until she begged. Her breath hitched, her toes curled, and she pleaded through gritted teeth, "Don't stop…" Not until her thighs trembled and her climax pulsed through her so hard that she nearly cried out his name.

When he slid inside her, it was slow. Deep. Bare. Her nails dug into his shoulders, and she instinctively tried to flip him. Out of habit, out of training.

He resisted. "No strength tonight," he whispered. "Just surrender."

His strokes were powerful but not punishing. His hands cradled her jaw. His lips kissed her neck. And when she came again, shaking under him, he smiled against her mouth.

"That's it," he whispered. "That's all I wanted from you."

She lay beneath him, legs still wrapped around his waist, breath erratic, heart racing. "I didn't think I'd feel anything again," she confessed.

And Ken—naked, glistening, eyes full of fire—kissed her forehead and replied, "Then I did my job."

"Oh, I didn't know I was hiring just yet" she said. They both laughed

"We might've overachieved."

———

The clock glowed 12:37 a.m. on Jean's desk. She was three espresso shots deep into James's SoCal schedule when a ping echoed across her monitor.

She squinted: *SPEAKER CONFIRMATION NOTICE: James King. Confirmed for 10:00 a.m. Following speaker Ellie Sinclair, 9:15 a.m.*

Jean froze. Mouse in hand. Staring. "…Oh hell no."

Three rereads later, she was already dialing. Danielle picked up mid-yawn. "If this ain't the Rapture or Ellie dying her hair again, I swear—"

"Check your email," Jean barked. "West Coast Tech & Leadership Summit."

Danielle: "Girl, I already know. Ellie's on at 9:15, she got the slot she wanted—"

"Yeah?" Jean cut her off. "Guess who's on at 10:00?"

Pause. Then a click. Then a gasp. "You lying."

Jean was spinning in her chair like a Bond villain. "She picked that slot thinking he turned it down, right?"

"He did! Or he said he did!"

"Lied."

"Deadass lied."

They both exhaled. Long. Heavy.

Danielle groaned. "We were just tryna get 'em in the same building. Now they back-to-back like a versus battle."

Jean cackled. "This ain't a summit. This is the season finale."

Danielle: "Oh, this is gonna be one of those. Either we get a crownin' or a clean execution."

Danielle chuckled, then grew thoughtful. "We did that."

Jean leaned back. "We just didn't expect it to work this well."

Danielle sighed. "Or for both of them to get all soft over somebody new."

Jean smirked. "Speaking of which, I finally looked up this Dr. Lane."

Danielle: "Uh oh."

Jean: "First of all, why he got the voice of a bedtime story and arms like he bench-presses trust issues? I started blushing like it was my Wi-Fi password."

Danielle laughed. "He's smooth. But let me tell you about Thalia…"

Jean perked up.

Danielle continued, "So, a while ago, Ellie sees her in the lobby, right? Gets up in her face a lil', all that queen shit."

Jean: "Oh lord."

Danielle: "Thalia doesn't flinch. Just smiles softly and says: 'You're stunning in person…like in your pictures.' And I'm thinking, 'okay, classic passive flex.' But then…"

Jean: "Oh no."

Danielle: "She lifts her phone, turns it real gentle-like. Zion's portrait of Ellie. On her lock screen."

Jean damn near choked. "Shut. Up."

Danielle: "I said the same thing. That bitch didn't point at the portrait, but she became the portrait. And walked away like nothing happened."

Jean leaned forward. "That bitch is smooth. Cold. My spirit animal."

Danielle: "Still Team Ellie though?"

Jean: "Till the last petal falls, baby."

Danielle: "Same. Even if Thalia's playing chess while we still putting checkers on the board."

Jean smirked. "Even if Dr. Lane got me ready to throw on a sundress and apply for heartbreak."

Danielle burst out laughing. "Still. Ellie and James? That's legacy love."

Jean: "Bond that survives battle, scandal, and bad decisions."

Danielle: "But can it survive the mic drop heard 'round the world?"

Jean: "We're about to find out."

Danielle: "Then clear the front row."

Jean: "And maybe get security on standby."

―――

The ballroom was quiet, reverent almost. Rows of chairs lined up like loyal subjects awaiting judgment. Dr. James King stood at center stage, still as a statue carved from resilience and fire.

Jean watched from the side, tablet in hand, eyes sharp as razors beneath cool lashes. The sound tech cleared his throat. "Mic check when you're ready, Dr. King."

James tapped the mic once. Then leaned in, voice wrapped in storm clouds. "Heavy is the head of the mad king that wears the crown."

Even the sound guy froze mid-sip of his coffee.

James's voice dropped deeper, darker. "My mother once told me, 'Fight like you're fighting for your life but not afraid to lose it…and you'll never lose. Even if you die trying'."

And then, it hit him. She was offstage crying. Torn apart by decisions even she didn't fully understand. Second-guessing herself for the first time in a long time.

James stood and looked at her, steady and still. "Are you a lion?" he asked, low and calm.

Ellie nodded, her voice breaking. "Yes."

"Then answer right," he said, stepping a little closer to her. "Are you a domestic cat, or are you a wild thing?"

She swallowed hard. "A wild thing."

His eyes locked on hers. His tone went velvet-deep, quoting from memory: "I never saw a wild thing sorry for itself. A small bird will drop frozen dead from a bough, without ever having felt sorry for itself."

He moved even closer, voice calm enough to hush a riot: "And you are no fucking bird."

James's final mic check wasn't even a check. It was a declaration. He added, almost gently, "Quoted from D.H. Lawrence…for her."

Offstage, Ellie gasped. Her fingers found the hollow above her heart. She wasn't prepared. But she knew he remembered. And that he knew she was there. James turned calmly to leave the mic.

Jean blinked and muttered, "Damn, James. You quoting G.I. Jane now? I didn't even know you watched movies like that."

He smirked without missing a step. "I'm full of surprises."

Danielle glanced at Ellie. "Still want to speak first?"

Ellie's eyes never left the stage. "Now more than ever."

Danielle grinned. "Go get your crown, Queen."

———

Later, the room buzzed with the anticipatory hum of excellence. Both sound checks were complete, and now the real show began. Jean and Danielle were front and center. Their heels crossed, phones silenced, and eyes glued to the stage like proud sisters at a family coronation.

Ellie stepped into the spotlight and the crowd erupted: standing ovation, camera flashes, whispers of admiration. She smiled, genuinely moved, and as the applause finally began to settle, she leaned into the mic with playful humility. "Are you all sure you're clapping for me? Dr. King is up next."

Laughter rippled through the auditorium. A few heads turned in James's direction. But he wasn't looking at them, he was looking at her.

Ellie took a breath and began, her voice fluid and powerful, filled with the confidence she once prayed for but now wore like a crown. And James watched, not just as a man, but as the architect of her rise.

Every word from Ellie was polished, profound. She didn't blink. Her delivery was flawless, the audience hanging on each syllable. She ended her talk with fire in her voice. "Audacity isn't always about speaking up. Sometimes, it's about standing tall when others expected you to fold." Thunderous applause followed.

As she made her way offstage, her eyes caught James, now standing at the side. Their gazes locked, intense, wordless. She gave a slight nod. James, in return, bowed gently with soft claps, a look of deep pride softening the edge of distance on his face.

Then he walked past her, and the moment he stepped on stage, the energy shifted. The room vibrated. Jean leaned over and whispered to Danielle, "They just saw the Queen. Now they're about to meet the Goddamn General."

Danielle whispered back, "I just hope the King remembers who built the kingdom beside him."

The host's voice boomed: "Please welcome to the stage, Dr. James King!"

The applause was deafening. A rockstar, a cyber warlord in a tailored suit, crisp voice, and quiet thunder in his walk.

James adjusted the mic once. "All great cybersecurity professionals understand that you have to know every part of your organization, down to the smallest, seemingly insignificant pieces. Because something that seems harmless—" He paused. Looked directly at Ellie from across the room. "—can eventually become a problem the size of the state of Texas."

Ellie blinked. Jean and Danielle both reacted internally.

Jean thought, "Did he just…? Oh he's petty-polite today."

Danielle thought, "He didn't just say that out loud."

Ellie thought, "Goddamn you."

But James never flinched. He moved through the rest of his presentation with surgical precision: funny, intelligent, commanding. He was everything.

He finished to deafening applause, nodding to the audience once and walking off stage, not to cheers or smiles, but to silence inside himself.

As he passed Ellie again, he looked at her one final time. Sadness lingered in the corners of his eyes. Pride too. He had always known how to walk away from a fight. But he had never run from one.

Ellie stood still, stunned by the ache building in her chest. He didn't make a scene. He didn't curse her name. He didn't even try to win her back.

And then it hit her. He made her believe she was brilliant. He made her feel like a queen. He gave her his devotion, his mind, his body, and the power to dominate him when she needed it most. Every desire she explored, he indulged. Every shadow she cast, he stood in. And he did it not to control her, but to help her soar.

Then, like a lightning strike, a memory returned. Ellie on top of him in bed. Playfully straddling him. Her tiny muscles flexing as she tried to hold him down.

He hadn't even resisted.

"Why aren't you tossing me off with all that power?" she asked.

James smiled, brushing her hair behind her ear and saying softly: "It takes even more power to let power go."

He did it for her, every single time. And now, he was gone. The King had relinquished the throne. And in doing so, made it clear: He was always more than the crown.

Chapter 13: The Gemini War Room

The sea of admirers was nothing new. James could command a room without speaking. Now, after his talk, the swarm moved around him like planets around a sun: leaning in, shaking hands, complimenting, snapping selfies. His name was on everyone's lips.

He offered polite smiles, nods, a quick photo here, a firm handshake there. But his eyes kept drifting toward the exit.

Jean trailed him like a shadow in heels. "You really dropped the 'Texas' line, huh?"

James turned, sipped his water, and raised a brow. "Did I?"

Jean narrowed her eyes. "That was a surgical strike, not a slip of the tongue."

"Guess I'll take your word for it," James said, cool and unbothered.

Jean smirked. "You play dumb like a man who graduated at the top of every class he ever sat in."

As they made their way out, Jean's phone buzzed. She glanced at the screen.

Danielle: Did she see him before he left?

Jean typed back quickly: Already in the car. Gone.

Danielle turned to Ellie, who sat silent, staring at her folded hands. She didn't even need to ask.

"He's gone," Danielle said gently.

But Ellie's nod wasn't agreement.

———

After leaving the conference, James let his mind drift back to his youth. Suddenly, he was there in the South Side, project apartments. The mid-afternoon sun was turning concrete into griddle heat.

Twelve-year-old James and CJ walked out of the corner store with empty pockets, and chilled king-size Snickers somehow acquired. They weren't stealing, not really. They were just living.

"Damn, these joints hit different when they cold," James said, already unwrapping his.

CJ held onto his, unopened. "Gotta wait for the right moment. You always rushing pleasure." James shrugged and took a bite. Sugar heaven.

That's when they saw him: Chance Curto. Thirteen years old, yet built like a grown man. A local Karate Kid turned street demon. Nobody fucked with Chance. Not unless they wanted a trip to the ER or a reputation rearrangement.

Chance spotted the candy in James's hand. "Where you get that from?" he asked, fake-casual.

James chewed slowly. "Store."

"You pay for it?"

James shrugged. "Nah."

Chance grinned. "You always doing something stupid, punk."

Then: Smack. He slapped the candy bar clean out of James's hand, sending it spinning into the dirt. CJ tensed beside him. James just looked at the ruined chocolate, quiet and cold. He didn't think, he didn't breathe. He was on Chance before the boy could blink.

Karate moves or not, it didn't matter. This wasn't a spar. This was rage, old and inherited, pounding like thunder. James had him on the ground, fists landing like sermons, fury untrained but unstoppable.

By the time Chance's parents ran out screaming, their son was limp, bloody, and broken. They pulled James off. He didn't resist. He bent down, picked up the candy bar—dust, dirt, and all—and shoved it into Chance's bleeding mouth. Then he whispered, with terrifying calm, "Now I've done something, motherfucker."

CJ said nothing and just walked with James back to their bikes. Then handed him half of his own untouched Snickers.

"Damn, man," CJ muttered. "You could've just had mine." They both laughed and rode off into the heat like nothing had happened.

But something had changed. A warrior had been born, not for sport or show, but for survival.

The roar of the highway reminded James that he was not in that simple time anymore, as he came back to the present. He sat back in the car seat, eyes closed. The city was behind him. Noise fading. And somewhere between then and now, that same fire was still there, coiled low in his chest, curled around his ribs like a reminder.

He hadn't fought for a candy bar since. But the right to love and to be loved? That fight never ended. Not for the Mad King or for what he built, even if the Queen forgot the fire.

James arrived at the penthouse. Inside, the lights were low, and Thalia was waiting, calm and prepared. The elevator chimed softly, and Thalia turned, barefoot in nothing but a silk robe loosely tied at the waist. The sound of James's keycard was all the confirmation she needed. He entered silently.

She smiled, not with seduction, but with knowing peace. "You called," she said, stepping toward him. "I thought you'd be too tired."

"I am," James said, pulling off his cuff slowly. "But not for the kind of peace you bring."

Thalia took his jacket and handed him a tumbler of bourbon without a word. Then, she disappeared into the bathroom, her hips swaying like temptation.

The bath was already drawn, steam curling up like fingers beckoning a weary king into a ritual. When James entered, the lights were dim, scented candles flickering. Thalia was now completely nude. Her robe lay like a whisper on the marble tile. She didn't step into the tub. Instead, she knelt beside it, dipping the loofah into the warm water and wringing it out slowly over his chest.

"I'm honored you came," she whispered, in Greek, "Se timáo me óli mou tin kardiá." (I honor you with all my heart.) She hummed something older than language, something that felt like it was sung by temple priestesses and war widows. A lullaby for warriors. Ancient and deep.

James sank deeper into the water, letting it claim his body. Thalia remained outside the tub. Nude, kneeling, baring herself. Not to seduce, but to serve. Her hands worshipped his scalp, her touch a sermon, her breath slow and steady.

James didn't ask for anything. She didn't offer anything more. And yet the air between them was charged, laced with something hotter than fire. Respect mixed with desire.

Thalia leaned close, her lips at his ear. "You deserve everything they said you'd never have. And I will make sure you have it all. Even if I'm never crowned."

———

When she arrived at home, Ellie made her way to her bedroom and was welcomed with silence. She lay in bed, her robe loosely cinched, skin still warm from a long bath that failed to wash away her ache. Her phone rested beside her. Still no word from James.

As she dozed, a soft moan slipped from her lips. In her dream, Ken was kissing her neck: slow, hungry, affirming her beauty with every word. Then came Camila.

Confident, stunning. Her therapist's voice, soft and coaxing, echoed, "You like to control, Ellie. But what if pleasure came from surrender?"

Camila's hand reached inside her legs, just as Ken lifted her into his arms. Ellie gasped in her sleep, wet, pulsing, and ashamed.

She jolted awake. Alone. She looked to the ceiling. Old desires, it seemed, died very, very hard.

———

The next day, back at Gemini, Jean walked into the office without knocking, her heels soft on the plush carpet but her energy sharp. She held two coffees and an iPad loaded with meetings, contracts, and chaos.

James stood at the window, hands in his pockets, watching the city stretch and breathe under the sun. He looked powerful. Calm. And completely hollowed out.

"You're too quiet," Jean said, setting the coffee beside him. "That's how I know it's bad."

James didn't respond at first. Then: "The quiet ain't bad. It's where I live."

Jean softened, her voice dropping. "It's where you hide."

He turned slightly. "Hiding would mean I'm afraid. I'm just finished pretending it didn't hurt."

Jean nodded, taking that in. "Schedule's been rearranged. You're cleared until 1:00. After that, it's Gemini meetings and the press wants follow-up from the conference."

James exhaled, rubbing the back of his neck. "Tell them I spoke yesterday. That's enough for the week."

Jean raised an eyebrow. "Understood. You want me to block everything?" She paused, watching him closely. "Anything else?"

"Yes. Get me a private table for dinner in San Diego. Low light. No noise. No press."

Jean tapped into her phone immediately. "Name?"

He didn't answer right away. Then, "Doesn't matter. Just make it peaceful." Jean didn't press.

———

Early in the evening, the low amber sun bleeds across Southern California's hills as Thalia glided through winding roads in her sleek black coupe. The stereo hummed with soft instrumental music, elegant and subtle, like her thoughts.

Her phone pinged with a single text from James. She didn't need to read it right away. She already knew it was him.

She smiled, lips parted just slightly. Her breath catching in her throat, not with surprise, but with anticipation. "He always comes back to warmth…He just doesn't know it yet."

She pressed her thumb to the screen and read: *Looking forward to that calm you promised, Thalia. Don't be stingy.*

She closed her eyes for half a breath, and thought to herself, 'I already love him. But he's not ready to love me back. Not yet. He still fights phantoms in the shape of her face. But this one…this one I will not lose. Not to history, not to heartbreak, and certainly not to a woman who needed him to bleed to prove his worth.'

She shifted gears and accelerated gently. Her body leaned into the road as her thoughts continued. 'He is not just a King, he's a warrior. A storm in tailored suits. A god…not Apollo, not Hermes. One who rivals Zeus himself, with power, wrath, and thunder wrapped in reason. And I am no mortal. I'm Olympus, and I will not crumble beneath him.'

Her eyes blink back into focus as the gate appears. She slows, punches in the code, and watches the wrought iron slide open.

A secluded Grecian-style estate perched above the Pacific with white columns, lemon trees, and bougainvillea curling over archways. The scent of sea salt and sage rides the breeze. Thalia stepped out, shoes clicking softly on flagstone. The door opens before she can knock.

"You still move like a woman with secrets," comes the voice, rich and weathered with wisdom. Kallista. A force of nature wrapped in black linen. Her silver-gray hair is swept into a careless twist. Her bare feet don't diminish her authority. If anything, they amplify it.

Thalia smiles and walks into the open arms of her oldest confidante. "I was taught by the best," she murmurs into Kallista's shoulder.

They move to the sunroom where a spread of figs, raw honey, soft cheese, and chilled white wine await. There, they sit, facing the open windows and the disappearing sun. "So," Kallista says as she pours, "Tell me about this King."

Thalia's smile fades into something more reverent. "He's fury dressed in silence. Gentle with me, but I've seen the monster caged behind his ribs."

Kallista sipped, never blinking. "And you want the monster?"

"No," Thalia says simply. "I want the man who knows how to keep it."

"Does he still bleed for the Queen?"

"She owns his past. But I…" she leans back, crossing her legs gracefully, "…I am the quiet of what's next."

"Still romanticizing the lion."

"No," Thalia corrects her. "Romanticizing his rebirth."

Kallista nods once, impressed, and proud. "You've learned. Patience isn't waiting. It's turning silence into sanctuary."

Thalia lifts her glass in a silent toast. "I am the sanctuary."

"And the throne," Kallista says softly.

"Exactly."

They sip. The wind rustles the lemon trees, and a scent like summer and war and ancient gods rides through the open windows. Thalia whispers something in Greek: "Όταν ένας βασιλιάς χάσει τον δρόμο του…επιστρέφει στη φωτιά ή στο φως." ("When a king loses his way…he returns to fire or to light.") And Kallista, the woman who once taught her how to turn whispers into weapons, smiled like a proud general. "Then be both."

––––

Back at Gemini in James's downtown SoCal office it was quiet, too quiet. The ambient hum of Gemini's server array pulses softly behind frosted glass, as he sat at the head of a long obsidian table, motionless, staring through a digital projection of the Gemini roadmap. Nothing on his face suggested fire, only a smoldering stillness.

Jean stepped inside the room with the same care one might show entering a lion's den, and said softly," I moved your 2 o'clock. Geneva's confirmed for tomorrow morning. You're clear."

James: "Appreciate it."

Jean added, "James…" But he didn't look up.

She continued, "Have you…seen it?"

James finally blinked, and a low smile creeps at the corner of his mouth, dangerous in its serenity. "The museum feature? Of course. Fifty thousand. That's the price of a masterpiece, apparently."

Jean exhales slowly. The article about Zion's painting of the Queen came out earlier, and she was dreading his reaction.

"She gave me fair warning, Jean. Maybe now she's content. How can I be upset about that?"

Jean said gently, "Because it's a private moment…during a time of weakness, now made public."

James stood, stretched his back with a slow roll of the shoulders, then walked to the window. Then said over his shoulder, "My bed wasn't cold, Jean. She just likes hers a bit hotter, I guess."

Jean stayed silent as James turned around, his voice soft. "But my heart? It still bled for her."

He rolled up the sleeve of his left arm, exposing the newly inked forearm: the sad-faced clown, painted in James's own likeness, weeping beneath his ever-smiling mask. And, just beneath it, he chaotic mouths of madness, screaming. The thorn from the heart tattoo, snakes around them all, binding each wound and image together. "Just so happens, I've got my own self-portrait."

Jean took a slow step forward, eyes flicking over the tattoo.

He continued, "I learned early that love is for suckers. Just one of those lessons that took all this time to finally click. From this point on, I will forever be sucka free"

Jean's face tightened, but she lets him finish. "Besides, my momma warned me. Said love ain't nothin' but a divine distraction. Something God put here to test how bad you really want to reach your goals."

He tapped his temple. "Took me thirty-something years, a kingdom, a queen, and a museum exhibit to finally hear her right." Jean watched him, aching for the man who gave everything away, thinking it would be enough.

James continued softly," I told her once she wasn't allowed to be a muse. She was a monument, a goddamn legend."

He walked past Jean and scoops up a leather folder from the table, flipping it open with ease. Diagrams. Timelines. Phase II of Gemini. "Now the world's seen the Queen through the eyes of a child who mistook lust for legacy."

Jean offered," She didn't know, James. She didn't pose for it."

James shrugged and spoke again. "The camera doesn't care who consented. It only captures what it sees."

He checked the time, then closed the folder with precision. "Reschedule dinner. I want something quieter. No guests. No press."

Jean asked, "Not even Thalia?"

James answered her without missing a beat. "No. Just me" then a pause, "on second thought if she is available extend the invite but don't push"

He walked toward the server room, his silhouette swallowed by the soft-blue hue of tech pulsing around him, then thought to himself, 'You can love someone more than your pride. But never more than your purpose.'

He wasn't mad, wasn't broken, wasn't even pretending anymore. And that terrified him more than rage ever could.

Later that evening at a rooftop lounge in SoCal, soft jazz under stars played, as a glass fire pit crackled low. A bottle of top-shelf bourbon sat half-empty on the table. James leaned back in a low-slung chair, jacket off, sleeves rolled, tie loosened. There's laughter in his voice, and light in his eyes.

Thalia sat beside him: calm, glowing, poised. Her silk wrap dress shifts with every leg cross like it's aware of its own power. She's close, but not clingy. Anchored, not territorial.

They clinked glasses. James said, grinning, "I swear...that last ovation? Sounded like a damn Super Bowl when I watched the recording of the speech on live stream"

Thalia smiled. "You are their quarterback, their king, and their war god, all wrapped into one."

James smiled and sipped his drink again, "Mmm. Don't gas me up. I'm tipsy enough to believe you."

She leaned in, brushing his shoulder. "Oh, I only deal in facts. And you were sovereign."

Suddenly, a voice behind them spoke up, "Well if it isn't two legends in one corner. I didn't know this place served royalty."

They both turned. Ava. Drenched in late-night glow, clad in black and gold, eyes glinting like trouble wrapped in temptation.

James smiled wide, bourbon warming every corner of his grin. "Well shit, Ava. I thought I left you back in LA. Is this an illusion, or am I just that drunk?"

Ava laughed, "Why not both?"

Thalia smiled," Always nice to see another woman who knows how to arrive."

Ava approached, eyes flicking between them. "You two look cozy. Something I walked in on?"

James said, "Nah. Just two grown folks enjoying the spoils of success."

Ava asked Thalia, "You always this composed?"

Thalia responded without blinking, "Only when I know the storm doesn't belong to me yet." Ava lifted a brow. Thalia's tone held no claim, just an elegant, dangerous 'maybe.'

James chuckled, swirling his bourbon. "Y'all trying to out-queen each other, while I'm over here just trying to survive being this pretty?" They all laugh.

Then a quiet settles between them. Electric. Thalia leaned in slightly, to Ava, "Freedom is the foundation of my kingdom. Loyalty is the currency. And pleasure…well…that's the crown." She sipped her wine.

Thalia's silky voice continued to Ava, "If you ever play your cards right, maybe one day, you'll get a taste of royalty too."

Ava lets the words hang in the air. "Well, damn. And here I was thinking I just came for a drink."

James leaned back, eyes closed with a grin, "Y'all are dangerous. I'm sitting between a storm and a sunrise."

Thalia smiled at him, "That's the point, my King. You were born to rule, but also to be worshipped."

James looked between them, eyes glassy but clear. "All my life I was taught to protect, provide, please. No one ever told me I deserved all of that back."

He raised his glass, "To building a kingdom where I am the pleasure. No compromise."

Thalia clinked, "To a crown that fits both your mind, and your mouth."

Ava finished her drink. "Well, if this is what power looks like, I might just submit for once."

Ava lingered beside their table for a beat longer, just as James finishes another sip of bourbon. He looked up, still grinning. "Before you go, I owe you an apology, seriously."

Ava raised an eyebrow, surprised.

James continued on, "For how I treated you. I was colder than I needed to be. Messy too. You didn't deserve that."

Ava looked at him a moment, expression shifting. "Thank you. That actually means something." She stepped closer, eyes playful, "But, I should probably apologize too."

James looked surprised, "For what?"

Ava grinned, "Because I lied to you. This pussy? Open and Juicy. Could've handled anything."

Thalia bursted into rich, stunned laughter. James laughed too, loud and honest and uninhibited. They all raised their glasses once more and James said, "To bold confessions…"

Ava added, "To thicker truths."

Thalia offered, "To men who learn how to rule…and how to receive." They clinked again, then she kissed the rim of her wine glass, watching the stars, and thought to herself, 'And only one ever learns to wait.'

Ava started to walk away, but paused and looked at both of them, "Don't be strangers." Thalia watched her go, expression unreadable. James leaned back again, a slow smile forming. "You know she's thinking about it. They all do, but only a few are worthy."

They didn't dare hope too loud. Not yet. But, in the stillness of the night, he felt it. The quiet making of a new kind of King. One who had mastered war, grace, and the art of ruling, and did it with a beautiful, knowing smile.

Chapter 14: Flesh and Fortune

The morning didn't arrive with sunlight. It arrived with flashes: camera shutters outside the lobby, reporters huddled like wolves just beyond the glass. Their breath fogged the clean windows of Ellie's downtown high-rise like the city itself was holding its breath.

Danielle was already waiting in the private elevator, hair pinned, voice sharp as she buzzed through media security on her Bluetooth. "No, I said back them off. The artist is the story. The woman is not the headline. There will be no comment."

She turned just as Ellie stepped in: dark sunglasses on, lips bare, hair twisted back like she didn't have the strength to wear it wild today.

Danielle went softer now, "They're vultures. But we knew they'd come."

Ellie said nothing, just breathed.

Twenty minutes later in the 34th floor conference lounge, the press release was already on the screen when they walked in. Danielle had it queued up on the projector in the private boardroom.

Headline: *From Muse to Movement: Zion Tate's NFT Collection Sells Out in 3 Minutes*. Image: Ellie's back: curved, golden, stripped of identity but not of intimacy. The replica painting. Sold. Licensed. Distributed. And now…forever.

Danielle looked at Ellie, waiting for the explosion. But there wasn't one. Instead, Ellie walked to the window, her arms folded tight. Then said quietly, "Do you know what it's like to be remembered for a moment you never agreed to exist?"

Danielle's heart cracked, "I'll bury it. Legal's ready. PR's already scrubbing. You want silence? We'll silence him."

Ellie shook her head. Just once." Let them see it. Let them look. Let them wonder."

Danielle became angry, "You can't keep letting people peel pieces off you and call it art."

Ellie turned, her eyes not red, but darker than usual. Heavy. "I just want to walk into a room without people knowing how I moaned for a man I never loved."

Ellie reflected on a time many years ago: The air was thick with weed and bad decisions. A cramped apartment in Inglewood. Heat sticking to the blinds. Music low and bass-heavy in the background.

Ellie was curled in her boyfriend Khalil's lap, freshly out of her first dorm room, and freshly in love with the wrong man. He grinned, "Yo, let me get just one shot of you like that. Look up at me real slow. That's it."

She laughed, nervous, half flattered. But he looked at her like she was a goddess and she wanted to be worshipped.

The photos came first. Her bare thighs, her lips parted. A slow striptease across old sheets and pillowcases that smelled like smoke and cologne. Then came the video.

He asked. She said yes. She wanted to please him, to trust someone. She straddled him, breathless and uninhibited. They laughed. They moaned. He whispered, "This is just for me, Queen. You my lil 'secret." She let him keep it.

Three days later, her phone rang non-stop. Girls from her classes were whispering. Guys were texting. Someone had transferred the video to a disc. Someone else had shared it during a campus party.

By the end of the weekend, everyone had seen it. No context, no apology. Just Ellie: nude, exposed, and riding a boy who didn't know what to do with a woman.

Classmates snickered, a cousin called. Her mother stood in the doorway that night, silent, face pale, rosary in hand.

Ellie didn't leave her bed for two days. By the end of the week, she'd changed her number, disconnected her laptop, and skipped every lecture She never dropped out, but she learned two things: Intimacy can be weaponized, and once the world sees you naked, they think they own what's underneath.

Snapping back to today, she sat in the conference lounge and thought about how the echo returned today. Through Zion, the painting, and the applause of people who called it art, when all she could see was another betrayal wrapped in brushstrokes.

Danielle broke the silence. "You want to fight this or own it?"

Ellie responded quietly, "Neither. I want it to disappear."

Danielle said gently, "That's not an option anymore."

Then came a knock at the door. An intern from the agency peeked in, clipboard in hand. "Miss Elena, the investment group from Tokyo is early. They're in the conference lounge."

Ellie nodded slowly, then asked Danielle, "How do I look?"

Danielle answered, "Like a woman about to teach them why you still wear the damn crown."

Ellie nodded, then walked out making her way to the conference lounge. As she stood at the head of the table, every CEO and investor seated with a translator, notebooks open. She spoke clearly with poise and command.

But somewhere between her third slide, and the market performance forecast, her voice cracked. Just once. Mid-sentence. Subtle, but undeniable. A pause. A breath. Then she continued. No one said anything, but everyone noticed.

Later on, in her office, the door closed behind her. Danielle followed quietly. Ellie sank into the couch. Finally, she let the sunglasses slide from her face. She stared out the window again. The crown hadn't slipped. But for the first time, it felt heavy in her hands.

———

In SoCal, the Gemini boardroom wasn't flashy. It was a weapon. Black marble, matte brass fixtures, custom ergonomic chairs. Tech-heavy, clean, and utterly without distraction. Just like the man currently commanding it.

James stood at the head of the long table, sleeves rolled, voice calm, eyes sharper than any knife in the room.

Twelve department leads, two founders, one CEO. And not a single person who dared interrupt him.

Behind him, the wall glowed with schematics. Project Gemini – Phase II. A digital empire in the making, designed not just to protect data, but to dominate the future of digital identity, surveillance, and legacy.

James spoke evenly, "We don't just protect corporations. We future-proof them. We are the wall before the threat, not the cleanup crew after it hits."

He tapped once on the remote. Diagrams shifted. Infrastructure expanded. Global market overlays appeared. "Phase II will require full-spectrum control: AI-backed anomaly detection, zero-trust authentication, and adaptive signal intercept systems. This isn't about paranoia. It's about sovereignty."

The room stayed silent. James turned slowly. "Gemini will be the shield and the sword. And when it's finished…there won't be a fortress in the world stronger than the one we build here."

He clicked off the screen. The room stayed breathless. Until the CEO of Gemini stood and walked over, extending his hand. "Dr. King. I'd like to make this official." James raised a brow.

The CEO smiled, "Seven figures. Base salary. Equity in Gemini. Full strategic partnership. We want you here. Permanently."

A few murmurs rippled through the team. James didn't rush to respond. He adjusted his cuff, nodded once. "I'll consider the offer."

Outside the boardroom, moments later Jean fell in beside him, matching his stride down the long hallway toward the executive lounge. Her expression was proud. Controlled.

But beneath the surface, a crack was forming. Jean quietly said," That was clean. Ruthless. Precise."

James responded without looking at her, "Thank you."

Jean said,: "And that offer…" He didn't say a word.

Jean continued softer, "So, it's real now. You're not just consulting. You're building again. We need bourbon, Beyoncé, and possibly an exorcist," Jean said. "In that order."

James finally met her eyes, "What else was I gonna do, Jean? Watch one kingdom burn and not prepare for the next?"

That hit her harder than she let him see. He disappeared into the lounge, leaving Jean standing alone in the corridor, iPad clutched to her chest. She tapped out a text to Danielle: *He got the offer. Seven figures. Equity. Strategic partner. He's not spiraling. He's building another throne.*

———

Elsewhere in the city, Zion sat at the center of a swanky downtown gallery, sunglasses on, surrounded by buyers and culture critics. People were fawning, Tweeting, quoting him. His phone wouldn't stop buzzing.

Articles asked about his "intentions." Forums accusing him of revenge porn dressed as expressionism. Legal experts weighing in on Ellie's potential countersuit. A text from his agent read: *Be careful. This fire can burn both ways.*

Zion scoffed. Then saw the new alert pop on his screen: *Controversial Artist Zion Tate Named in Ethics Inquiry Over Unlicensed Image Distribution.* He stopped scrolling, the smile faded, and for the first time, his jaw tightened. Not in arrogance, but in unease.

While the Queen stood in silence, the King forged a new castle in the fire. And the court jester who thought himself a god was learning that some storms are drawn by hand, but some come for you on their own.

———

Dinner had been soft. Ken cooked. Ellie watched him move in the kitchen, appreciating the domestic ease he brought with him. His wine selection was thoughtful. His laugh was warm. His hands were gentle.

It should've been perfect. They talked about travel, family, and poetry. He even quoted something by Baldwin that made her close her eyes for a second and think, 'maybe.' But when he leaned in to kiss her on the couch, it felt safe. Too safe.

Later, in his bedroom, Ken made love like a man with time. His lips traced her collarbone. His hands moved reverently over her body. He whispered affirmations between kisses, and told her she was soft, divine, resilient. Like he was blessing her, not fucking her.

And at first, she let it happen. Closed her eyes. Let his rhythm slow her pulse. But then, her breathing shifted. Her hips moved faster than he was offering. She opened her eyes, and suddenly, she wasn't in the room anymore.

A fantasy entered her mind where Camila joined them: She knelt at the edge of the bed, hair loose, eyes daring. Her lips parted as she crawled forward. She purred softly, "Don't let him lead you. You don't need peace, Ellie. You need fire."

Ellie moaned under Ken, but her gaze was locked on the image of Camila, her imaginary hands sliding over Ellie's hips, cupping her from behind. Camila leaned in, whispering as she kissed Ellie's spine, as she said, "Take it. Show them you're still the Queen. Still the one who owns every gasp in the room."

In reality, Ken was still making love to her like she was fragile. But in her mind, Camila kissed the back of her neck, reached around, and grabbed her throat, tight enough to thrill, loose enough to tempt.

Ellie whispered, "Yes…" and rolled him over.

Ken blinked, surprised, then said softly, "Ellie—"

Ellie commanded, "No."

She pinned him beneath her and rode him like a queen mounting a throne, not for connection, but for domination. She imagined Camila behind her again, now naked, tongue trailing fire between Ellie's shoulder blades.

Ellie moaned louder. Bit her own lip, and began to tremble. She pictured Camila breathing in her ear, "Let him drown. You deserve to finish on your terms."

Ken said gently to her," You're not here with me."

Ellie gasped, "Shut the fuck up and drink." He blinked, confused.

She grabbed the back of his head and forced him lower.

Ken muffled, "Ellie—"

Slap. She hit him. Not hard, but hard enough. Her voice cracked," Just shut up. Please. Just, please." She came violently.

Her eyes still closed. Camila still whispering in her mind. But when the wave crashed, the vision vanished. And all that was left was Ken staring up at her. Confused, ashamed, visibly hurt.

She stood, grabbed her robe with trembling fingers and barely audibly said, "I'm so sorry."

Ken was still seated and stunned." Ellie…"

"No. Don't say anything." She backed away like she was leaving a crime scene, didn't put on her shoes, just grabbed her purse and left barefoot. The elevator ride down felt like a funeral. She got into her car and didn't even bother turning on music.

By the time she hit the freeway, her hands were shaking and the tears finally came. She thought to herself, 'I'm not who I used to be. But I don't know who I am now either.'

She pulled into her driveway with mascara streaked down her cheeks and the taste of bitterness on her tongue. She gripped the steering wheel for 23 straight minutes before moving.

Then finally whispered: "God, I miss who I was with him."

———

At a club on the other side of the city, the night was champagne and ego. Zion leaned back in a corner booth at EJC's, a posh rooftop club in West Hollywood, dressed in a sleeveless designer turtleneck, iced-out ring on every finger, surrounded by his latest fans.

Two influencers were hanging on his every word. A producer offered to connect him with a gallery in London. A model from Prague whispered something filthy in his ear.

He laughed and waved the bottle of Dom Perignon for another round, and chuckled to the server," Keep it flowing. It's all legacy, baby."

More laughter. More flashing lights. Until the check came.

The server seemed apologetic, "Sir, your card's been declined."

Zion blinked, drunk and confused. "Run it again." They did. Again, declined.

He pulled out his phone and opened his banking app, staring at the balance: -$437.00

His drunken grin slowly faded. Then immediately he received a long text from his lawyer:

Zion, we have a serious problem. You publicly referenced exposure and used her name during a recorded panel. That gave her team legal leverage to seize proceeds from the initial portrait and NFT run.

They've filed an injunction and started asset freeze protocols under civil code. It's airtight. You brought up the sex. The consent is now a legal weapon.

Also, I just found out she hired Mark Spade. Yes, THAT Spade. Start apologizing. Immediately.

He dropped the phone. The champagne he'd just swallowed turned bitter in his throat. He whispered to himself, "No fucking way." He looked around. The crowd still laughed, still drank, still danced. But it all felt a mile away.

He wasn't the artist tonight. He was the target. The last image in his mind before blacking out was Ellie's portrait, and the fact that it no longer belonged to him. Shortly after, Zion laid unconscious in the back of a black SUV, two men from his label dragging him to a hotel under an alias.

———

As the night continued for others, Jean was sitting in her Gemini office, heels off, feet on the desk, swirling a glass of red wine. The skyline glows behind her, cold, calculating beauty.

Danielle was at home in sweats and a comfortable tee with her laptop open, glowing with receipts, eating dried mangoes and sipping a ginger mule through a gold straw.

The call connected. No greetings, just war energy. And Jean said, "You look way too comfortable to be sitting on that kind of intel."

Danielle smirked, "Oh, baby…I'm not sitting on it. I'm sitting in it. Zion's shit just went from scandal to soap opera."

Jean said, "Talk to me."

Danielle scrolled through her phone. "Ellie's lawyer sent Spade everything. Threats, screenshots, post timestamps, phone logs. All of it. Said it was 'so clean it could frame itself'."

Jean nearly spit out her wine. "Wait. Spade as in Mark Spade?"

Danielle grinned. "THE Spade. The legal grim reaper. Pro bono."

Jean replied, "Jesus. Zion better not even breathe around an ATM."

Danielle said, "He can't. Spade already seized all his money. Accounts frozen. Royalties paused. NFT payments rerouted. I even heard his card got declined at a posh club."

Jean gasped, as Danielle continued, "Yup. Server ran it three times. Zion had to check his phone in front of influencers. Found out exactly how hard we go around here."

Jean smiled, "Good. He wanted to turn her into a trophy. Now he's watching the case get engraved with his name."

Danielle leaned back, "And the scary part is, Ellie didn't even ask for blood. She just asked for it to stop. That's why Spade stepped in."

Jean added, "He saw a queen being hunted."

A pause. Both women drink at the same time, their sync effortless.

Jean softly spoke again, "He's really building it without her, D."

Danielle knew she was talking now about James, and quickly replied, "I know."

"Gemini made him an offer. Seven figures. Equity. Full strategic partnership. Permanent," Jean said.

Danielle was stunned and said simply, "Damn."

Jean went on. "I told myself it didn't mean anything. But when he said he'd consider it…"

Danielle quietly offered, "You knew."

Jean agreed. "He's not spiraling. He's reconstructing."

Danielle finished her drink. "And she's still unraveling."

A silence stretched between them. Not judgment, just the painful truth.

"They built so much together, but he'll hand her every piece if she asks. She just has to stop hurting him first." Jean noted.

Danielle replied, "She doesn't even know she's still holding the knife."

Jean countered, "But Spade does. So now the vultures are clipped."

"What's next then? We stay out of it?" Danielle was unsure of their next move.

Jean shook her head. "We maneuver. Let the fire burn down. But when it's time…"

Danielle finished the thought, "…we'll have the foundation ready."

Jean smiled and raising her glass, "To the court."

Danielle toasted with her straw, "To the quiet ones who never left the throne room."

That evening, in James's office the night was still. Only the glow from the city beyond the glass and the low hum of Gemini's standby servers keep the darkness from swallowing the room whole.

Jean sat at James's desk, organizing the last few documents for his morning meetings. She wasn't snooping, just managing. Her fingers danced across keys, updating permissions and syncing project folders.

Until something caught her eye. A document, tucked deep in a personal directory she never touches. It's not labeled as anything official. Just the date: *1/19*. No subject, no header. Just content. Jean clicks it. And reads: *1-19*

My last breath approaching, can't believe what I'm saying.
All I can do is say to God, "I know You see me down here praying.

How are You just gonna act like I ain't there?
Shit, You watched Your own son die, so I guess this is fair

I guess I should believe and have some faith
My heart is beating so fast; this ain't heaven I taste

I close my eyes tight, though my mind says keep them open,
But every time I do, I see what can't be spoken

Death looks like death combined with an angry small child,
With a million insects and animals that live in the wild Death smells like a bed of roses covered with large dead flies,
Hard to imagine how fast time flies

Don't paint a rosy picture as you speak kind words at my eulogy,
Just remember me screaming for help, saying, "Look at how you're doing me."

Something wicked this way comes,
Or is it the cocktail of pills and weed going down with the rum?

Lay down and die, or shut up and live,
Like damn, motherfucker, those are the only options you give?

Fuck it. Then kill me, then again, nah. Death, you can't have me
Who will find my body lying here first, screaming out, "Oh my God, what a tragedy?"

Wake up, wake up, someone call 911.
Sorry, can't you smell the death all over my body? This thing is done

I'll find a cool place for you somewhere in this fire,
Part of me is saying 'fuck I't because my ass is so damn tired Tired of being strong,

tired of hiding in plain sight,
Tired of fighting what some would call the "Good Christian fight."

Ever wonder why there are so many animals tied to the devil,
Ever wonder why we have to get high to go to another level?

Ever wonder what drives someone to take their own life,
Ever see something so dangerous, you find yourself asking to roll the dice?

Am I high, or did my brother and sister just hug me,
Did my grandmother just tell me that everybody loves me?

Did my grandfather just tell me to get myself up,
Did I really just look in his dark black eyes and say 'I don't give a fuck'?

How am I writing, when I should be texting for help
Maybe I don't want any 'cause no one can relate to how I may have felt Or how
they make me feel, or how that creates hurt
I remember my whole plan was once to buy a Versace shirt

To buy a nice car, and to buy a nice house
Only to be empty inside and full of self-doubt

I'm dying, and I can feel it; what will my last words be,
I lived for everyone else; now fuck you, I'm free.

Jean doesn't breathe. The silence in the room turns surgical, cutting straight through her ribcage. She sat alone at the desk, wine in hand. The glow of Gemini's Phase II interface danced on the glass wall behind her.

She stared at the crown he now wore, and not the one Ellie gave him. The one he forged in blood, ink, and silence.

Jean thought to herself, 'You almost left us. And no one even saw it coming. Except me…now.'

She looked down at her reflection in the black glass of the desk, then whispered, "They think I'm his assistant. But I'm the last knight left at this table. And I don't fucking fold."

———

The morning sun had barely stretched across the glass of James's penthouse office when his phone buzzed. A text from Thalia: *Does it fit?*

He snapped a photo of his pinky, the ring resting snug and cool. A brushed silver band with an obsidian center, engraved inside with: *You are the kingdom. Not the weapon.*

He called her, and as she answered, he said, "I love the ring."

Thalia smiled through the phone. "I meant every word. It's not a leash. Just… acknowledgment. You don't owe me anything."

James countered, "But I do. You've been a force. Kept me from falling all the way off."

Thalia said, lightly teasing, "Well, I had help from bourbon and clean sheets."

James laughed. "Still. I'm completely drained, in the best ways."

Thalia's voice became sultry, "Speaking of…I thought of you this morning."

James smiled, "Did you now?"

He looked at his phone and, damn. Three pictures. Nothing explicit, just suggestion: Her hand in her thighs, nails red; Her back arched in silk; A mirror pic of her bare, only his ring visible on her finger.

"Something to keep your mind stimulated," she teased.

James's voice started softly, then began to roughen, "I'm very, very inspired."

Thalia asked breathily, "So, should I expect you tonight?"

James didn't answer immediately. He let the moment breathe. "No. A car's picking you up tonight. Pack a bag."

Thalia: "Oh?"

James replied, in a mock-serious tone. "It's time you see my place."

Thalia was already smiling. "Mmm…I must warn you, King, if I come, I'm not just packing a bag, I'm bringing intention."

James paused dramatically. Then dropped into full Eddie Murphy-Hakeem voice, "I must warn you, my apartment is very, very poor."

Thalia laughed without missing a beat, "Hakeem, if I wanted to be with someone with money, I'd be with Darrayl. Not with you."

They both laughed, deep, rich, and completely unscripted.

Jean was watching from the doorway, and whispered to herself, "Damn. This bitch is a diabolical love villain. I need to get in her master class."

Thalia ended the call and sat in silence, letting the heat swirl low in her belly. She stood, stretched, and turned toward her closet like a woman preparing for to receive a king. Then said to herself, smiling, "Tonight, we reset the throne."

She packed with elegance and fire in equal measure. She wasn't showing up to be seen. She was arriving to be remembered.

———

Danielle and Ellie stepped into the marble lobby of the law firm, heels, confidence, and coffee in hand. Danielle said, "They said to go to the twelfth floor, and someone would meet us. Be cool."

Ellie replied, "I'm always cool."

"Girl, last time you said that, we had to bribe hotel security," Danielle teased.

They both smiled. But Ellie's breath caught when she stepped off the elevator and saw him. Back turned, hands in his pockets, that stature, that posture.

Danielle said in a hushed tone, "Whoever he is…damn."

Ellie's lawyer appeared, carrying two iced lattes. I brought your favorite. Caramel almond milk, right?"

They both took their drinks as the man turned. Mark Spade. It was him, the one from the club. The one whose body Ellie could still trace with her eyes closed. She nearly choked on her first sip. Mark said calmly and composed, "It's a pleasure to finally meet you. I'm Mark Spade."

Ellie caught herself fast, "Pleasure's mine, Mr. Spade."

Mark smiled. "Please. Call me Mark."

Danielle watched Ellie closely, and thought, 'Is she really wrapping this man up right now?'

Mark's eyes didn't wander, but there was an energy, one both Ellie and Danielle clocked instantly.

Ellie lifted her chin, "Thank you for moving so fast. I wasn't expecting this kind of turnaround."

Mark replied, "I don't enjoy seeing a Queen with a damaged crown."

His voice was smooth. Just loud enough for Ellie, just low enough to make Danielle squint in suspicion. Mark continued," My PR division is finalizing the NFT fallout and cleaning up any digital leak points. Zion's attorneys are backpedaling so fast they're tripping over their own exhibits."

Ellie raised a brow, "That quick?"

Mark smirked. "When it comes to your name, Ellie, I don't play chess. I knock the damn board over."

He turned to leave but paused. Handed her a small card. "Careful not to spill your coffee, mine was spilled on me once and, ouch." And just like that, he was gone.

Danielle leaned in and whispered, "Okay but like, who the hell is he? And how did you just flirt with him like that in a law office?"

Ellie was breathless and laughing, "Long story. Also, do not Google him."

Danielle replied, "Oh, it's already too late."

The King didn't fold, he simply chose a different game. The Queen didn't run, she just stopped explaining her throne. And somewhere between bourbon and bodyguards: Two people who once ruled together were becoming rulers in their own right. But fate has a funny way of reminding you who you crowned first.

Chapter 15: England and Spain

James had left the door unlocked. Not because he was careless, but because he didn't need locks where trust lived. Thalia stepped into his penthouse like she wasn't visiting but arriving home. She didn't wander, didn't snoop. She studied silently, thoroughly and respectfully.

A bottle of cologne she hadn't seen before sat on the bathroom counter, masculine but elegant. His cufflinks were still aligned in their tray. His desk had a fresh Gemini folder resting atop a closed laptop.

And on the bookshelf, a photo. James and Ellie, captured in black and white, mid-laugh. Her head tilted back, his hand resting on the small of her back.

Thalia didn't flinch. She paused only long enough to smile. Not bitter, but reverent. She wasn't pretending the past didn't matter. She was here to write the future.

She placed her bag on the bench at the foot of his bed, peeled off her heels, and slowly undressed. Silk slipping down bronze curves, hips swaying with a grace even the silence bowed to.

She stepped into the bathroom and turned the water hot, just shy of unbearable. In the mirror, she studied herself. Full breasts, high cheekbones, lips that curved like promises. Hair piled loosely, collarbone glistening in the rising steam.

Thalia said softly, to her reflection, "Not one of many. The one who stayed." She stepped into the shower. The water kissed every inch of her skin, down the arch of her spine, grazing her thighs, over her shoulders like anointed oil. She soaped slowly, luxuriously, like preparing herself wasn't hygiene, it was ritual.

As she rinsed, she imagined it: James entering the apartment, loosening his tie, and setting down his keys. Then finding her. Bare, soft, waiting. With wine poured and a quiet smile that said, "I'm yours. The world can wait."

She pictured him kissing her neck from behind, inhaling the jasmine scent still clinging to her. His voice low, grateful. Her body shivered. Tonight, she would remind him. She wasn't just here to rest beside a king. She was here to bless the throne.

——

Jean was home and sat barefoot in a silk robe, scrolling through a private Gemini executive brief. The screen glowed with a signature line in gold font: *James King – Principal Advisor & Permanent Partner (Pending Terms)* Jean exhaled. Scrolled to the footnotes: *Clause 9c: Appointment of Jean Richardson. as COO – full strategic access and executive authority. Salary to exceed prior base by 4x, immediate retroactive equity vestment upon contract ratification.*

She didn't smile, not really. She picked up her phone and hit Danielle's contact and initiated a video call. Danielle was lounging in leggings and a tank, sipping from a wine tumbler, her lashes still intact.

Jean said flatly, "I think it's permanent."

Danielle paused mid-sip, "Like…permanent permanent?"

Jean nodded. "He listed me as COO. Big pay bump. No wiggle room. That man has no intention of circling back."

Danielle sat forward, now focused.

Jean said quietly, "I think I'm giving up, D."

Danielle asked, "Giving up what?"

"On the kingdom we tried to save." She closed her laptop gently. Then Jean sighed. "It's like James is England, and Ellie is Spain. Both strong. Both proud. They just don't answer to each other anymore."

Danielle didn't speak for a beat. Then said softly, "Can I tell you something you probably won't like?"

Jean smirked, "Always."

Danielle continued reluctantly, "Mark Spade might've lit something in her. I haven't seen Ellie with this much fire since, honestly, maybe ever."

Jean laughed lightly, "Don't tell me you're Team Spade now."

Danielle shrugged, "I'm team 'let her win again.' However that has to happen."

They both went quiet. And in that silence, no bitterness. Just acceptance. After a pause, Jean raised her tumbler "To new kingdoms."

Danielle raised hers: "And a new court." They clinked glasses through the screen.

One Queen lay her claim not through seduction, but through presence. One court stepped down from the battlefield, not in defeat, but in grace.

And two empires that once warred together, began to rise apart.

———

Ellie was sitting in her office, eyes on the screen, reviewing the countless emails and documents from Mark Spade's team. Her phone buzzed softly against the glass desk.

Mark Spade: *I know we just met formally but I really need a date for this gala. Would you consider it? Please forgive me if it comes off as too presumptuous.*

Ellie paused. She hadn't even thought about the upcoming gala. She smiled slightly to herself as she typed a quick reply: *Not presumptuous. Bold, maybe.*

Mark: *Bold, I can handle. I actually wanted to take a moment to apologize for that day at the coffee shop. You were right about me. I tend to carry arrogance and confidence as armor.*

Ellie leaned back, her lips curving slightly. She typed back quickly: *It wasn't my best day. I may have been a bit harsh.*

Mark: *Harsh is honest. Honest is rare. I appreciate both.*

She felt a gentle flush warming her cheeks, smiling despite herself. Before she could respond, another message arrived.

Mark: *I'm lucky you didn't dismiss me entirely.*

Ellie laughed inside at the thought of Ava using the word, *lucky*. She shook her head as she typed swiftly. *Please don't ever say that fucking word again.*

Mark: *Noted. Now formally, would you do me the honor of joining me at the gala? Feel free to bring Boss...Danielle, was it?*

Ellie: *Bringing me out in public has its disadvantages.*

Mark: *Who said anything about public? I thrive on discretion.*

A shiver of intrigue ran through her, a soft ache blooming in her core as she read his words, seeing elements of James in the subtle flirtation and assuredness. She paused for just a moment, savoring the sensation before replying. But it wasn't James. And maybe that was the point.

Ellie: *Then I accept. Danielle will come too. She'd never forgive me otherwise.*

Mark: *Then it's settled. I'll handle everything.*

Ellie exhaled slowly, setting her phone aside with a soft smile, warmth pooling in places long left untouched.

"So, we're officially going," Ellie announced to Danielle, who had just entered her office carrying paperwork.

Danielle's eyes widened with excitement. "With Mark Spade? The mysterious legal assassin? Girl, this is getting spicy."

Ellie laughed, shaking her head. "Calm down. He's intriguing. And yes, it's him."

"Well, at least you're finally intrigued again," Danielle said, eyebrow raised knowingly. "But we better make sure Jean tells James. He doesn't need to find out from someone else."

Ellie nodded slowly, expression neutral but thoughtful. "You're right. Better from us than from some random."

Danielle quickly grabbed her phone and sent a swift message to Jean: *Gala confirmed with Spade. Tell James please. Let's not have surprises.*

Jean's reply came swiftly: *Understood. I'll handle it.*

As James gathered his belongings to leave the office for his evening with Thalia, Jean stood at the doorway, eyes steady but clearly hesitant.

"James, hold up a sec," Jean started, clearing her throat.

He turned, raising an eyebrow in question. "What's up?"

"Ellie's going to the Legal Gala, with Mark Spade," Jean said directly, watching his face carefully for any hint of reaction.

James absorbed the news, expression remaining calm and controlled. "I've never met the man, but good for her. She deserves to come out on top after all the Zion mess. I even offered to help handle it; she refused, so clearly she's capable."

Jean nodded, still assessing him. "You know, you have an invite to that gala too, considering all your cyber and AI connections. I can decline it if you prefer."

James shook his head softly, meeting her gaze directly. "Nah, I'll go. If we're both truly moving forward, it shouldn't bother either of us."

Jean sighed softly. "Look, you both got destroyed—" she paused, mumbling softly, "—over bullshit. But you both made your way back, proving no one made the other. You're both still King and Queen, and all that rich bullshit."

James laughed lightly, amusement lighting his features. "Jean, I genuinely like Thalia. She'll never replace Ellie because no one replaces anyone. It's about having the power to let power go and stop fighting for something that's no longer yours."

Jean shook her head in mock frustration. "But you two were meant, damn it. You rich motherfuckers be making up your problems. This is straight-up 'Love and Hip Hop' for people that actually got money."

James laughed deeply now, "You're too much, Jean. But seriously, I'm going. Besides yourself, just make sure I'm allowed a plus one."

Jean rolled her eyes dramatically. "Damn, James," she sighed with exaggerated resignation. "Will do."

James drove toward his place with one hand on the wheel and the other resting lightly over his thigh. The city lights blurred beside him, but his thoughts were crystalline. For the first time in a long time, he felt clarity. He was moving forward. Maybe not yet healed. Maybe not yet whole. But forward, nonetheless.

Thalia was waiting for him at his place. She had texted earlier that she would be ready for whatever he had planned and dressed accordingly. That thought made him smirk.

He pulled up, grabbed the paper bags of groceries, and stepped into the building. As the elevator climbed, he exhaled, releasing more of the weight he'd carried for far too long.

When the doors opened, she was there. Thalia stood near the window in a form-fitting, wine-red dress that clung like a second skin. Her long hair fell softly over her shoulders, her heels sculpting her already flawless legs.

James whistled low. "Damn, woman. You trying to take me out before dinner?"

She grinned. "Well, if I knew dinner was optional…"

He held up the bags. "I came to cook, but seeing you like this, maybe we should go out instead."

Thalia stepped forward, placing a gentle hand on his chest. "No. Stay in. Show me what you've got planned in the kitchen, Chef King."

James chuckled, setting the bags down. "Okay, but I'm warning you, it might get ugly."

He pulled off his shirt and handed it to her. "Here. Get comfortable."

She didn't hesitate. With the grace of a woman who knew exactly what she was doing, she unzipped her dress and let it fall to the floor in a silken puddle. Wearing nothing else but her heels, she slipped into his oversized shirt. It swallowed her up and she inhaled deeply like it was oxygen itself.

"Smells like sin and safety," she murmured.

James, shirtless and humming, moved into the kitchen. He turned on a smooth jazz playlist, the saxophone curling around the room like smoke, and started unpacking ingredients.

Thalia leaned against the island, watching every flex of his back as he moved. Then it hit her, a smell that stopped her breath.

"Wait…" she said, stepping forward. "What are you making?"

James turned to her with a playful smirk. "Σου φτιάχνω μελιτζάνα, όμορφη ελληνική θεά μου." ("I'm making moussaka for you, my beautiful Greek goddess.") Her eyes sparkled. "Ξέρεις να μιλάς Ελληνικά;" ("You know how to speak Greek?")

James winked. "Φυσικά, αγάπη μου. Είμαι άνθρωπος των θαυμάτων και του κόσμου." ("Of course, my love. I am a man of marvels and world travel.") and laughed. She was smitten. And soaked.

As James stirred the pan, he glanced at her. "I was invited to a gala next weekend. I'd love for you to come with me."

Thalia asked, "Formal?"

"Black tie. Jean says there will be press, and big names…including Ellie."

She held his gaze. "Do you want me to say no?"

"No," he said sincerely. "But I want to be transparent. I must be sure the fire is gone. Not because of you, but because of me."

He turned away for a moment, then added in Greek, "Πρέπει να ξέρω πριν χτίσω το νέο μου βασίλειο, με εσένα ή μόνος μου." ("I need to know before I build my new kingdom, with you or alone.") She stepped closer, hands brushing his waist. "Take what time you need. I'm not expecting you to have no feelings left. You're human…an incredible one. And feelings don't leave us just because we want them to."

Her voice dipped to a whisper. "But I'll shine for you. Shine to match the glow of your kingdom."

Then, even softer to herself, "And when I'm done, even a Queen will know she's no match for a King…and his soon-to-be Queen." Thalia turned, phone in hand, texting back and forth, her smile one of playful satisfaction.

James set the table with careful precision, plating the dish with practiced hands. But Thalia couldn't wait another moment. She rose, barefoot, the oversized shirt brushing mid-thigh, her eyes locked on his. "Forget dinner," she whispered. "I want you now, my King."

Their lips met with searing heat, her body melting into his as they collided with purpose. She pulled him toward the couch, unbuttoning the last few buttons of his pants, moaning into his mouth as he lifted her in one swift motion.

The shirt was the only thing separating them, his scent on her skin, his breath now at her throat. Her legs wrapped around him instinctively as he sat, pulling her down onto his lap.

Her hands explored his chest, her hips grinding gently against his growing erection, her moans feathering into his ear as she whispered, "Take me."

He didn't hesitate. What followed wasn't just sex. It wasn't just making love. It was a ritual.

Their souls reached for each other in the silence between moans. Each thrust, each gasp, each whispered name carried weight and reverence.

He kissed her as if he were giving thanks. She clung to him as if worshiping. It wasn't a possession, it was permission. It was creation, where forevers begin.

Thalia cried out as she unraveled, her body shuddering with pleasure. James followed, holding her tight, forehead pressed to hers as he gasped her name like a prayer.

They didn't collapse; they settled. Whole. Still. And for a moment, in the quiet after, they both knew: Something just began.

—

The next afternoon after a long day in the office, Jean sat curled on the far end of the leather sectional in James's penthouse, tablet in hand, face drawn in that determined, obsessive mode she got into when something didn't sit right.

"You ever notice how this Mark Spade guy just kinda materialized?" she asked.

James, lounging shirtless in tailored slacks, didn't even glance up from his glass of water. "He's a lawyer. They always slither in when the blood hits the water."

"I'm serious," Jean insisted. "No recent pics. Nothing on social media. The man moves like a shadow. Even his press photos are polished but impersonal. It's giving ghost in Tom Ford."

James chuckled quietly. "Sounds like Ellie's type."

Jean shot him a look. "Okay, rude." She kept scrolling.

"Boom," she finally said, triumphant. "Three years ago. Some charity gala in New York. He was on a panel for equity in the arts. Old archives had a photo."

James didn't even glance her way. "I'm sure he's beautiful."

Jean ignored him. "I mean, yeah. Actually, he kinda is. Tall, clean lines, built like a man who owns a full gym and uses every piece. His beard game is strong too. If I wasn't allergic to drama, I'd say—"

"Jean." James sighed, amused.

"I'm just sayin'. Wanna see?"

"Nah," he waved her off. "You said he's fine, that's enough."

Jean rolled her eyes, then zoomed in on the photo. "Damn. I bet he smells like wealth and judgment. If Ellie shows up on his arm, the press is gonna eat it up."

She angled the tablet his way. "C'mon. Just look. I'm curious if he's got the kinda vibe women fall for, or if I'm just bored."

James took the tablet with a lazy motion. And then instantly froze. His entire body stiffened, glass hovering halfway to his lips.

Jean noticed instantly. "Okay…wow. You good?"

He didn't answer right away. He just stared. Not at the man's suit. Not the beard. Not the easy posture of power. The face of the man in the picture was the same one from the club that night. The one James had bumped into. The one whose coffee he'd knocked out of his hand. The one Ellie had said she didn't know and said was no one.

That moment flashed in his mind: Her eyes darting away, the way her voice caught when she swore it was nothing. I wasn't nothing. It had never been nothing.

Jean watched his face twist into something unreadable. "You…really mad that he's hot?"

James didn't answer. He set the glass down carefully and handed the tablet back like it was fragile.

Jean blinked. "Wait. What just happened?"

James stood up, slowly. He adjusted his waistband, voice even. "Yeah."

But he was lying. Later, alone in his room, James sat at the edge of his bed, fists resting on his knees. The silence was brutal. The ghost she said she didn't know. The stranger she claimed was nothing.

And now he was showing up everywhere: at Ellie's side, in her inner circle, in her goddamn gala plans. James exhaled through his nose. Slow. Controlled. But the rage behind his calm had claws.

Back in the living room, Jean sat with the tablet in her lap, replaying James's reaction. Her smile faded into a frown.

That wasn't jealousy. It was recognition. She didn't know what the hell had just clicked inside him, but she knew one thing for sure.

Mark Spade wasn't just some smooth-ass lawyer anymore. He was a problem. And a problem wearing Ellie's favor was a damn threat.

Chapter 16: Fire or Light

Later, in Thalia's loft, the smell of jasmine, cedar wood, and something ancient clung to the air, soft and sacred. James entered to the echo of Sade playing low from her vinyl setup, the kind of melody that wrapped around your spine instead of your ears.

She greeted him in a silk wrap, barefoot but regal, her thick curls piled atop her head like a coronet. Her skin glowed under candlelight, not from makeup, but intention.

"Take your shoes off," she said softly.

He raised an eyebrow. "Since when do you do house rules?"

"Since you became someone who needed a place to land."

James smirked, then obeyed.

A robe, a fresh towel, and a basin of warm water waited at the foot of her low platform bed. Next to it, a gold-etched bottle of oil. She poured it into the basin, the scent rising instantly: oud, clove, rose.

"What's all this?" he asked.

Thalia looked up slowly. "Preparation."

He didn't push. James wasn't a man who trusted easily, but his body was tired, and his soul quieter in her presence than anywhere else. So he sat.

She knelt, as she washed his feet in silence. Not because he needed cleansing, but because what she was about to do demanded it.

———

Back in LA, Ellie stood at her vanity like it was a battlefield. Danielle sat on the window ledge, sipping white wine and watching her boss try not to look bothered. "He knows," she said, flatly.

"He knows who Mark is. Probably has since earlier tonight. Jean found the photo and—"

"I don't care," Ellie cut in. "I told him that night the man was no one. And he was. Then."

Danielle cocked her head. "But now he's someone?"

Ellie turned, eyes flaring. "I need him to be someone."

Danielle said nothing. Ellie looked away. "James is gone. He made his choice. He sent me into exile, remember?"

Danielle set the glass down. "Girl, you are not exiled. You're just prideful. So is he."

"Good," Ellie snapped. "Let him stay gone. Let him believe I've been sleeping with Mark this whole time. Let him choke on it."

But the edge in her voice was hollow. Even she heard it.

She sat at the edge of her bed, her gown still on the hanger. Her phone buzzed Mark, again. Confirming pickup time. Confirming dinner after the gala. Confirming everything James once would've just known to do without asking. Ellie stared at the screen like it insulted her.

Danielle approached slowly, crouched down, and adjusted Ellie's heel strap. "You don't have to care, El."

"I don't."

"But you also don't have to lie to yourself."

Ellie stayed silent. Her fingers tightened around the phone, but she didn't respond.

——

Back in Thalia's loft, James lay stretched out on the floor cushions in loose linen pants, no shirt, eyes closed as Thalia ran a single line of scented oil down the center of his spine.

"You have forgotten you are royalty," she whispered in Greek. Her tone anchored him.

She placed one hand over his heart, the other over his shoulder blades, as if holding a crown made of silence. "You give. You serve. You build. But when's the last time someone called you to the throne, James?"

She wasn't asking to be worshipped or even offering sex. She was offering remembrance, and it shook him.

Thalia moved slowly around him, lighting a ring of tea lights that matched no religion but honored every sacred thing he carried.

"I have no kingdom to offer you," she said, now in English. "But I offer you this: Tonight, you are not building, not chasing, not performing. You are simply King." James exhaled, eyes still closed, a single tear slipping past his temple without permission.

——

Miles away Ellie zipped up the gown herself trying it on for the gala next weekend. No fanfare. No pretense.

Danielle watched quietly from the side, then finally spoke. "You look like vengeance in couture." Ellie didn't smile. But she didn't need to. As she gathered her purse and headed toward the door, Danielle asked carefully, "If James shows up, and Thalia's with him…"

"She will be," Ellie replied. "And that's fine."

Danielle paused. "You sure about that?"

Ellie turned, looking her assistant square in the eye.

"Thalia's not some groupie. She's smart and elegant. She doesn't just follow, she leads. So no, I'm not worried about her because she's not worthy. I'm worried because she is."

Danielle nodded, respectful.

Ellie adjusted her earrings one last time. "But let's be clear. I'm not going to that gala to fight for James."

"No?" Danielle asked.

"I'm going to let the kingdom see what kind of queen survives when the crown is ripped away."

——

Back at Thalia's loft, James was reclined now, a thin golden sash around his neck that Thalia had placed there without explanation. She kissed his temple, not as a lover, but as a priestess would anoint flesh.

"When you walk in next weekend," she whispered, "walk in like you're not reclaiming anything. Walk in like you never lost it."

But something in his heart still burned. Because even as he surrendered to her care, even as the crown she offered felt weightless on his head, James King knew the truth. He had once given away his throne to a woman who never asked for it. And somehow, he still hadn't gotten it back.

——

Days passed as usual, and the evening of the Midas Foundation Gala finally arrived.

The chandeliers glittered like suspended galaxies. Rich mahogany panels climbed the ballroom walls, and waiters moved in synchronicity across polished marble floors, their silver trays reflecting the kind of wealth that had never known hunger.

The guests had arrived in layers of prestige: legacy names, politicians, cultural titans, heirs, and designers, all dressed like gods pretending to be people. But no one was ready for the coronations tonight.

Ellie and Mark Spade entered. They descended the central staircase slowly, each step echoing as the crowd parted instinctively.

Ellie was poured into emerald silk, high-slit, low back, custom embroidery catching the light like whispers of royalty. Her makeup was sharp and cruel, lips a wine-stained blade. Her expression, 'un-fuck-with-able.'

Mark wore deep navy with black lapels, a single emerald pin at his collar to match her. Minimalist, confident. The kind of man who didn't need to speak when the room was already trying to decipher him.

They didn't just enter. They arrived. Like a kingdom reuniting and fire meeting its twin flame. The whispers started immediately. "Is that Ellie? Is that Mark Spade with her? Since when were they…? God, look at them."

Cameras swiveled. Photographers stepped back without being asked, this was a moment.

Danielle followed two paces behind, wearing midnight-blue velvet and an expression that dared anyone to breathe wrong.

Ellie scanned the crowd once they reached the ballroom floor. Her body language screamed, "You are witnessing a rebirth." Inside, she kept repeating the mantra, "Bury him. Let him rot in what he believes." She was armored. Untouchable.

Everything slowed. The music changed, subtle, almost imperceptible at first. Strings dropped into a lower register. Lighting adjusted slightly, casting a faint golden hue on the entrance archway. James King entered. Time didn't stop, but it bent around him.

He was midnight in motion. A black tuxedo tailored to strangle the soul. Skin aglow with the bronze hue of self-forged power. He didn't smile, didn't posture. He walked with the exact energy of a man who had nothing to prove, because the proof was walking beside him.

Thalia floated in ivory silk, structured, statuesque, and devastating. A woman who looked like she wrote peace treaties in blood and scented oil. One hand rested on James's arm like it belonged there, like she had guided him through fire and placed the crown on his head herself.

But it was the second figure on his other arm that detonated the room.

Ava. Her red gown slit to the hip. Diamond chain draped across her bare back. Hair slicked and pulled tight, revealing cheekbones sharp enough to commit war crimes. Her smirk was surgical. She wasn't trying to steal the scene, she simply was the scene.

And together, James, Thalia, and Ava. The most dangerous kind of symmetry. A holy trinity of dominance, destruction, and desire. The crowd gasped in silence. The flashbulbs flared.

Ellie whispered, "What the actual fuck?" Her fingers clenched the stem of her champagne glass as her eyes locked, not with James, but with Ava.

Ava smiled. That same smug, hypnotic expression from months ago. And then, she mouthed it. "Lucky. Bitch."

Ellie's face didn't move, but her heart detonated behind her ribs. She was supposed to bury James. But he came to burn down the cathedral, with her and Mark locked inside.

He hadn't just shown up, he'd declared war. And he wasn't trying to reclaim the crown. He was proving he never gave it away.

Thalia leaned in, whispering to James without looking toward Ellie. Her voice as soft as smoke. "This is what it means," she said. "To have the power and let it go."

James nodded once. Not to agree, to confirm. He wasn't here to fight Ellie. He was here to remind everyone, even her, that he'd already won the war by walking away whole.

Ellie didn't break. Not in posture or breath. But she turned her head slowly toward Mark, eyes glazed, smile faint. She whispered, "Well, I guess I underestimated him."

Mark looked across the ballroom with narrowed eyes, reading everything. "Looks like he didn't come for peace," he said.

"No," Ellie replied. "He came for fire." Then she politely excused herself from Mark for a moment.

The door shut behind her with a soft click. Ellie locked it. Not for fear nor secrecy. But because she needed the kind of silence that came with solitude, the kind no one could witness or interrupt.

The private powder room was bathed in soft amber light. A crystal chandelier above, gold fixtures, art-deco wallpaper, and a velvet chaise in the corner like it belonged to some forgotten empress.

She leaned against the door for a breath, then another. And then her body moved like it had been waiting all night to release the lie of composure. She kicked off her heels. One, then the other. The gown stayed on, but she unzipped the back just enough to breathe.

Her reflection stared back at her from the grand mirror: flawless, glowing, powerful. But her eyes were glass, breaking.

No words yet. Just breath. Heavy. Slow. Tight. And then, finally, her lips parted, barely moving as she whispered into the mirror: "What did I expect?"

The answer didn't come. Because she already knew. She had wanted him to break. To see her on Mark's arm and collapse inside. To crawl. Instead, he had ascended.

Her fingers found the edge of the marble sink, white-knuckled. She blinked, and a tear slipped without permission. Another followed.

She turned away from the mirror like it betrayed her. Moved to the soft bench. Sat with both hands in her lap, unsure whether to hold herself together or let herself fall apart.

And that's when the memories flooded: His arms, his voice. The way he used to hum when he cooked. The first time he told her she scared him, in the best way. The way he kissed her palm before every major meeting like it was ritual. The way he never once asked her to be less.

Her face crumpled, not in rage, not in shame. Just grief. Raw, woman-born grief. Grief for the way she let distance answer questions that only love could've clarified. Grief for never telling him how much it really gutted her to find Ava's card. Grief for being so afraid of needing him that she destroyed him for making her feel that way.

Tears rolled in silence. No sobs. No shaking. Just slow, devastating descent.

She sat like that for several minutes. Maybe more. And then, like a queen rising from rubble, she stood. She zipped her dress back up. Wiped her face with soft tissues scented like lavender and ego death, smoothed her hair, and took a long look at herself again.

Still beautiful. Still powerful. Still Ellie. But not untouched. And definitely no longer unbothered. She stared into her own eyes and whispered one thing: "You let him go." Not because she had to. Not because he deserved it. But because she didn't know how to hold him and herself at the same time. Someone else did.

Back in the gala, the balcony was soaked in candlelight and decadence, the city skyline reflecting in James's glass like fire trapped in crystal. He stood flanked by

Thalia and Ava, and if anyone believed this was chaos, they didn't understand what orchestration looked like.

Thalia was not here to parade a prize. She was here to crown her King. Her gown hugged her curves like it had been sewn by sin itself, and her voice slid between them like warm oil.

"Tell me," she said, brushing James's chest. "Is she joining us tonight?"

She didn't look at Ava. She didn't need to. She knew her answer. James studied her for a long beat, then replied, "Are you sure about that?"

Thalia smiled, slow and sure. "Are you?"

She stepped even closer, her body flush against him, one hand trailing down his arm like a whisper that remembered every secret. "You've been fantasizing about us all night," she whispered. "But you're not the only one."

Ava returned then, hips gliding, a fresh glass of champagne in her hand and audacity in her smile. She stood beside James, then leaned in, her breath hot at his jaw.

"He isn't," Ava said. "Because I've been imagining how it'd feel too. Both of us. Every taste, every scream, every turn."

Thalia chuckled. "Are you hungry, Ava?" she asked softly.
Ava purred. "Starving." She sipped, then let her lips curl into something filthy and gleaming. "But I do hope you're thirsty, Thalia…" she cooed. "Because I've got quite the fountain. And when I spring, it comes in waves: wet, hot, and messy. You might drown."

James choked back a laugh, heat rising behind his eyes.

Thalia looked up, eyes dark. "Mmm. I guess James will be swimming in a rough and wet ocean this evening."

Ava giggled. "Do you have a life vest, baby?"

James smirked, voice low and deliberate. "I never need one. I stroke for my very life until I hit the shores. And I never drown."

The three of them laughed: low, sultry, rich with sin and royalty. There was nothing awkward. No guilt. No shame. Only power. They were playing, plotting, and welcoming each other in.

Inside the ballroom, Ellie reappeared. But this time, she wasn't walking into her moment. She was walking into his.

James didn't look back. Ava didn't even blink. They were immersed in each other, not despite Ellie's presence, but because they didn't need to notice it anymore. Ellie wasn't the ghost haunting the memory. She was simply no longer relevant to the kingdom she helped birth.

James stood still, towering and grounded, the weight of Thalia's devotion anchoring him while Ava's energy flared like gasoline on a flame. Thalia touched his wrist gently. "Look at you," she whispered. "Worshipped by fire and submission."

"Which is which?" James murmured.

Thalia leaned closer. "That's the magic. You don't have to choose."

Across the room, Ellie was frozen in place. She thought she was watching a war of lust and ego. But what she was really witnessing was a coronation. And she was the one who handed over the crown.

Mark. Zion. Ken. None of them could ever stand beside this. Not this man, not this presence, not this display of quiet, blistering dominance.

She had tried to protect her pride. Had armored herself in distance and had let James think she didn't care. And now she was watching him become a god. Not because she gave him power. But because he never needed her permission to reign.

The car was silent on the way to Mark's estate. Not awkward. Not tense. Just quiet. Ellie leaned her head against the tinted window, watching the city blur in smudges of gold and black. Mark sat beside her, relaxed, confident, sipping from a crystal tumbler poured from the bar between them.

"You sure you're alright?" he asked, voice low and even.

"I'm fine," Ellie said, lips barely moving.

"You were quiet back there."

"I had a lot to see."

Mark nodded. "He looked…different. I'll say that."

James's laughter echoed in her memory, wrapped in heat and sin, surrounded by women who didn't just desire him, they belonged to his orbit. She had once been that orbit. She was just passing through his sky.

Mark's estate was everything she expected: gated, sculpted, modernist, cold and beautiful in the way art galleries often are. He guided her through glass doors and into a space filled with curated jazz, rare whiskey, and muted seduction.

He poured her a drink, but she didn't touch it. Instead, she stepped out of her heels. Mark approached behind her. "Do you want to talk, or forget?" She kissed him. It wasn't desperate or planned. It was acceptance.

They moved through the house slowly, undressing between rooms. A belt here. A clasp there. Mark was attentive, gentle controlled. He worshipped her the way men who read too much and talked too little often did, with quiet awe and practiced precision.

Ellie turned, reached for his collar, and kissed him again, slow at first, then deeper, her tongue slipping past his lips like a promise she wouldn't keep. He followed her lead, slipping his jacket off, guiding her through the wide glass hall like a man trying to memorize every step.

By the time they reached the bedroom, she was already stepping out of her gown, letting it puddle at her feet. Mark paused, his breath visibly caught in his throat. "You're stunning," he murmured.

Ellie climbed onto the bed without replying. She spread her legs slowly, deliberately, her body arched like an offering she didn't owe.

Mark dropped to his knees at the edge, kissing her inner thighs, his hands sliding up the backs of her knees as his mouth found her center. He licked with discipline: firm, circular strokes, tongue flicking just enough to pull a moan from her lips.

She gripped the back of his head, anchoring him there, hips rolling gently, but it wasn't out of need, it was out of control. He was good, calculated. She came softly on his tongue, legs trembling, her breathing short, but her mind was somewhere else.

Mark kissed up her body, positioned himself, and slid inside her with reverence. He moved slowly and passionately, like a man who valued worship over destruction. And it felt good.

The rhythm was tender. The sound of skin meeting skin echoed in the high ceilings. Her nails traced his back, then dug in a little harder when he angled deeper.

She came again. Harder this time. But even as her body spasmed, her lips parted in silence: No name, no prayer, no king. Just, a wave, followed by stillness.

Mark collapsed beside her, breathless, his hand over his heart. Ellie lay on her back, blinking up at the ceiling, her legs still parted, her skin damp. And then she felt it. The tears. Not sadness nor guilt. Just the realization that this wasn't what she wanted.

It had felt good. But it wasn't him. She rose from the bed slowly, nude and glowing in moonlight. Mark stirred, eyes opening. "Where are you going?"

She didn't answer, just stepped toward the window, stared out at the city she used to command, and whispered faintly to herself, "I want my King back."

———

Meanwhile, James's whispers would prove much different. The elevator doors hadn't even closed behind them before Ava kissed James hard, one leg hitching up around his waist. He grabbed her thigh, lifted her effortlessly, and backed her into the nearest wall.

Thalia stepped out of her heels slowly, watching them. She didn't interrupt. She planned this.

James's penthouse was dim and warm, lit only by low amber bulbs and the flicker of a fire pit in the corner. Thalia moved through the space like a queen returning to her throne.

Ava pulled James toward the bed, her dress already halfway unzipped. Thalia followed, her robe slipping from her shoulders like silk surrender.

When they reached the mattress, Ava shoved James back onto it and climbed on top, grinding against him, her mouth dragging along his throat.

Thalia knelt beside them, cupping James's jaw. "You ready to be worshipped like a god, my King?"

He just exhaled and then submitted. Clothes vanished. Breath shortened. Time melted.

James kissed Thalia deeply, hand tangled in her curls, while Ava crawled lower, her lips leaving a trail down his abs, her nails scratching his thighs just enough to raise goosebumps.

Ava swallowed him whole. James groaned, body arching, one hand still tangled in Thalia's hair as she kissed his neck, his chest, his jaw.

"Fuck," he growled.

"She's just getting started," Thalia whispered, licking his earlobe. And she was right. Ava's mouth was greedy, skilled, obscene. She slurped and sucked like she wanted to milk his soul, her throat swallowing every inch, her hand stroking what her lips couldn't take.

Then Thalia moved down, replacing Ava at his base, tongue lapping, licking both him and Ava at once, until James was a shaking mess between their mouths.

203

They devoured him like royalty does a feast. In sync. In control. And then they flipped him. Thalia mounted his face, dripping, trembling. And Ava straddled his hips, guiding him back inside her with a loud, throaty moan.

James gripped both thighs like reins and took control. He ate Thalia like he'd been starved for years, groaning into her, his hands spreading her wider as her cries turned feral.

Ava rode him in deep, bouncing, her tits in his face, her nails clawing his chest. "I want her taste on your tongue while you fuck me," she gasped.

He roared, thrusting harder, his face still buried in Thalia, devouring every drop. Thalia screamed, her body convulsing, juices dripping down his chin, soaking his beard.

Ava cried out as she came again: squirting, legs shaking, thighs slick with the mess they'd made. Their fluids mixed, slicking every stroke, every breath, every cry. And James didn't stop.

He flipped Ava next, pressed Thalia's face into her soaked folds, and slid back inside, fucking her while Thalia tongued Ava until she was leaking again, into Thalia's mouth, onto the sheets, down her thighs.

James growled like thunder, his body a machine, his hips slamming into Ava as he looked Thalia in the eyes and said, "Show me how you are owning this." Thalia moaned and swallowed Ava whole, licking, drinking, destroyed by the taste of both of them. Ava bucked and screamed, writhing between the two of them.

When James finally came, it was with a roar and a curse, as his entire body jerked, hips grinding, his seed flooding Ava as Thalia moaned beneath them both, licking her lips.

The three collapsed. Sweat. Heat. Pulse. They lay tangled in one another, ruined and divine. Thalia lay on James's chest, her fingers tracing invisible crowns into his skin. Ava curled at his side, body twitching from aftershocks, her lips swollen and slick. James stared up at the ceiling. It had been perfect.

And yet, Ellie's face still lingered.

Thalia looked at James, reading him instantly. "You doing okay?" she whispered. But his silence said something else. Because power had been restored. Bodies had been worshipped.

But Ellie was still the ghost in the room. And the room was still. Too still.

———

After a moment at the window, Ellie made her way back into bed with Mark. Mark's breath was slow and even beside her, one arm draped across her hip like he thought it meant something. His warmth didn't reach her skin.

She stared at the ceiling, motionless, naked under the sheets. Her body was quiet now, but her mind was back there. Back with James.

Mark had made her come. Twice. And still, nothing inside her had unraveled. There was no surrender, no thunder rolling beneath her skin, no afterglow that left her shaking, broken open and adored. There was only satisfaction, yet hollowness.

She turned her head away from him and reflected for a moment. She could still feel James. The weight of his body pressing her into the mattress like he owned time itself. The way he didn't just take her, he unleashed her. Made her primal and feral. The way he used to whisper in her ear, just before she came undone, "I would burn every kingdom just to taste this again."

Her breath trembled. She slid one hand inside herself. Mark didn't move. She exhaled, long and slow, fingers slipping through slick heat. She was already wet. Of course she was, because James still lived inside her skin like a secret she couldn't scrub out. Her body remembered him more clearly than her mind ever could.

Her other hand gripped the sheet. Her hips rose slowly, grinding into her own touch, and her memory filled with James's voice, his breath, his hands forcing her knees apart just to watch her shake.

He used to demand her pleasure. Used to tell her, "Don't you dare come quietly. I want the whole damn city to know this pussy belongs to me." She came with a tight gasp, biting the pillow to stay silent. Her toes curled. Her thighs clamped. And the wave broke. Shattering, blinding. But also, lonely.

When it passed, she slipped out of bed, careful not to wake Mark. She padded barefoot across the cool marble floors, pulling one of his robes around her body. The house was dark, modern, breathtaking.

But it was also lifeless. Art hung on every wall. Books lined tall shelves. Even the air was scented like curation. But none of it felt like home. Because home had always been James. She walked through it quietly, letting memory do the damage.

He took her the way she needed, without fear, without apology. James didn't just love her body. He loved everything that made her hard to love: The parts that barked, the pride, the fire, the throne. He wanted it all.

And somehow, when he held her down and made her come so hard she couldn't breathe, it didn't feel like he conquered her. It felt like he offered her a place to be unmade.

She stepped outside, the robe fluttering behind her in the breeze. The city stretched below. Quiet. Golden. Indifferent.

She reached for a cigar from Mark's private humidor. Lit it, inhaled, exhaled. And stood there, naked beneath silk, dripping with the weight of everything she'd tried to forget.

Her thoughts didn't whisper anymore. They screamed: He was mine. He loved me with nothing hidden. No angle, no leverage. Just need, just fire. Just me. No one had ever made her feel like that. Not Mark. Not Zion. Not Ken.

They'd all wanted to win her. But James? He wanted to worship her. His pleasure came from her cries. His obsession had been her pleasure, not because it proved anything, but because it was hers. And that was enough for him.

She stared at the night sky for a long time before she whispered the truth out loud. It didn't tremble. It didn't crack. It just was.

The city was still asleep. The sky had softened into indigo, with only the faintest streaks of light beginning to flirt with the horizon. Inside James's penthouse, the heat of the night still hung in the air, thick with sweat, moans, and the scent of sex that hadn't been quiet.

They were asleep now. Thalia lay curled in one corner of the bed, her nude body stretched in a slow, satisfied sprawl, Caramel silk and power, with a waist that curved like poetry and hips that could crush a man's will. Her ass, round and high, still faintly quivered from being ravaged the night before. Her nipples were dark, taut, and marked with the memory of his teeth. She looked like she'd been worshiped and wrecked, and she had been.

Ava, tangled in the sheets near the foot of the bed, looked like lust incarnate. Pale and flushed, her thighs still glistened with a mess of juices: hers, Thalia's, and his. All dried in streaks across her stomach and down the inside of her legs. Her blonde hair was a wild halo, her lips swollen, her neck bruised with pleasure. Her full, natural breasts rose and fell with every breath, the skin across her chest streaked with fingernail trails.

They were perfect. Ruined. And gloriously satisfied.

James couldn't sleep. He rose slowly, sliding from the bed without a sound. His body was sore. His cock still twitched faintly with the memory of being drained by two mouths, two holes, two women who had made it their mission to destroy him in worship.

But the ache in his chest was worse. He grabbed a pair of silk drawstring pants from the back of a chair and padded barefoot through the quiet, past the empty living room, toward the balcony. The doors slid open with a whisper. Cool air kissed his skin. And James stepped out into the stillness, alone.

The city was quiet. Lights blinking like stars had fallen and built themselves into towers. He leaned against the railing, jaw tense, arms crossed over his chest. Everything should've felt perfect. He had been desired. Served. Devoured by two goddesses who knew how to feed a king.

But the storm inside him hadn't passed. Because when he looked across that ballroom, and saw Ellie on Mark's arm, something in him died. And worse, something in her might have too.

'She started it,' he reminded himself. 'She let me believe it was nothing. She stood by that man like I hadn't built a kingdom for her to sit on a throne, and she knew how much it would hurt.'

And then his fists clenched on the railing. 'But so did I.' Because what he delivered last night wasn't strategy. It was vengeance. It was cruelty wrapped in grace. It was a man who came to burn the kingdom with her still inside it.

And for a moment, he had smiled doing it. The smile was gone. And all he could think about was her face. The way she looked at him: shocked, wide-eyed, not broken but ghosted.

Mark stood beside her, composed and quiet, passive. That man didn't move, didn't shield her, didn't see the dagger coming.

James exhaled through his nose. He would've saved her. He would've stepped between her and the fire, and carried her out, even if it meant burning too. Because that's what James always did. Even when she hurt him. Even when she ran. He protected her. But, last night he destroyed her.

The ache in his chest sharpened and his soul screamed. But he didn't say it. Not out loud. The balcony door opened behind him. Soft steps approached. Thalia's voice, like silk brushing his spine, "You alright?"

He turned slowly, meeting her gaze. She was radiant in the morning light. Hair messy, breasts full, body glistening faintly in the dawn. He nodded once. "Yeah. I'm good."

He reached out, brushing her arm gently. "Thank you," he said. "For everything. For last night. For making me feel good again."

Thalia smiled, slow and knowing. She followed his gaze down and saw his cock stirring beneath the waistband of his pants. Still thick, aching, and ready. She bit her lip. "I'm not done making you feel good yet."

She extended a hand. Nude, elegant, and undeniable. James, torn and haunted, still took it. Because desire could be louder than grief, even when grief wore the face of a Queen.

As they walked back inside, Ava was already sitting up, stretching like a lioness waking from sacred slaughter. Her eyes caught James. Then Thalia. Then she smiled. "Finally. I was getting thirsty again."

James stepped into the room and let the door shut behind him. They came for him again. Lips. Mouths. Breasts. Clenched thighs. Slick tongues.

But even as Ava straddled him, even as Thalia guided his hands back between her legs, James's soul screamed. For Ellie. For his Queen. For the woman nobody could replace.

And the women? They tried to fuck her ghost out of him. Because deep down, they knew: The Queen wasn't dead.

Chapter 17: The Fire's Not Out

"Okay, first of all, why the hell didn't you tell me Ava was the dirty-ass surprise guest of the night?"

Danielle didn't even wait for her espresso to finish brewing before she went in. Jean sat across from her on video chat, hair wrapped in a silk scarf, sipping tea like she hadn't just helped orchestrate a visual war crime at a gala.

Jean shrugged, deadpan. "Thalia sent her a separate car, never mentioned it. I thought she was bluffin'. Then boom, bitch appears like a Bond villain in red."

Danielle squinted. "You thought she was bluffing and still didn't tell me?"

Jean raised a brow. "You know damn well I wouldn't have told you that shit even if I did know."

Danielle blinked, nodded. "Fair."

They both sipped in silence. Then Danielle spoke first. "Still gotta give her credit."

Jean leaned back. "She smooth as fuck."

Danielle said, "I haven't seen anything that slick since, shit, since The Count of Crisco."

Jean paused mid-sip. "The what?"

"You know that movie with the French dude that escapes prison and comes back to destroy everyone."

Jean blinked. "*The Count of Monte CRISTO, Danielle.*"

Danielle laughed. "Shit, same difference. Slick-ass revenge." They both cackled.

Jean pointed a finger. "But let's be real…Ellie?"

Danielle's smile faded. "Looked lost."

"Lost and outclassed," Jean echoed.

Danielle exhaled. "I told her not to play petty when her heart was still all wrapped up in James. That's not the kind of man you play at."

Jean nodded slowly. "And Mark Spade? Fine as hell, sure. But the second James walked in…"

Danielle raised both brows. "Whew."

"…like he was walking into a player's ball," Jean finished, smirking. "And not only did he not look outta place, he showed up with two bad bitches flanking him like he invented confidence."

They both shook their heads.

"Didn't say a damn word," Danielle added. "But everything about him screamed, 'I don't belong to nobody but I'm still the motherfucking king'."

Jean held up her tea like a toast. "Facts."

Danielle leaned back with a sigh. "I feel bad for Ellie though. You could see it in her eyes. She didn't expect that. She really thought she had control."

Jean nodded. "Thalia's not one to underestimate. Ellie: zero. Thalia: two."

There was a long beat, then Jean whispered, "That bitch might be the Wonderful Wizard of Oz. And Candyman. With a hint of evil flying monkey."

Danielle covered her mouth, wheezing. Jean kept going. "But why do I kinda wanna grow up to be that bitch?"

Danielle pointed at the screen. "Real shit? Me too." They both laughed, the kind that shook their shoulders but also carried a quiet sadness underneath.

Jean sighed, sipping. "We done meddling."

Danielle nodded. "Yup. No more puppet strings. No more middle-woman missions."

"Forever friends."

"Forever."

A long pause. Then, together, like gospel: "Still Team King and Queen. Original cast only."

——

When she arrived home, Ellie walked into the house barefoot, heels dangling from her fingers like discarded armor. No lights on, just the soft hum of the security system. She set her heels down without ceremony, unzipped the black gown she had worn like war paint and stepped out of it slowly, letting it pool at her feet like a memory she wasn't ready to release.

Her bare skin prickled with the cool air as she wrapped herself in one of James's old robes, the dark gray one he used to wear when he cooked breakfast shirtless, towel slung around his hips. She had washed it a dozen times, but it still smelled faintly like him. Lavender oil. Sweat. Bourbon.

She moved through the house on instinct: dim lights, candle in the bathroom, cold water on her face. She didn't need to cry. The ache lived beyond tears now, somewhere deeper.

Ellie's phone buzzed once on the marble counter: Camila. She had forgotten she even dialed her earlier. She lifted the phone with a trembling hand and answered. Camila didn't flinch. "You keep waiting for closure. But what if survival is the only ending?"

"Ellie?" Camila's voice was calm, present. Like she already knew Ellie was unraveling from the inside out.

"I don't really know why I called," Ellie said.

"You don't have to," Camila said gently. "Just speak."

Ellie sat on the edge of the tub, robe pulled tight across her chest. She glanced down at the burn mark across the suit jacket in the trash. Her voice dropped to a whisper.

"It's not just heartbreak. I've felt that before. I've survived that before. This is…" She swallowed hard. "It feels like I took the match and set fire to something holy. And now I'm pretending the ash was part of the plan."

There was silence on the line, the kind that only comes from someone who's listening without judgment. Then Camila asked softly, "Do you still want him, Ellie? Or do you just want to win?" The question cut through every layer of pride she'd tried to drape herself in.

"I want him," she said, voice cracking. "I want to not want him. But I do, still, even after all this."

Camila's tone was gentle but resolute. "Then let's unpack that. Tomorrow morning, early. I don't usually see clients on Mondays, but this feels like the kind of weight you shouldn't carry into another week."

Ellie paused for just a moment, then said, "I'll be there." They hung up without goodbye. Some bonds don't need closure. They just need clarity.

After she showered, back in the bedroom, Ellie pulled on one of James's Gemini launch shirts. Soft cotton, faded design, his scent clinging to the collar. She tucked her knees beneath her at the edge of the bed and stared at the shredded business card still barely visible from the trash bin. She didn't pick it up. The woman's voice still echoed in her head: "Lucky."

She had built this man from wreckage. Held him when he was all fire and no foundation. She had kissed his bruises. Protected his name. Let his pain live inside her body when he couldn't hold it anymore.

She didn't win him, she earned him. She didn't feel lucky, she felt haunted.

Her gaze shifted to her desk, still cluttered with unread press releases and court updates about Zion. She opened her laptop anyway.

Started to respond to an email. Then paused. Her fingers hovered over the keys. And instead, she opened her journal app. Not the one the publicist would someday quote, but the private one. The sacred one.

She titled the page: *All the Things I Still Love About You, Even Now*

And then she let the truth speak:

I love the way you say my name when you're calm, like it's the first time you've ever tasted peace.

I love how you used to press your forehead to mine before we made love. Not because it was romantic, but because it was real. Like we were syncing up so the world wouldn't break us.

I love how you always smelled like bourbon and war. Like a man who's battled for everything but still makes room for soft things.

I love the sound of your voice when you're defending me, even when I didn't ask you to. Especially when I didn't.

I love how you held me when I broke and didn't ask questions. Just brought food, rubbed my back, and waited for the storm to pass with me.

I love the way you looked at me when I walked into a room, like you had already won, just because I was yours.

I love that you let me trace the Spartan on your back like it was scripture. That you let me see you, even in your silence.

I love the way you said "My Lady" like it was a vow and a confession all at once.

I love how you worshipped me when the world said I should've been harder, colder. But you knew that I just needed to be safe.

She stopped. Her hands were trembling. She typed one final line.

I love you even now. Even when you don't see me. Even if you never do again.

She didn't save it. She didn't delete it. She just closed the laptop, but left the page open, like a door not fully shut. And whispered into the silence: "Please, still see me."

———

It was late afternoon by the time James pulled into Thalia's driveway, his car grumbling low as it coasted to a stop under the awning. The sun was dipping low behind the trees, casting amber light across the slate-gray exterior of her home, warm and still like the exhale after a storm.

He stepped out, hoodie tied around his waist, chest still damp with the sweat of iron therapy. His arms were swollen, his knuckles pink, his breath steady, but his heart wasn't. He rang the bell.

She opened the door almost immediately, barefoot and backlit by the warm light inside. A pale green romper hugged her hips softly, her skin kissed by sun, her curls falling over her shoulders. There was something ancient in her calm. Something sovereign.

"You're early," she said simply.

"I needed quiet. And clarity," James replied, stepping inside.

She moved with a quiet grace to the kitchen counter where a steaming mug waited. "Tea?"

He shook his head. "No. Just this." He gestured between them.

Thalia inclined her head gently and led him into the living room. She didn't sit. She remained standing, spine tall, energy poised. She wasn't performing. She was preparing, for truth.

James stood across from her, breathing a little heavier now. The silence between them wasn't awkward. It was pregnant. Waiting.

"I know what last night meant," James began. "What it cost you. The planning. The performance. The precision."

"I chose it," she said calmly. "And I'd choose it again."

"But that kind of sacrifice…" he said, voice low, "it doesn't come without expectation."

Her eyes narrowed just slightly, not in suspicion, but awareness.

James inhaled. "Are you saying you love me?"

Thalia didn't blink. She stepped forward slightly, chin raised. "I'm saying…" she began, voice rich and unwavering, "I am love, James. Every fucking bit of it."

She stood there fully now, in front of him, glowing like dusk and defiance. "My light is as bright as the darkness I see inside you. I've seen it, felt it, and I'm not afraid." He didn't interrupt her, didn't blink.

"I don't need a thing from you," she continued, her voice honeyed but sharp. "I am self-made, accomplished, respected. And smart enough to know that those things, and beauty, won't make a woman like me whole."

James's voice came quiet, deeper now. "Then what will?"

She stepped closer. Inches away. "Everything, love," she said softly, "and everything from absolutely nothing takes time."

The space between them thrummed. James's jaw flexed, as if he was trying to keep something from unraveling. Thalia smiled gently and lowered her gaze for a breath.

She reached up and brushed a speck of something from his shoulder. The gesture was so maternal and intimate, it made his lungs lock. Then, with a light laugh, she pulled back. "I'm going to make you a post-workout dinner." James lifted a brow.

She turned and walked toward the kitchen, hips swaying lightly beneath the soft cotton of her romper. Her voice floated over her shoulder, playful now, "I took the liberty of buying a few new pairs of your favorite joggers. Left them in the guest room closet, with those soft cotton tank tops you like."

He watched her disappear behind the wall. "And I would have gotten you some socks, love," she added, laughing, "but you seem to hate them as much as I hate panties."

James stood alone in the living room, the echo of her words still burning in the air. He exhaled through his nose, jaw tight, arms loose at his sides. He hadn't felt this kind of peace in months. But peace didn't mean clarity.

And as her laugh trailed through the kitchen like incense, he closed his eyes and whispered beneath his breath, "Don't ruin this."

———

The walls of Camila's office were painted a quiet blush, the kind of pink that didn't beg for softness, but commanded calm. Sunlight warmed the space through high, narrow windows, and the smell of palo santo lingered like a prayer that had already been answered.

Ellie sat curled on the loveseat, shoes off, posture relaxed, but her energy was coiled. Like a serpent that hadn't decided if it wanted to strike or simply rest. Camila sat opposite, tablet in hand but gaze firmly on her client.

"I'm here because I don't want to be reckless again," Ellie said, fingers wrapped around the cool glass of water.

"And how are you defining reckless today?" Camila asked, voice even.

Ellie stared at the sunlight etching patterns on the floor. "Letting my pride script my love life. Letting someone else's silence write my rage before I've even processed the pain. Letting vengeance feel like strategy when all it is, is grief in lingerie."

Camila replied, "That's a hell of an answer."

"It's a hell of a truth." They sat with that for a moment.

Then Ellie added, her voice softer now, "I slept with Mark."

Camila didn't flinch. She only raised one brow. "And how was that experience?"

"Good," Ellie admitted. "He was gentle. He tried. He wanted to make me forget."

"Did he?"

Ellie smiled faintly. "No. Because even with everything he has, the money, the pedigree, the intelligence, he didn't have the strength. Not that night. He couldn't save me from what I was spiraling into. Couldn't even stand between me and my own unraveling."

She inhaled deeply. "But James would have watched me set an entire house on fire with me inside it, then walked into the flames, saved me, and nearly destroyed himself putting it out. And he would've done it without blinking. Never mentioned it again. Never needed credit. Never told the world he was the reason I still had skin left."

Camila nodded slowly. "That's a powerful metaphor."

Ellie's throat tightened. "It took me this long to understand that he wasn't a King because I was a Queen. He was a King who made me a Queen. And then let me live the illusion that I built that throne myself."

Camila didn't interrupt.

Ellie smiled sadly. "I was so busy being dominant that I never stopped to honor the man who let me feel powerful without asking for any of it back."

"You loved him," Camila said.

"I love him," Ellie corrected. "And I don't want to lose myself trying to win him again."

Camila softened. "Then don't. Let love be strategy. Not surrender."

Ellie looked up. Her smile crooked now, sly at the corners.

"You know…" she said as the session wound down, "If you weren't so damn professional, I think you almost could've gotten this."

Camila smirked. "Ellie, please. You couldn't handle all this woman." They both laughed, deep, feminine, knowing. Ellie stood, grabbing her purse, a little lighter in the chest.

As she walked toward the door, she chuckled to herself, "Damn, that bitch still makes me wet." Old habits.

———

Danielle was driving through Echo Park and slowed her car as the breeze caught something ragged stapled to a nearby telephone pole. She eased to the curb. Something about it pulled her curiosity, and when she stepped out and saw it fully, her jaw tightened.

A flyer. Homemade. Smudged: *PRIVATE ART LESSONS – PORTFOLIO CONSULTATION $40/HR (NEGOTIABLE) "Learn From a Legend" Contact Zion* (Phone number scrawled messily) And below that? A faded black-and-white photo of him: shirtless, posed like a catalog model clinging to an expired dream. His eyes looked sunken. His body gaunt. The caption tried to sell confidence, but the paper whispered desperation.

Danielle blinked. Laughed once. Snapped a picture and texted Jean: *Art of the motherfucking FALL.*

Jean replied, Damn. *From gallery god to fucking handyman on a flyer. Poetic.*

Danielle stood there a moment longer, letting the quiet humiliation of the image settle in her bones. She almost felt bad. Almost. Then she remembered what he did to Ellie.

She got back in the car, sunglasses sliding back into place. And drove off. No music, no commentary. Just the breeze peeling Zion's face from the pole as she disappeared down the block.

———

At his Gemini office, James sat alone in his corner suite, sun pouring across the edge of his desk. A signed lease agreement lay open in front of him. Permanent relocation to Southern California, a new beginning.

The pen sat in his hand. His grip never moved. Thalia's voice echoed in his mind like a soft chant, "I am love, James. Every fucking bit of it."

He rubbed the back of his neck. His gym bag was still on the floor. The fabric smelled like sweat, like steel, like silence. Like the weight he'd been lifting wasn't just physical.

His phone buzzed on the desk. A text from Jean: *They're expecting your signature on the paperwork first thing tomorrow. They accepted all your conditions. It's all ready.*

James stared at the message, then the screen dimmed, but he didn't respond. He leaned back in the chair, exhaled through his nose, and thought, 'I don't know if I'm running from something or toward something. And I'm not sure it matters.'

He opened the lease folder again. Read every line slowly. He'd asked for equity, full brand control, partial board autonomy. And he got it all. "But still," he murmured to the room, "Would this even be hard if it was all in the same place?" The question echoed.

"Is it the distance that helped me move forward? Or was I already done and just needed a clean excuse? I keep saying I'm not looking back," he whispered.

Then stared out the window, the sun dipping low. "But I haven't really taken a step forward either."

He looked down at the lease again, then stood. "I need clarity," he said to himself. "Not more sunshine and strategy. Just clarity."

———

That evening in Ellie's penthouse, she lit a single candle and turned off every light in the room. The robe she wore slid off one shoulder as she stood by the window, wine glass in hand.

Her laptop was open on the bed. One journal entry still sitting unsaved: *He didn't have to come back for me to be whole again. But God, I hope he does.*

She closed it. She didn't smile. She whispered, "He knows where home is."

Chapter 18: Heaven's Hunger

The final act didn't open with an explosion. It opened with a hush. The kind that settles before the storm, before everything you thought was buried claws its way back to the surface.

It had been weeks. Long enough for the world to believe the fire was out, but it wasn't. It was waiting.

Ellie's empire thrived. Headlines named her a visionary, investors called her indispensable, her quarterly reports shattered expectations and turned doubters into disciples. Photos of her graced magazine covers again: poised, radiant, unbothered.

But behind the curated strength was a woman who hadn't slept through the night in almost a month. She hadn't cried either. Because tears would mean it was over, and Ellie refused to mourn what still lived in the marrow of her bones.

So, she smiled for cameras, signed deals, held court in meetings with the kind of poise that made men question their place in the room. But every time she was alone, she reached for her phone.

Because if she said aloud, "I miss you. I need you. I was wrong, too", that would mean admitting she'd helped burn the kingdom down. And Ellie had never known how to apologize with grace.

———

James woke before dawn. He trained harder than anyone, ate clean, slept little, and pushed the Gemini project forward like his life depended on it. Because maybe it did.

He was sharper now. Colder, and more deliberate. His smile had changed. It was rarer, quieter, but no less devastating. People noticed, but no one asked.

Jean watched him from a distance, quietly adjusting schedules, fielding inquiries, protecting his space. She never asked about Ellie.

Because sometimes, when James thought no one was watching, his hand drifted to the watch she gave him. The one he still wore. The one that never stopped ticking, even when everything else did.

He never listened to her last voicemail. But he never deleted it either.

———

Thalia moved with intent. She made herself invaluable at work. Attentive, present, soft in the right ways, but strong when needed. She never asked James for more than he could give. And he gave what he could: dinners, soft laughter, the comfort of not having to explain himself. He liked her. Respected her. Needed her, even.

But he didn't crave her. Not the way he still craved the woman who once made him laugh so hard he choked on a shrimp cocktail in Miami. The woman whose voice could still wake him from sleep like a song he'd forgotten the words to but never the melody.

——

Mark Spade waited. Not idly or impatiently. But with precision. He was everything James wasn't. Calculating, controlled, and af little dangerous in a way that didn't scream but whispered. And Ellie intrigued him. Not just her power or her face. Her restraint.

He could see the ache in her and didn't try to fill it. He only offered her one thing: Choice. And when you've been starved of agency, choice is seductive as hell.

——

Zion was finished. The lawsuit, the scandal, the art world turning on him like wolves circling a wounded lion. His accounts were frozen and his assets seized. His calls went unanswered, and no one returned his messages. Especially not the Queen whose image he tried to sell.

He watched the empire move without him. And he realized too late that you don't get to steal a crown and wear it without consequence. The fire's not out, it's waiting. In the silence between texts not sent. In the touch that never came, the name still whispered by lips too proud to tremble. It's there. Coiled. Patient. And when it rises again, it won't ask permission. It will simply burn.

——

The building buzzed with ambition. Deals closed. Designers delivered. Staff spoke her name with reverence and precision. Ellie Sinclair was still Ellie Sinclair.

Her empire hadn't slipped, not even by a thread. Her public persona remained pristine, a goddess carved from silk and steel. She still moved like royalty, still ruled like prophecy. The world had no idea that beneath her fitted blazers and signature stilettos, she was quietly bleeding in places no one could see.

But Ellie was learning the difference between winning and healing. Each day was one more day further from James. And maybe that wasn't the worst thing. But it wasn't the best either.

She wasn't in love with Mark Spade. And he wasn't necessarily in love with her. But their dysfunction functioned. They worked on paper. They didn't spark like wildfires, but they didn't burn the house down either. He stimulated her mind, mirrored her composure, and never touched the places in her spirit still reserved for the man whose name she hadn't whispered in weeks.

Tonight, a text arrived as she wrapped a pitch meeting for a brand she'd built from dust into dominance: *Dinner's done. Car's waiting. Thought we could try something a little elegant and depraved.*

Her eyes skimmed the message. *Desirable Decadence. An exclusive night. A place where names were whispered but never spoken. Where power moved in shadows and pleasure wore high fashion.*

She stared at the message and didn't flinch. Maybe tonight she'd let go of the man who never really let go of her. Maybe tonight she'd be remembered for something other than what she'd lost.

Later that evening, outside Ellie's building, the silver Maybach glided to the curb like something summoned. It didn't idle. It waited.

Ellie emerged from the building with the kind of elegance that had become legend. Her black dress clung to her body like it had signed an NDA. A thigh-high slit moved like it had rhythm. Her stilettos were sharp enough to draw blood. Her lipstick, a deep crimson, looked like a warning sealed with a kiss.

She slipped into the backseat wordlessly. On the seat beside her was a black box, wrapped in ribbon. Mark Spade sat relaxed, tailored in a suit so dark it stole light. His shirt collar was open just enough to whisper sin. And the scent of him, clean spice and aged scotch, hung heavy in the air between them. "Evening, Queen," he said, voice all smooth and suggestion.

Ellie glanced at the box. "You're getting predictable."

He tilted his head slightly. "Only in the packaging."

She unwrapped it slowly, sliding her fingers beneath the ribbon like it might unravel more than silk. Inside was a red key. Sleek. Antique in shape. New in feel. Weighted with intention. "What is this?" she asked, turning it between her fingers. "The key to the vault?"

Mark's smile didn't break. "No, but maybe we can unlock a few doors with it. I see the woman again, the one who silences rooms and forgets the names of her enemies. Maybe it's time she remembered how to take." She slipped the key into her clutch and didn't reply. Because something in her did remember.

The Maybach drove through the city like it was part of the architecture, windows dark, quiet inside except for the low thrum of music, and the ache she didn't dare name.

They stopped outside a building without signs. Just the heat of mystery pulsing beneath a gothic façade: smooth obsidian stone, arched iron windows, and golden sconces flickering with real flame.

Etched into the massive double doors, blood-red and embossed, was a crooked crown. Not perfect, not polished. Just real. The kind of place you don't enter, you surrender to.

Mark stepped out first, rounding the car like a ritual. The doormen said nothing, just opened the doors as if they already knew her.

The concierge bowed slightly. "Welcome back, Mr. Spade. And welcome to you, ma'am."

Ellie didn't blink, didn't smile. She stepped forward. And the world changed.

Inside, the air was warm and thick with moans and murmurs, the scent of sandalwood, sweat, and something floral but untamed. The lighting was low, cut through with jeweled beams: red, gold, indigo, spilling across smooth floors, and mirrored columns.

Bodies moved like smoke. Everywhere. Nude, half-draped, leather-bound. Skin of every shade gleamed with oil and tension. Men with thick thighs and chiseled abs leaned against curved walls, their cocks heavy and swinging between their legs, some already gripped by eager mouths.

Women, full-bodied and lithe alike, arched in pleasure across fur-covered benches, fingers inside each other, eyes closed or wide with invitation.

One woman rode a man's face on a crystal table, her moans rising over the hum of bass like a gospel choir. His arms were locked tight around her thighs, muscles flexing as he devoured her. Her body writhed, wet and glistening, nipples pierced and shining in the chandelier's reflection.

A tall, caramel-skinned man with gold rings on every finger stood behind another woman, as her ass lifted and her back arched, then plunging into her slow and deep while she sucked a second cock in front of her, drool spilling onto her chest.

A Black woman with a bald head and dark tattoos across her collarbone reclined in a clawfoot chair, legs spread, fingers dipped in her own wet heat, eyes locked onto Ellie as if she'd been waiting for her.

The sound was a symphony of sin, moans layered with gasps, low music threading between cries of pleasure and the slap of flesh on flesh. She felt it like a rush of blood behind her eyes.

Desire. Dark. Raw. Buried so deep she'd almost convinced herself it didn't exist anymore. But here, it pulsed again, and rose up like a storm she used to dance in.

Behind her, Mark didn't speak. He just watched her as her breath caught. Watched her eyes flick from one scene to the next, studying lips parted in pleasure, cocks stretching open mouths and holes, fingers drenched in orgasm and hunger.

And when her hands clenched around the clutch in her lap, he knew. She remembered what it felt like to let the world fall away. What it meant to be the one everyone watched.

Not because she was untouchable. But because she was insatiable. Ellie's heartbeat thundered beneath her ribs. She didn't reach for Mark, didn't turn to him. But he stepped closer anyway.

And when she turned her head slightly, eyes wide and lips parted, he didn't say a word. He didn't have to. She was ready.

They walked deeper. The crowd parted, not out of submission, but anticipation. And then she saw them: Three doors. Massive, arched, each one guarded by a stunning woman. Goddesses carved in desire.

One door red. One black. One blue.

The woman in front of the red door had midnight skin and a body like poetry: hips generous, breasts full, nipples pierced and glinting beneath a sheer mesh corset. Her hair was in braids, long and heavy, cascading down her back like a whip. Her lips were full and painted the same shade as Ellie's. Her gaze was possessive.

The woman at the black door was tall, androgynous, covered in ink, wearing only a leather harness and thigh-high boots. A coiled crop hung from her belt. Her eyes were kohl-lined and unreadable. Her body didn't promise sex. It promised submission, or punishment.

And the woman at the blue door was soft and golden, her blonde curls wild, her body round and irresistible. She was nude, unbothered, her hands resting on the curves of her belly and thighs. Her smile was warm, maternal even. But her eyes held secrets older than lust.

Ellie stood still, breath shaky, pulse racing. And for a moment, she wasn't Queen, or boss, or ex-lover. She was just Ellie, wondering if she was ready. She turned to

Mark, her lips parted in silent awe. He smiled, slow and knowing. And then reached into her purse, the red key glinted in his hand.

——

Back at Gemini the office was quiet, bathed in amber shadows and the distant hum of productivity slowing for the night. Most of the staff had already cleared out, their energy long spent on boardroom fire drills and power lunches. But James King stayed behind, tying up the last threads of the day like a man who never stopped building.

He stood by the window of his corner office, gazing out over the skyline with the same intensity he once gave to street corners and survival plans. The view was different now: cleaner, higher, but no less earned.

Thalia texted: *You want Chinese or Spanish tonight?*

James smirked and tapped a reply: *Oh, you're not cooking one of your super calorie-packed meals that threaten to be the end of my abs every day?*

Three dots danced. Then her message appeared: *Ha! You may just have to make "ab day no flab day" multiple days. But seriously, babe—pick one. No, I'm not cooking. You get Greek every night. Tonight will be no different. But besides that…*

James laughed quietly, thumb pausing before he responded: *Alright. I can do some spicy Spanish food.*

Perfect, she sent back. *I was thinking the same. And grab me something sweet on your way home?*

You got it. He sent, then pocketed the phone, still smiling when the door opened. Jean stood there, arms full of folders and authority.

"You're not going anywhere yet," she said, already marching toward his desk. "You promised I could pick out my new office now that I'm officially part of the C-level mafia."

James arched a brow. "You know damn well you already picked it out." Jean grinned and pointed across the hallway at an office that was not only already claimed, but currently occupied.

"That one," she said unapologetically.

James chuckled. "Done."

She leaned on the edge of his desk. "Now, are you going to start the admin interviews next week?"

"For you and for me," he confirmed, pulling on his jacket.

"They better not be lying on their resumes," she said.

"They always lie on their resumes."

He headed for the door, but Jean called after him one last time.

"Hey," she said, suddenly more serious. "You're doing good. You've built something impossible."

James paused, hand on the doorframe. "I used to dream about this life," he murmured.

He left the office to the sounds of the city breathing through glass walls. The Bentley rumbled to life, and he tapped his playlist. Nas filled the speakers, the track smooth and classic, something old-school enough to remind him of where he came from. 'Only a King can survive what I've seen,' he thought.

But then, his mother's voice echoed in the back of his mind. Soft, Southern, fierce in faith. "Not yourself, baby. But with the help of the Good Lord. Nothing is possible without God's unchanging hand in it."

James's eyes softened. His hand tightened briefly around the steering wheel.

The house was quiet when he arrived. No aromas of dinner in the air. No soft jazz or clinking pans. He walked in and called out, "What happened to Spanish food, babe? Did you change your mind?"

A voice drifted from the other room, smooth, sultry, laced with wicked amusement. "Of course not."

He turned the corner and dropped his bag to the floor. Thalia stood like temptation in a sheer, see-through bodysuit, the kind made for sin. It hugged every curve with surgical precision, but it was the crotchless detail, with her full, natural bush peeking through, that stopped his breath.

Her nipples were hard, barely concealed beneath the sheer mesh. The garment left nothing to the imagination. Not her taut stomach, not the curve of her hips, not the strength in her thighs.

And beside her? Another woman. Latina, beautiful, and sinfully real. She wore a black silk robe, open and falling off one shoulder. Her skin was sun-kissed caramel, smooth and glowing. Breasts full and natural, tipped with deep brown nipples. Her stomach soft but tight, adorned with a gold chain that dangled into the V of her waistline.

She licked her lips slowly when she saw him, her mouth glossy, full, and painted in a shade almost identical to Ellie's.

Thalia stepped forward. "Dinner will be served," she purred, placing a hand gently on the Latina woman's hip, "with a show…"

Her eyes dragged down his body, landing on the bulge already straining in his slacks. "…and dessert," she whispered, "for a King's appetite."

Because in that moment, as the women began to move toward him, he realized, this wasn't just pleasure. This was power. And Thalia knew exactly what she was doing.

———

Back at the club with Mark, the red door closed behind her with a slow, resounding thud. And then Ellie stepped into fire.

The room beyond was drenched in scarlet shadow and golden heat, all soft, pulsing light and deep, erotic rhythm. The air itself felt thick, laced with moans and musk, the raw scent of desire clinging to every surface like sin. Two men and three women stood waiting, presenting.

The first man was tall, obsidian-skinned and breathtaking, with a chest carved from pure dominance. His thighs were thick, cords of muscle twitching slightly as he adjusted himself. Already hard, his cock curved upward like it was sculpted to wreck.

The second was bronze and feline, eyes golden, jawline sharp. Tattoos kissed the inside of his forearms, trailing up to a neck thick with lust. His cock hung low and heavy, half hard, a promise unspoken but certain.

The three women were divine. One draped herself across a low bed, her body covered in sheer netting, breasts full and kissed with dark rose nipples, her fingers trailing lazily between her legs as she watched Ellie with open hunger.

Another knelt on the floor, pale-skinned and flushed, her plump ass in the air and her mouth already parted, waiting for orders, or permission.

The third was honey-toned, muscular and soft in perfect contrast, her bare breasts jiggling gently as she danced to a rhythm no one else heard, one hand already pressed where she needed it most.

Ellie stood at the center like lust had returned home. Mark entered silently behind her, with his eyes locked onto her every move. He didn't touch, didn't speak, he just watched as she slowly unzipped her gown and let it fall.

No undergarments, no hesitation. The Queen stood naked in heels, her body perfection not because it was untouched, but because it was used, worshipped, broken, healed, loved. And now, hers.

Her nipples were tight with arousal, her skin flushed. Her bush was neatly groomed, thick, soft, a crown for her throne. Her lips were parted, her breath already shaky.

She turned her head slightly, locking eyes with Mark. And in her voice, low, commanding and wicked, came her first words of the night, "Watch your Queen be devoured."

One of the women rose and crawled toward her, hands slow and reverent as she kissed Ellie's ankle, then calf, then inner thigh. Ellie stood still, her hand slowly sliding through the woman's hair as that soft mouth reached her pussy and licked gently, just once.

Ellie shuddered. This time deeper. Firmer. With need. Another woman came behind her, tongue trailing from her spine to the back of her neck, whispering in her ear, "Can I taste too, my Queen?"

Ellie moaned her permission. The caramel-skinned man moved forward now, fingers brushing Ellie's jaw before kissing her: open-mouthed, slow, intoxicating. Her hand found his cock and wrapped around it like it had belonged there in another life. She pulled back from his kiss, breathless. "Lie down." He obeyed instantly.

She straddled his face, one knee on either side of his head, her wetness already slick and dripping onto his tongue before he even fully opened his mouth. "Drink," she whispered. "And don't stop." As he licked and sucked with reverence, her body trembled. But she didn't break. The second man moved behind her, lifting her hair and kissing her back slowly. His cock pressed between her ass cheeks, thick and ready, but he didn't enter. He waited.

"Mark," she called out, voice thick with pleasure, "what do you really want to do?" He stepped forward at last, finally removing his jacket, revealing broad shoulders and a frame that had been sculpted in silence.

"I want to see you take what's yours," he said. Ellie smiled. A wicked, royal thing. She pulled off the man's face, glistening with her arousal, and turned to the second man. "On your knees," she commanded.

He dropped instantly. She stood in front of him and lifted one leg onto the chaise, exposing her pussy again: already swollen, wet, demanding. He leaned in to taste her, but she stopped him.

"No," she said. "Taste her first." She pointed to the woman who had started on her earlier, now flushed and needy.

The man leaned in, tongue lapping between the woman's legs, moaning as he devoured her. Ellie watched, one hand massaging herself as she controlled the pace, the rhythm, the very temperature of the room.

Mark moved. He stood behind her, fingers wrapping around her hips, pulling her gently to him. His cock was hard, hot, ready.

"Mine," he whispered against her ear. "All of this. Mine to protect. Mine to serve." And he pushed into her: slow, thick, stretching her until she gasped, her walls gripping him instantly.

One of the women rose and knelt before Ellie, her tongue circling Ellie's clit while Mark fucked her from behind. Ellie moaned louder now, body suspended between the tongues of women and the cock of a man who worshipped her without ego.

Mark held her tighter, thrusting harder, deeper, as she reached down to the man kneeling and guided him to her breast. His mouth wrapped around her nipple while the other woman licked her slick clit like it was holy.

Her orgasm built fast and hard. She came with a cry: loud, animalistic, beautiful. Her body pulsing as Mark kept moving, never breaking stride, fucking her through it, keeping her aloft in the storm of sensation.

And then he came too. Growling against her back, his thrusts deep and final, claiming her without caging her. They collapsed together, surrounded by moaning, panting bodies. Some still writhing, others watching in awe.

Ellie stood first. Unshaken, naked, glowing. She turned, pulled Mark up by the collar, kissed him hard. Then whispered, "Long live the Queen."

But they weren't done. The room was alive now, with everyone partaking. Women riding men. Men bending over for women. Bodies intertwined in variations of hunger Ellie couldn't even name.

She looked toward the dark-skinned dancer she'd been eyeing earlier and began to walk, but Mark caught her hand. "Not her," he murmured.

His eyes flicked toward the tall, quiet man who had been leaning near the post, and watching Ellie all night like a wolf waiting to be called to the feast. Ellie's mouth curled.

She walked toward him, slowly. She knelt, took him in her mouth, and he gasped, then growled. Moments later, he had her bent over a chair, one arm wrapped around her waist, the other in her hair, fucking her with ruthless control.

Her breath left her in ragged cries, her cheek pressed into the soft cushion, her legs wide, shaking. He wrecked her, and she smiled through the pleasure. As she came again, violently and beautifully, her eyes turned toward Mark.

He was behind one of the women now. A petite blonde. He had her on all fours, one hand pressed between her shoulder blades, the other gripping her ass as he pounded into her. She screamed his name, wild and grateful.

Ellie smiled because Mark wasn't done. After he finished with the blonde, he moved from her like water and walked toward the bronze Adonis, who had finished making a woman squirt across a mirrored floor.

Mark grabbed him and kissed him. And the man melted. Mark turned him, bent him slightly forward, and gripped his hip. He didn't wait, he just entered him like it was nothing new. Like it was truth.

Mark fucked him with the same power, the same elegance, the same authority. The man moaned, trembling, accepting every stroke with pleasure. Ellie's mouth parted, frozen. Not in horror, but in realization. Mark was free, and so was she.

He looked at her as he finished: deep, hard, still inside the man, his eyes locked on hers. And he smiled a slow, wicked, satisfied smile.

Ellie lay back. Transcendent. Holy. She was no longer haunted. She was Queen again.

———

On the other side of things, James's mind was trying to catch up with what his body already knew: This night had changed everything. Thalia turned slowly, beckoning the Latina goddess forward. "Strip for him," she said softly.

The woman obeyed, fingers brushing her robe from her shoulders with delicate control. It fell in a whisper. And there she stood: full curves, heavy breasts, slim waist, and hips made to be held. The golden chain she wore draped on her body shimmered with movement as she approached James like prey offering itself to a predator.

Thalia circled behind her, brushing her hands down the woman's arms as she whispered in her ear in Greek. The woman nodded. Then Thalia turned to James. "Sit."

He sat in the center of the room, in the high-backed chair once meant for solitude, he now sat like a King among offerings. And they were not meek. They were powerful, intentional, and erotic. They were a temple, and he was the altar.

The Latina woman straddled him, pressing her warmth against the bulge in his pants, grinding slowly, teasingly, as she kissed the corner of his mouth. Her breasts brushed his chest. She whispered, "Don't worry. I know exactly how to make Kings beg."

James grunted as she licked a slow line from his jaw to his ear. Thalia dropped to her knees between them. Her fingers unfastened James's belt, unzipped his pants, and pulled out his cock. Thick, veined, already throbbing.

She kissed the tip, just once. Then took him fully into her mouth. James's head fell back with a groan as the Latina's hips rolled against him and Thalia's mouth worshipped him with the patience of a saint and the sin of a siren.

Her hands never rushed, her lips never lost rhythm. Her bush still glistening, untouched, yet charged with control.

Thalia pulled off and looked up at him, lips swollen, breath warm. "You've carried the weight long enough," she whispered. "Let me carry you."

And then she stood. She helped the Latina rise too, and then, she climbed onto James's lap, facing him. Her arms wrapped around his neck.

She lowered herself slowly, his cock vanishing into her body with one smooth, aching glide. She didn't moan. She breathed, like she was tasting the first inhale after being underwater for years.

James gripped her hips. Hard. But she leaned forward, pressing her lips to his ear. "You don't have to hold me. I'm not going anywhere."

She began to ride. Slow, deep, controlled. Every lift of her hips, every drop, was calculated. She wasn't chasing a climax. She was building a cathedral.

James tried to buck up into her. Thalia pushed his shoulders back with both palms and said softly, "No. Let me." And it ruined him.

She rolled her hips in perfect circles, her full bush brushing against his pelvis, her clit grinding into his base. He felt everything. The heat, the wet, the love and the mastery. Then, without warning, she stopped.

He slipped free, cock wet and angry and pulsing. She nodded at the Latina woman, who immediately dropped to her knees and took him in her mouth, deep, fast, greedy.

James cursed. His fingers tangled in her hair, but he didn't thrust. He couldn't. Because Thalia had turned around and bent over the chair in front of him, presenting herself.

Her body was an invitation. Her hips, arched. Her ass, round and soft. Her full, glistening lips were slightly visible. Pink. Soaked. Spread.

"Come," she said. And he did.

He stood and entered her in one brutal stroke that pulled a deep growl from his chest. Her cry echoed like a hymn. He fucked her hard, both hands gripping her waist, thrusting into her with the kind of power that made the air leave the room.

She took it. Every stroke. Every thrust. Every growl.

Her hands braced on the back of the chair as he slammed into her, cock slick with spit and honey, his balls slapping against her soaked heat. As she began to shudder, her body breaking open around him, she cried out, "Now, my King. Now!"

He spilled into her, hips jerking, body convulsing. Not just from orgasm. From relief, from devotion, from 'Goddamn, this is mine'.

They collapsed together. Breathing, sweating, clinging. And just when James thought it was over, Thalia crawled onto the floor between his legs and licked him clean, every drop. Then she looked up at him, smiling, calm, and unmoved.

James's chest still heaved. The room was heavy with the scent of sex and something sweeter: surrender. He lay half-reclined in the oversized armchair, naked, thighs slick with Thalia's essence and his own. His cock twitched against his stomach, as if it hadn't just fed on the divine.

Thalia knelt between his legs, licking the last traces of him from her lips like they were sacred. She looked up with a smile that said she was nowhere near finished. "Still hungry?" she asked.

James exhaled, wrecked. "You're unbelievable."

Her smile deepened. "I thought you might be."

Suddenly, a knock at the door caused James to turn his head slowly toward the bedroom door, half-dazed, half-wary.

Thalia stood, her full bush glistening with their pleasure, hips swaying with lazy confidence as she walked over the plush carpet to the door of his bedroom.

She cracked it open. And in walked more heat: A woman. Petite, sharp, entirely composed. Chinese, sexy, and fully tattooed. Ink kissed every inch of her visible skin: dragons along her hips, lotus petals blooming across her chest, winding koi from her back down her thighs.

Her body was art in motion, all toned muscle and fluid grace. Her breasts were small, pierced with silver rings that bounced as she stepped forward barefoot on painted toes.

Her eyes locked on James. She strutted to the bed like she'd already had him inside her. Before he could sit up, she climbed onto the mattress, straddled his face, and lowered herself onto his mouth.

Her pussy was bare, smooth, and already dripping. She smelled like heat and jasmine. James groaned, because she didn't just sit. She rode, gripped his head with both hands, ground her clit against his tongue, rolled her hips slowly as if she were painting her pleasure across his face.

Behind her, Thalia approached. She leaned in and kissed the woman on the mouth, slow and sensual, tongues teasing. Then Thalia reached down between the Latina woman's thighs, still slick and aching from earlier, and slid two fingers inside her like she owned her.

The Latina moaned instantly, her knees buckling, body trembling again. "Stay open for me," Thalia whispered. "Let him hear how much you love being filled."

The Latina collapsed to her knees beside the bed, hand in Thalia's hair, body arching as she begged through gasps, "Please…just like that…oh my God…"

The tattooed woman gasped as James's tongue flicked faster. "Yes…fuck…your tongue…he's—oh, fuck!"

James's hands gripped her thighs, his tongue working like a machine, nose buried in her softness as she came on his mouth—hard and wet, her cries cutting the air.

And still, James wasn't done. The tattooed woman climbed off, legs shaking. She tried to steady herself. He stood, and his cock was steel again. Thalia didn't flinch. She smiled, dragging her soaked fingers up his chest. "Go ahead," she whispered, licking her fingers clean. "Break her."

He didn't need to be told twice. He spun the Chinese woman around, bent her over the mattress, and slammed into her with one perfect, brutal thrust. She shrieked in pleasure. James grunted, deep, low, animalistic.

He fucked her like a man possessed, both hands gripping her hips, slamming into her until the mattress creaked and she cried out again, squirting down his thighs, legs shaking.

Still he moved, and she took it. Beside them, Thalia lowered the Latina onto the floor and straddled her face, holding her breasts as the woman licked and moaned and begged.

Thalia whispered, "That's it, baby. Feed me. You already know how." Her thighs trembled as the woman sucked her clit, licking her in tight circles, obeying every command. James watched it all. He fucked harder. Deeper.

Until the Chinese woman cried out again, another orgasm wracked her and she collapsed into the mattress, moaning into the sheets.

James came with a roar, flooding her, gripping her hips so hard he knew she'd bruise. It was over. The women trembled in silence.

The Chinese woman crawled off the bed and lay on the floor, gasping. The Latina collapsed beneath Thalia, still twitching with the last waves of climax. James was exhausted, nude, his cock glistening. Chest rising and falling like thunder.

Thalia stood. Glowing. She helped the women dress: robes, kisses, soft touches. "You were divine," she whispered to each. She walked them to the bedroom door, pulled it open, and guided them out with the grace of a high priestess escorting angels home.

Then she turned. The room was dim, candles low. James, wrecked, was sprawled across the bed, one leg dangling off the edge, arm over his forehead, a satisfied smile ghosting across his lips.

She padded softly across the rug, pulled the silk sheet up over his waist, and sat on the edge of the bed. Her eyes traveled the length of him: his body sculpted, his muscles twitching in sleep, his soul finally at rest.

She leaned in close, brushed her lips against his ear, and whispered, "Now you're full, my King."

Then she curled beside him, body against body, her head on his chest, and whispered a soft lullaby in Greek. Not to soothe him. To honor him.

Chapter 19: Thorns in the Crown

He could count her absences like pay periods. It had been too long. James stirred before the sun had fully crested the skyline.

The air in the bedroom was thick with the residue of pleasure. The warmth from three different bodies still lingered in the linens, but the room had quieted. The only sound now was the gentle hum of the city below, muffled by the heavy glass windows and the slow rise of his breathing.

He was naked. Sore in the best possible ways. Spent, but not broken.

His head turned to the left where Thalia slept, half-curled beneath a silk sheet, her hand resting across his bare chest, her face relaxed and unconcerned. Her lips were parted slightly in sleep. Content. She looked like a woman who had served her King and been crowned in return. And she had.

James lay still for a moment, his arm draped behind his head, his cock resting heavily against his thigh. There was no shame. No regret. Just that quiet voice in the back of his head, familiar, relentless.

He exhaled through his nose and whispered to the ceiling, "Damn though…that was fantastic." He chuckled. But it didn't erase the truth underneath.

James had never been one for excess when it came to sex. Before Ellie, he'd barely made it to his second hand counting past lovers. Not for lack of opportunity, but because he valued what he gave.

He could still hear his mother's voice from back when he was a young man, somewhere between curiosity and recklessness. "If you give that thing to everybody, how special is it?" she'd said. "You only get one of those things, baby. And if it's all used up, what the heck are you gonna have left when God blesses you with the love of your life?"

That line stayed with him. It wasn't just about sex, it was about integrity, sacrifice. Legacy.

Last night was unforgettable. And the man who once told the love of his life that watching another man touch her would tear him apart from the inside out, let his thoughts trail.

———

This reminded James of something that took place about two years ago. A local underground spot just outside of Oakland. One of those hush-hush, amateur sex clubs that looked like nothing from the outside but was packed with sweat and temptation inside.

Ellie had walked in first, wearing a trench coat over a sheer, thigh-length lace bodysuit. Her heels clicked with audacity. James followed behind her like a storm dressed in muscle and purpose.

The room was full of sound: wet noises, groans, gasps, people moaning against walls, across benches, tied to posts.

Ellie turned to him, arousal clear in her eyes, but so was something else: boundaries. "Let's get this straight," she said softly, almost laughing. "The idea of another man touching me? Disgusts me."

James's jaw clenched. "Good. Because no fucking man touches what's mine."

She leaned in, whispering against his neck. "But a woman?" She smiled. "I wouldn't mind some big tits in my face. Maybe tasting one. Being tasted."

He let out a slow breath. "That's a fantasy I can live with." Then his voice darkened. "But anything else? Any man trying to fuck you? That's a wrap. Game over. You'd see me on the evening news." Not because it was possessive. But because it was honest.

They stepped into that club hand in hand, and for the rest of the night, they explored everything together: her tongue between thighs, his mouth on her, no one else allowed inside the sacred perimeter of them.

James opened his eyes. And just like that, his phone buzzed and lit up on the nightstand.

Jean: *You coming in today or just running your own damn kingdom from bed now?*

He groaned. Checked the time. 9:43 a.m. "Shit." He sat up, rubbed his face, already reaching for his pants.

Yes. Rushing out the door now. Hold down the fort.

Jean replied instantly: *I always do. But if I gotta cancel one more breakfast meeting for your Black ass, I'm changing my title to Empress.*

James laughed, dragging a hoodie over his head and stuffing his feet into sneakers. As he stepped out of the bedroom and headed for the kitchen, he looked back once. Thalia hadn't moved. Still draped in silk and glory. Still everything she said she'd be.

And still not the reason he felt that emptiness creeping in around the edges. He shut the door gently behind him.

Ellie's eyes opened slowly. The sun bled through the silk curtains of the penthouse, warm against her bare skin. The windows framed the Los Angeles skyline like a living painting: steel and light, silent and watching. The bedroom still smelled of jasmine, perfume, and the kind of sex that made you forget what planet you were on.

Her thighs were sticky from the night before, her muscles sore in places she hadn't stretched in months. The scent of lust and sin clung to her pulse points. Her fingers grazed one breast and she smiled: primal, sated, owned.

Mark had pushed her to new limits. The kind of raw, carnal pleasure that stripped the polish off her power. No title, no expectations. Just her. Screaming, sweating, devoured. And when she returned the favor, when she climbed on top and made even him beg, she felt limitless.

She loved that about him. The way he looked at her like she was the last woman left on Earth. How his restraint wasn't weakness, it was reverence. His wealth could wrap cities in gold. His body? Straight out of a Tyler Perry fantasy. That kind of chest didn't belong under a suit. That mouth had no business doing PR.

Everyone wanted him. But he wanted her. And that was intoxicating.

Still, as she lay there in the aftermath, draped in luxury sheets and smeared lipstick, her smile began to fade. Because the pleasure had faded too.

And all that remained was the echo of a quiet, unspoken truth: She didn't want to be worshipped all the time. Sometimes, she just wanted to be Ellie. No empire, no crown, no curated expressions or crafted power stances. Just a woman who could laugh with someone who didn't want anything from her but loved everything about her.

James had understood that. He was the master of the reset. A walk in the city, a drive with the windows down and Prince playing loud. A dumb inside joke about Trader Joe's parking lots. He could have her screaming one minute and giggling into his shoulder the next. He never competed with her, he protected her.

With Mark, she explored freedom. But she was learning freedom isn't always safety. And safety doesn't always mean small.

Her mind drifted, not to James again. But to a darker place. A version of herself from a long time ago. They weren't together long, but long enough to leave damage. He was charming at first, handsome. The kind who looked good in photos but disappeared in real life.

He told her what men often told women with power and curves they didn't know how to respect: "You got a nice body and half-ass decent pussy. That's it. You ain't nothing deep. You ain't smart. You're corny. You lucky I'm even dealing with you."

Ellie remembered those words like a brand. Like they were carved under her skin. She didn't cry when he said them. She just folded them up and tucked them somewhere cold.

But they took root. And for years, no matter how much she conquered, there was always a part of her that feared he might've been right. Until James.

Another flash: Their first major event together. He was introducing her to political power players, billionaire investors, cultural icons. And she, Ellie Sinclair, felt like a fraud in a custom gown. She could command stages, silence men in boardrooms, but standing next to James that night, she felt small.

He must've seen it in her eyes. That flicker of doubt. That instinct to shrink. Because he grabbed her hand, turned her toward him and said, "You are every fucking thing that I am tonight. And so much more. Pick that chin up, you beautiful bitch."

She stared at him. Then grinned, and pulled a playful fist back like a movie villain, and quoted one of her favorite Queen Latifah lines from UNITY: "Who you callin' a bitch?"

And right then, right there, the Queen was born. Not because of the dress. Not because of the cameras. Because the man beside her saw her. And made her see herself.

"Ellie…" Mark's voice pulled her back to the present. He stepped back into the bedroom with two mugs of steaming coffee, shirtless, his sweatpants hanging dangerously low.

He leaned in, kissing the slope of her neck, warm lips trailing against her collarbone. "You want some coffee?" he murmured, brushing her hair off her shoulder. She ran her fingers through her curls to smooth them out and sat up slightly.

"Yeah," she said softly, "yes please." Mark handed her the mug, then sat on the edge of the bed.

"I was gonna let you sleep longer," he said, sipping his own. "But something about the way you look in that sunlight…"

Ellie asked playfully, "Dangerous?"

"Divine."

"Got plans today?" she asked, smiling at him.

"Downtown meetings," he replied, standing and stretching, the light catching the lines of his abs like sculpture. "A few suits trying to figure out what to do with old money."

He leaned down and kissed her forehead. "Don't let the world take too much from you today."

Ellie held his gaze. "Thanks. For reminding me I don't have to give it all away."

"You never do," he said, heading toward the bathroom to grab his things.

Moments later, she heard the front door click shut behind him. The penthouse was silent again.

Her eyes traced the skyline one more time before she rose, wrapping a robe around her body. She walked toward the mirror, coffee in hand, her reflection staring back: bare-faced, wild-haired, still flushed from memory.

Not Queen Ellie. Just…Ellie.

She smoothed her hair, tightened the robe's belt, and took a breath. She whispered to the mirror, "Chin up, bitch." Because broken or not, Queen or woman, she had shit to do.

————

James stepped into the building just after 10:20 a.m., hoodie half-zipped, sunglasses on, and coffee gripped hard. His body still ached, in the best ways. But his soul was quieter now.

The receptionist gave a soft, knowing smile. He didn't return it, but he dipped his chin, half greeting, half warning. His vibe said, 'Yes, I had a night. No, I don't want to talk about it.'

The elevator opened to the executive floor, and as James stepped out, the sound of cardboard scraping tile caught his ear. Then he saw it. Across the hall from his own office: chaos. Organized, glitter-laced chaos.

Stacks of labeled boxes sat outside the corner office. A cart filled with sad fake plants leaned against the wall. And a woman in beige heels, beige pearls, and a beige attitude stood in the hallway with her arms crossed, lips pinched into a line of pure disapproval.

She glared at the movers, glared at the boxes. And then, she glared at him. What the hell? He moved closer, coffee raised halfway to his lips, trying to put the pieces together. That's when he saw it. The maintenance guy painting the new name on the glass office door.

In bold, looping cursive, a fresh coat of shimmering gold spelled out: *Jean Richardson – Chief of Organized Chaos* And underneath that in a thinner, sassier font: *Empress. Don't call her unless you got snacks.*

James choked on his coffee, then laughed out loud. Just as a pair of movers strolled past him, one of them hauling in a pink and black cheetah-print chaise lounge, the other wheeling a bar cart stocked with mini champagne bottles, La Croix, and Sour Patch Kids.

Behind them came a full-size framed poster of Prince holding a Yorkie. James rubbed his face and muttered, "What the actual…"

"Good morning, King." Jean appeared beside him, dressed in high-waisted slacks, a silk floral blouse, and six-inch stilettos like she was running the Met Gala—and maybe the country.

She took a sip from her own mug that read, *I already know I'm right.*

James turned to her. "Tell me this is temporary."

Jean sipped. "Tell me you plan to ever show up before 10 again."

He looked back at the nameplate. "Chief of Organized Chaos?"

She grinned. "Promised. Delivered."

James pointed toward the boxes. "And her?"

"The previous occupant of my new office?" Jean raised a brow. "She said, and I quote, 'I didn't know assistants could apply for C-suite roles.' So I let her know, and I quote, 'I didn't know White mediocrity still had the audacity to speak unprovoked in 20-20-fucking-five'."

James snorted into his coffee. "Jean…"

"She's lucky I didn't summon Beyoncé to personally escort her out."

"Cheetah print though?"

Jean placed a hand over her heart. "It's not just cheetah. It's feminine ferocity with lumbar support. A throne, James. For the real backbone of this place."

James smirked. "So, we're glam rock-meets-Fortune 500 now?"

Jean looked at the poster of Prince being hung behind her new desk. "We are whatever I say we are. This is a kingdom. You the King. I'm the Empress. That office?" She pointed across the hall. "That was just my dressing room. Now? It's my fucking stage."

He was amused. Then he looked back at the scowling woman now being handed a cardboard box by a bright-eyed intern. "She's pissed," he muttered.

Jean shrugged. "Let her be. She had seven years to make that space hers. I made it mine in seven minutes."

James watched the furniture continue to roll in: fluffy rugs, a Himalayan salt lamp, a framed quote that read "You can't unseat a woman who built her throne while standing."

He exhaled a low chuckle. "You really are the glue around here."

Jean arched a perfectly sculpted brow. "No, baby. I'm the Gorilla Glue, the glitter, and the GPS. You may be King, but don't ever forget who keeps this castle upright."

James walked into his own office, still grinning, still wrecked from the night before, but lighter than he'd felt in days.

As the door shut behind him, Jean turned to the intern now holding a pink feathered pen and a clipboard. "Write this down," she said. The intern nodded. Jean grinned. "Under my portrait, I want the plaque to read: *Empress of Everything. Break room tyrant. Keeper of the coffee codes. And proud protector of the crown.*"

——

On Second Thought HQ pulsed with curated chaos: interns double-fisting iced matcha, stylists rolling garment racks across marble, and a photographer chasing the light through the atrium.

Ellie walked through it all like a sovereign in Gucci slides and oversized black shades, her coffee in one hand and her silence weaponized.

Danielle followed close behind, her top knot tight, her vibe looser. She held a tablet in one hand and a protein bar she had no intention of eating in the other.

"Okay," Danielle said, scrolling, "you've got a call with legal at eleven, your brand team wants to push the Jade line launch by two weeks, and some influencer named, 'Sunflower Justice' is trying to start a Twitter thread about you stealing her whole aesthetic."

Ellie said, "Tell her I invented her."

"Already did," Danielle said, flipping to the next tab. "Also told her our lawyers have the resources to do more than thread."

They stepped into the executive elevator. Danielle hit the top floor button with practiced flair. Silence settled between them briefly. Then Danielle turned to her boss, her friend, and eyed her over the rim of her tablet. "So."

Ellie, not missing a beat, replied coyly, "So?"

"So you're glowing. And not your regular CEO-slays-a-press-run glow. I mean that I've-had-multiple-orgasms-and-one-of-them-might've-included-a-headboard-breaking kind of glow."

Ellie's lips curved. "You're annoying."

"I'm correct."

The elevator chimed. They stepped out into a hallway that smelled like eucalyptus and ambition. Danielle lowered her voice, eyes still scanning the tablet. "Just tell me, was it as good as it looks?"

Ellie stopped and turned to face her. "It was…" she paused, finding the word, "spectacular."

Danielle let out a soft whistle. "Talk about an upgrade, E. I mean, damn. Mark Spade is all man."

Ellie took another sip of her coffee, sunglasses still on. Then she murmured, more to herself than anyone, "Mmm…maybe not all."

Danielle froze. "Wait, what?"

Ellie blinked slowly. "Nothing."

"Maybe not all?" Danielle repeated. "Ellie, what does that mean? Did you find a ring in his nightstand? A Grindr notification? What?"

Ellie just walked forward, cool as fog. "Danielle."

"I'm not judging! I'm just…clarifying."

"I didn't say anything."

"You said everything!"

Ellie opened the door to her office and stepped inside. Danielle followed her, still buzzing.

"I mean, he gives masculine energy, but also, I noticed he moisturizes his cuticles. That's a level of precision you don't usually see in emotionally available straight men."

Ellie pulled off her shades, set them down. "He's perfect, D. Wealthy, fine, discreet, and dangerous. What more could a girl ask for?"

"Maybe a man who only wants dessert and not a taste of the appetizer tray too?"

Ellie laughed, finally. "You're going to hell."

Danielle grinned. "I've got a booth reserved between Eartha Kitt and Diana Ross."

Ellie sat on the edge of her desk, finally letting herself exhale. Danielle leaned on the doorframe, tablet now forgotten. For a moment, the mood softened.

"You good, though?" Danielle asked, quieter this time. "I mean…not just in the thighs."

Ellie looked out the window. The city moved like it always did: loud, distracted, ambitious. "I'm trying," she said finally. "He makes it easy to forget. But sometimes? I miss…the silly, the quiet, the us-against-the-world stuff. Not just the world-in-my-hands kind of love."

Danielle nodded. "That kind of love don't hit the same."

Ellie sipped her coffee. "No," she whispered. "It doesn't."

———

The restaurant hummed beneath candlelight and jazz, the kind of background noise that knew how to fade politely when two people shared something too personal to announce.

Thalia sat across from James, sipping the last of her wine, skin glowing under the warm tones of the booth's low lighting. Her heels were off, legs tucked beneath her, and she looked content.

James smiled faintly as he wiped his mouth with the linen napkin and leaned back. "This was good," he said, voice low.

Thalia studied him. "You sure you don't want to stay the night?"

He reached for his jacket, already sliding one arm into it. "I need my own bed tonight. Got an early morning."

She raised a brow. "Since when do you run on structure?"

He chuckled. "Since Jean turned into a damn Empress."

He pulled out his phone and flipped it around to show her a photo of Jean's new office: A chaotic burst of pink cheetah print, neon lighting, and a glitter-drenched nameplate. *Jean Richardson – Chief of Organized Chaos. Empress. Don't call her unless you got snacks.*

Thalia blinked. "No she didn't."

"She did." He kissed Thalia gently on the cheek. "If I'm late again, she'll probably have my parking pass revoked and my emails redirected to Jesus."

Thalia smirked, but she watched him. "You okay?"

He nodded, not lying, but not telling the full truth either. "Yeah. Just tired of noise."

———

That night, in Ellie's loft, the moment she shut her front door, silence fell like a silk robe over her skin. No stylists, no calls, no Danielle. Just her, barefoot, and fresh-faced. Wrapped in the oversized robe James used to hate because it swallowed her frame.

She wandered to the kitchen, poured a glass of wine, then stood there for a while, one hand on the counter, the other wrapped around the stem. The city blinked through the windows, but her home was still. The first stillness she'd felt in months.

———

James arrived back at his place at 10:43 p.m. He placed his keys in the dish, peeled his hoodie halfway, and walked barefoot to the couch, sinking into it with a quiet groan.

His body was still recovering from indulgence. Now there was no background music, no breathy voices, no expectation. Just him, his thoughts, and that silence: the one he didn't know how to fill anymore.

He grabbed his phone. Opened, scrolled, paused. Memories started to hit like static.

———

Ellie thought back to a fundraiser she attended in a burgundy gown. High bun, her skin like polished bronze. They were standing by the hors d'oeuvres. People all around, quiet admiration, veiled envy.

James leaned in, lips at her ear. "If all these people knew this fine, innocent-looking woman had such a greedy pussy, they would just fall over and die."

Ellie choked on her champagne. Laughed so hard she had to turn away. "James," she hissed, still giggling. "You are disgusting."

He teased, "You love it." She did.

Back in the present at home, Ellie sipped her wine. She stared at her phone and opened the screen. His name: still pinned. She hadn't texted him in months, hadn't dared. But tonight, the silence didn't feel peaceful, it felt sharp.

Ellie finally lay down, phone in hand. No new notifications. Still, she opened the last message from him, read it, then closed it again.

———

He thought now of another memory of him and Ellie. He leaned in, sweat-soaked, trying to kiss her. Ellie wrinkled her nose and pushed him back. "Uh uh. I know you're not about to try me like this."

James laughed. "What?"

"You're gonna go wash all those reps off first." He looked confused.

She folded her arms. "Do you want me to die from high blood pressure from those salty-ass balls, or get killed by the poison gas cheese ball smell you got marinating under there?"

James gasped, hand to chest. "Damn! No gas mask head? That's how they did it in the old days."

Ellie nodded. "And that's how they died." They laughed until it hurt.

He loved her most in moments like that, when she could throw fire with one sentence and then smile at him like he was still the only man in the world.

Still thinking of Ellie, he opened his voice messages. Her voice. He pressed play: "I know you better hurry up before I start Power without you. You know that's my boyfriend waiting for you to fuck up right? I love you."
James sat still. Breath trapped somewhere in his chest. He opened his texts. Typed. Deleted. Typed again.

Then, he copied something instead: *I won't pretend that I intend to stop living. I won't pretend I'm good at forgiving, but I can't hate you. Although I have tried. Mmm…I still really, really love you. Love is stronger than pride. I still really really, love you.*

———

Ellies phone chimed. And just like that, her heart froze. His ringtone. She never changed it. "The champ is here…the champ is here…"

She dropped the wine glass onto the bed. Stared at the screen: *I still really, really love you.*

Did he find out about the club? This man has eyes everywhere.

Another message arrived: *I know you've moved on, and I know I've tried to. But damn if I don't have this whole world at my fingertips and nothing feels like home,*

E. You were my Queen, but you were my homie-lover-friend first. I'm dying inside. And I wouldn't have minded if I was dying for you. But to live without you is worse than death itself.

She didn't reply. Couldn't yet. She read it over and over. Tears rolled down her cheeks.

——

Ten minutes later, James just stared at the screen: *Don't be late or I'm ordering shit you hate.* Thalia. James shook his head.

He tossed the phone onto the nightstand. But before it could even settle, her ringtone: LL Cool J's "Headsprung."

"They call me Big Ellie…Big Cellie…" His heart slammed into his chest. He lunged for the phone. Fumbled, dropped it, then scooped it up like it was oxygen on a crashing plane.

One message: *Interesting.*

And for the first time in too long, James shed a tear. Not dramatic. Just real. He turned off the ringer, rolled onto his back, and finally let go. Heart open. The King. Waiting for his Queen.

Chapter 20: The Long Road Home

The moment Ellie hit send after, *Interesting*, her screen dimmed. Flickered once. And died. "Shit," she hissed.

The room was still dark, lit only by the low hum of city light spilling through the blinds. Her wine glass was half full on the nightstand. The sheets were still tangled around her thighs. Her hair was wild and damp, but her mind was buzzing.

She fumbled off the bed, bare feet hitting cool hardwood, and yanked open the drawer next to her vanity. The charger was there, knotted like a mess of tension she didn't have time to unravel.

She plugged it in and stared. The screen stayed black. Ellie exhaled. Leaned back in the chair and waited. 8 minutes later, the Apple logo finally glowed. The screen blinked to life, and she went straight to her texts. No reply yet.

Her finger hovered above the keyboard. Not anxious, not desperate. Just… unfinished. She typed quickly, *Sorry. My phone died. What I was saying was "interesting", because damn, I was literally just thinking of you.*

Then added: *How have you been, James King?*

She waited another 10 minutes hoping he would respond before texting him. *Ok. I guess you had a moment. Moment over, huh? Good night.*

Then set the phone face down, and laid back in bed, her heart thumping a little too loud against her ribs.

The next morning, in James's apartment, the light broke through the blinds, soft and slow. He rolled over, hand grazing the nightstand. His phone vibrated gently against the wood. He reached for it, eyes still half-shut.

Three messages, all from her. His thumb hovered over her name before he even opened them. It wasn't smug. It wasn't triumphant. It was real. Something inside him stirred. Not lust, not guilt, something good. The way it used to feel when she sent him dumb memes at 2 a.m, or when she'd call him King James with a wink after a workout.

He rolled onto his back, held the phone over his head, and whispered, "There she go."

That morning, Ellie sat in her sunlit kitchen in an oversized tee, barefoot, legs pulled up on the stool. Her phone rested next to her coffee cup. She hadn't even touched her latte. Because she kept checking for a reply. Nothing yet.

Something in her felt different. It wasn't hope, it was closer to gravity. Like something was pulling her home, and she wasn't sure whether to run from it, or open the damn door.

———

Hours later, they both go about their day. He cancels a meeting he wasn't focused enough to lead. She skips a call she didn't feel ready to fake through.

They both keep their phones close. They both type messages and delete them. They both want to say: *Can I see you? Can we talk? Are we okay?* But neither does.

Because when you've been royalty, losing your crown is one thing. But losing your person? That's the war, and neither of them is sure the battlefield is safe.

———

Jean's new office looked like someone had dared Cardi B to design the Situation Room, with input from Tracee Ellis Ross and a sprinkle of RuPaul.

Pink cheetah print on the chaise lounge. A custom LED sign that read: *Mind Your Business & Moisturize.* The gold-framed portrait of Prince sat dead center on the back wall. And right underneath it, was a black fabric bulletin board titled: *People Who Tried Me.*

But Jean was bored. She'd organized her inbox down to the emojis. She'd eaten six sour gummies in a row and alphabetized her pens. At one point, she seriously considered doing yoga, until her left ankle cracked and reminded her she was too old for that "ocean flow" nonsense before noon.

So she did what she always did when she was bored. She went to annoy James.

He sat at his desk, hoodie on, AirPods in, pretending to review something important. But his phone was right beside the screen, lit up, idle.

Three messages from Ellie, still unanswered. Jean pushed the door open without knocking. James didn't look up. "You know, one day I'm gonna lock this door."

Jean flopped onto the chair across from his desk. "And on that day, I will pick the lock with a bobby pin and a purpose."

He sighed. "You here to harass me or just redecorate my office in protest?"

"Neither," Jean said, sipping her matcha. "I'm here because I've already run out of things to color code, and I'm dangerously close to converting our break room into a hookah lounge."

Jean blinked. "Don't test me."

He chuckled, then hesitated, and closed his laptop. But his eyes didn't follow. They stayed on the phone, and something in them looked stuck.

And after a long pause, he said, "I texted Ellie."

Jean sat up straighter. "Wait. For real?"

James held up a hand. "Before you start. I didn't say I wanted your opinion."

Jean narrowed her eyes. "James King, if you really didn't want my opinion, you wouldn't have opened your mouth. You want the commentary. Just admit it."

He looked down at the phone again. "I haven't responded to her last messages yet."

Jean blinked. "You texted her and ghosted after that? What, are you trying to audition for season three of Toxic and Terrified?"

James smirked. "It's not like that. I just needed space to think before I say more."

Jean leaned forward. "Stop acting like you don't know her. That woman's seen your whole soul, and probably your colon. Didn't y'all have sex in this office at least once a month?"

James cleared his throat, looked around. "First of all, don't put that out into the air. Second, it was more like every other month."

Jean laughed so hard she had to put her mug down. "Exactly! So stop acting like she's some woman you met at a WeWork."

James ran a hand over his jaw. "It just feels different now. Like, I care about Thalia, a lot. But the longer you're away from your person, the more the bad fades. The good shit? That starts showing up everywhere. You remember the laugh, the silence that wasn't awkward, the way they said your name like it had purpose."

Jean nodded slowly. "I mean, I get it. Thalia's dope. She's like the five-stone Thanos of romantic warfare. That woman has timing, tact, and titty placement down to an art form. She's my petty spirit guide."

James smiled as Jean continued.

"We've been cleaning up this mess since Q1. I want hazard pay, or Beyoncé tickets," Jean snapped. But then said gently, "But Thalia ain't Ellie,"

"That was Ghost and Angie. Messy, magnetic, but you felt it. Thalia's more like Tasha. Reliable, strong, classic. But not the person you'd burn a kingdom down for."

James squinted. "Tasha was a short-vision bitch though."

Jean snapped her fingers. "And we all rooted for that bitch, right up until she turned crazy with the bad wigs and even worse decisions."

They both cracked up. Then quiet returned, softer this time. James exhaled. "It's wild, though. How memory works. The smallest things hit me now. A song, a coffee shop, that voicemail she left me about Power…"

Jean's brow rose. "Oh Lord."

James smiled wistfully. "You know she used to make me wait for her so we could watch it together? She'd say, 'You better hurry up before I start Power without you. That's my boyfriend waiting for you to fuck up'."

Jean held her heart. "We loved that show until they made Ghost's beard weird."

James laughed. "Facts."

Jean stood and grabbed her sour gummies off the desk. "You gonna text her back?" She popped a candy into her mouth. "Just remember clarity, not cleverness. You want her back? You better stop playing poet and start speaking human."

She pointed toward his phone. "And if you don't text her back, I'm texting her myself, on your behalf, and telling her you cried watching Encanto."

James chuckled. "I did cry watching Encanto."

Jean nodded. "Because that damn song hits. We don't talk about Bruno is a cultural wound." They both laughed as she walked out.

James stared at his screen again. Still unread. But something inside him felt clearer, less haunted. Because sometimes the scariest thing isn't admitting you still love them. It's realizing they might still love you, too.

———

Ellie sat at her desk, long after the sun dipped behind the skyline. Her office glowed in amber lamplight, blinds drawn halfway, and her speaker played a soft loop of Sade's "Love is Stronger Than Pride."

The lyrics filled the air like a scent. *I still really, really love you…*

For a moment, Ellie relaxed, letting the words hit. Soft. True. Unapologetic.

A knock tapped once before Danielle walked in, tablet in one hand, a thick stack of client notes in the other. She stopped just inside the door and cocked her head. "Oh no. You got the Sade on? Sade-Sade? That's either wine mood, man trouble, or you just signed a life-changing licensing deal and didn't invite me."

Ellie smirked, barely lifting her head. "Door three."

Danielle set the papers on the desk and pointed. "These are for action and signatures, which you still insist on doing with ink like it's 1997, even though you swore three years ago we'd go paperless."

Ellie arched a brow. "And yet you printed them. Interesting."

Danielle grinned. "I'm here to support your hypocrisy, not fix it."

Ellie flipped through the first few pages, then paused, and looked up. "James texted me last night."

Danielle froze mid-scroll. Her mouth dropped open like someone pressed mute on her whole system. Ellie continued, calm as the music. "Actually...he sent a lyric. From this song."

Danielle sat down without asking, blinking fast. "Wait, you are serious?"

Ellie nodded. "Then he followed it with another message. Told me everything and nothing all at once."

Danielle let out a breath. "I was hoping to hear back from him today. I knew you wouldn't say it out loud, but I saw it all over your face this morning."

Ellie sipped her tea. "I wasn't going to say anything at all."

Danielle squinted. "You literally just did."

Ellie gave her a pointed look.

Danielle smiled. "And that's why you told me. Don't lie. I don't meddle."

Ellie raised an eyebrow. Danielle raised hers higher. Ellie sighed. "Yes, you do."

Danielle crossed her arms. "And yet here we are." They both laughed softly, but it quieted fast.

Ellie set her mug down. "When I saw his name on my phone last night, I felt like... like my heart opened. Like one of those scenes in nature documentaries where they time-lapse a whole garden blooming."

Danielle leaned in, "Baby, I've seen you command a boardroom full of men twice your age. I've watched you turn heartbreak into an empire. But this 'I'm free, I'm strong' shit. That ain't you."

Ellie blinked. "I thought it was."

"It's cute when we pull it out like armor. Slip on the crown, rule the day, ignore the texts, keep our heels sharp and our hearts locked up. But Ellie..." She paused. "You made that your real life."

Danielle moved in closer. "And that's not who you are. Not really."

Ellie's voice was soft. "You think he still loves me?"

Danielle didn't even hesitate. "That man loves unlike anything I've ever seen. James is a fine bitch. Better looking than you fine bitch. Bulletproof. Walks in a room and people stop breathing. But he's never looked at anyone, anyone, the way he looked at you. Even when you weren't looking."

Ellie smiled through a sudden mist in her eyes. She looked down at the signature page. Then whispered, "When we'd cross the street, he'd always move me to the inside. Closest to the building. Even if I didn't notice. Even if I was mid-sentence."

Danielle clutched her heart. "That's some old-school, Southern-boy-in-the-body-of-a-city-man kind of shit. That's rare." She paused. "And now, a man will push you into traffic just to save his kicks."

Ellie laughed, hard. Danielle nodded. "Had a man do me like that once at a party. Haven't touched a man since. I said if I'm gonna get trampled, it better be by someone who smells like cocoa butter and says thank you after."

The moment was full and glowing. Sisterhood, truth, and that sacred space where vulnerability didn't mean weakness.

Then Ellie's phone buzzed. She glanced at the screen. Mark.

Danielle peeked. "Is that your cologne in a suit?"

Ellie nodded. "He's downstairs."

Danielle stood. "Want me to say you're buried in work?"

Ellie looked out the window. "No," she said softly. "I'll go."

She gathered her coat and bag, pausing as the Sade track looped again. Danielle gave her one last look. "You good?"

Ellie nodded. But the bloom from earlier? It hadn't fully faded. And it wasn't for Mark.

Danielle barely made it to her office before her phone buzzed. Jean on FaceTime: She grinned and answered with a swipe. Before the screen fully loaded, Jean's voice burst through: "Bitch! Yesssss, bitch! I know."

Danielle laughed and flopped into her chair. "You knew all day and didn't tell me?"

Jean held up a hand. "Swear to God. I just found out myself. This morning."

Danielle narrowed her eyes. "You waited till after I left?"

Jean leaned into the camera, eyes wide. "Danielle. James loves Ellie so much that even super bitch Thalia can't win with all her mystic pussy powers of the galaxies from far, far away."

Danielle howled. Jean continued, "That woman got planetary rotation in her hips and James still hit send like a slow jam apology."

Then Jean said, with mock solemnity: "I really hope they get back together."

Danielle asked, "You '90s DJ torn, or 'this is my song and I'll kill you if you change the station' torn?"

Jean nodded slowly. "Team Kool DJ Red Alert vs. Marley Marl torn."

Danielle gasped. "Juice Crew vs. BDP torn. And lowkey hoping Big Daddy Kane walks into the battle."

Jean threw her hand over her heart. "Nas vs. Jay-Z post-'Ether 'torn."

Danielle leaned back. "LL and classic Moe Dee. Or Ice-T. Or Canibus."

Jean snapped her fingers. "And Cool J crushed all of them. Licking his lips in tribute to me the whole time."

Danielle choked on her sparkling water. Jean grinned and kept going. "Biggie versus 2Pac torn."

Danielle: "I was team Biggie, but 2Pac slept with his woman, made a whole song about it, and introduced us to Thug Passion like it was therapy."

Jean threw up the West Coast "Dubs."

"West west, y'all. Ice Cube vs. all of N. W. A.!"

Danielle: "Damn. The Lynch Mob was a hidden gem."

They both paused. Then, Jean whispered: "Okay, bitch. We gotta end this right."

Danielle narrowed her eyes. "You won't."

Jean leaned in: "Eazy-E versus Dre."

Danielle slammed her desk. "That wasn't even a battle! Eazy just got body-bagged with braids."

Jean pointed at the camera. "Final round."

Danielle smiled. "Drake versus Kendrick. Choose."

Jean gasped. "You dirty."

Danielle folded her arms. "Don't stall. Loyalty is on the line."

Jean sighed. "Team Drake, bitch. Champagne Papi is my future husband."

Danielle nodded slowly. "He not like us."

Jean narrowed her eyes. "Umm, bitch, he's kinda like you. You are White."

Danielle clutched her imaginary pearls. "Don't make me angry, bitch."

Jean smirked. "Red Room, No Way You End On There Will Angry? Or All Eyes On Me, 2Pac Angry?"

Danielle stood up. "Tyreek shot Ghost angry and he never coming back!"

They both screamed with laughter. Then they paused. Breathless. Jean's tone softened. "I really love them, D. James and Ellie. Like truly."

Danielle nodded, now calmer. "They belong together for sure."

Jean looked off-screen. "I don't even know where James went after work. But I'm guessing Thalia's somewhere nearby, slipping amnesia meds in his drink or mouth."

Danielle cackled. "That woman is the memory foam mattress of seduction. Soft, deep, and makes you forget your back ever worked."

They both leaned back into their chairs, riding the last wave of laughter. Then Danielle quieted. "I don't know what's up with Mark," she said, taking a sip. "But Ellie kinda hinted he might be a bit…um…"

Jean leaned in. "Torn?"

Danielle shrugged. "Between her and someone else."

Jean's face twisted. "Bitch. Noooo."

Danielle sipped her coffee like it was tea. "Nothing confirmed, but Ellie said something about his freak freaking her freak."

Jean gasped, full tilt. "You mean, freak freaked the freak?"

Danielle nodded slowly. Jean sat back, stunned. "Girl, if this man pulls a 'surprise I'm fluid' plot twist after all this, Ellie gon' write a memoir and call it 'The Queen, The Dick, and The Closet Door'."

Danielle dropped her head on her desk, laughing. Then silence stretched between them again. The weight of love unspoken, of history repeating, and of time folding in on itself.

Jean's voice softened. "We joke a lot," she said. "But I mean it. I want those two to find their way."

Danielle nodded, whispering, "Me too."

———

The rooftop restaurant glimmered under strings of fairy lights, wine glasses half full. Mark looked pristine in a designer button-down, and a wristwatch that could pay off someone's debt.

Ellie was quiet, her mind somewhere else. Mark asked something. She didn't hear. "Ellie?"

She snapped back. Sorry. What?"

He smiled. "Long day?"

"Yeah."

He didn't press. didn't want to.

——

Thalia lay curled beside James on the couch, blanket over her legs, a romantic movie flickering on screen. He sat beside her, arm around her shoulders, but he was somewhere else. Not emotionally, not consciously. Just…drifting.

Thalia kissed his shoulder. "You okay?"

"Long day," he said.

She smiled and nodded. But deep down, he wasn't tired. He was tethered, to something or someone he never truly had let go.

——

Mark snored softly beside her, one arm draped over the edge of the bed like he'd claimed the night. But Ellie lay wide awake, eyes open, her body still and buzzing.

The screen of her phone glowed faintly in the dark, waiting. Then moved: *Let's talk tomorrow, E. Tired of replaying messages to hear your voice.*

The dots appeared almost instantly: *I would love that, Jay.*

And just like that, tomorrow couldn't come fast enough.

Ellie was up before the sun. Hair wrapped, silk robe tight, face freshly washed and glowing. The playlist was light and nostalgic: Janet, Anita, the quiet confidence of knowing something good was coming.

She moved through the morning like it was her first day at a new job. Or more like it was prom and she already knew she was winning prom queen. She hadn't hustled this fast since trying to catch the premiere of a new Michael Jackson video in the '90s.

Mark stirred under the covers as she breezed through the room, grabbing her keys and bag. "You already leaving?" he murmured.

She leaned over and kissed his cheek. "I have a long day. I'll text you." The door clicked shut behind her before he could answer.

———

At work, Danielle watched her boss speed through client briefs like her soul was caffeinated. "Okay, I'm gonna just say it," Danielle said, holding a coffee cup with both hands. "You need to stop pretending like you ain't watching that phone.

Ellie didn't look up. Danielle rolled her eyes. "You already pegged his schedule. You waiting for that 10 a.m. post-workout text like it's a stimulus check."

Ellie smiled but didn't deny it.

———

At James's place, Thalia lay curled under the duvet. James stared at the ceiling. Then flinched, and gasped, when her mouth wrapped around him from beneath the sheets.

She was soft. Precise. Warm. He groaned. She'd done this a hundred times before. But today, he enjoyed it differently. Not with guilt, but with distance. His hand ran over her curls as she finished. She emerged, kissed his chest.

They showered together in silence. She washed his back, but she felt it: the way his eyes weren't fully here.

"Everything okay?" she asked softly.

"Yeah, just trying to finalize some things on the deal for staying," he lied.

She nodded but didn't push. They kissed once more before he left. Brief, familiar, forgettable.

At James's office, Jean stood in his doorway before he even got to his chair. "Well?" she asked.

He hung his coat. "I'm calling her after my 10:30."

Jean tapped her iPad like it was her baby. "It's been rescheduled."

She turned dramatically, walked to the door, then looked back, raised her hand, and made a motion like she was answering a damn phone. Then closed the door behind her. James smiled.

———

In Ellie's office, Danielle waved a folder in front of Ellie's face. "Stop refreshing your life and just call him."

Ellie narrowed her eyes. "I'm not—"

"Girl." Danielle smirked. "Call him and say, 'Get your Black ass home. Enough is enough, Anna Mae'."

Then her phone buzzed. She looked down, and her mouth moved soundlessly. "It's him."

Danielle backed up toward the door, grinning. "I'll take my leave, your highness." She slipped out.

Ellie's phone rang and she picked up and answered softly. "Hello…"

James's voice lit up on the other end. "Oh, so I get the soft, seductive hello now?"

She laughed. He smiled. "Damn, E. I missed hearing your smile. It sounds like… the color 16 to my soul."

She said, "The…what?"

James laughed. "Exactly. Indescribable."

She bit her lip. "You trying to butter me up, Dr. King?"

"Nah," he said, his voice low and real. "I'm just glad to hear your voice."

"Same here, Jay."

He paused. Then, "I know you're with Mark. But you're forever with me."

Ellie took a breath. "And you're not with Thalia?"

James paused. "Just as much as you're with Mark."

Another silence. He broke it first. "No one's the same."

Ellie whispered, "No one is us."

He smiled softly. "Was there ever a time we weren't?"

Ellie didn't speak, but it wasn't from shock, she was hiding tears.

"I'm coming into town this week," James said.

"Oh? You have things to do out here?" she asked, lightly teasing.

"Yes," he said. "To see you."

Ellie's chest tightened, but she kept it cool. "Well, that would be nice."

"I'll let you know when. But let's make it a point not to be strangers again."

She nodded. "I'd like that."

There was a quiet lull. And just as she was about to say goodbye, James's voice broke through again. "Ellie."

"Yes?"

He smiled into the phone, voice tender and nostalgic. "When did you fall in love with hip hop?" Ellie's smile was instant.

With a laugh soft as breath, she replied: "Who you callin' a bitch? U. N. I. T. Yyyyyyyyy." And said nothing else. Just ended the call.

———

"Okay, something's in the air," Jean said, spinning slowly in her office chair, her pink cheetah-print heels resting on her desk. "Either Mercury's out of retrograde or James finally exfoliated the chip off his shoulder."

Danielle's face popped up on the corner of the video call screen. "Ellie's the same. She's humming again."

Jean's eyes lit up. "Humming?! Like full vocal cords?"

"She had on a lip gloss this morning that didn't scream 'I dare a man to speak to me'. It whispered, 'I might smile if the vibe's right'."

Jean gasped. "Bitch, we are entering a new zodiac era."

Danielle laughed. "But seriously, they're different today."

Jean stopped spinning. "Yeah. I love it."

Danielle nodded. "Same."

———

At On Second Thought headquarters, later that day, Mark leaned against Ellie's desk, posture relaxed, but eyes reading her carefully.

"You look amazing today," he said, adjusting the cuff of his blazer. "I was thinking, tonight, maybe we hit the club again. Just us. Something decadent. Private."

Ellie glanced up from her screen. Her expression softened but didn't bend. "I think I'm going to go home tonight," she said gently. "Sort out a few things. My head's full."

Mark gave a small, understanding nod. "Another night, then. I'm just in the mood for something dirty tonight. Not gonna lie."

Ellie returned the smile, but it barely touched her eyes. "Yeah," she said. "I could be too. Just, not tonight."

Mark accepted that with grace. But he felt it. A shift.

———

At James's office that evening, he leaned back in his chair, half-reading a proposal, half-watching the city soften through the tinted windows.

You want me to come over tonight? James stared at the message from Thalia. Brows furrowed.

He typed back: *Since when do we ask?*

Three dots. Then her reply came: *Since I know when something's shifting. I've got laundry and errands anyway. I'll come tomorrow. Rest easy, King.*

Thalia didn't press. She never did. She believed in the power of space. In the art of absence. And tonight, James didn't fight it.

——

In Ellie's loft, the lights were low. No music, no screens glowing in the background, just the sound of her shoes clicking across hardwood as she paced, phone in hand.

She'd changed into something soft. Nothing tight, or structured. Just comfort and memory.

The kind of night you spend alone on purpose. But tonight didn't feel lonely. It felt suspended.

——

When James got to his place that night, he walked in, kicked off his shoes, and dropped his keys in the ceramic dish Ellie bought two Christmases ago. The scent of Thalia's perfume still lingered faintly in the room, but the weight of her absence felt heavier than her presence.

He sat down on the couch. Opened Ellie's contact and stared. And somewhere across the state, Ellie did the same.

Split Screen: FaceTime Ringing. It happened without coordination. A single thumb pressed. Connecting.

Ellie sat up straighter. James cleared his throat. The screen came to life. Two faces, both changed, both familiar. Neither sure what to say first. But everything already being said in the silence between them.

James was lounging in a soft black tee and gray sweat shorts, the dangerous kind with a loose fit and a reputation for letting his member peek out the bottom whenever the fabric shifted just right.

His bald head caught the glow from a floor lamp like it had its own gravitational pull. That sharp, dark beard framed his jaw like a crown of shadow, the kind of beard that whispered secrets in silence.

Ellie was curled on her couch in an oversized tee, no makeup, just balm on her lips, and honesty in her eyes. Her curls were pulled into a high puff. She looked like comfort. And peace. And a woman in the middle of remembering how love once felt.

She smiled first. "Hey."

James nodded. "Hey."

A breath passed. Not awkward, just loaded.

He looked her over. "You look…rested."

She smiled softly, "You look like temptation."

He laughed, scratching his jaw. "It's just the shorts."

She arched a brow. "It's never just the shorts, Jay."

James chuckled, then looked down, a little shy. "I wasn't gonna call. I didn't want to push."

Ellie answered softly. "You didn't. It was good. The messages."

He met her eyes again. "I meant every word."

She nodded slowly. "I know."

Another pause, heavy but warm. He sat up a bit, adjusting the phone in his hand, which definitely didn't help the shorts situation.

Ellie's eyes flicked down for half a second and came back up. It was quick, but he caught it. James grinned. "You still remember everything?"

Ellie leaned back, fingers curling around her wine glass. "Even the stuff I tried to forget."

He exhaled. "Like?"

She took her time. "The way you'd pull me closer by my ankle while we watched a movie, like you couldn't even wait for the credits. Or how you used to run your thumb down my spine when you thought I was sleeping."

James swallowed. "You weren't sleeping?"

"Never. Just memorizing."

He looked away for a second, then back.

She softened. "You okay?"

He nodded. "Just missing you in the quiet."

Ellie's throat caught. She tried to lighten it. "So…no Thalia tonight?"

James said, "Yeah, she sensed something shifting. Said she'd come by tomorrow."

Ellie raised a brow. "Smart woman."

"She is. But she's not us."

Ellie didn't flinch. "Mark asked if I wanted to go to the club again."

"Did you?" he asked.

She answered, "No, I told him I wanted to go home. Sort through a few things."

James studied her face. "Same."

Another pause. "I mean what I said, I'm coming into town this week," he said.

Ellie felt that. Deep. She said nothing for a long moment. "That would be really nice."

"I'll let you know for sure when, but likely the weekend. But let's not be strangers again."

She smiled gently. "We never really were."

Right before she could say goodbye, she asked, "I know you wanted to FaceTime me earlier."

James said playfully, "No, I didn't."

He leaned back slightly, his arms stretched behind his head. His shorts shifted in a way that made Ellie avert her eyes quickly.

"I just figured, let me go ahead and do it now."

Ellie grinned wide. "You ain't got to lie, Craig. You ain't got to lie!"

James let out a laugh, full and boyish. And just before he hit the red button, he looked into the screen and said, with all the playfulness of a man who knew exactly what he was doing. "Bye, Felicia."

The screen went black. And they both sat there, smiling into nothing. Hearts stirred like old songs, where they still knew the lyrics by heart. They had been a King and a Queen in exile. Not from each other, but from themselves.

James King, the architect of empires, had carved power from pain. Bald, beautiful, and built like a prayer answered in flesh, He had once sworn off softness because it reminded him of everything he couldn't protect.

Ellie Sinclair, the woman with no crown but all the fire, had once folded her heart into steel just to survive. She had been loved publicly and lost privately and still walked like nothing had ever cracked her.

Together, they were unstoppable. But love is not armor. It's the wound and the weapon. The pause and the pulse. And when you don't water what grows between you, even the strongest roots pull back from the soil.

So, time passed. She found Mark and he found Thalia. Two people who were good, kind, even dazzling. But not each other. And here they are now. Not back together, not broken. Just...present.

Talking again, laughing again. Letting the silence fill in the blanks that time had carved out. There's no timeline here. No plot twist. Just a slow return.

The kind where a man texts a woman not because he's lonely, but because her voice is the sound he wants to fall asleep to.

The kind where a woman smiles at her screen not because she misses the attention, but because she still memorizes his pauses when he speaks.

The club has gone quiet. The war rooms have been cleared. Peace treaties signed in texts, FaceTime calls, and quiet admissions.

But the kingdoms? They remain unclaimed. Not lost, not conquered. Just waiting.

Because some love stories don't burn down and rise from ash. Some love stories drift apart like continents and spend years drifting back.

And when they do, not even the gods dare interrupt it.

Chapter 21: Where Loyalty Lives

A few days passed. Not many, just enough for the dust of silence to settle into a rhythm of something else. A year ago, she wouldn't have imagined this version of herself, hardened, but standing.

Between James and Ellie there had been no grand plans. No declarations. Just text threads. Hundreds of them.

Emojis, memes, soft sarcasm, dumb inside jokes. Voicemails that didn't say much but meant everything. That familiar "…" typing bubble popping up and disappearing like breath.

And suddenly, both of them were on their phones more than they'd been in months. For something other than work. For something that felt like memory dusted off and put back in heavy rotation.

The kind of attention that only used to belong to each other.

In downtown L.A. Thursday evening, the restaurant Mark had chosen was dim and expensive. Not flashy, just elegant in that very specific way that money never needed to announce.

He looked perfect, as usual. Trim beard, tailored suit, scent like dominance and detail. He was off.

Ellie sat across from him, sipping slowly from a glass of something floral. She wore soft pastels, curls pinned loosely, face glowing, but her eyes drifted often. To the tablecloth, her water glass, her phone screen.

Mark noticed. He always noticed. "I thought we could do something private this weekend," he said, cutting a slice of his duck. "Maybe go back to the club. You seemed powerful there."

Ellie looked up, smile polite, and voice calm. "I think I'm going to stay in this weekend. Maybe tonight too. I've got some things to sort out."

Mark set his fork down slowly. "I see."

She didn't explain. He didn't push, but he felt it. The subtle slippage of something he'd thought he had full grip on. Then he leaned forward, elbows on the white linen.

"I've been thinking," he said. "About us. About you not needing to be everywhere all the time. About maybe letting go of your estate."

He continued, smooth as marble. "Move in with me. You'd have your space. Hell, I could give you your own wing if you need it. I'm busy enough that I'd barely be around during the day."

Ellie sat straighter. "Mark…"

"I'm not trying to crowd you," he added quickly. "I just want to make it easier. For you, for us."

Ellie paused thoughtfully, a smile playing at her lips that didn't reach her eyes. "There's still a lot James and I have to sort through," she said carefully. "I can't just ignore that."

Mark leaned back, a flicker of something darker in his gaze.

"How much do you think all that is worth?" he asked. "Ten million? Twenty?"

Ellie stilled. Then gave him a slow look.

"Stop," she said, her voice even. "Not that much. I wish."

He blinked once. "Right."

The air grew dense between them. But Ellie didn't flinch. She didn't soothe him, and she didn't offer anything.

Mark, sensing the edge of the cliff but not ready to leap, or be pushed, held up the menu and said, lightly, "Okay. No heaviness. How about we just order some dessert?"

Ellie nodded, softly. Relieved. Because while she wasn't ready to break it off, she knew with everything in her that Mark was not the one. Not anymore. Maybe not ever. That answer was still unfolding.

———

James leaned back in his chair, phone tucked between his shoulder and ear, a smile already tugging at his lips before the call even connected.

Thalia answered with a soft, sultry lilt. "Yes, we're still on. I'm doing my own rendition of Roscoe's chicken and waffles, Greek style."

James barked out a laugh. "Greek style? What does that even mean?"

She giggled. "It means I'm pulling the recipe straight out of my ass and hoping for the best."

They laughed together. That easy, comforting rhythm they had formed over months. "I'll be there in an hour," James said.

"Perfect," she replied.

They hung up, and James was still grinning when Jean stepped into his office like she owned more than just her pink glitter nameplate.

"Well, well, well," she said. "You got your sexy phone voice on. That for Thalia or someone else?"

James rolled his eyes. "Dinner plans."

Jean folded her arms, already reading the subtext. "You know what I'm gonna say."

"I already do," James replied, standing and reaching for his keys.

"Then say it with me," Jean challenged. "Tell her. Let her know Ellie's back. Let her move on."

James paused. "Ellie's not back. Not yet. But we're…trying to find our way there."

Jean looked at him with some suspicion, "So you're halfway home but still hosting another woman at the door?"

He sighed. "Everything's been perfect with Thalia. I mean it. Peaceful. No explosions. No chaos. Just…good."

"But?" Jean pressed.

"But I'm scared," he admitted. "Scared to let go of this kind of perfect for that other kind Ellie brings."

Jean's voice dropped an octave. "Since when did you start being scared of anything?"

She leaned forward. "Don't tell me this magical temptress turned you into some kind of punk bitch too."

James pointed at her playfully. "Watch it now."

Jean grinned. "You know I say it with love."

James exhaled. "I've really grown to love Thalia. But I never had to grow into anything with Ellie. It just…was."

Jean nodded. "That's how you know."

She turned to leave, calling over her shoulder, "You better take that bourbon. You're gonna need it."

Later that night at Thalia's loft, the moment James walked in, he was greeted by the scent of spiced honey and something frying in olive oil. Jazz played low in the background.

Thalia stood at the stove, apron tied neatly at her waist, and a black thong peeking out from underneath. She wore comfortable wedge heels, the kind only confident women bothered to cook in.

James walked up behind her, wrapped an arm around her waist, and kissed her bare shoulder. She leaned her head back against his. "Dinner's almost ready."

He whispered into her skin, "Smells good."

"Wait 'til you taste it," she teased.

James poured himself a bourbon, loosened his shoulders, and sank into the couch. He slipped off his shoes, rubbed his temples, and exhaled. He loved the quiet here. But tonight, it felt heavier than usual.

Thalia brought out the food moments later, two plates arranged beautifully, no shortcuts. But instead of calling him to the table, she sat beside him on the couch. Calm. Still. Gorgeous. She looked into his eyes and asked, "James…do you love me?"

He didn't flinch. "I do," he said. He was about to say more when she gently cut in.

"Before you ruin that," she said, "Just know, I never expected you to forget Ellie." She held his hand in hers, warm and firm.

"I never expected you to stop loving her to love me. God knows I know that big heart of yours has enough love to hold us both. I never asked you to be exclusive with me. I simply prayed for it."

James stared at her, jaw tight, throat thick.

She smiled softly. "But I also know you will never truly be mine, unless she is never not yours."

She leaned forward, kissed him on the cheek. "I want you to enjoy this dinner," she said. "And enjoy me tonight. And then…"

She glanced toward the bedroom. "…you'll find I've packed all your things. Take them. Think. Decide."

James opened his mouth to protest, but she raised a hand. "I've already taken my things from your place too."

"Damn, baby," he whispered. "Don't you think that's a bit extreme?"

She smiled. "Absolutely. But I've always been prepared for the worst. And I'm enthusiastically hoping for the best."

He reached for her hand. She didn't let it go. They stood, walked to the table together, and sat. They laughed over dinner like it was any other night. Like the heaviest conversation in the world hadn't just happened. But it had, and neither of them would ever forget it.

Back at home later that evening, the city was quiet in that way only midnight could bring, when even the neon signs went to sleep and traffic lights blinked with no one watching.

James kicked off his shoes, laid back across his bed, and picked up his phone. He opened their thread. She was already typing.

Ellie: *Did you watch the new Kanan episode?*

James smiled. His thumbs hovered for a second, then typed back: *No. I was kinda waiting to watch it with you.*

Her response came almost instantly: *Well, you're all the way over there.*

James sat up a little, propped against his headboard: *Since when has that ever stopped you from doing anything, King E?*

Ellie bit her lip as she lay down, grabbing her remote and adjusting the pillows. She looked at the time on her phone: *Okay. Time check. On three we hit play.*

James: *Say less. I'm ready.*

Ellie: *One…two…three.*

Across the city, in two different beds, their screens lit up with the same opening scene. The same music. The same familiar universe of betrayal, bullets, and plot twists.

They watched, they reacted, they laughed at the same parts, cursed at the same betrayals, and both shouted "Noooo!" at the same exact turn.

For a while, they forgot they weren't together. It just felt like home.

Somewhere near the end of the episode, James said softly, "Damn. I missed this."

Ellie sat up, her voice trembling as the words finally spilled. "Yes, James, I missed this. And I love you."

She paused, the tears already sliding down her cheeks. "I love you so fucking much. And I never knew how strong you were until now."

James's breath caught.

"I never knew how much grace it took for you to let me go. To let me believe I was stronger than you. And then—" her voice cracked "—you took the strongest parts of yourself apart and gave them to me so I could stand up and walk. So I could survive."

More tears. More truth.

"And even then, James, I was never a fraction as strong as you. Not even close."

There was silence on the other end. No breath. No movement. Ellie stared at the screen. "James…?"

But the screen had gone dark. She looked down in horror. "NO—no, no, no!" Her fucking phone had died.

She scrambled, swearing, grabbing her charger and slamming it into the port like she was giving CPR. Hands shaking, she plugged it in and sat in the dark, begging it to come back on. Apple logo. Loading.

Her heart raced. Buzz. Incoming FaceTime. James.

She picked up so fast it nearly slipped from her hands. James's face filled the screen. "Yo…what happened?"

Ellie's mouth parted, panicked. "Oh my God. You didn't hear any of that?"

James squinted. "Any of what?"

Ellie inhaled sharply. Then spoke softly, "I love you, James. I love you so fucking much." James's lips curled slowly into that maddening grin.

"Ohhh…" he said. "I thought you were talking about the part where you were crying and telling me how I gave you all my strength and put you together and shit."

Her jaw dropped. "You motherfucker—"

James burst into laughter. She wiped her eyes, still crying. "I hate you."

"No, you don't."

"You knew you heard me."

"I told you to charge your damn phone."

She laughed, shaking her head. They both fell quiet again. But this time? It wasn't silence. It was everything.

They didn't say what came next. didn't make promises. didn't confess anything more. But in the dark, two beds, two cities. One call. They felt something stronger than hope. And they both knew.

They were still scared to say more than a whisper. This was louder than love.

——

The next day the morning air was still soft when Ellie walked into her office, coffee in hand, lips glossed in quiet confidence.

Danielle trailed behind her, reading off emails between sips of oat milk cold brew.

"Clients are chill, board wants a Q3 teaser, and Jean sent you a meme about glitter-stained coffee cups and your tragic attempt to go paperless."

Ellie grinned. "Tell her I'm still evolving."

Danielle was about to launch into a rundown on brand approvals when there was a knock on the glass. A courier stood there: suited, solemn, and holding a flat black envelope with a gold seal.

Danielle opened the door. "For Ellie?"

The man nodded. Danielle raised a brow and took it. "From…?"

"Mr. Mark Spade," he said before walking away.

Ellie turned. "Mark?"

Danielle held the envelope like it might detonate. "Probably some whirlwind trip like Italy or Morocco. You know, rich people shit. Like, 'Pack nothing. Your soul is the luggage'."

Ellie let out a breathy laugh and peeled the seal. Her smile evaporated.

Danielle squinted. "Okay, you look like you saw a ghost. What is it?"

Ellie didn't answer. She reached inside the envelope and pulled out two deposit receipts: crisp, formal, and styled to look like certified checks.

Danielle walked around the desk.

One check: *Pay to the order of: Ellie Sinclair.*
Amount: $20,000,000.00

The other: *Pay to the order of: James King.*
Amount: $10,000,000.00

Danielle's mouth dropped open like someone had unplugged her.

"What in the Powerball Black Excellence just happened?!"

Ellie set the checks down carefully, like they were glass. She unfolded the letter tucked behind them:

Walk away. Let him keep everything. Here's further incentive for him to keep everything. Only pack what's dear to you. There are no strings. No conditions. No terms. I just need to know the Queen who stands beside me doesn't need a thing from me. We can talk about it over dinner tonight.

Ellie laid the note flat on the desk. Danielle snatched it up like it was a holy scroll. "Girl," she whispered, reading it again. "That's not just a love move. That's player-level diplomacy." She pointed at the checks.

"Not only did he write you a check for twenty million, but he cut one for James, too. That says, 'Pardon me. I just stole your bitch'."

Ellie looked stunned. "I...I can't believe he did this."

Danielle leaned back. "You're not gonna take that, are you?"

Ellie blinked hard. "I can't."

She touched the checks again. "Not because it's twice what I'm worth..."

She turned slowly to Danielle. "...but because it's twice what James is worth. And he just wrote two checks and said, 'Stop this bullshit. You're mine'."

———

James sat across from Jean, who was biting into a blueberry scone like it owed her answers. "So...you home now?" she asked, crumbling the pastry all over her iPad.

James nodded. "Yeah. I brought my things back. She took hers."

Jean raised a brow. "So...y'all done?"

James shrugged. "I don't know. I love her. I really do. But if we're finished, it won't be because she packed up a few things and told me to think."

Jean chewed slowly, then swallowed. "So let me get this straight. She packed your shit. Said, 'Take it. But come back if you want to'."

She leaned back and sighed. "Goddamn. I'm running out of evil genius titles for that woman."

James chuckled. "She's a lot."

Jean smirked. "Are you going back there tonight?"

He said, "Probably not. I'm thinking of heading to L.A. this weekend."

Jean's interest piqued. "L.A.?" She grinned. "What the hell's in L.A.?"

James just smiled and leaned back.

———

Ellie stood at the window in her office, holding the letter like it might disappear. Her fingers hovered over her phone. Then she dialed.

Mark answered, smooth and amused. "Yes, Queen?"

Ellie exhaled. "I can't take this. I don't know. It feels like pressure. We said we weren't going to do that."

Mark's voice was calm, even. "As I said in the note," he replied, "No pressure. No terms. Just real."

"If you look at the back of both checks, they've already been deposited. Yours and his."

Ellie's eyes widened. "You what?"

Mark chuckled. "Whatever you do is whatever you do." And he hung up.

At work, Jean's phone buzzed. A text from Danielle: *Tell James to check his account. Tell him it's not a joke. Mark deposited $10 million. No strings. For real.*

Jean read it twice. She sat down slowly and said to herself, "Oh, this shit just got real." She stood by the glass conference room wall, one brow raised, mouth twisted in a smirk that could slice steel.

Inside, James was mid-sentence, commanding the room without a stutter, until Jean raised her hand and waved like she was signaling an aircraft.

James shook his head slightly. Not now. Jean didn't budge. Instead, she tapped her phone, turned it to face the glass, and mouthed: "Check. Your. Account."

James looked confused but then reached toward the corner of the table where his phone had buzzed quietly under a folder. He unlocked it mid-sentence.

His face didn't change. Not even a blink. But Jean saw it. His jaw flexed. Eyes narrowed, thumb paused. Then, stone faced, he put the phone down like it was a receipt for gum and returned to his pitch.

Jean, grinning like a villain at intermission, mouthed again through the glass: "Ooooh. This shit is good."

Back at Ellie's office, Danielle leaned against the window. "So…anything from James?"

Ellie said softly, "Nope."

Danielle arched a brow. "And you're really about to sit across from Mark tonight? With that receipt on the table?"

Ellie stood, grabbed her purse. "No. I'm not. I'm not letting him script a perfect dinner to make me feel grateful for a power move I didn't ask for."

She grabbed the envelope off the desk. "I'm going to his place. Now."

Danielle stood straighter. "You sure?"

"Yeah. And while I'm gone, call my bank. Ask them about reversing the deposit. I'm not keeping his money."

Danielle clutched her imaginary pearls. "A moral queen. We love to see it."

Ellie rolled her eyes. "Just call." She walked out without waiting for more questions.

In James's office post-meeting, he barely made it back to his chair before Jean stormed in. "Okay," she said, tossing her tablet onto the desk. "What the fuck did you say to this man to make him drop ten million dollars into your account?"

James rubbed his temple. "Not a goddamn thing. I've never spoken to him. Not even that night."

Jean sat down. "Wait—ever?"

James shrugged. "Never met the man as who he is, but a brief encounter when I helped him with his coffee. I don't know what this is."

She blinked. "You think it's a mistake?"

"I don't know," James said. "But if it is, I'm not giving it back."

Jean laughed so hard she wheezed. "There should be a Jean Fee for all this bullshit. I've earned it."

James grabbed his phone. "I'm calling Ellie."

Ellie was driving. She answered quickly, breath tight. "James?"

"You know what this is about?"

"I do," she said. "And it's not a gift. It's pressure."

James's voice was sharp. "What the fuck do I have to do with it?"

"Because," Ellie said, "he's that wealthy type that thinks money can buy anything. Forgiveness. Closure. Or silence."

James let out a short breath. "Well, he can't buy you. You're fucking priceless, even when you're on sale. And he can't buy me either," he said. "But if he wants to drop millions like he's the rich Black Thanos, I'll take that shit."

"No," Ellie said firmly. "Don't. In his mind, it's charity. It's control."

James sighed. "Fine. I'll send it back. But I'm not happy about it."

"Neither am I," Ellie whispered.

They hung up.

Jean looked at James. "He's worse than your Greek magic-coochie Medusa." She continued. "Damn. What do I gotta do to get on 'Love is Blind: Billionaire Bitches Edition'? Somebody sign me up." She walked out shaking her head.

Late that afternoon at Mark's estate, Ellie stepped out of the car, the gates closing behind her. The driveway curved like a secret she wasn't supposed to know.

She slipped off her heels at the door. She didn't want him to hear her. She walked through the foyer, past the living room, through the hallway with quiet fury building in her chest. Around the corner, she heard music and the rhythmic thump of something hitting gym mats.

She opened the gym door. And stopped breathing. Mark was naked, bent over an incline bench. Behind him, a tall, sculpted, blonde-haired, blue-eyed man was fucking him with slow, deliberate strokes.

Mark looked up, sweat beading along his temple. His eyes met hers calmly. He reached back mid-thrust and said, without flinching, "Can you close the door? I'll be out in about twenty." Then he moaned and dropped his head again.

Tears filled her eyes, not from heartbreak, but confusion and pain. A hollow grief she couldn't name. She walked out, fast. Back in her car, she sat behind the wheel, shaking. She thought, 'Why am I crying? I didn't want him. I didn't even want him...'

She tried to remain calm, but inside her heart was splintering anyway. At home, minutes later her phone rang. She answered. "What do you want, Mark?"

He sounded normal. Like nothing happened. "Why'd you leave?" he asked. "I was almost done."

Her voice cracked. "Was I supposed to sit around while you get fucked and then have dinner like nothing happened?" and then mumbled softly to herself, "dick-in-the-booty-ass, bitch."

"If you can say we were exclusive, I'll apologize. If you haven't been talking to James, I'll apologize. If you didn't love him the entire time, I'll apologize."

Mark's voice was smooth. Practiced. "But if you can't say those things, I'll pick you up at 8. And we'll talk like adults."

Ellie opened her mouth. No sound. He continued. "That's what I thought. See you at 8." He hung up.

———

James sat alone and stared at the wall, the bank confirmation still open on his phone. Ten million. Ten million reasons to make a decision.

He took a long sip of his bourbon and leaned back. Tonight, one door had to close, for good.

Either the kingdom he tried to build, or the one still standing in ashes, waiting to be rebuilt from truth.

Chapter 22: The Return of the King

The day had thinned to dusk by the time James stepped out of his office. The wind hit different when you were carrying something on your heart. It didn't cool you off, it cut right through you.

He walked toward his car, slowly. The door shut behind him with a weight that didn't feel like the end of a workday.

He didn't start the engine right away. His phone sat in the console. Silent. The direct deposit being reversed. The money untouched. But still, his hands didn't reach for the wheel.

Instead, he sat there and thought: Love doesn't always ask your permission. And it sure as hell doesn't always stop when it should. That's what hurt the most.

He pushed the button to start the car, and the speakers lit up with the gritty boom of classic Jay-Z. "Streets Is Watching…"

He nodded once, then settled back. He thought back to a hard lesson he learned as a child: "Don't answer it," James whispered, peeking around the kitchen door. "It's Nikki. I already know."

The phone rang again, sharp and insistent from the wall-mounted cradle. His mama side-eyed him over her pot of red beans. "Boy, I know I didn't raise no coward."

"She calls like every day," James muttered, arms crossed.

"Pick up that phone and face that girl like a man."

James folded. "I don't even like her like that."

"Did you tell her?"

He hesitated. "I didn't wanna hurt her feelings."

POP! She slapped the back of his head lightly. "How do you expect her to know if you don't tell her?"

The phone stopped ringing for half a second. Then started again. This time, she grabbed the receiver, handed it to him, and held onto his arm when he tried to bolt. "Tell that girl you don't like her."

James put it to his ear, voice low and cracking. "I…I don't like you."

She took the phone and hung it up with a swift click, then she turned and looked at him, not angry, but eyes full. "A woman's time," she said, "is her beauty."

She kept going. "Don't you ever take a woman's beauty from her. That's all we got in this world, James. Our beauty is our time, our grace, our effort."

She stirred the pot slowly. "Let that girl give her beauty to someone who wants it. Who'll see it. Don't let her waste it on someone who only holds it out of guilt."

James couldn't speak. He just nodded, then he whispered, "I'm never gonna waste nobody's time, Momma."

James blinked back into focus, the bass from Jay-Z still thumping in his chest. He turned off the music, and turned off the hesitation, and he drove.

He arrived at Thalia's loft early in the evening. She opened the door before he knocked. Wearing a long, soft black wrap dress that made her skin look dipped in moonlight. Her curls were up. Her eyes were warm.

She smiled, pulled him in, kissed him like welcome and pause all at once. But when she stepped back, she knew.

She reached for his hand, squeezed it once, then led him inside. The lights were low. A single glass of wine sat untouched on the table. No second one in sight.

He didn't speak. She sat beside him on the couch. And before he could find the words, she wrapped her arms around him and pulled him in, tight. The kind of hug that says, 'I already know'. She whispered into his shoulder, "I understand."

And then, softer: "I really love you for coming to tell me."

James pulled back, eyes misting. "Thalia…"

She put her fingers to his lips. "No explanation needed."

He shook his head. "But I do need to say this." He placed his palm gently on her cheek. "I love you. I do. But I love you enough to not take another moment of your beauty."

Her eyes glistened. Because she knew what he meant. Because she remembered being that girl with no answers from someone else. She nodded, blinking through it. "Only real men do what you did today."

She lifted his chin with her finger when his head dropped. "I'll never forget you for it." Then she kissed him, softly. No fire. Just thanks.

And James walked out the door. He didn't close it hard. He didn't look back. But he knew that door would stay open longer than it should. And the one he was walking toward? There were no guarantees, no certainty.

Just the sound of his mother's voice whispering in his chest, "We don't do what's easy. We do those things that are hard like they are easy."

Later that evening, Ellie drove herself to dinner. That alone was the first flag.

She never drove when she was with Mark. He always sent the car. Always had the route mapped, the valet tipped, the table reserved, the wine pre-selected.

She needed control. Of the wheel. Of the exit. Of herself.

The restaurant was immaculate, posh, polished, warm lighting, waiters in tailored vests. Mark was already seated, of course, sipping something amber from a crystal glass.

He stood as she approached, that smooth, unbothered smile on his face. He leaned in to kiss her. She shifted, just enough. "I don't want anything to do with where that mouth's been."

Mark paused. Then smirked like he'd been told a clever joke. "Ouch," he said, putting both hands up as if surrendering. "Alright then."

She sat across from him, crossing her legs slowly, gaze steady and sharp. He sipped his drink again. "I saw the money came back today," he said casually. "Surprised me. I was even more surprised James returned most of his."

Ellie's eyes didn't move, but something flickered behind them. "Most?" Her inner voice kicked in: 'This motherfucker…' and laughing inside. Still, she only smiled.

"I didn't need your money to figure out whether I wanted you or not."

Mark nodded once. "Fair." "But," he added, leaning in a little, "you had no choice. I knew I'd get you eventually. You love power, Ellie. You crave it. It's not a flaw, it's a feature. And that beast inside you, that edge, it's what makes you perfect for me."

Ellie blinked once. Mark smiled wider. "I've never seen it in a woman before. That hunger. It's beautiful. You're beautiful. I watched you make a king behave in a room as everyone watched and I knew then I had to have you."

He sat back, casually swirling his drink. "When I'm not monogamous," he said, "I don't pretend to be. I just make sure the woman knows she's the favorite."

Ellie exhaled slowly through her nose. Her tone didn't rise. "It wasn't seeing you fuck a man that changed anything for me."

Mark tilted his head. "It was realizing," she continued, "that you can only save what you can buy, charm, or control."

Now he blinked.

"And you won't die on a sword for anyone. Not for a cause. Not for a person. Not even for yourself."

She folded her napkin slowly. "I can't build the next part of my life with someone like that."

Mark nodded slowly, then said without missing a beat: "That's fair. Suit yourself," And then without saying it he said it: 'Dimissed.'

Ellie stood. Mark didn't. He didn't even look up. He stared at his phone, took a sip of bourbon, and tapped at the screen like he'd been dining alone all night.

No tears. No grand scene. Just a woman reclaiming her time, her power, and her exit.

The night air folded behind them as they each left the places that had once felt full. James drove in silence. No music. No phone calls. Just breath and wheel. He pulled into his garage and sat for a moment in the car, staring at the dashboard. Then, he smiled. Not from joy, but from the sudden, uninvited memory of her laugh.

Ellie thought back to a Halloween and melted at the thought of her being mid-yell, tangled in a pile of costume pieces scattered across their old bedroom. "James! Where the hell is my Bo Peep hat?"

James leaned against the dresser, shirtless, watching her with that cocky half-grin. "You know Little Bo Peep ain't got no business yelling like that."

She turned, hand on hip. "Don't test me."

He tilted his head, narrowed his eyes. "Wait, did you really just put on that dress without any—" Her eyes widened.

"You out here Little Bo Peepin' commando?!"

She grinned, faux innocent. "Maybe. So?"

James stepped closer, voice deepening. "So how you gon 'tell the Big Bad Wolf that when he's tryin 'to eat you?"

Ellie burst out laughing. "No! The Big Bad Wolf wants to eat the sheep."

James smirked. "Oh shit. I didn't know Little Bo Peep was a sheep."

They both doubled over in laughter, falling onto the bed in a mess of fake lambs and tangled sheets.

James shook his head as the memory faded, a soft smile still lingering on his lips as he stepped out of the car.

———

Back at home, Ellie kicked off her heels and let the door close behind her. She didn't even turn on the lights. She stood in the soft glow of the city coming through the window, her breath catching before she even realized why.

She sat on the couch and remembered back to a time with her phone face down, pretending to scroll through emails. But she wasn't okay. Her smile was brittle. Her spirit exhausted.

James walked in, took one look, and didn't even ask. Instead, he raised his voice just slightly. "I swear to God, Ellie, if you don't stop moving my charger I'm throwing your whole purse in the goddamn sink."

"Excuse me?"

"You heard me," he said, grabbing her phone. "Let me show you something."

She jumped up, ready to fire back. And he caught her in his arms mid-rant, lifted her off her feet, and kissed her like the world had tried to break her and he refused to let it.

"There's a Queen hiding behind all those sad faces," he whispered. She cried quiet, shaking tears. And instead of taking her to the bedroom, he carried her to the kitchen and cooked a full three-course meal. He recited poetry with every plate like she was a goddess starving for words.

Ellie's phone buzzed: *One night to be an old-school superstar…you wearing shell toe Adidas or bright suede Pumas?*

Her lips cracked into a full smile before she even unlocked it. She texted back in all caps: *MY ADIDAS.*

Seconds later: *It's like that…And that's the way it is.*

She laughed, alone, but not lonely.

Back at James's place, he set his phone down, stretched across the couch, and waited. Both of them, miles apart, memories between them, hope beneath them, felt something lift.

The sorrow of the night softened. The weight didn't disappear. But it got lighter, one message at a time. And in those messages, they were finding each other again. Not like before, but maybe something better.

——

Some mornings don't feel like morning at all. They feel like breath after drowning. Like a long exhale in your own bed, before you even open your eyes. That was today.

James woke up with his chest lighter than it had been in months. The air tasted different. His movements were sharper, smoother. No hesitation in his brushstrokes, his suit selection, his step.

He didn't check his phone until he reached the elevator.

James walked in, and before Jean even turned on her playlist she narrowed her eyes. "You're early. Who died?"

James tossed his briefcase onto the sofa. "Nobody. But if things go the way I need them to, we're headed back home."

Jean sat up straight. "Thank God. I don't know how you do this C level shit. I've been bored since my office been done. And FYI, my salary is staying the same."

James nodded. "Done. I'll walk out of here and never look back."

————

Meanwhile, in Ellie's office, Danielle was stretched across the couch like a pop culture prophet, sipping her matcha like it held the secrets of the universe.

"So let me get this straight," she said. "Ten million returned. Mark ghosted. You cooked dinner for yourself. And James is texting like y'all back in high school?"

Ellie smirked. "It's not that simple."

Danielle agreed. "No, E. It never is. But it always involves a super-fine, rich motherfucker doing the absolute most."

She sat up, dramatic. "Mark Spade would fuck an alien if it dropped out the sky with pussy and teeth. If it had an ass with thorns and a scent called Martian Lust, Mark would still be backstage with a candle and a playlist trying to serenade it." Ellie burst out laughing.

"I swear to God," Danielle went on. "He'd be like, 'So what if she's radioactive? It's the radiation that makes her real'."

More laughter, loud and full. She was storm and stillness, the same woman. And yet not at all. Ellie wiped a tear. "Honestly, no matter what happens with me and James, I'm proud of who I've become. I'm the woman I always wanted to be. Not the one I had to be."

Danielle's smile softened. "And James? He'd love your ass with a snotty nose and a bad COVID cough." They both howled again.

Late that morning in James's office, Jean was typing furiously on her iPad while James mapped out logistics on the whiteboard.

"Alright," Jean said. "We can finish this out in style and still pivot home before the quarter ends."

James nodded. "Let's do it. We'll leave behind the contracts but take the crown."

Jean sipped her drink. "Everything good with Thalia?"

James paused, then smiled. "Yeah. She appreciated the honesty. Refused to settle for anything less than our kingdom."

His phone buzzed, and he picked it up. The grin was instant. Jean didn't even blink. "I don't have to ask who the fuck that is."

She waved her hand. "Tell El I said what's up."

James read the message out loud: *If you had to pick between two hot heartthrobs to be for a day... George Michael, Faith-era, 5 o'clock shadow and tight jeans. Or Christopher Williams, pre-New Jack City, still dreaming, not yet dissed?*

Jean dropped her tablet. "Damn. I'd fuck both of them."

James nearly choked on his coffee. Jean stood up, dramatic as ever. "One wore cologne like commitment. The other moaned in full falsetto."

James typed his response. *Gotta go with George Michael. Rockstar. Made the 5 o'clock shadow iconic. And that song? Faith. Come on.*

Jean snapped. "Good. Cause if you'd said Chris, I was about to tell you to sit your five-dollar ass down before I make change."

James leaned back in his chair, laughing. "Nino Brown reference? Seriously?"

"Classic beginning of the end," Jean said, sipping. "Stay woke."

She teased, "You ever gonna stop texting and actually go home?"

James shrugged. "Soon, young grasshopper. It's not easy getting all your demands met."

Jean smirked. "You're ridiculous."

James grinned. "Mine were all settled about an hour ago, I am fighting for your crazy shit, like candy and coffee allowance, really?"

That afternoon in Ellie's office, her phone lit up. James Calling. She answered with a playful breath. "What's up?"

James's voice dropped into that tone. That Jay tone. "You tryna catch up on BMF tonight or what?"

Ellie checked her watch. "Absolutely. Don't be fucking late." She hung up before he could say anything else.

And just like that, the evening was set. Two homes. One show. And a love story being rewritten, one carefully crafted moment at a time.

Meanwhile, Jean's face filled the top half of the screen, her curls piled high and her expression already three seconds from an eye-roll. "You see this shit?" she said, sipping from a mug that definitely didn't contain coffee. "Ellie's got James wrapped around her finger already."

Danielle, calling in from her L.A. office, didn't miss a beat. "And for the first time in a long time, I think she's finally appreciating James being wrapped around anything."

Jean grinned. "I swear, we really did that."

Danielle leaned back in her chair. "We really did. All this reconnection? All us."

"Even though," Jean said, "We didn't do a goddamn thing."

"Not a damn thing," Danielle echoed. They raised imaginary glasses to themselves.

Danielle reached for her drink. "Also, let me tell you. Mark Spade? That man's taste in pleasure is like his bank account, limitless."

Jean widened her eyes. "I knew it. It's always the fine ones that cant make up their mind, do you want pussy-pussy or man-pussy?."

Danielle pointed at the screen. "Said the exact same thing."

Jean waved a hand. "From now on, if you don't have a missing side tooth, cologne that can't be found on the clearance rack at Walgreens, and a little gut, don't even speak to me." They both burst out laughing, wheezing into their mics.

Jean composed herself. "And girl, Elliott Technologies? Thrilled James ain't leaving. Gave him everything but the deed to the company. I added a car service for myself, to and from, and he signed that shit like it was a fan letter."

Danielle gasped. "How do you not love James King?"

Jean sipped. "Exactly."

Danielle sat forward. "Ellie gave back all that money. Made James give his back too."

Jean coughed, long and pointed. Danielle squinted. "Bitch, what you mean cough?"

Jean tried to look innocent. "I said she made him give back his money."

Danielle's eyes narrowed. "Not all?"

Jean shrugged. "James figured if we are moving back, we should move back debt-free. Left a little something for the inconvenience."

Danielle's mouth fell open. "How much is a little something?"

Jean said it with a straight face. "Few hundred thousand. Mark Spade needed to pay for his disrespect to me, Don James, and all of the five families."

Danielle fell back in her chair, hand to her chest. "I take this as a sign of disrespect!" she said in a perfect Godfather rasp. "How dare you come for my queen and not even say excuse me?"

They laughed so hard the FaceTime glitched.

———

Ellie and James were all set. The episode of BMF was hitting its wildest twist yet. Someone got betrayed. Someone got shot. A car exploded. They were watching in sync, FaceTime minimized, volume synced perfectly.

Ellie glanced at the screen. "Okay. Why are you acting like I'm not waiting for you to tell me when you're coming to see me?"

James paused the show. Enlarged the screen. Stared at her dead-on. "Well," he said, cool as sin. "Since bitches wanna be thirsty, I guess I can get out there tomorrow."

Ellie blinked. "Really? Bitches wanna be thirsty?"

James shrugged, smirking. "That's what I heard."

Ellie leaned closer to the screen, grinning. "Fine. I am thirsty. I can't wait to see you."

James sat forward, eyes serious but soft. "Don't forget who caved first, my love."

They both broke into full-body laughter. Then James leaned back, voice lower now. "Real talk, E…say less. I'll see you tomorrow."

Ellie smiled like she hadn't in months. They went right back to watching BMF. Two screens. One heartbeat.

And a story slowly finding its rhythm again, not perfect, but finally honest.

Chapter 23: The Lightness After

Some stories don't need retelling. They need honoring. And this one, James and Ellie, was never about a perfect love. It was about a true one. Two people. Both brilliant. Both bruised.

She built an empire from the shards of her silence. He built a kingdom from the weight of his name. They let each other go when love still lived between them. They stitched themselves back together, separately, quietly.

There were betrayals. There was healing. There was laughter so loud it made grief jealous. And somewhere between miscommunication, missteps, and missed calls, they never stopped choosing each other. Not officially.

But in the way you wake up and hope their name's on your screen. In the way you remember the softness of a goodbye more than the sharpness of a fight. In the way your body still turns toward the empty side of the bed. Because even when the castle crumbled, the crown never stopped being heavy.

It just sat there, waiting to be earned.

That morning in his office, the bag was already open. The sun was already rising as James stood at the edge of his bed, fingers resting on the duffel like he was still deciding. But he wasn't.

He knew. He folded two black tees and a long sleeve tee, a pair of jeans, a hoodie that still smelled like a time when things made more sense, and a pair of sneakers, nothing flashy.

He wasn't going back. He wasn't trying to fix what had already broken, he was going to give them both the thing they deserved after all this time: An answer. He thought to himself: 'I don't know how she's gonna look at me when I walk through that door. I don't know if her eyes will be soft or guarded. Don't know if she'll ask me to stay or tell me it's too late. But I do know this: I'm done running from the parts of myself that only exist when I'm next to her. I'm not coming with promises. I'm not coming with poetry. I'm coming with presence. With the truth in my eyes. because we both loved in different languages. And maybe we never stopped. Maybe the real strength wasn't walking away. Maybe it's walking back without knowing what the hell is waiting for you on the other side of the door. I'm not moving back. But I'm moving forward. Toward her. Not as her past. But maybe, just maybe, as her answer.'

———

Ellie didn't dust the bottles of bourbon, didn't chill his favorite glass, didn't light the candle he used to say smelled like success and sex and safety.

This time, she wasn't trying to recreate anything. She was trying to feel everything.

She pulled out a small bag from the back of her pantry, and one by one, laid it all on the kitchen counter like sacred relics from a different kind of temple: Chico Sticks. Boston Baked Beans. Lemonheads.

And then she reached in again and smiled. Tahitian Treat. The soda that could rot enamel before the halfway point but tasted like red heaven and childhood freedom. She popped the top and set it gently beside the snacks. Not on a tray, no fancy napkins.

Just real. Just them.

The king-size Snickers bar, his all-time favorite. She held it in her palm for a moment, shaking her head with a smirk. "Maybe I should rub it in the dirt a little first," she whispered, laughing to herself.

James had once told her about the first fight he ever earned his name in was the time when Chance Curto knocked his king-size Snickers bar out of his hand and into the dirt. That was all it took. James didn't yell, didn't threaten. He just kicked his ass. That day didn't just start a fight, it made James King a warrior.

"Over a candy bar?" she'd asked once.

"No," he'd said. "Over thinking he could get that off, and I was dying to destroy that shit."

She placed the Snickers down beside the rest of the treats, like she was laying down armor.

She fluffed the pillows on the couch, not to perfection, but to comfort. She wiped down the coffee table, put on the playlist that used to score their arguments, their makeups, and the days when laughter came too easy to question.

She didn't look at her phone. Not yet. She was busy creating space for him, not the version who left, not the one who'd been buried under guilt and pride. But the one who once danced with her in the kitchen with syrup on his fingers and music in his mouth.

She told herself, 'I'm not laying out bourbon. I'm not curating mood lighting or playlists that hint at old patterns. I'm not even expecting him to say the right thing.

I just want him to show up like he used to. Before the boardrooms and broken silences, before the headlines and heartbreak, before we got so good at surviving that we forgot how to simply exist beside each other.

I want to remember what it felt like to just be. I want to look at him and not see what we lost, but what we might still find. This is not about being ready, it's about being open.

This is about making room for the King. Not the one I lost, but the one who remembered where the hell his throne was.'

She glanced at the counter one last time and laughed to herself. It looked like a gas station snack aisle. It looked like middle school mischief. It looked like hope. She sat down.

————

The FaceTime rang once before Danielle answered with a smirk already loaded. "Don't even say it," she said, pulling her bonnet tighter. "I know. I know. The prodigal dick returns."

Jean, sprawled across her couch in San Diego with a bowl of popcorn and a glass of boxed red, grinned wide. "Oh, we're calling him 'penis with purpose' now?"

Danielle lifted her mug. "He's coming for the Queen. That ain't just dick. That's destiny." They both hollered.

Jean sat up straighter, tossing popcorn at the camera like she was baptizing it. "Alright. Important business. When James walks through that door, what song should be playing?"

Danielle's eyes widened. "Ooh. You want to score the moment?"

Jean nodded like it was gospel. "This shit is cinematic. We need a soundtrack."

Danielle leaned back, considering. "Okay, first thought? That classic Chicago joint."

Jean asked, "Chicago?"

Danielle started singing: "Everybody needs a little time away…I heard her say…"

Jean jumped in. "Even lovers need a holiday! Yesssss!" They harmonized horribly.

Jean wiped a tear. "He was gone. Now he's back, Queen!" More laughter.

Danielle laughed loudly, "No, no. It needs to be more dramatic. Like, teenage love story meets adult breakdown."

Jean raised a brow. Danielle straightened and sang: "Is this the end…are you my friend…"

Jean gasped. "Not New Edition!" Jean laughed so hard she slapped the arm of her couch.

"Okay but wait," Danielle continued. "If we're going there, how do we not throw in 'End of the Road'?"

Jean flailed. "Bitch, this is a reunion. Not a funeral! We are not walking away from each other!"

Danielle giggled. "I'm just saying, if the universe gives us Boyz II Men, we listen."

Jean paused, then softened. "You know what I'm digging in the crates for this one. Stevie Wonder. All in Love Is Fair."

Danielle squinted. "That's deep as hell."

Jean looked proud. "Classic. Legendary. No skips."

Danielle asked in mock surprise, "No John Legend? No Chris Brown? Not even a notable White boy singer? What happened to balance?!"

Jean shrugged. "Not tonight."

She stood up, walked toward her Bluetooth speaker like a preacher approaching the pulpit. "Okay, bitch. I got it."

Danielle sat forward. "Alright. I'll give you the last word. What is it?"

Jean didn't say a thing. She hit "play", and the speakers cracked with soul. That unmistakable voice crooned through: "Love 'em and leave 'em…That's what I used to do…"

Danielle threw her head back. "Oh bitch…you win."

Jean grinned. "Rick James, Fire and Desire. There is no other answer."

Danielle leaned back. "Set the table, dim the lights, cue the redemption."

Jean nodded. And on two different screens, in two different cities, they both knew. This wasn't the end, it was the return.

———

James arrived and had only two bags. One was his usual duffel, soft leather, worn in the corners. The other, a plain brown grocery bag, bulged with familiar shapes and nostalgic weight.

When the door opened, Ellie was already walking toward him, barefoot in the quiet, her curls pulled back, smile tucked into the corners of her mouth like she wasn't ready to show it fully just yet.

She leaned in for a kiss. James lifted the grocery bag and cocked a brow. "Are you trying to kiss me, or do you want my arm to fall off?"

Ellie paused mid-lean, then rolled her eyes with a grin. "Billy Dee had good hair when nobody else did. You're not that smooth, Dr. King."

They both laughed as she reached for the bag. But as she turned to walk it to the kitchen, James reached out and pulled her gently back.

The bag slipped from her hands, hitting the floor with a soft thud. And then, his arms were around her. Strong. Familiar. Final.

Ellie melted instantly. There was no monster in the room big enough to scare her when James King was holding her.

Her breath left in one long exhale, her forehead pressing against his collarbone. His own chest lifted and dropped like the air had been waiting to come home too.

When he finally let go, she blinked back full eyes, no tears falling. Just warmth. She kissed him softly. A single peck. Then pulled back, whispering, "Got me dropping groceries and shit." They laughed.

In the kitchen, they moved without thinking. The space still knew them. Still remembered the arguments, the makeups, the meals that changed the course of dreams. The kitchen was the unofficial war room, the sanctuary, the confessional.

James reached into the cabinets and pulled out the pans. Ellie watched him like she'd forgotten the ritual, how he always tapped the bottom of the skillet once before placing it on the burner. How he always rolled his sleeves exactly twice.

It was muscle memory, love memory. Until he wiped his hands on his pants, walked over, and picked her up. Ellie squeaked, laughed, wrapped her arms around his neck.

He sat her on the island gently, kissed her forehead, and walked back to the stove. No fanfare. No declarations. Just the sound of oil heating, vegetables being chopped, something simmering that had nothing to do with food.

They talked about everything. Missed memes, terrible office coffee, and random memories neither of them thought they remembered.

Not once did they say, 'I'm sorry.' Not once did they say, 'I'm back.' Because nothing had to be said. There were no thrones tonight. Just two royals, finally at peace.

James turned off the last burner and plated the food. Ellie watched him. "So, are we binge-watching something tonight?"

James smirked. "No. I have something else in mind."

She smiled, eyes playful. "Oh?"

He looked her over and laughed. "I'm not that easy."

She coughed into her fist, grinning. "Okay. So, what do you have in mind?"

James walked over and stood between her knees, hands on her thighs. "I'm gonna wash your feet," he said softly. "Then I'm going to wash your hair. And while I do, I'm going to read you every poem I wrote for you."

James continued. "The ones I memorized. Just in case I ever got the chance again."

She didn't speak for a moment. "Well, they better be good," she teased. "I know how much you hated reading out loud in school holding everybody up."

He threw his head back and laughed. And so did she. The night was full. Of laughter, of healing, of a love that needed no ceremony.

No crowns. Courting each other the way real royalty always does: In the quiet, in the kitchen, in the places that never stopped feeling like home.

The next morning, nothing looked different. But everything was. There were no parade banners, no golden throne to reclaim, no fire-lit declarations. Just two people making eggs and splitting a soda that could rot teeth on sight. Laughing like there hadn't been months of silence between them.

———

Weeks passed.

James wrapped the Gemini SoCal project with the same relentless precision that had built his name into something whispered with reverence.

He delivered under budget, ahead of schedule, and with a closing meeting that ended with one of the directors calling him a "walking system upgrade with a pulse."

Then, without announcement, he submitted his exit documentation, handed off final approvals, and walked out of that building for the last time. They didn't return to Elliott Global Technologies with trumpets or titles. Just presence.

James was already back at the desk before anyone had time to miss him. Ellie slipped into her office quietly. Jean was waiting by the security desk with a list of demands for her upgraded C-suite space, and Danielle had already reorganized Ellie's calendar to include "mandatory vibe resets" every Thursday.

They didn't reclaim the kingdom. They resumed it. Wiser, softer, still sharp.

Jean and Danielle were still guardians of the gates. Still swearing they were the reason the crown came home.

There were new rules now. Fewer calls after hours. More laughter during them. Ellie stopped answering emails in bed. James stopped apologizing for showing up late when he'd stayed up writing poetry he wasn't quite ready to share yet.

Some nights were filled with music and food and bad reality shows. Others were silent. Healing. Just breath and shoulders and sleep. There was no announcement. No official "we're back." But they were.

———

One night, months later, James walked past Ellie's office just as she closed her laptop. She looked up, he looked back. She didn't speak, just smiled.

And he gave her that signature nod. The one that said, 'I've been yours.' The one that meant 'I still am.'

They weren't perfect. They weren't poetic. But they were present. And sometimes, that's the most sacred thing two people can be.

They didn't rule like King and Queen anymore. They lived like partners. And in that, they found something heavier than power. Peace.

The kingdom didn't fall. It simply evolved. No longer made of gold and thrones, but of kitchens and laughter, text threads and side glances, midnight snacks and Sunday silences.

The crown was never meant to be worn alone. And love, real love, never needed an audience. It just needed room. They had all the room in the world.

———

Heavy is the Crown.

The end.

Author's Note—The Kingdom Was Never Safe

I didn't write "Heavy is the Crown" because I had a cute story to tell. I wrote it because I've never known how to do anything halfway. I've never been satisfied with "just enough."

When I entered the tech profession, I was told to be grateful for a job, any job. That just making decent money was enough, but it wasn't. Becoming an executive was supposed to mean I'd made it.

But I didn't want the job, I wanted the theater, I wanted more than I had. And I wanted it so bad the hunger never let me sleep. That same hunger bled into this book. It still hasn't let go of me.

I didn't grow up dreaming about being average. I didn't bust my ass to make a quiet entrance into the publishing world. I came into this with one of two goals: Either I would succeed so loud they couldn't ignore me, or I would fail in front of everybody, daring the whole world to watch.

There was never a middle.

This book started as a short story. I turned it into a full novel in under a month. I stayed up nights, writing five chapters at a time with no plan, just purpose. And I didn't stop until I hit top 10 in three genres: Urban erotica, African American fiction, and literary drama…On my debut. And I'm not done.

I'm not some overnight genius. I'm not some publishing darling. I'm a product of hard work, hunger, and hustle. And I'm proof that when you move with purpose, it doesn't matter who you're up against. Hunger beats talent. Every. Fucking. Time.

I've been this way my whole life. Whether it was tech, publishing, or walking into a room where nobody looked like me. I've always had to fight to be seen. I don't chase attention anymore, I command it.

So you don't have to believe in me. You don't have to clap for me. Just watch what happens when I crown myself.

—Dr. James E. Lorraine

Author. Kingmaker. Unapologetic.

THANK YOU FOR READING

You just finished a story that's part of something bigger: the Crown Cipher Universe. If this book made you feel something, the next story might finish the sentence.

☐ Join the House: Get early access, giveaways, and exclusive letters from your favorite authors.

Join now → https://crowncipherpublishing.com/join

CONTINUE THE STORY

Every story under this crown is connected. Different voices. Same house. Protect it.

If You Loved…	Next, Read…	Author	Link

Heavy Is the Crown	Letters in Silence	Omari Vale	https://crowncipherpublishing.com/books
Letters in Silence	The Monster Beside the Silence	Alonzo J. Crippen	https://crowncipherpublishing.com/books
No, Not That Email	No, Not That Wedding (2026)	James E. Lorraine	https://crowncipherpublishing.com/books
The Lies We Inherit	CounterFactual (Coming Soon)	Angela R. Key	https://crowncipherpublishing.com/books
We Touch Through Strangers	Heavy Is the Crown	James E. Lorraine	https://crowncipherpublishing.com/books
The Monster Beside the Silence	The Silence of the Pack (2026)	Alonzo J. Crippen	https://crowncipherpublishing.com/books

MEET THE AUTHORS

James E. Lorraine:

The flagship author of Crown Cipher Publishing, architect of the Kingdom Universe, and the voice that built the House.

Angela R. Key:

Author of The Lies We Inherit and CounterFactual. A master of psychological thrillers and gothic realism.

Omari Vale:

The lyrical craftsman behind Letters in Silence and We Touch Through Strangers, bridging silence and connection.

Alonzo J. Crippen:

The dark heart of The Wolf Gospel Series, creator of The Monster Beside the Silence.

Read more → https://crowncipherpublishing.com/books

BECOME A CROWN CIPHER AMBASSADOR

Review, share, and earn rewards as part of the Royal House.

Apply here → https://crowncipherpublishing.com/ambassadors

REVIEW & FOLLOW

Your words build the House. Review wherever you read.

Follow @CrownCipherPublishing on all platforms.

#ProtectTheHouse #CrownCipherAuthors

We protect this F**king House.